THE MONSTER FROM 1,000,000 A.D.

A high-pitched, ragged screech came from behind the house, a caterwaul of fright. Boone started running toward the sound. But as he was rounding the corner, something going fast and hard struck him in mid-stride, tumbling him nose down into the soft dirt.

He pawed at his face to wipe off the dirt and pulled himself to his feet. Emma was streaking for the traveler, with the others close behind. It was Emma, he thought, who had knocked him down.

Then he saw what was chasing them. It was like a living spider web, more than twelve feet across, with pulses of energy throbbing across the tiny threads of the web. Behind the threads was a disk of some sort that might have been an eye. And he saw mechanical appendages . . . things like arms were already reaching out for him.

Enid's voice shrieked at him. "Boone, you fool! Run! It's a killer monster!"

By Clifford D. Simak
Published by Ballantine Books:

Highway
of
Eternity

Clifford D. Simak

A DEL REY BOOK
BALLANTINE BOOKS • NEW YORK

A Del Rey Book
Published by Ballantine Books

Library of Congress Catalog Card Number: 85–26826

ISBN 0-345-32497-8

Manufactured in the United States of America

First Hardcover Edition: June 1986
First Mass Market Edition: June 1988

Cover art by David Schleinkofer

Table of Contents

New York

1

The cable reached Boone in Singapore:
NEED A MAN WHO CAN STEP AROUND A CORNER. CORCORAN.
He caught the next plane out.

Corcoran's driver was waiting for him as he came through Customs at Kennedy. The man took Boone's bag and led the way to the limousine.

It had been raining, but the rain had stopped. Boone settled back comfortably on the well-upholstered seat, watching the scene unwind through the windows. How long had it been, he asked himself, since he had been in Manhattan? Ten years, perhaps more than ten.

By the time they reached Corcoran's apartment building, it had begun raining again. The driver gathered Boone's bags, held an umbrella for him, and ushered him to a private elevator to the penthouse. Corcoran was waiting in the library. He rose from a chair in the corner and came across the heavy carpeting with hand outstretched and a look of relief on his face.

"Thanks for coming, Tom. Had a good flight?"

"Good enough," Boone told him. "I slept on the last leg."

Corcoran nodded. "I remember you could always sleep on planes. What are you drinking these days?"

"Scotch with a splash of soda." Boone sank into the indicated chair and waited until the drink was handed him. He took a long pull of it, glancing about at the appointments of the room. "You seem to be doing well these days, Jay."

"Quite well. I have wealthy clients who pay for what they get. And operatives all over the world. If a diplomat sneezes in Bogota, I hear of it within hours. What's doing in Singapore?"

"Nothing. Just a layover between jobs. I can afford to be selective about the stories I take to cover these days. Not like it was when we used to see each other."

"How long ago was it?" asked Corcoran. "When we first met, I mean."

"It must be fifteen years or more. That unpleasantness in the East. You came in with the tanks."

"That's it. We got there too late. It was a massacre. Bodies all piled up and no sign of anyone alive." Corcoran grimaced at the memory. "Then suddenly, there you were, unruffled, standing among the dead. You wore that jacket with all the pockets for your notebooks, recorder, tapes, camera, and films. You carried so much stuff you seemed to bulge. And you told me you'd just stepped around a corner."

Boone nodded. "Death was half a second away. So I stepped around a corner. When I stepped back, there you were. But don't ask me to explain. I couldn't tell you then and I can't tell you now. The only answer is one I don't like—that I'm some kind of a freak."

"Let's say a mutant. Have you tried it since?"

"I've never tried it. But it's happened twice more—once in China and again in South Africa. When I did it, it seemed natural—the kind of thing any man might do. And now, what about you?"

"You heard what happened to me?"

"Some," Boone answered. "You were a spy—CIA and all that. You were trapped, but you got word back, and a fighter snatched you up. A daredevil landing out of a grade-B movie. The plane was shot to hell and gone, yet it made it back . . ."

"That's right," said Corcoran. "Then it crashed. The whole back of my head was smashed in, and I was so close to dead it didn't matter. But I had information that was vital, so they performed miracles saving my life . . . Anyhow, they had to do some strange things in fixing my head. Apparently some of the wiring in my brain got crossed or something. I see things differently now sometimes—things others don't or can't. And I think in quirky ways. I tie little items of information together in a sort of sneaky deduction that defies straight-line thinking. I know things with no reasonable way to know them. I've made it pay, too."

"Fine. And does that have anything to do with your calling me here from Singapore?" Boone asked.

Corcoran leaned back and took a sip of the drink he'd mixed for himself, considering. Finally he nodded. "It has to do with one of my clients. He came to me about six years ago. Said his name was Andrew Martin. Maybe it was."

Martin had come in, aloof and cold, and wouldn't shake hands. He refused absolutely to answer any questions. Then, when Corcoran moved to show him out politely, Martin reached into his breast pocket, took out an envelope, and pushed it across the desk. Inside were one hundred thousand-dollar bills.

"That's just a retainer," he stated. "For any work you do, I'll pay double your usual rates."

What he wanted were rumors from all over the world. Not the usual political things, but unusual or outrageous rumors—the sort that seemed to make no sense at all. He wouldn't say how he could be reached. He'd phone in daily and tell Corcoran where to find him—always at a different place.

There weren't too many of the kind of rumors he wanted, but for those he paid well, usually more than double rate, and always in thousand-dollar bills. It went on that way for years.

Corcoran checked on him, of course. But there wasn't much to be learned. Martin seemed to have no past and no discoverable occupation. He had a respectable office with a part-time receptionist, but she had no idea what he did. He seemed to have no business dealings at all.

He also had a corner suite at the Everest, but he didn't live there. At least, when Corcoran's operative got into the suite, there were no clothes in the closets nor any other sign of occupancy.

On occasion, Martin was seen around town with a woman named Stella, as mysterious in her way as he was in his.

Then, a few months ago, Martin and Stella vanished into thin air.

Boone sat up abruptly. "What?"

"That's right—or they seemed to. After the last time I reported to him, he left me and was seen making a phone call. A short time later, my operative at the Everest saw Stella leaving and followed her. She and Martin went into an old warehouse near the docks. They never came out. And they haven't been seen since."

Boone took a pull on his drink and waited. Finally he prompted Corcoran. "That last rumor . . ."

"It came from London. Had to do with someone searching frantically for a place called Hopkins Acre."

"That seems innocent enough."

Corcoran nodded. "Except for one thing. In all of Britain, there is now no place called Hopkins Acre. But there was, four, five hundred years ago. Located in Shropshire. I checked. In 1615 it disappeared while the family that owned it was off on an European tour. It was there one day, gone the next. No sign left to show it had ever existed. The whole estate—the land, even the landscape—all of it gone, along with the people who farmed it or worked as servants in the house. Even the house. Not even a hole in the ground was left.''

"That's impossible," said Boone. "A fairy tale."

"But a true one," said Corcoran. "We established beyond question that it had once been there and had disappeared.''

"And that's the end of the story?" Boone asked. He shook his head. "But I still don't see why you sent for me. I'm no good at tracing missing persons or locating houses that disappeared almost four hundred years ago.''

"I'm coming to that. I had other business, and Martin was gone, so I tried to forget him. But a couple of weeks ago, I read that the Everest was to be dynamited.''

Corcoran raised his eyebrows questioningly. Boone nodded. He was familiar with the way they placed shaped charges around a building that was to be demolished. When the process was done right, the structure simply came apart and fell as rubble for the shovels and bull-dozers to clear away.

Corcoran sighed. "That brought Martin back to my mind. I went down to have a final look at the building. I'd left it to my operatives before, which was a mistake. Remember I said I saw things differently now?''

"You saw something?" Boone asked. "Something your men didn't see?''

"Something they couldn't possibly see. Only I can see it, and I have to catch it just right. I—well, I can't step around a corner, but sometimes I seem to see around a corner. Maybe on a wider spectrum, maybe a little way into time. Do you think it's possible for a man to step or see a little way into time, Tom?''

"I don't know. Never thought about it.''

"No. Well, anyhow, there it was—a sort of enclosed balcony like those you see plastered to the sides of apartment houses, just outside the suite Martin had occupied. Sort of out of sync with normal perception, half in and half out of our world. And since Martin never lived in the suite, I'm sure he must have lived in that balcony or box.''

Boone picked up his glass and drained it. He put it back carefully on the table. "You expect me to step around a corner to get into that box?"

Corcoran nodded.

"I'm not sure I can," Boone told him. "I've never used the trick consciously. It always happened when I was in extreme danger—sort of a survival mechanism. I don't know whether I can do it on demand. I can try, of course, but . . ."

"That's all I ask," said Corcoran. "I've exhausted every other possibility. The hotel is empty now and guarded, but I've arranged to get in. I've spent a lot of time there, probing, tapping, prodding, and drilling, trying to find a way into the contraption. Nothing. I can look out of the window against which it's stuck, and there's no sign of anything between window and street. But when I go outside and look up, there it is."

"Jay, what's your big concern? What do you expect to find in that so-called balcony?" Boone demanded.

Corcoran shook his head. "I don't know. Maybe nothing. Martin became sort of an obsession with me. I probably spent a lot more trying to find out about him than his business paid. This is worse. Tom, I've *got* to get into that box!"

He paused, studying his empty glass. Then he sighed and looked up again. "The trouble is, we haven't much time. This is Friday night, and they're planning to blow it Sunday morning, around dawn, when everyone is off the streets."

Boone whistled softly. "You cut it fine."

"I couldn't help it. You were hard to locate. When I learned you were heading for Singapore, I cabled every hotel where you might stay. Now, if we're going to do anything, we have to move fast."

"Tomorrow—Saturday," Boone agreed.

"Make it tomorrow evening. They're holding some kind of media thing on the last day of the old hotel during the day. Television and press will be all over the place. We'll go in when it quiets down."

He stood up and collected the glasses, going back to

the well-stocked bar. "You're staying with me, of course," he said.

"I figured on it," Boone answered.

"Good. Then we'll have one more drink and maybe do a bit of reminiscing on old times. After that, I'll show you to your room. We'll forget the box until tomorrow evening."

2

David had roamed the fields since early afternoon, accompanied by his favorite setter, enjoying the quiet satisfaction of being alone in a beautiful and ordered world.

Out of the stubble at his feet a grouse came storming up. Automatically, the gun came to his shoulder and his cheek was against the stock. The sights lined on the bird, and he jumped the barrel sharply to the left. "Bang!" he said and knew that if a shell had been in the chamber and he'd pulled the trigger, the bird would be tumbling to the ground.

The setter came galumphing back from chasing the bird

and set himself on the ground in front of David, looking up and laughing in his way, as if to say, "Aren't we having fun!"

It had taken a long time for the setters of Hopkins Acre to adapt. They had been bred to flush the birds and bring the dead ones back. They had not understood this new procedure. But it was different now, after many generations of setters. They no longer expected the crack of the gun or to find dead birds.

So, he asked himself for the thousandth time, why did he carry the gun? Was it fondness for the feel of its weight and the way it fitted to his shoulder? Or was it to reaffirm to himself that he was a truly civilized creature, though of a line with a long history of cruelty and brutality? But that would be an unjust pose. He would not kill the sheep, but he ate the mutton. He was still a carnivore, and a carnivore was a killer still.

It had been a good day, even without the birds, he reminded himself. He had stood upon the hill and gazed down on the straw-thatched houses of the village where the tillers of soil and husbandmen of the sheep and cattle lived. In the pastures he had seen the animals, sometimes quite alone and sometimes with a boy and dog keeping watch. He had encountered the grunting hordes of swine in the heavy woods, wild as deer and rooting for fallen acorns. But he had not ventured close. Even now, he could find no fellowship with the happy clods who worked the land. He had seen the colors of the woods changing in autumn and had breathed the chill air. He had come down to the brooks that flowed through the woods and had drunk from them, watching the darting shadows of trout.

Earlier, he had caught sight of Spike playing some ridiculous game, hopping carefully in erratic patterns. David had watched him, wondering once again what manner of creature Spike might be.

Tiring of his game, Spike had taken off, moving toward a patch of woods, but bounding in a random pattern which had more grace and spontaneity than the restricted hopping of the game. The sun of the autumn afternoon had glinted off his globular body, with the sharp points of his spikes spearing the sunbeams and scattering them in sparkles. David had called out to Spike, who apparently had not heard him and had finally disappeared into the woods.

The day had been full, David told himself; now the shadows lengthened and the chill deepened. It was time to be turning home.

There would be a saddle of mutton on the board tonight. Emma, his older sister who was married to Horace, had told him so and had warned him to get home on time.

"Do not be late," she told him. "Once done, mutton cannot wait. It must be eaten warm. And be careful of that gun. I don't know why you take it. You never bring home anything. Why don't you bring back a brace or two of grouse? They would be tasty eating."

"Because I do not kill," he told her. "None of us ever kill. It's been bred out of us."

Which was not true, of course.

"Horace would kill," she told him, tartly. "If there were need of food, Horace would kill. And once he had brought it home, I would dress and cook it."

She had been right, he thought. Horace, that dour and practical man, would kill if there were need of it, though not for simple fun; Horace never did anything for the fun of it. He must have a reason to assign to everything he did.

David had laughed at Emma's worries. "The gun can't do me harm," he told her. "It's not even loaded."

"You'll load it when you put it back on the rack," she said. "Timothy will insist you load it. If you ask me, our brother Timothy is a little gone."

They all were a little gone. He and Timothy and perhaps, in a different way, Horace and Emma. But not his little sister, Enid. She, of all of them, was the free spirit and the thinker. She thought longer thoughts, he was sure, than any of the rest of them.

So, remembering the mutton that could not wait and must be eaten warm, he headed for home with the dog, done now with fun and laughter, trailing sedately behind him.

Topping a knoll, he saw the house from a distance, set in a green rectangle of lawn among the tawny fields. Heavy growths of trees, many of them resplendent in their autumn foliage, ran all around the perimeter of the park, in the center of which stood the house. A dusty road which was now no more than a double cart track ran in front of the park, a road that ran from nowhere to nowhere. From the road, the access entrance ran up to the house, flanked by rows of towering poplars that through the years had become the worse for wear and which, in a little time, would die away and fall.

Trailed by the faithful dog, David went down the knoll and across the brownness of the autumn fields, finally coming up to the entrance road. Ahead of him lay the house, a sprawling two-storey fieldstone structure, with its mullioned windows turned to subdued fire by the setting sun.

He climbed the broad stone stairs and struggled momentarily with the heavy and reluctant latch on the massive double door before one of the doors swung smoothly open on well-greased hinges. Beyond the foyer lay the extensive drawing room, lit only by a brace of candles set upon a table at its farther end and beyond it the many-candled brightness of the dining room. From that second room came the subdued murmur of voices, and he knew the family already was foregathering for the evening meal.

He walked into the drawing room and turned to the right to come into the gun room, filled with shadows made alive by the flickering of a single candle set upon a bar. Going to the gun rack, he broke the shotgun and fished out of a pocket in his hunting coat the two shells he carried, clicking them into place and closing the breech with a single motion. That done, he put the gun in its place and turned around. Standing well inside the gun room was his sister, Enid.

"Did you have a good day, David?"

"I didn't hear you come in," he said. "You walk like thistledown. Is there something that I need to know before I walk into the lion's den?"

She shook her head. "No lion tonight. Horace is almost

human, as close to human as he ever gets. We had word today: Gahan is coming in from Athens.''

"Gahan I have no liking for," said David. "He is so intensely scholarly. He lords it over me; makes me feel useless."

"And mc as well," said Enid. "Maybe the two of us are useless. I don't know. If you and I are useless, I enjoy being useless."

"So do I," said David.

"Horace likes Gahan, though, and if his coming makes Horace livable, we'll gain from the visit. Timothy is ecstatic. Gahan told Horace he would be bringing Timothy a book—probably a scroll—written by Hecateus."

"Hec—well, whatever the name may be. I've never heard of him. If it is a him."

"A him and a Greek," said Enid. "Hecateus of Miletus. Fifth or sixth century. Scholars are of the opinion that Hecateus was the first man to write serious historical prose, using a critical method to separate out the myth content of history. Gahan thinks the scroll he has is an unknown book, one that had been lost."

"If it is," said David, "that's the last we'll see of Timothy for some time. He'll lock himself in the library, have his meals brought in. It'll take him a year to mull his way through it. He'll be out from underfoot."

"I think," she said, "that he is being led astray, that he is becoming mired in history and philosophy. He is looking for the basic errors we humans made and he thinks that he will find the roots of them in the first few thousand years of human history. He has found a few, of course, but one does not need to study history to be aware of them: the problem of surpluses, the profit motive, and the war motive which arises from one man or tribe having more than another man or tribe may have; or the need of huddling—the need of men and women to huddle in tribes, nations, and empires, reflecting that terrifying sense of insecurity that is part of the human psyche. You could go on and on, of course, but I think Timothy is deluding himself. The meaning that he seeks is a deeper meaning and it is to be found otherwhere than in history."

He asked, quite seriously, "Enid, do you have some idea? Even a faint idea?"

"Not yet," she said. "Perhaps never. All I know is that Timothy is looking in all the wrong places."

"Maybe we should be going in to dinner," he suggested.

"Yes, I think we should. We can't keep the others waiting. Emma has been in a tizzy that you would be late. Timothy has been sharpening the carving knife. Nora, out in the kitchen, has been in a flutter. The mutton's almost done."

He offered her his arm and they went across the drawing room, carefully threading their way between the shadowed, half-seen furniture.

"Oh, there you are!" cried Horace when they came into the dining room. "I have been wondering where you were. The mutton cannot wait, you know. Here, you must, each of you, have a glass of this port. It is quite the best I have tasted in years. It is really excellent."

He poured and stepped around the table, handing each of them a glass. He was a squat man, short and powerful of body, and with the appearance of excessive hairiness. His hair and beard were so black that the blackness seemed to shade into blue.

"You seem in excellent spirit," David said to him.

"I am," said Horace. "Gahan will be here tomorrow. I suppose Enid told you that."

"Yes, she did. Will he be alone or will someone else be with him?"

"He didn't say. There was reception trouble. Interference of some sort. That is something that has not been perfected. Teddy, back in the Pleistocene, thinks it has to do with stresses in the duration alignment. Maybe something to do with directional anomalies."

Horace knew nothing about the problem, David told himself. He might have some slight knowledge of time techniques, but certainly no grasp of the theory. However, on any stated subject, he was an instant expert and could talk convincingly and authoritatively.

Horace was about to expand further on the matter, but

was interrupted when Nora came in from the kitchen, bearing in triumph the platter of mutton. She placed it in front of Timothy and went bustling back into the kitchen. The rest of them found their places at the table and Timothy began the carving of the saddle, making an occasion of it, plying knife and fork with his customary flourish.

David tasted the port. It was excellent. Occasionally, on certain small matters like the selection of a good bottle of port, the law of averages, unassisted, would make Horace right.

They ate in silence for some time. Then Horace judiciously wiped his mouth on his napkin, stuffed the cloth back into his lap, and said, "For some time I have been worried about our twentieth-century outpost in New York. I don't trust this Martin fellow. I've been trying to raise him for the last few months and the blighter does not answer."

"Maybe he has gone away for a while," suggested Emma.

"If he were going," said Horace, "as our security man, he should have kept us informed. He has this woman, Stella, with him. If he's not there, at least she could answer."

"Maybe she went with him," said Emma.

"She shouldn't have gone. The post should be manned at all times."

"I would think," said David, "that it might be poor policy for us to keep too persistently trying to get in touch with him. As a measure of security, we should keep our communications to a minimum."

"We are the only ones in this time segment," said Horace, "who have time capability. There is no one monitoring."

"I wouldn't bet on that," David told him.

"What difference does it make?" asked Emma, forever the timid keeper of the peace. "There is no reason for us to be sitting here arguing about it."

"This Martin almost never talks with us," Horace complained. "He never tells us anything."

Timothy laid his knife and fork down on his plate, making more of a clatter than was necessary. "Despite the fact," he said, "that we know nothing of this man and do not entirely trust him, he still may know what he is doing. You are making something out of nothing, Horace."

"I met the man and Stella," said David, "when I went to twentieth-century New York several years ago to run down some books that Timothy wanted. That was the time," he said to Timothy, "when I brought back the shotgun and rifle for your collection."

"Splendid pieces, both of them," said Timothy.

"What I can't understand," Emma told him sharply, "is why you must keep them loaded. Not only those two, but all the rest of them. A loaded gun is dangerous."

"Completeness," said Timothy. "Certainly even you can appreciate completeness. The ammunition is an integral part of a gun. Without it, a gun is incomplete."

"That reasoning escapes me," said Horace. "It always has."

"I wasn't talking about the guns," said David. "I am sorry now that I mentioned them. I was only trying to tell you that I met Martin and Stella. I stayed at their place for several nights."

"What were they like?" asked Enid.

"Martin was a cold fish. A very cold fish. Talked very little and when he did, said nothing. I saw him only a few times, briefly each time. I had the feeling he resented my being there."

"And Stella?"

"A cold fish, too. But in a different way. Bitchy cold. Watching you all the time but pretending that she wasn't."

"Either of them seem dangerous? Dangerous to us, I mean."

"No, not dangerous. Just uncomfortable."

"We may be too complacent," said Emma in her timid voice. "Events have gone too well for us for a number of years and we may have fallen into the notion they will keep on going well forever. Horace is the only one of us who stays alert. He keeps busy all the time. It seems to me that the rest of us, instead of criticizing him, should be doing something, too.''

"Timothy keeps as busy as Horace," said Enid. "He spends all his time sifting through the books and scrolls that have been gathered for him. And who has gathered them for him? It has been David, going out to London and Paris and New York, taking the risk of leaving Hopkins Acre to collect them for him.''

"That may all be true, my dear," said Emma, "but, tell me, what might you be doing?"

"Dear people," protested Timothy, "we should not be quibbling with one another. And Enid, in her own way, does as much as all the rest of us, or more.''

David glanced down the table at Timothy, his soft-spoken, easy-going brother, and wondered how he put up with Emma and her lout of a husband. Even under the utmost provocation, he never raised his voice. With his saintlike face rimmed by his white and wispy beard, he was the quiet voice of reason before the tempests that at times rocked the family circle.

"Rather than argue," said David, "about which of us is doing the most to solve the dilemma that we face, it seems to me that it might be better to admit that no one of us is really doing much that bears upon the problem. Why don't we, quite simply and honestly, admit that we are refugees, hunched here, huddling, hoping that no one finds us out. I would suggest that none of us, if our life depended on it, could define the problem.''

"I think some of us here may be on the right track," said Horace, "and even if we're not, there are others looking for answers. The people in Athens and the Pleistocene . . .''

"That's exactly it," said David. "Us, Athens, the Pleistocene, and New York, if Martin and Stella are still there. How many of us altogether?"

"The point," said Horace, "is that there must be many other groups. Our three groups—our four groups, really—know of one another. There must be many, bound together as are our four groups, who do not know of us or other groups. This makes sense. Revolutionaries—and we, in a sense, are revolutionaries—are segregated in cells, with only minimal knowledge of one another."

"For my part," said David, stubbornly, "I still think we are pure and simple refugees—the ones who got away."

They had finished with the mutton by this time and Nora came in to pick up the platter, returning with a steaming plum pudding that she placed in the center of the table. Emma reached out and pulled it closer.

"It's already cut," she said. "Pass your dessert plates to me. There's sauce for those who wish it."

"I saw Spike today," said David, "when I was in the fields. He was playing that silly hopping game of his."

"Poor Spike," said Timothy. "He got sucked in with us. He came visiting. He was not one of the family, but he was there when it was time to go. We couldn't leave him there. I hope that he's been happy with us."

"He seems happy enough," said Enid.

"We're not about to find out if he is or not," said Horace. "He can't talk with us."

"He understands more than we think he does," said David. "Don't ever make the mistake of thinking he is stupid."

"He is an alien," said Timothy. "He was a pet—no, that's not quite right—he had an association of some sort with a neighboring family. In those days there were some strange associations with the aliens, not all of them entirely understandable. At least to me they weren't."

"With Henry it is different," said Enid. "He is one of the family. His connection may be a little distant, but he is one of us. He came along willingly enough."

"At times I worry about Henry," said Timothy. "We don't see much of him."

"He's busy," said David. "Having a good time. Roaming the countryside beyond Hopkins Acre, scaring the hell out of all the villagers and country folk and perhaps some of the gentry who are still benighted enough to believe in ghosts. He brings in a lot of local information. Because of him, and only because of him, we know a great deal of what is going on out beyond the Acre."

"Henry is no ghost," said Emma, primly. "You shouldn't talk about him the way you do."

"Of course he is no ghost," David agreed, "but he looks enough like one to fool anybody who doesn't know."

By common consent, they ceased their talk and settled down to the pudding, which was heavy, but exceedingly good.

I heard you talking of me, said a thought that was not a voice, but a thought so strong and clear that all at the table heard it.

"It's Henry," Emma screeched, all flustered.

"Of course it is," said Horace, croaking a little in his throat. "He delights in startling us at unseemly moments. He may be gone for days and then be at one's elbow, shouting in one's ear."

"Pull yourself together, Henry," said Timothy, "and sit down quietly in a chair. It is disquieting to be conversing with someone who is invisible."

Henry pulled himself, or most of himself, enough together so that he could be seen, though dimly, and sat down in a chair at the foot of the table, opposite Timothy. He was a misty sort of thing, somewhat like a man, although carelessly shaped. But what he pulled together did not stay together too well; it kept drifting back and forth so that the shape of the chair which still could be seen through his tenuous substance wavered with his drifting back and forth.

You have enjoyed a disgustingly heavy meal, he told them. Everything heavy. The mutton heavy. The pudding heavy. It is this heavy eating that makes all of you as heavy as you are.

"I am not heavy," Timothy told him. "I am so thin and stringy I totter in the wind."

You never walk in the wind, said Henry. You never leave the house. For years, you have not felt the warmth of honest sunlight.

"You are almost never in the house," said Horace. "You have more than your full share of sunlight."

I live by sunlight, Henry told him. Certainly you are

aware of that. The energy I pluck from the sun is what keeps me going. But it's not only the sun; it is other things as well. The sweet scent of pasture roses, the singing of the birds, the feel of naked soil, the whisper or the howling of the wind, the great, sweeping bowl of sky, the solid majesty of trees.

"You have an impressive catalog," said David, drily.

It is yours as well.

"I have some of it," said David. "I know of what you speak."

"Have you seen Spike?" asked Horace.

Off and on I see him. He is confined to the bubble around Hopkins Acre. I am the only one of you who can pass through the bubble without the help of time. I do some wandering.

"The wandering's all right, if that is what you want to do," said Horace. "But I wish you would cease your pestering of the natives. They look on you as a ghost. You have the neighborhood in a continual uproar."

They like it, said Henry. Their lives are dry and dull. They enjoy being scared. They huddle in their chimney corners and tell one another tales. If it were not for me, they'd not have those tales to tell. But that's not what I am here about.

"What are you here about?"

There are those who are curious about the bubble, Henry answered. They don't know what it is, they're not sure of its exact location, but they sense it and are curious about it. They are sniffing all about.

"Not the natives, certainly. There's no way they could be aware of it. It has stood here for almost a century and a half and . . ."

Not the natives, Henry told him. Something else. Something from Outside.

A deep and solid silence clamped down upon the room. They all sat, glued to their chairs, staring back and forth at one another. An ancient fear came out of the darkness of the house, centering on this one well-lighted room.

Finally Horace stirred. He cleared his throat and said, "So it has finally happened. I think we knew all along that some day it would. We should have expected it. They have tracked us down."

New York

3

A wrongness persisted, a sense of aberration, some factor not quite right, the feeling of a *corner*. But Boone could not pin it down; there seemed no way to reach it.

Corcoran had been going over the wall of the outermost room of the suite with his flashlight held only inches from the wall, bent forward in his effort to detect any sort of indication of a break in the smoothness of the wall. Now he halted and turned off the flash, swinging around to face Boone. Light from the street outside saved the room from darkness, but it was too dim for Boone to see Corcoran's face.

"It's hopeless," Corcoran said. "There is nothing here. Yet I know that outside those windows over there, a structure of some sort is pasted to the outside of this building. I can't be wrong on that. I saw it."

"I believe you, Jay," said Boone. "There is a wrongness here. I can feel it."

"You can't put a finger on it?"

"Not yet," said Boone.

He walked to one of the windows and looked out into the street. With a start, he saw that it was deserted. No cabs slid smoothly along it, no one was on the sidewalks. Peering more closely, he saw movement in a darkened doorway of the building across the street, then another, darker bulk; and, for only a moment, a glint of light reflected off one of the bulks.

"Jay," he asked, "when did you say they'd blow this building?"

"Sunday morning. Early Sunday morning."

"It's Sunday morning now. There are cops across the street. I saw light flash off a badge."

"Four or five o'clock. At first dawn. I checked other operations like this one. Always at first light, before a crowd would have a chance to gather. It's only a little after midnight. We still have several hours."

"I'm not sure of that," said Boone, "They could steal a march on us, do it before anyone thinks they'll do it. This is an old, socially historic place. The end of the Everest would be sure to draw a crowd. But if they blew it early, before anyone expected it . . ."

"They wouldn't do that," said Corcoran, moving over to him. "They simply wouldn't . . ."

A dull thud hit them, buckling them at the knees, and the plaster of the suite began to crack, fissures starting at the corners of the ceiling to run obliquely across it. The floor began to sag.

Boone grasped desperately at Corcoran, throwing both arms around him tightly.

And they were in another place, in another suite, a suite where there was no plaster cracking, no slumping of the floor.

Corcoran pulled angrily away from Boone. "What the hell was that?" he shouted. "Why did you grab . . . ?"

"The Everest is going down," said Boone. "Look out the window. See the dust."

"It can't be. We're still in the Everest."

"Not any longer," said Boone. "We're in that box you saw. We stepped around a corner."

"What the hell!" cried Corcoran. "You mean to say . . ."

"It took a crisis, Jay. I should have realized that. I can do it only at the last moment, at the crisis point, when there is no hope."

Corcoran looked at Boone accusingly. "You played a dirty trick on me. You didn't warn me."

"I didn't know, myself. This freakness of mine is a survival trait. It doesn't work until there is a threat. That's the way it always happened. It's an instinctive response."

"But always before you apparently were gone only for a while. You came back again. Will we be coming back . . . ?"

Boone shook his head. "I don't think so. I only came back when it was safe. Here we'll be hanging in the air with a building falling underneath us. If we step back around the corner, we'll be falling, too. And before, I had no real place to go. Every time before, I stepped into a sort of limbo—a gray, flat world of some kind of fog, with no real features. But this time, we stepped into a real place—this box. I can't be entirely sure, but I think I'm right."

"So this is it," Corcoran said. "We are in Martin's hideout. What do we do now?"

"That's up to you," Boone replied. "You wanted me to step around a corner. I did and took you with me. You are the one with all the questions. So start hunting for the answers."

He looked around the room in which they found themselves. The furniture was strange—familiar as to form and function, but very oddly structured. Against the farther wall stood what could have been a fireplace, but which, he told himself, probably wasn't one. Above it hung a rather massive rectangular form that could have been a painting. But it was so far beyond even the wildest, most twisted works of the latest artists he had known that he fought against the thought that it could be a piece of art.

The room seemed to be on a steady keel; it did not sag or shift. And how could that be? It had been somehow attached to the building that now was in the process of crumbling into an unsightly, shattered pile. Yet seemingly it held in place. Without the support of the blasted building, it still kept position, some hundred feet or more above the street.

Boone moved swiftly to a window and looked out. In the faint light of the street, a billowing cloud of mortar and plaster dust swirled above the surface of the pavement, while broken bricks, splintered wood, and shattered marble skittered along the sidewalks. There was no doubt that the old hotel had fallen or was in the process of falling.

The room in which he stood lurched suddenly, one end dropping, then regained its steadiness, while a shiver ran through it. Boone spun back from the window, holding his breath.

The lurch had unhinged the painting or whatever it might be, and it was swinging back to uncover a black panel set into the wall. The face of the panel was filled with gleaming instruments. In the center of it, a red light was flashing on and off.

Corcoran stood spraddle-legged, staring at the panel. The red light kept on blinking.

A voice came out of the panel, speaking gibberish. It kept on speaking gibberish. It spoke fast and angrily.

"Speak English!" Corcoran roared at it. "Speak English. Don't you know the language?"

The red light ceased its blinking and the voice said in English, a rather strangely accented English, "Of course, we know the tongue. But why speak in English? This is Martin, is it not? Where have you been? Why have you not answered us?"

"This is not Martin," Corcoran said. "Martin is not here."

"If you are not Martin, then who are you? What business have you answering? How come you are in Martin's place?"

"Friend, whoever you may be," said Corcoran, "the story is a long one and there is no time to tell you. The hotel has been razed, and here we hang in Martin's place, suspended in thin air and about to crash at any moment."

The speaker from the panel drew his breath in sharply. Then he said, "Don't get excited. We can set things right."

"I am not excited," Corcoran said, "but I think we may need a bit of help."

"We'll help. Listen carefully."

"I am listening carefully."

"You see a panel. You must see it. It's activated when the screening cover is unhinged. It must be unhinged."

"Damn it, it is unhinged. Cease this kindergarten silliness and tell me what to do. The panel's here. What does it do? How does it operate?"

"On the lower left-hand corner there is an array of—I suppose you could call them buttons. On the bottom row, starting from the right, count three and push the third button."

"It's pushed."

"Now count two up from that third button and push the second button."

"It's pushed," said Corcoran.

"Now—but don't do this until I tell you. Count upward at an angle to your right the space of three buttons. Do you understand?"

"I understand. I have my finger on the designated button."

"Don't push it yet. I have to know when you are about to push it. When you do push it, you give over control to me and I'll get you out of there."

"You mean you'll take control of this place we are in and move it elsewhere?"

"That's what I mean. Do you object to it?"

"I don't like it," Corcoran said. "But we're in no position to do much quibbling."

"You keep saying we. Are there more of you?"

"Two of us."

"Are you armed? Do you carry weapons?"

"No, of course not. Why should we have weapons?"

"I wouldn't know. Perhaps . . ."

"You're wasting time," shouted Corcoran. "We could crash at any time."

"You have the proper button?"

"Yes, I have."

"Then push it."

He pushed it. Darkness clamped in on them, a darkness that brought instant disorientation—as if they had been divorced from all reality. There was no sense of movement—no sense of anything.

Then there was a slight bump. The darkness fled and there was sunlight pouring through the windows and from the widening edges of a door, or port, that was opening downward, pivoting on its lower edge.

"I suppose," said Boone, "this is where we get off."

He stepped to the door. Beyond the port that had become an inclined exit he saw a lawn. Up the lawn was a house—an old house of considerable extent, built of weathered fieldstone that showed, here and there, a growth of moss.

A man who wore a hunting coat was coming down the lawn toward them. Over a crooked arm he carried a shotgun. He was flanked, on his right side, by a happy dog, a beautiful golden setter, and on his left by a globular monstrosity that stood almost as high as he did. The monstrosity was rolling sedately along beside him, matching its pace to his. Over all its surface, it was studded with extremely sharp-pointed spikes, gleaming and flashing in the sun. But the spikes, despite their sharpness, did not sink into the turf. For an instant, Boone had the strange feeling that it was walking on tiptoes, which was replaced almost immediately by the realization that it was floating, revolving slowly as it floated.

Boone walked down the slope until he reached the end of it and stepped down on the lawn. Behind him, Corcoran had halted and was staring at the scene, moving his head from side to side to take in all of it.

Up the lawn, several other people had come out of the house and were standing on the broad stone steps, watching what was going on.

The man with the shotgun, still flanked by the happy dog and the monstrosity, halted a dozen paces away and said, "Welcome to Hopkins Acre."

"So this is Hopkins Acre?"

"You have heard of it?"

"Just recently," said Boone. "Just the other day."

"What was said of it?"

Boone shrugged. "Not much. Nothing actually. Simply that someone had developed a sudden interest in it."

"My name is David," said the man. "This grotesque alien is Spike. I am happy that you made it. Horace is not the sort of technician into whose hands I would want to place my life. He is fumble-fingered."

"Horace is the one we spoke with?"

David nodded. "He has been trying for months to get in touch with Martin. When our panel alerted us this morning, he thought Martin was trying to reach him."

Corcoran came down the incline to stand beside Boone. "My name is Corcoran. My companion is named Boone. We are both immensely curious about what has happened to us. I wonder if you could explain it."

"You are no whit more curious than we," said David. "Let's all go up to the house and talk. I think Nora will be serving lunch soon. Perhaps a drink or two before we gather at the board."

"That would be excellent," Boone told him.

Shropshire: 1745

4

"**T**he one important thing for you to realize," Horace told them, "is that you can never leave this place. If there *were* any possibility of your leaving, we would have been forced to kill you."

"Horace is so dour," said Enid. "He has no sense of grace. He is like a hammer. He hammers everything. He could have said that he was sorry you could never leave, but assure you we are glad you're here."

"I'm not sure I am glad they are here," said Horace. "It is only another indication the situation is getting out of hand. Martin and Stella disappearing into thin air and no trace of them and the story that Ghost . . ."

"Henry!" Enid said. "Henry, not Ghost."

" . . . The story that Henry told us last night about something snooping all around the Acre, sensing a certain strangeness and trying to sniff out the strangeness. I tell you, they are closing in on us. Now here come these two from New York, with a not entirely satisfactory explanation of how they gained entrance to Martin's traveler and knowing, of all things, about Hopkins Acre."

"We've been here too long," Emma complained. "We should have broken the trail by going someplace else. No one should stay in one place for a century and a half."

"Moving to some other place would have involved some danger in itself," said Horace. "We'd have had to make arrangements for a team of technicians who could handle such an operation. We would, first of all, have had to scout another place to go. We could have done the scouting for ourselves, but we could not, unaided, have made the move to another place. We do not have the skill by half."

"I was under the impression," said David, rather nastily, "that you, unaided, can handle any sort of job."

Horace hunched his shoulders like an angry bull.

"Stop it," said Timothy, in his gentle way. "Stop it, the both of you. Instead of arguing among ourselves, we should be seeking to explain, as best we can, the situation these visitors have stumbled into as our guests."

"I sincerely wish you would," said Corcoran. "You tell us we can never leave, and yet David—it is David, is it not?"

"Yes," said David. "I am David and I leave occasionally. London and Paris mostly. Once to New York."

"And you mentioned that someone would be coming in from Athens. So there are comings and goings."

"The comings and goings, as you call them," said Timothy, "are by means of vehicles we call travelers. The traveler Martin lived in brought you here from New York, but that's not the entire story."

"I pushed buttons," said Corcoran.

"You could have gone on pushing buttons and still the traveler would not have stirred. What you did was push

certain buttons that tuned in the traveler with the control
panel in this house. Once that was done, Horace could
operate Martin's traveler."

"You mean only certain people can operate the
travelers?"

"The point is," said Horace, "that you're inside a time
bubble—a simplistic term, of course—through which no
one can pass, not even us. The only way to get through
it is by traveler."

They all sat silent for a moment.

"I forgot," said Horace. "Ghost is the only one who
can get through unaided and he is a special case."

"Henry," Enid reminded him. "Henry. Not Ghost."

"It seems to me," said Boone, "that we must accept
as gracefully as we are able all that you have told us. We
are here, you say, and we are not about to leave. I don't
understand much of what I've heard. There are a lot of
questions, but I suppose there'll be time later to voice all
of them."

"I am pleased you see it that way," said Timothy. "We
ourselves are bound by certain restrictions we cannot ignore. We hope you will be able to live a pleasant life with
us."

"There is one further question that seems to me too
important to wait. Who are you?" Boone asked.

"We are refugees," said David. "Refugees cowering
in the depths of time."

"Not so," Horace shouted. "You keep babbling about
us as refugees. We are revolutionaries, I tell you. Some
day we'll be going back."

Enid said to Boone, "Pay no attention to these two.
They are always at one another's throats. What you
meant, I'm sure, is where we came from. We are people
who once lived a million years from now. We are from
your very distant future."

Nora spoke from the door that led into the dining room.
"Lunch is on."

Lunch was civilized and pleasant with no bickering.
David talked of the few days he had spent in twentieth-
century New York and asked Boone and Corcoran about

the city. Timothy talked about some of the reading he had been doing. Enid said little. Emma was sweetly silent. Horace sat hunched over, occupied with his own thoughts. Finally he was moved to speech. "I wonder what has happened to Gahan. He should be here by now."

"Gahan is from Athens," said Emma. "He is bringing Timothy a new book."

"We always say Athens," Timothy explained. "But they're really not in Athens, although quite close to it."

"We also have a small group in the Pleistocene," said David. "Southern France. The early days of the last glaciation."

"Neanderthals," said Boone.

"Yes, a few of them. Early Neanderthal."

"What I can't understand," said Horace, still tied up in worry, "is why Martin should have left so hurriedly. And Stella, too. Apparently he had a small traveler hidden in a warehouse and he used that to get away, alerting Stella so that she could join him. He should have used his residence traveler to get away. But he didn't. He panicked. The damn fool panicked. He got scared and ran."

"He was afraid of being trapped at the hotel," said Enid. "That seems quite clear to me. Perhaps he did not place complete trust in Mr. Corcoran."

"There was no reason that he should have," said David. "According to Mr. Corcoran's own admission, he had men watching Martin and Stella. They were watched at every move."

"He bought my trust and paid very well for it," said Corcoran. "I'll work for anyone wholeheartedly if he pays me for it. Never, in all my life, have I ever double-crossed a client."

"But you didn't trust your client in this case," said David.

"I can't say I did. He gave me no reason to. I watched him not to do him harm, but to be certain he did no harm to me. He was a curiously secretive man. He was a slippery character."

"He must have known the hotel was to be razed," said Horace. "Surely the tenants would have been notified.

To have left the resident traveler, knowing that, facing the possibility that its presence might have been revealed, is inexcusable."

"Maybe he didn't know about the hotel," said Corcoran. "The tenants were not notified until the last possible legal moment. And even then, there was no public announcement. It was one of those quiet deals. It was long after Martin left that I heard of it. And there is little rumor that I miss."

"Then," said David, "perhaps he left on some quick errand, thinking he'd soon be back. That may be why he left the residence traveler."

Horace rumbled at Boone, "What you have not fully explained is how the two of you were able to get into the traveler. Not how you detected it; that I can understand. But how you got into it."

"I told you what I could," said Boone. "I stepped around a corner. I can't tell you more. I don't understand myself how I do it. All I know is that it can be accomplished only under stress."

"That is no explanation," said Horace. "Surely a man knows what he does."

"Sorry," said Boone. "I can't help you further."

"And since we are getting down to fine points," said Corcoran, somewhat out of sorts, "tell me what all that gibberish meant when I first contacted you."

"On that point I can answer you," said Timothy. "As you must perceive, we are very furtive folk. Perhaps at times too committed to a cloak and dagger ethic. We think our communications system cannot be tapped. But arrayed against us are forces that are powerful and most wondrously intelligent. We can't be sure how safe we are; we never can be sure. So when we talk among ourselves on the communication system, we employ a very ancient language, the speech of a small and obscure group of humans. By this method, we hope that, even if our communications could be penetrated, there is little possibility that the listener could decipher what we're saying."

"This," said Boone, "is the most insane setup I have ever come across."

"You know not the half of it," said Timothy. "You do not know the Infinites. If you knew the Infinites . . ."

A shriek sounded from the kitchen. Timothy and Emma leaped to their feet. Nora, still shrieking, appeared in the kitchen door. Her cap was awry upon her head and her hands were twisting the apron that was tied about her waist.

"Visitors!" she screamed. "There are visitors. And there is something wrong. The traveler landed in the flower bed and tipped over on its back."

Chairs screeched and everyone was charging for the kitchen, heading for the outside door.

Corcoran looked at Boone. "Could it be that Athens chap?"

"I suppose it could," said Boone. "We had better go and see."

They halted on the kitchen stoop and stared at what was happening in the flower bed. A great gash had been plowed across the bed by a rectangular object, some twelve feet in length and half as wide, its nose buried at an angle in the soil. David, Horace, Enid, and Timothy were shoving and tugging at it. Emma stood to one side, loudly lamenting.

"We should give them a hand," said Corcoran.

Boone and he loped across the lawn.

"What do you want to do with it?" Boone asked a panting Horace.

"Pull it free," gasped Horace. "Get it right side up."

With the extra manpower, the craft was wrenched free from the soil and turned over.

Horace and David attacked what seemed to be a panel set into the side of it. Slowly the panel yielded to their clawing fingers, then popped open. David threw himself into the opening, crawled for a ways, then began backing out.

"Give me some help," he yelled. "I have hold of Gahan."

Horace wedged in beside David, fumbling for a hold, then the two of them began backing out, hauling a limp human figure. They hauled it across the flower bed and laid it in the grass.

Gahan lay upon his back. He was bleeding at the mouth. One arm hung limp; his chest was sopped with blood. Horace knelt beside him, lifting and cradling him. The eyes came open and the bloody mouth moved, but only gurgling came out.

Enid rushed in and knelt beside him. "It's all right, Gahan. You are safe. You are at the Acre."

"What happened?" Emma screeched.

Words and blood came from the mouth. "It's gone," he said, then choked on the blood.

"What is gone, Gahan? What is gone?"

He struggled to speak and finally said, "Athens." That was all.

Timothy said, "We had better get him to the house. He is badly hurt."

"How could it have happened?" Emma shouted.

"He crashed, damn it," said David. "He was hurt and lost control."

The wounded man struggled, trying to speak. Horace raised him higher. Enid tried to wipe the blood off his mouth with a filmy handkerchief, only smearing it.

"Athens," came the blood-choked whisper. "Athens base gone. Destroyed."

He slumped more deeply into Horace's arms.

Boone pushed closer to Horace and laid his fingers on Gahan's throat, feeling for a pulse. He took his hand away.

"This man is dead," he said.

Reverently, Horace withdrew his arms and let Gahan slump onto the grass. He rose slowly to his feet and the silence of the group was deadly. They looked at one another, not quite understanding.

Timothy said to Boone, "We shouldn't leave him out here. Will you help me carry him?"

"We'll have to bury him," said Emma. "We'll have to dig a grave."

"We have to talk," said Horace. "First, before anything, we will have to talk."

"Where do you want to put him?" Timothy asked Emma.

"A bedroom," said Emma. "Upstairs. The back bedroom to the right. We can't put him in the drawing room. All that blood will spoil the furniture."

"How about the gun room? That would be easier. We wouldn't have to haul him up the stairs. There's a leather couch in there. We can wipe off the leather."

"All right, then. The gun room."

Boone and Timothy picked up the body, Boone by the shoulders, Timothy by the feet. They made their way across the kitchen and through the dining room, with David shoving aside the pushed-back chairs to clear room for them. At the far end of the drawing room, they reached the gun room door.

"Over there," said Timothy. "Over there against the wall."

They laid the dead man on the couch and Timothy stood looking down at him.

"I don't know," he said. "I don't know how to handle this. There has been no death in this house since first we came. It's a new experience and we are not ready for it. We're very close to immortal, you know. The time mechanism keeps it that way."

"No, I hadn't known," said Boone.

"Inside the time bubble we do not age. We age only when we are outside of it."

Boone said nothing in reply.

"This is bad," said Timothy. "This is one of the crisis points that you run across in history. We must decide what we should do. Decision and no mistakes. That's important—no mistakes. Come with me. The others will be talking."

The others were not talking. Gathered in the dining room, they were shouting and screaming at one another.

"I knew it," Emma screamed. "I knew it. I just knew it. We were getting along too well. We thought it would keep on that way forever. We should have been looking ahead, making plans . . ."

"Making plans for what?" yelled David, drowning her

out. "How could we know what to plan for? How could we know what might happen?"

"Don't you yell at my wife!" roared Horace. "Don't you ever again use that tone of voice to your sister. She is right. We should have imagined all sorts of contingencies and worked out models for our reaction to them. We shouldn't be standing here, like we are right now, caught unawares and trying to figure out the best course to follow."

"I think," said Timothy, adding his voice to the squabble, "that what we had better do is just settle down and do some quiet thinking on it."

"We haven't the time to do any quiet thinking on it," yelled Horace. "Not the leisurely kind of thinking that you mean. I know you, Timothy. You just put things off. You won't face up to anything. You never would face up to anything. I remember the time . . ."

"I agree we should be doing something," David shouted. "I think Timothy's approach is wrong. It's no time for sitting back and waiting for something to happen. Certainly there are measures we could take. But each of us can't just keep shouting what he or she may think and . . ."

"We've got to get away," screamed Emma. "We have to get away from here."

"There is no good," yelled David, "in simply running. Run, yes, if we have to, but we must have a plan."

"I will not run," shouted Horace. "I'm not about to run. Running is for cowards and I will not have it said . . ."

"But we have to run," screamed Emma. "We have to get away. We can't wait for whatever's coming. We have to find a safe place."

"You won't find a safe place running," Horace bellowed. "We have to use our heads."

"I still think," said Timothy, "that we are reacting too precipitously. A few days more or less will not make that much difference."

"In a few days you could be dead," yelled Horace.

"At least we have to give Gahan a decent burial," protested Timothy.

"Gahan doesn't count," yelled Horace. "Gahan's dead. Nothing more can happen to him. We are still alive, and what happens does matter to us and . . ."

Boone stepped on a chair and from the chair to the table, kicking china and glass aside.

"Shut up, all of you!" he thundered. "Shut up and sit down!"

All of them stopped yelling and turned to stare at him.

"You have no place in this," said Emma, tartly, "You're not one of us."

"You made me and Corcoran part of your group," said Boone, "when you told us we could never leave this place. We both have the right to speak. We're in the same boat with you. So shut up, all of you, and sit down."

Startled, they all found chairs and sat down.

Boone said to Corcoran, who still stood against a wall, "Jay, if anyone starts yelling, if anyone gets to his feet, will you shut him up?"

"Quite willingly," said Corcoran.

"I understand," said Boone, "that this is no more than a healthy family squabble and that most of you didn't mean half of what you said. But you were not about to get anywhere and I think you do have to make some plans. Whether you like it or not, I'll serve as referee."

Horace stood up. Corcoran pushed himself away from the wall and started toward him. Horace sat down.

"You had something you wanted to say?" Boone asked Horace.

"What I was about to say is that you understand none of what is going on. You have not the background that is required of a referee."

"In that case," said Boone, "perhaps you'll fill me in."

"Horace won't," said Enid. "He'll tell it as he sees it. He will shade the meaning . . ."

Horace stood up. Corcoran pushed off the wall. Horace sat down again.

"All right, Miss Enid," said Boone. "Perhaps you'll proceed with your unbiased version." He said to Horace,

"You'll have your chance later on. But the rules are one at a time and no shouting and no shoving."

"We are a group of refugees," said Enid. "We are . . ."

"Not refugees!" yelled Horace.

"You shut up," said Boone. "Enid, please go on."

"As I told you earlier," said Enid, "we are from a million years into your future. In that million years the human race has changed."

"Was encouraged to change," said Horace, interrupting. "On its own, the race would not have changed."

"You can't be sure of that," said David. "For example, there is Henry."

"I can be sure," said Horace. "The Infinites . . ."

Boone raised a hand to stop him. Horace stopped.

"You used that word," Boone said to Timothy. "I was about to ask you more about it and then the Athens traveler came. Tell me, what are these Infinites?"

"The Infinites are another intelligence," Timothy told him. "They are from somewhere in the galactic center. They are not biological. Maybe they were at one time and changed to what they are."

"As a matter of fact," said David, "we know little about them."

"I wouldn't say that," objected Horace. "We know, at least approximately, what they are."

"All right," said Boone. "We have wandered from the point. Enid was about to tell us how the human race had changed in a million years."

"They changed," said Enid, "from corporeal beings, from biological beings, to incorporeal beings, immaterial, pure intelligences. They now are ranged in huge communities on crystal lattices. They are . . ."

Horace broke out, "The obscenity of it! The immorality . . ."

"Shut up!" Boone roared at him.

He turned to Enid. "But you are human beings. The people in the outpost near Athens were human beings. Biological and . . ."

"There were some who rebelled," said Enid. "Some who fled to escape incorporeality."

"The incorporeality was, to many of the human race, something akin to a new and exciting religion," said Timothy. "There were, however, some who protested most violently against it. We number ourselves among those protestants. There are many other protestants hiding out in various time periods. We maintain small, widely separated groups. It is harder to find us that way. The protestants fled, and now the Infinites or their agents hunt us down. I think the belief that the incorporeality process was a religion was an entirely human idea. With the Infinites, I am convinced, it was not a religion, but a plan, a universal plan. The Infinites are convinced that one thing, and one thing only, can survive the death of the universe. That is intelligence. So the Infinites are busily at work creating a corpus of intelligence. Certainly not the human race alone, but including many other intelligences in the galaxy, perhaps in the universe. The Infinites in this galaxy may be no more than one primitive mission of many missions spread throughout the universe, working diligently with the benighted, heathen populations."

"It is mad!" yelled Horace. "I tell you, it is madness!"

"You understand," said Emma, "we never saw the Infinites. Some people did, I guess."

"What Emma means," said Horace, "is that none of us, here in this room, saw them. Other humans did and became convinced that the entire human race should allow itself to be turned into pure mind entities. This belief of theirs became an insane article of faith. Those who rebelled against it became outlaws."

"What you must realize," said Timothy, speaking softly, "is that our race was ripe for such a development. Even before the Infinites put in their appearance, the human race had changed. By that period from which we fled, viewpoints and philosophical concepts had been vastly altered. The race had gotten tired, was bored. It had made too much progress, had accomplished too much. Progress no longer meant a great deal. Dilettantism was, by and large, the norm."

"But you?" asked Boone.

"Not we," said Timothy. "Not we and certain others. We did not fall into the trap. We were the outlanders, the backwoods rednecks, residing far beyond the fringe of the shining society which humanity had become. We wanted to stay human. We distrusted the new ways. That is why we were outlawed."

"But the time travelers?"

"We stole the time concept from the Infinites," said Horace. "We still were human enough to do anything necessary to protect ourselves. The Infinites do not lie or steal. They are great and noble."

"And stupid," said David.

"Yes, that is right," said Horace. "And stupid. But now they have found us out and we must get away again."

"I can't leave," said Timothy. "I have decided that I will not go. I will not leave my books or my notes, the work that I have done."

"What Timothy is trying to do," Enid explained to Boone, "is get an inkling of where, and how, the human race went wrong, how it could have gotten itself into the situation that convinced the people of a million years from now to go along with the scheme of the Infinites. Timothy thinks that back here, close to the roots of our civilization, he may find a clue through a close study of history and philosophy."

"I am close to it," said Timothy. "I am convinced I am. But I can't carry on my work without my books and notes."

"There won't be room," said Horace, "to take along all your notes, let alone your books. Our traveler capacity is limited. We have Martin's resident traveler and I am glad we have it. We have our own small traveler and Gahan's traveler, if it still operates . . ."

"I doubt there is much wrong with it, if anything," said David. "Gahan lost control of it, that's all. It made a fairly soft landing in the flower bed."

"We'll have a look at it," said Horace.

"Now we are beginning to make some progress," said Boone. "But there are decisions that have to be made. If you are convinced that we have to go, has anyone any idea where we should go?"

"We could join the group in the Pleistocene," said Emma.

Horace shook his head. "Not that. Athens is destroyed and Henry says something is sniffing all around us. The possibility is good the Pleistocene people have been located as well. If they have not been, our going there could lead whoever is looking for us to them. My suggestion would be to go back deeper into time, beyond the Pleistocene."

"It seems to me we should go into the future," said David, "and try to find out what is going on."

"Back into the hornet's nest," said Emma.

"If that is what it takes," said David. "There probably are some people like us still up there, those who did not leave, who are skulking around, toughing it out, making out as best they can."

"Martin might know something about what is going on," said Horace, "but where the hell is Martin?"

"We need some time to think it out a bit," said David. "We can't make decisions on the run."

"Two days, then," said Horace. "Two days and we're gone."

"I hope you understand," said Timothy, speaking slowly and decisively, "that I intend to go nowhere. I am staying here."

The Monster

5

Boone sat on a low stone fence that ran between a pasture and a field. In the field, two setters ran in happy frolic, chasing one another, giving chase to the birds their gamboling flushed from the stubble. The late afternoon sun was warm, and the cloudless sky arched like a great blue dome.

For a couple of hours, Boone had prowled the Acre, accompanied by the happy dogs. He first had set out with a solid determination to find the time bubble, to locate the wall of differentiating time that somewhere must come down to earth. He had tried to walk a straight line, stopping every now and then to realign the landmarks he had

set up to insure his going straight. But after an hour or
more of walking his straight line, he had found, with some
astonishment, that he had come back approximately to
that point where he had started out.

The walk, however, had not been entirely pointless nor
a complete failure. During the hour or more, the countryside through which he walked had seeped into him. It
had been a long time since he had gone for a walk in any
countryside, and the walk had brought back memories of
other walks in other years and in other lands. He had come
upon a flock of complacent sheep that stood and watched
him with mild question in their eyes, then trotted off a
ways, but stopped and stood to watch him as he ambled
past them. He had stepped across small, swiftly flowing
brooks with water that had a crystal look; he had walked
through small, neat groves of trees; he had noted with
deep satisfaction the autumn wild flowers that grew along
the brooks, nodding above the mirror of the water and
along the hedges.

And now he sat upon the low stone wall, not far from
where he had clambered over it to begin the walk. Behind
him was the road that ran up, between the rows of dying
poplars, to reach the house; the sweep of stubbled field
before him. And sitting, he thought with muted wonder
of what he and Corcoran had been told by the people of
the house. It was so fantastic and so beyond all imagination that he had found much difficulty in bringing it to
grips. He could find no starting point to begin a logical
consideration of it. Far down the field, at the edge of a
grove of trees, he caught the flicker of something moving.
Watching it, he finally made out that it was a man, and
a short time later recognized Corcoran. As he watched,
Corcoran came striding up the slope toward him.

He waited on the wall until Corcoran finally came up
to him.

Boone patted the wall beside him. "Sit down, Jay," he
said. "Tell me what you found."

For Corcoran, he knew, had not gone walking without
purpose; he had been seeking something.

"I found the edge of the bubble," Corcoran told him.

"I am sure I did, although it was very hazy, and I would not take an oath on it."

"I hunted for it myself," said Boone. "I walked a straight line and ended up where I had started out. I did not find the wall, but you have different eyes."

"That's it, I suppose. I do have different eyes. But also I have a witness. Henry, go ahead and tell him."

"Henry? Jay, you're stark raving. There is no one with you. You came up the slope alone."

"I met a friend along the way. I forgot that you can't see him in the sun. Henry, move over into the shadow of that tree so my friend can see you."

He made a thumb toward a small tree growing beside the wall. "You can see him in the shade."

Boone looked at the tree. There was nothing there— and then he saw a hazy flickering, dancing in the air like dust motes dancing in a narrow sunbeam coming through the slats of a window blind.

A soundless voice addressed him out of the shadow of the tree, the unspoken words impinging on his brain.

I am glad to meet you, sir. I am Henry, although at times Horace calls me Ghost, much to the uneasiness and wrath of other members of the family. Ghost I do not mind at all. Ghost might even be the proper name for such as I. For, after all, who is there to say what is and what is not a ghost. Although, if I am a ghost, I am not a ghost out of the past, as I suspect most other ghosts would be, but a ghost from the future.

"Well, I'll be damned," said Boone, "And yet, in light of other things, you're almost commonplace. Earlier in the day there was mention of you by the family. By the way, I'm Boone. Tom Boone. Jay and I are friends from long ago."

What your friend told you of his seeing of the time wall is true, Henry said in Boone's mind. I know he saw it, although imperfectly. Your friend is most unusual. So far as I know, no other human actually can see it, although there are ways of detecting time. I tried to show him a sniffler. There are a number of snifflers, trying to sniff out the bubble. They know there's something strange, but don't know what it is.

"Did you see the sniffler?" Boone asked Corcoran.

"I saw something. A rather small thing. No larger than an ordinary dog. But I did not see it well. All I knew was that there was something there."

I know not what the snifflers are, said Henry. But in our situation we must be at least marginally concerned with anything that transpires beyond the ordinary.

"How are things going at the house?" Corcoran asked Boone.

"When I left they were talking. Not shouting at one another. Horace and Enid were off to one side, arguing about where they would bury Gahan. But the rest were talking, discussing things."

"I think it was wise for both of us to leave," said Corcoran. "Give them a chance to talk among themselves without outsiders being present."

Boone agreed. "This is their show. It should be up to them to make their own decisions."

"Back there, when you jumped up on the table, you damn well made it your show."

"It wasn't that," said Boone. "I wasn't trying to horn in. But they weren't getting anywhere. They were yelling at one another, that was all. They could have kept it up all day. They needed someone to knock some common sense into them."

You think ill of them because of their bad behavior, said Henry. I readily admit that it is bad, but you must understand the stake they have in all of this. They fled the future a century and a half or so of your years ago. They fled for their lives, of course, but they also fled so that men and women might not live as bodiless abstractions, so that the race might be more than theoretical or hypothetical thought processes. Look upon me. I was halfway to being the nothing that all humans would be if the Infinites had their way. With me it did not take. The procedure stuttered and I was spat out and was free; in my present form, I can not be snared again. I am beyond everything except, perhaps, some extraordinary harm of which I am not yet aware. And having escaped, I came back to the family, and with them I fled. By reason of my unorthodox form, I was able to be of some assistance to them. And out of their recognition of me as still a member of the family, the family flies to my defense when Horace, whose only family association is that he cowed and persuaded my sister Emma to marry him, pays me less respect than is due a member.

"Your tale is fascinating," said Corcoran, "and adds to our comprehension of the situation that we find here. You must be aware how difficult it is for us to grasp all the nuances of what has happened a million years beyond our time."

Indeed I do, said Henry, and I must admit I am amazed at how well and solidly you have accepted what you have learned of us in the last few hours. You have not been bowled over by our revelations.

"It is because we are too numb to be bowled over," said Boone.

I think it is not that at all. You have betrayed no numbness. Your reactions have led me to believe that basically our race is far more rational than we might have expected to find so deep in our ancestral roots.

"I'm curious," said Corcoran, "how you could have performed significant services for your family in their flight."

I acted as a scout, said Henry. I am admirably fitted to act as such. Who would suspect a flittering moonbeam or a slight glitter in the sunlight? Even seeing this, any reasonable man would lay it to a momentary aberration of his visual faculty. So I went into the past, all by myself. Unlike the others, I need no traveler; space and time are open roads to me. I went as an advance agent, a feeler-outer. The others made arrangements and waited on my word. But before I could get back, they were forced to flee precipitously, with no direction and no plan. I finally found them in the depths of the so-called Dark Ages, when large areas of Europe were deserted, dank and desolate. A perfect place to hide, perhaps, but most disagreeable.

"It was you, then, who found this place, Hopkins Acre."

That is right. There were other locations that might have done as well or better, places that I liked much better. But this one was made to order for our taking over. The owner and all his family were absent on a tour of the Continent. Even before I went hunting for the others, I tracked down technicians in my own time who could secure this tract for us. So there it was, as you see it now, waiting for my family once I had found them in that noisome fen that was Dark Age Europe.

"I can't help but wonder about the Hopkins family," said Corcoran. "They came back from vacation and their home was gone as if it had never been here. And the rest of the neighborhood—a house, a farm, an estate with all the people who lived on it, wiped out overnight—what was the neighborhood reaction?"

I do not know, said Henry. None of us ever knew or thought of it. It was no concern of ours. All we took was property that we needed. Property is not sacred.

David's voice came from behind them. "I saw you sitting here," he said, "and I came down to tell you the funeral is at sundown."

"Is there anything we can do?" asked Boone. "Help with the grave, perhaps?"

David shook his head. "No need of help. Horace is a husky man and can move a lot of dirt. A little labor will do no harm to Timothy, much as he may loathe it. A few blisters on his soft and uncalloused hands would be a great education for our brother Timothy. Emma's helping, too."

David climbed the wall and sat down with them.

"Henry is here with us," said Corcoran. "We've been talking with him. An enjoyable and instructive conversation."

"I thought he was," said David. "I caught the sense of him. Henry, I am glad you're here. All the family should be on hand for the burial. All of us now will be there, barring Spike. Do you have an idea where he is? Could you go and find him?"

I have no idea, David. No one can keep track of him. He could be anywhere. After all, it matters little. He is not exactly family.

"By now he is," said David.

"One thing I am curious about," said Corcoran. "Was any determination made of how Gahan died?"

"Horace had a look at him. His chest was torn open, as if a great taloned claw had struck him and torn it all away. How he lived long enough to warn us, I do not comprehend. He was close to death when the traveler crashed."

"How long would it have taken? I mean the trip from Athens to here."

"It would have been almost instantaneous."

"That sounds right. On our trip from New York, there was a momentary darkness, then almost immediately the bump of landing."

"Horace, I suppose," said David, "is the only one of us who would have thought to examine Gahan. Horace beats out his brains getting to the bottom of things, planning ahead. But he has no capacity for the long range. Right now he has all three travelers lined up on the lawn. Gahan's traveler is operative. The landing in the flower bed damaged it not at all. So Horace has them all stocked with food and some of Timothy's weapons."

"I take it, then, that you have decided to leave."

"Well, yes, I would suppose so, although not exactly when or where to. Horace has each of us assigned to specific travelers."

"And when you leave, are we going with you?"

"Why, most assuredly. Our numbers are not large. Quite possibly, we will have need of you."

"I suppose we should be grateful."

"Grateful or not, you are going with us. The both of you."

"I don't think I would enjoy staying here," said Corcoran, "trapped on a few acres inside a displaced segment of time."

"It is strange how it has all worked out," said David musingly, as if he might be talking to himself. "With the family, I mean. Horace, the hardheaded, practical lout, the organizer, the schemer. Emma, the moaner, the keeper of our consciences. Timothy, the student. Enid, the thinker. And I, the loafer, the bad example, the one who makes the others feel virtuous."

"There is one thing you said," Boone told him. "Enid is the thinker. It seemed to me you put a special emphasis, almost a special meaning . . ."

"In the time from which we came," said David, "there was finally time to think. There was no need to break one's back to make a living or to get ahead. We had made our progress and we had no great regard for it. So, given the time to do so, many turned to thought."

"Philosophy?"

"No, just thinking for the sake of thinking. A way to kill one's time. It was an activity held in very high regard. It brought about many great ideas, discussed most learnedly and politely, but never put to use. We were tired of putting things to use. The great thing about thinking is there's never any end to it. You could spend a lifetime thinking, and many people did. Perhaps that was the reason so many of us could equate ourselves with the Infinites' idea of turning ourselves into units of incorporeal intelligence, thinking entities unhampered by the grossness of a biological body."

"You come close to sounding as if you approved of the program pushed by the Infinites."

"Not at all," said David. "I am only trying to tell you the situation as it applied to many of the race."

"But Enid . . ."

"With her, it is slightly different. Look at it this way. Timothy is a student, studying mankind's past in an attempt to find the basic, early flaws in the human culture, in the hope that the future remnant of the biological race can set up a way of life that has a better chance of reasonable survival. Enid is trying, by the exercise of deductive thought, to arrive at independent scenarios that may serve as guides for the new culture that must be established if any of our race are to survive as biological beings. Both Timothy and Enid are trying to lay out new paths for us. Give them time and they may come up with a new human pattern."

Here comes Enid now, said Henry.

The three sitting on the wall clambered off it and stood, waiting for her.

"We are about to begin," said Enid.

"Henry's here, with us," said David.

"Good," she said. "Then all of us will be there. Even Spike is here. He came rolling in just a while ago."

They started up the slope toward the house, Corcoran and David walking ahead, Boone falling in beside Enid. She took his arm and spoke in a confidential voice.

"There is no coffin," she said. "No time to build one. We wrapped him well in a new white muslin sheet and Timothy found a length of canvas that Emma and I sewed into a shroud. It's the best that we could do. Horace is in a dither. He thinks we should get away at once."

"And what do you think?"

"I suppose he's right. We probably have to go. But I hate to leave this house. It's been home for a long, long time. We are burying Gahan at the foot of an old oak tree back of the house."

"You have a fondness for trees?"

"Yes. It's not an unusual love. Many people love them. Would it surprise you if I told you trees will come after men? The trees will supersede us; they will take our place."

Boone laughed. "That's as fine-honed a conceit as I have ever heard."

She did not answer and they went up the slope in silence. As they came up to the house, she gestured to her right. "There the travelers are," she said. "All lined up and waiting."

And there they were on the lawn before the house— the two smaller ones the closest and the large one that had served Martin as living quarters a little distance off.

"You and your friend will be going with us," she said. "Had anyone thought to tell you that? I hope that you don't mind. I am sorry that you got mixed up in this."

He said grimly, not entirely joking, "I wouldn't have missed it for the world."

"Do you really mean that?" she asked.

"I'm not quite sure," he told her. "One thing I do know. When you leave, I'd rather go with you, wherever you may be going, than stay here in this place, unable to get out."

Corcoran and David had turned to the left to go around the house.

"Right after the funeral," said Enid, "we'll get together and make a final decision what to do."

A high-pitched, ragged screech came from somewhere behind the house. It cut off for a moment, then took up again, a caterwaul of fright which kept on and on, its pitch going up and up.

Boone started running toward the sound, sobbing as he ran, for suddenly the terror in the shrieking closed down all about him and seemed to grasp him by the throat.

As he was about to round the corner of the house, something going fast and hard struck him in mid-stride and bowled him over, tumbling him across the grass until he brought up in a thicket of rosebushes, half in, half out of the thorny clump. He tipped forward into the soft earth that extended beyond the clump and landed nose down in the dirt.

He pawed at his face to wipe away the clinging dirt, scrabbling with the other hand to claw himself free of the bushes, which was not an easy thing to do, for the sharp and solid thorns had snagged into his clothing and resisted all attempts to pull loose.

With the dirt partially off his face, he saw Emma streaking for the Martin traveler, with some, perhaps all, of the others close behind her—all running as if the very devil were nipping at their heels. It was Emma, he thought, who ran into me.

He lunged desperately to pull himself free of the bushes, but a clinging rose sprout with a grip still on his trouser leg tripped him so that he sat down solidly upon the ground, facing back along the left side of the house.

Something was coming along the side of the house, a

sort of thing he had never seen before nor would have believed possible. It was like a living spider web a good twelve feet or more across. It throbbed with pulses of energy, or what he thought of as energy, running all across it, flickering and sparkling and flashing all along and across the tiny threads that made up the web. Behind the threads was a mirror, or a disk of some sort that might have been an eye. Through the flashing energy, Boone dimly saw what could have been mechanical appendages that were beginning to reach out and down toward him. There were other things immersed within the web, but what they could be he could not imagine.

A voice shrieked at him. "Boone, you fool! Run! I'll wait for you."

He lunged to his feet, jerking his trouser free of the bush, and spun about, beginning to run.

There was only one of the smaller travelers left upon the lawn, standing with the port wide open and Enid beside it.

"Run!" she shouted. "Run!"

He ran as he had never run before. Enid leaped into the traveler. From the entrance, she beckoned at him desperately.

He reached the traveler and sprang into the port, catching his toe on the edge of it and sprawling on top of Enid.

"Get off me, you dunce!" she shouted, and he flung himself to one side. The port banged shut. As it closed, he glimpsed the web, almost on top of them. Enid was scrambling frantically toward a glowing instrument panel in the front of the traveler.

Boone started to crawl forward, but there was a sudden shock that pinned him to the floor, and with the shock came darkness, the utter, unnerving darkness he had experienced when the Martin traveler had left New York.

Enid and Boone

6

Light came back—blinking lights on the panel and faint sunlight from a small observation screen.

Boone struggled to his knees, tried to rise to his feet. He bumped his head rather painfully on the ceiling.

"These vehicles are cramped," said Enid, speaking easily, unexcited. "You crawl on your hands and knees."

"Where are we?"

"I'm not sure where. I had no chance to pick a location or a time. I simply told it 'go!' "

"That was taking a chance, wasn't it?"

"Sure it was. But would you rather I had stayed and let that monster wreck the traveler?"

"No, of course not. I implied no criticism."

"I am getting a reading," said Enid, bending low over the panel. "A time reading, that is. I still don't know where we are."

"And the reading?"

"Measured from where we started, more than 50,000 years into the past—54,100 to be exact."

"50,000 B.C.?"

"That's right," she said. "Open country. A plain. Hills in the distance. Funny looking hills."

He crawled forward, crowded in beside her, and looked through the forward vision plate.

Scant grass flowed toward bald, squat hills. In the distance were dots that looked like a grazing game herd.

"America, I think," he said. "The western plains. Somewhere in the southwestern United States, more than likely. I can't tell you how I know. I just have a feel for it. Desert in my time, but 50,000 years before that, it would have been good grassland."

"People?"

"Not likely. The best bet is that men first came to the continent 40,000 years before my time. Not sooner. The scientists could be wrong, of course. In any case, Ice Age America. There would be glaciers to the north."

"Safe enough, then. No bloodthirsty tribesmen. No ravening carnivores."

"There are carnivores, but there's good feeding for them. They shouldn't bother us. Any idea where the others are?"

She shrugged. "It was each man for himself."

"Timothy? He said he wouldn't go."

"I think he went with the others. Your friend, Corcoran, held back, arguing, seeing what was happening to you. David picked him up and heaved him into the other small traveler. They all took off, not waiting for us."

"You waited for me."

"I couldn't leave you to that monster."

"You think it's the one that destroyed the base at Athens?"

"Probably. There is no way of knowing. You know this place we are in?"

"If it's the southwestern United States, I've been there. Spent a couple of vacations there. It looks like it to me, unless some other places have that kind of butte. I've never seen any that resembled them in any other part of the world."

"The food and whatever else Horace threw in the traveler should be somewhere in the back. He put some supplies in each of the travelers, but he was in a hurry and he probably paid less attention to what he included than he should have. I think he threw the rifle that David brought Timothy from New York in this one."

"You want to go out now?"

"I think we should. It's terribly cramped in here. Get out and stretch our legs, have a look, take a little time to decide what we should do."

"Have you any idea what we should do?"

"None. But in this sort of place it should take a while to track us down, if it can be done at all."

Crawling the length of the traveler, Boone found the rifle, a rucksack, a roll of blankets, and a few other packages bundled up in haphazard fashion. He got them all together while Enid opened the port.

Crouching in the doorway, Boone examined the rifle. One cartridge was in the breech and it had a clip of five. There was, he hoped, more ammunition in the bundles.

"You stay here for a moment," he told Enid. "Give me a chance to check what's out there."

He jumped out of the port, straightening swiftly when he landed, the rifle up and ready. It was all damn foolishness, he told himself. There was nothing here. If it was southwestern North America of 50,000 years ago, there'd be only the game herds and the prowling predators; those would not be lying in wait for stray humans who might come stumbling in and who, in any case, probably would make poor eating.

He was right. There was nothing. The land was empty

except for the black dots that he had spotted earlier and had recognized as grazing game herds.

The traveler lay at the foot of one of the buttes that thrust up here and there across the plain. Somewhat less than halfway up the slope stood a small grove of scraggy trees—junipers, more than likely. Except for the clump of trees and ragged haphazard carpets of grass, the butte was bare. Occasional stratified ledges of sandstone poked out of the bareness.

Enid came up beside him, saying nothing.

"We have it to ourselves," he said. "The traveler knew what it was doing. Except for a desert area, it picked the most out-of-the-way place it could find."

"The traveler had nothing to do with it," she said. "It was just happenstance."

The sun was halfway down the sky—Boone took it to be the western sky. Why he thought so, he didn't know.

A lone bird drifted above, not moving its wings, coasting on a thermal; a scavenger out to spot a meal. Small boulders lay here and there. Out from behind one of them came a wriggler. It wriggled its way across the sand, moving away from them.

"He and his kind are what we have to watch out for," said Boone.

"A snake? What kind?"

"A rattler. A rattlesnake."

"I never heard of that kind. My acquaintance with snakes has been limited. I don't think I have seen more than one or two in all my life."

"Some of them can be dangerous. Not necessarily deadly, but dangerous."

"The rattlesnake?"

"Dangerous. Sometimes deadly. But he warns you, buzzing at you with the rattles on his tail. Not always, but usually."

"You asked what we should do. I said I had no idea. How about you?"

"It's early yet," said Boone. "We've barely gotten here. You bought us some time. Let us use it."

"You mean to stay here?"

"Not for long. There is nothing to keep us, nothing here at all. But here we can sit quietly for a while, collect our thoughts, and talk things over. In the meantime, let's look around a bit."

He started off, along the base of the butte. Enid trotted to keep up.

"What are you looking for?"

"Nothing, actually. Just the lay of the land, to get some idea where we are and what might be here. It's just possible there might be a spring flowing out of the butte. That's sandstone up there on the slope. Water percolates down through sandstone. Sometimes, when it hits a less porous stratum, it flows out."

"You know the strangest things."

"Just simple woodcraft. Knowing how nature works."

"You're a barbarian, Boone."

He chuckled. "Yes, of course I am. What did you expect?"

"Our people were barbarians, too, up in the time we were born in. But not like you. We had lost touch with what you call nature. Up in our time there is little nature left. Wild nature, that is."

A jagged spur of limestone jutted out of the side of the butte. As they were circling around it, a gray animal jumped out from behind the outthrust of stone, ran for fifty feet or so, then swung around to have a look at them.

Boone laughed. "A wolf," he said. "One of the big prairie wolves. He's puzzled about what we are."

The wolf did look puzzled. He sidled cautiously away from them, dancing a humorous little jig, then, apparently satisfied that they represented no danger, sat down with all deliberation, wrapping his tail comfortably around his feet. Watching them closely, he lifted his upper lip in the beginning of a snarl, then let it relax, covering the fangs he had displayed.

"There will be others around," said Boone. "Ordinarily, wolves don't travel alone."

"Are they dangerous?"

"Hungry enough, I suppose they could be. This one looks well fed."

"Wolves and rattlesnakes," said Enid. "I'm not sure I like this place."

As they rounded the spur of sandstone, Boone halted so suddenly that Enid, following close behind, bumped into him.

The spur of sandstone curved inward, back into the butte, then curved out again, forming a rocky pocket. On the inside curve of the pocket stood a massive beast.

A great, black, woolly head with a pair of heavy horns, six feet or more from tip to tip, faced them. Its head hung low. A heavy beard hanging from the lower jaw swept the ground.

Boone grasped Enid by the arm and slowly backed away. The red-rimmed eyes of the beast glared at them out of a tangle of wool.

"Easy," warned Boone. "No quick moves. He could charge us. The wolves have been pestering him. He is old and desperate."

Reaching the point of the spur they had rounded to step into the pocket, Boone stopped. He let loose of Enid's arm and, using both hands, lifted the rifle to ready.

"A buffalo," he said. "A bison. Americans called them buffalo."

"He's so big!"

"An old bull. He'll run a ton or better. Not the bison of the twentieth century. An earlier type. *Latifrons*, maybe. I don't know."

"But wolves, you say. Wolves are no match for him."

"He's old and probably sick. In the end they'll wear him down. Wolves have the patience to wait. He's got his back to the wall, making his last stand."

"There are a couple of wolves over there. Another part-way up the slope."

"I told you," said Boone. "They hunt in packs."

"That poor bull," she said. "Is there anything we can do to help him?"

"The kindest thing would be to shoot him, but I can't do that now. He still may have a chance to get away, although I doubt it. You see that bird up there?"

"I saw it a while ago, just floating in circles."

"He's waiting. He knows what the end will be. Once the wolves are done, there'll be something left for him. Come on away. We'll look for water elsewhere."

A short time later, they found water, a small seepage trickling out from under a sandstone ledge. It went nowhere, soaking into the thirsty ground, forming a small spot of wetness before it disappeared into the soil. Boone scraped out a hole into which it could collect. They went back to the traveler to find something that would serve as a water bucket. All they could find was a small saucepan. When they returned to the pool Boone had dug, enough water had collected to fill the pan.

Boone saw that he had been right about the sun. It had been in the western sky. It had moved appreciably closer to the horizon.

"There'll be wood up in that juniper thicket," he said. "We'll need a fire."

"I wish we had an axe," said Enid. "I went through the stuff Horace flung into the traveler. Food, blankets, this saucepan, a frying pan, a fire-starter, but no axe."

"We'll get along," said Boone.

They made two trips to the junipers, hauling in more than a night's supply of wood. By that time the sun had set. Boone started a fire while Enid rummaged through the rucksack to find food.

"I think the best bet is the ham," she said. "There also is a loaf of bread. How does that sound to you?"

"It seems excellent," said Boone.

Sitting beside the fire, they munched ham sandwiches as night closed down. A wolf was lamenting somewhere nearby, and from farther off came other sounds Boone could not identify. As the dark deepened, stars came out, and Boone, staring up at them, tried to make out if there were any changes in the constellations. In a couple of instances he thought there were, but he was not well enough acquainted with the constellations of his own time to determine if there were changes or not. Some distance out beyond the fire, spots of light, side by side, showed up.

"Those are wolves?" asked Enid.

"More than likely. It's possible they may never have seen fire before. And they've never seen or smelled a human. They are curious, probably frightened as well. At least apprehensive. They'll sneak in and watch us. That is all they'll do."

"Are you sure of that?"

"Sure enough," he said. "They have the bull staked out. When they get hungry enough, they'll close in on him. Maybe one or two of them will die, but the rest of them will eat. They're waiting for him to weaken a bit more before they have a try at him."

"It's horrible," she said. "This eating one another."

"Just like us. This ham . . ."

"I know. I know. But the ham's a little different. The hog was raised for slaughter."

"But when you get right down to it, one thing dies so that something else may live."

"When you get right down to it," she said, "none of us is very civilized. There's another thing I have wondered about. When you got free of the rosebush and were legging it for the traveler, with the monster breathing down your neck, I had expected you to disappear."

"Disappear? Why should I disappear?"

"You told us about it, you remember. How you can step around a corner . . ."

"Oh, that. I guess the monster wasn't any real danger. You were waiting for me and the port was open. The stepping around a corner seems only to be a matter of the last resort."

"And something else. In New York you stepped around a corner, hauling Corcoran with you, and were in Martin's traveler. Where did you go those other times?"

"Strange," he said. "I don't actually remember. I probably was wherever I went for only a very short time. A moment or so and then I was back again. Into my own world."

"It had to be more than a moment or two. You had to stay there long enough for the danger to get over."

"Yes, you're right, but I never tried to get it figured out. I guess I didn't want to face it. It was so damn confusing, so unbelievable. I remember telling myself once that there must have been some factor of time disparity, but I didn't follow it up. It was too scary."

"But where were you? You must have had some impression."

"Each time it was terribly fuzzy, as if I were standing in a heavy fog. There were objects out there in the fog but I never really saw them. I only sensed there was something there, and it scared me. Why are you so interested?"

"Time, that's what I am interested in. I thought that probably you had moved in time."

"I can't be sure I moved in time. I only thought I might have. It afforded an easy explanation for a procedure that was impossible. One always seeks for answers, usually easy, simple answers. Even when the easy answers aren't understandable."

"We have time travel," she said, "and none of us, I am sure, really understands it. We stole it from the Infinites. To steal time travel was the one way we could fight back, the one way we could flee. The human race had far space travel before the Infinites showed up. I think it was our far travel that aroused the interest of the Infinites in us. I've often wondered if some of the very primitive principles of time might not have made our many-times-faster-than-light travel possible. Time is somehow tied into space, but I have never known quite how."

"You stole this time travel you have now from the Infinites. Yet you call yourselves barbarians. Hell, you're not barbarians. Anyone who can steal time factors and make them work . . ."

"There were others up there in the future, I am sure, who could have used time travel better. But they weren't interested. Mechanisms, even the sophisticated mechanism of time travel, were no longer concerns of theirs. They had reached a higher plane."

"They were decadent," said Boone. "They gave up their humanity."

"What is humanity?" she asked.

"You can't believe that. You are here, not up there million years from now."

"I know. And still how can anyone be absolutely sure Horace is always sure that he is right, of course, but Horace is a bigot. Emma is sure Horace is right. That's blind, stupid faith on her part. I'm not sure about David. He's happy-go-lucky. I don't think he really cares."

"I think he does," said Boone. "When it comes down to the crunch, he'll care."

"There was so much else the human race could have done," she said. "So many things yet that could be done. And then, if history is right, quite suddenly humanity lost interest in doing things. Could there have been some inherent braking system built into their intelligence, something that warned them to slow down? I've thought about it and thought about it. I go around in circles. I'm cursed with the kind of mind that is forced to see and consider all sides of a question, all the approaches that I can puzzle out."

"You had better slow down," said Boone. "You're not going to solve it all tonight. You should be getting some sleep, back in the traveler. I'll stay out here and keep the fire going."

"The wolves will sneak up on you."

"I sleep light. I'll wake at regular intervals to tend the fire; so long as there is a fire, the wolves will keep their distance."

"I'd rather be out here with you. I'd feel safer."

"It's up to you. You'd be safer in the traveler."

"I'd suffocate in there. I'll go and get some blankets. You want a blanket, don't you?"

He nodded. "As the night goes on, it could get chilly out here."

The moon was coming up, a great, bloated, yellow moon swimming up over the naked, ashen buttes. The land seemed empty. Nothing moved, nothing made a sound. Even the watching wolves were gone; no glowing eyes stared in from beyond the campfire. Then he saw the soft movement of a shadow through the moonlight. They still were out there, like so many drifting shadows.

He felt some of the emptiness and the loneliness lift from the land.

Enid came back and gave him a blanket.

"Will one be enough?" she asked.

"Enough. I'll drape it over my shoulders."

"You mean you'll sleep sitting up?"

"It'll not be the first time. It keeps a man alert. You might doze off, but if you do, you wake."

"I've never heard such foolishness," she said. "You *are* a true barbarian."

He chuckled at her.

Half an hour later, when he rose to his feet to place more wood upon the fire, she was asleep, wrapped in her blanket.

The fire replenished, he sat down again, pulled the blanket close about his shoulders, wrapping it well about him and placing the rifle in his lap.

Later, when he awoke, the moon was well up the sky. The fire had burned down somewhat, but still had plenty of fuel. He let his head droop and was half asleep again when, rousing for an instant, he saw someone sitting across the fire from him. The sitter was wrapped in an indistinct covering of some sort and wore what seemed to be a conical hat that had fallen down across his face. Boone sat quietly, not moving, still fogged with sleep. Through slitted eyes he watched the one across the fire from him, wondering vaguely if there was actually someone sitting there, or was it no more than sleep-hazed hallucination? The other did not stir. A wolf so distorted by the mist of sleep that he seemed a sitting man—a wolf companionably sitting across the fire? It was no wolf, Boone assured himself. Forcing himself out of his lethargy, he struggled to his feet. At his first motion, the thing across the fire was gone. There had been nothing there, he told himself; it had been no more than a waking dream.

Using a stick of firewood to rake scattered coals and the half-burned wood together, he piled on more fuel. Then, wrapping the blanket closely about himself, he fell asleep again.

He woke gradually, as a man would normally wake, but

with a warning growing slowly from somewhere inside himself. Tensed against the warning, he opened his eyes a slit and there was a wolf, sitting in front of him, almost nose to nose with him. Opening his eyes a little wider, he found himself staring into yellow, feral eyes that glared back unblinkingly.

His startled mind screamed for action, but he held his body firm. If he made any sudden motion, he knew, those heavy jaws could take off his face.

The wolf lifted its upper lip in the beginning of a snarl, then let the lip drop back. Otherwise it did not move.

Unaccountably, Boone felt insane laughter rising in him at this grotesque situation in the midst of primordial nothingness—a wolf and a man sitting nose to nose. He spoke softly, barely moving his lips. "Hiya, pup." At the sound, the wolf wriggled back a little on its seat, increasing the distance between them by a foot or so.

The fire was almost out, Boone saw. The alarm clock inside his brain had failed him and he had overslept.

The wolf's lip twitched as if to begin another snarl, but there was no snarl. Its ears, which had been laid back, tipped forward, like those of an inquisitive dog. Boone felt the urge to reach out a hand to pat the seemingly friendly head. Good, hard sense restrained the impulse. The wolf wriggled back a little farther, sliding on its bottom.

Out some distance beyond the fire stood several other wolves, ears pitched forward, watching closely to see what might happen next.

With a leisurely movement, the wolf rose to its feet and backed away. Boone stayed sitting, his fingers closing hard upon the rifle, although, he told himself, there was no need of that. The incident was over. Both he and the wolf had played it cool and there was no danger now, if there had ever been a danger. More than likely the wolf had never meant him harm. The fire had gone out, and the wolf had moved in closer, intrigued and puzzled by this new kind of animal that had suddenly appeared in its hunting ground, driven by canine curiosity to see what kind of thing it was.

The wolf was retreating, moving easily and deliberately, with a sidewise motion. Then, with a fine nonchalance, it turned its back on him and went loping off to join the other wolves.

Boone shook off the blanket and rose to his feet. The fire was not dead as yet. Brushing away the overlying ash, he uncovered a tiny core of fire, fed it with tiny twigs of dead juniper. It blazed up, and he fed it other fuel. When he rose from the flames, the wolves were gone.

Exploring in the rucksack, he found a package of oatmeal. Water was still left in the saucepan, and he poured it into the skillet. He dumped oatmeal into the saucepan, added water from the skillet, found a spoon, and stirred the gruel. When Enid awoke and sat up in her blanket, he was squatted by the fire, cooking breakfast. The eastern sky was beginning to lighten and the air was chill.

Enid came to the fire and squatted beside it, holding out her hands to warm them. "What have you there?"

"Oatmeal. I hope you like oatmeal."

"Ordinarily, I like it. But I suppose there is no sugar or milk. Horace wouldn't have thought of those."

"There is still some ham. Maybe other stuff as well. When I found the oatmeal, I looked no further."

"I can gag it down," she said. "At least it will be warm."

When it was cooked, they both gagged it down. She had been right; there was no sugar or milk.

Finished with breakfast, Boone said, "I'll go to the spring and wash the dishes, then bring back more water."

"While you are doing that, I'll pack everything back into the traveler. We don't want to leave it lying around."

"Do you want me to leave the rifle with you?"

She made a face. "I have no idea how to use it. Besides, I doubt there is any danger."

He hesitated, then said, "I don't suppose there is. In case something does happen, get into the traveler and close the port."

At the spring he met two wolves, who were lapping water from the spring hole. They retreated politely and let him wash the dishes and fill the pan with water. After he left he glanced back. The two had moved in on the spring again and were busily lapping water.

Back at the camp, Enid was crouched beside the fire. She waved her hand in welcome when she saw him coming. Standing beside her at the fire, he asked, "Do you have any idea what we should do?"

She shook her head. "I haven't even thought about it. If I had some idea where the others could be, we could go there. But they probably did the same as we did—left as quickly as they could, just anywhere to get away."

"There's an awful lot of time to flounder around in if we have no idea where to go," he said. "Not much sense in leaving here, it seems to me, until we know where to go."

"Eventually Henry will sniff us out. I assume he is with one of the other two travelers."

"Eventually could be a long time," said Boone. "I'm not about to spend the rest of my days in a continent empty of people. I'm sure you must feel the same. We could go someplace else more to our liking."

"Yes, we could do that," she said. "But not for a while. If we left a trail somehow that could be followed, we should not break it. We should stay here and hope that Henry finds us."

He squatted down across the fire from her. "There could be worse places," he said. "We're in no danger here. But I suspect that after a time it could become a little boring. Just plains and buttes, buzzards in the sky, wolves, and bison on the hoof. Nothing ever taking place."

"We'd run out of food," she said.

"There is plenty of food. Bison and other meat animals." He patted the rifle. "We'll live as long as this holds out. After the last cartridge, we can make lances, perhaps bows and arrows."

"It won't come to that," she told him. "Before it does, we'll leave."

He reached for the pile of wood, laid a few sticks on the fire. "We'll have to go for more of this. Our supply is running low."

"Let's get in a good pile of it this time," she said. "We don't want to have to run up to that thicket every day to bring in wood."

A low rumbling, from somewhere close by, brought both of them to their feet. The rumbling ceased, then came again, changing to a bellow.

"It's the bull," said Boone. "He's in some sort of trouble."

Enid shuddered. "The wolves are moving in."

"I'll go and see," said Boone. He started and she trotted along beside him.

"No," he said. "No, you stay here. I don't know what I'll find."

Loping along, he came to the sandstone outcropping, ran around it, and into the rocky pocket where they had found the bull. The bull was backed against the sharp incline of the spur, his rump pressed tight against the rock. Facing him were half a dozen wolves, darting in at him with short rushes, then spinning about and away to escape the slashing of his horns. The bull was bellowing angrily, but with desperation in the anger. His head was held low; his bellowing came in short, hard gasps. He kept swinging his head from side to side to bring his horns in play against the menace of the wolves. His beard swept the ground as he swung his head. His flanks were quivering and it was apparent that not for much longer could he stand at bay, fighting off his enemies.

Boone lifted the rifle, paused for a moment before he brought it to his shoulder. The bull swung its head to stare at him, its red eyes peering out of the matted fur. Boone lowered the rifle.

"Not now, old man," he said. "Not yet. When they close in, you'll get one or two of them and I owe you that."

The bull's stare was unblinking. His bellowing sank to a mumble. The wolves, disturbed by Boone's intrusion, moved off.

Boone backed slowly off, wolves and bison watching him intently. I'm the intruder here, he thought. I'm an unknown and unexpected factor introduced into this environment. And I have no business here, no right to interfere. For untold centuries old bull bison, robbed of their strength, grown slow with years, had fed the wolves. Here wolves were the certified predators, ancient bison the certified victims. It was the scheme of life, the way that things were done, and no referee was needed to pass judgment.

"Boone!"

At the cry Boone spun about and raced around the spur. Enid was standing by the fire and pointing up the hill. Coming down the slope rapidly, heading straight for the camp, was the unlikely monster that had driven them from Hopkins Acre. The spiderweb glinted in the morning sun. Peering over the top of the web was the huge, shining eye and some sort of dark mechanism was emerging from the web.

He had no chance to cover the distance to the fire, Boone knew, no chance to do anything at all to stop the monster.

"Run!" he shouted. "Into the traveler. Go!"

"But, Boone . . ."

"Save the traveler," he bellowed at her. "Save the traveler!"

She ran for the traveler, leaped into it. The monster was almost on top of it, not a great deal more than a hundred yards away from it.

Sobbing, Boone raised the rifle. The eye, he thought, that great, round, shining eye. Probably not the way to do it, but the best that he could think of.

His finger tightened on the trigger, but, even as he began the squeeze, the traveler disappeared—the space it had occupied was empty.

Boone eased his finger and lowered the rifle. The monster overran the area where the traveler had been, then swiftly swung around so that it faced Boone. The great eye, now raised above the web, stared at him, the web glittering in the sunlight. The mechanism was receding back into the web of brightness.

"All right," Boone said to it. "Now I'll take you on."

He had six cartridges; he could fire at least four of them before it could reach him. First the eye, then the web . . .

But the monster did not come at him. It did not move at all. He knew that it must be aware of him; he could feel it seeing him.

He waited for it and it made no move. It knew that he was here and it knew him for what he was. But would it know, he asked himself, that he was not one of those it was hunting down? If the monster was what it seemed, a hunting robot, then it was entirely possible that it could be very narrowly programmed to its targets. But on the face of it that did not appear too probable. The logical assumption would be that it would include among its targets any human associating with the people from the future.

Boone took a slow step forward, then waited. The monster did not stir. Was it, he wondered, playing a game of cat and mouse, waiting until he was close enough to catch him in a rush before he had a chance to employ a defensive mechanism?

He didn't have to go back to the campfire, he remembered. There was nothing there except the saucepan and the skillet. While he had gone to the spring, Enid had packed the rest of the provisions into the traveler—the food, the blankets, the rucksack, everything they had. All he had was the rifle and the cartridges it carried.

Realizing this, he felt a terrible nakedness. He was on his own. Enid would do her best to come back and pick him up. But would she be able to? He knew nothing about the capabilities or the operation of a traveler or how proficient Enid might be in its operation.

The monster moved, but not toward him. It moved slowly, tentatively, out toward the plain, as if it might be uncertain what to do. Maybe, Boone told himself, it was worried. It had botched its job, that much was certain. It had failed at Hopkins Acre and here it had failed again.

The monster moved beyond the fire and went out onto the plain, a twinkling object of sunburst glory against the drabness of the level land and the dusty buttes.

Keeping a wary eye on it, Boone walked to the fire and

piled more wood on it. Before too long he would have to climb the butte and bring in more wood from the clump of juniper. Elsewhere he might find a more convenient campsite, but he could not go too far. When Enid returned—if she returned—she would come here. When the traveler reappeared, he would have to be here, waiting for it.

He knelt beside the fire, laying down the rifle, and went through his pockets, taking inventory. He pulled a handkerchief from his hip pocket and spread it out, laying on it the items that he found in other pockets. A lighter, a pipe, a half-empty packet of tobacco, a jackknife that he had carried for years for sentimental reasons, a small notebook, a ball-point pen, a pencil stub, a couple of paper clips, a handful of coins, his billfold with a few bills, credit cards, his driver's license—and that was all. He had traveled light when he had gone to the Everest with Corcoran, leaving the rest of the junk he would normally carry on his person in the drawer of the nightstand beside the bed. But he had two essentials: a lighter, which he would have to use sparingly; and a knife—a poor, cheap knife, but still a knife, a cutting edge.

He restored the items to his pockets, then rose, dusting off his trousers.

The monster, he saw, had changed directions. It had circled and now was moving back toward him. Boone picked up the rifle, hoping that he would not have to use it. He had only six cartridges and none of them could be wasted. But where did one shoot a robot to bring it down?

From the other side of the spur of sandstone that extended out beyond the pocket where the bull stood at bay came occasional bellowing. The wolves must be at the bison once again.

It was unreal, thought Boone—all of it unreal. Even knowing it was happening, he still found some intellectual difficulty in believing it. Any minute now it would go away and he would find himself in a world he knew, among friends and without any thought of a killer robot, an embattled bull, or a wolf nose to nose with him beside a dying campfire.

The monster was much closer now, heading straight for him. It was much bigger than he had thought it was and still not quite believable. The monster seemed in no hurry. The bellowing from the direction of the sandstone spur became thunderous, filled with rage and rising desperation.

Boone shifted his feet, planted them solidly. He raised the rifle, but did not snug it to his shoulder. He was ready now, he told himself, set for whatever happened. The great eye first and, if it seemed necessary, the center of the web.

The bull burst into view in a mad gallop around the sandstone spur. He was no longer bellowing. His head was carried high, the sun glinting off the six-foot spread of horn. Behind him loped the wolves, not trying to close in, taking their time. They knew they had him now; out in the open they could come at him from all sides and pull him down.

Suddenly the bull shifted direction and his head came down. The monster tried to dodge away, but its movement was too late. The full impact of the bull's charge caught the monster low and lifted it. A vicious twist of the bison's head speared it in midair on one sweeping horn. It spun in the air and the bull's head twisted the other way. One horn came clear and the second caught it as it came down. The gleaming eye burst into shards, the web hung loose and twisted. The monster fell to the ground and the bull rushed over it, the driving hoofs striking and shattering it still further.

The bull stumbled and fell to his knees. With a great effort he regained his feet and swung away, bellowing in blind fear. Behind him lay the monster, a heap of shattered wreckage. The bull came to a stop, swinging its massive head from side to side in an effort to locate its tormentors. The wolves, which had retreated when the bull had struck the monster, halted their flight, turning about and waiting, tongues lolling out of the sides of their mouths. They danced in anticipation. The bull was quivering—quivering all over—weak and ready to collapse. One hind leg buckled and he almost went down, but stiffened the leg and stayed erect.

Boone lifted the rifle, lined up the sights for a heart shot, and pressed the trigger. The bull fell so hard he bounced. Boone jacked another cartridge into the breech. He said to the bull, "I owed you that cartridge. Now they won't eat you alive." The wolves were scurrying, frightened by the sound of the shot. In a little while they'd come sneaking back again; there would be feasting this night out beyond the campfire.

Boone walked slowly over to the monster, kicking aside broken fragments of it that lay in his path. It was a tangled mess. Looking down upon it, Boone was unable to reconstruct in his mind the shape that it had taken. The shock of the bull's charge and the ripping thrusts of the horns had scrambled the robot. The gleaming eye had disappeared; the web was torn beyond recognition. Lying in distorted fashion were twisted lengths of metal that at one time could have been operable appendages.

The monster spoke inside his mind.

Mercy, it said.

"The hell with you," said Boone, speaking before astonishment could dry up his speech.

Don't leave me here, the monster pleaded. Not in this wilderness. I did no more than my job. I am a simple robot. I have no basic evil in me.

Boone turned about and shuffled back to the campfire. Quite suddenly he felt drained. The tension had snapped and he was limp. The monster was dead and yet, out of the midst of its death, it spoke to him. He stood at the campfire undecided for a moment and then went up the slope to the clump of juniper. He made three trips, hauling in a good supply of wood. He broke it into proper lengths and stacked it in a neat rank. Then and not until then, he squatted beside the fire and let his mind dwell upon his predicament.

He was marooned in primitive North America, with no other human being closer than hither Asia, across a land bridge that would, in later years, become the Bering Strait. If he finally were condemned to stay within this time frame, he quite possibly could walk those thousands of miles to hunt out other humans—and to what end, he asked himself. The chances were that they would either kill him or make of him a captive.

There was a better way—to wait for someone from Hopkins Acre to come hunting him. Enid, he was sure, would return if it were possible. Jay, he was certain, would move heaven and earth to rescue him, but Jay would need the help of others.

At the best, he admitted, his circumstance was not too hopeful. On the face of it, he probably would not be important to the people of the future. He was, after all, no more than an intruder, perhaps an unwelcome intruder, who had come blundering in on them.

The monster spoke to him again, a faint and distant voice.

Boone! Boone, please have mercy on me!

"Go chase yourself," said Boone, muttering to himself rather than to the monster, for he had no faith in the monster's voice. There probably was no voice; the words were no more than his own perverse imagination.

The wolves had come back to the bull—seven of them now, where he had never seen more than six before—and were tearing at the carcass.

"Good eating to you," he said to them. Both the hide and the meat of the ancient animal would be tough. It would take some effort to rip through the hide to get at the flesh, which would not be the best of eating. But to a wolf it would be meat to fill an empty gut.

Before the day was over, Boone would need some of the meat; he had nothing else to eat.

It would be dangerous to walk out to the carcass and drive the wolves away so that he could slice out some meat. The only tool he had was a jackknife of the very cheapest sort, put together so shoddily that any undue pressure might break it all apart. He'd have to wait a while until the wolves were less hungry and therefore less possessive. By that time, perhaps, they would have so torn the hide as to expose areas of flesh from which he could hack a chunk for his own consumption. He'd be, he decided, the scavenger to the wolves.

He rose from his squatting position before the fire and began walking, beating out a path from the fire to the sandstone spur and back again. Pacing, he tried to formulate a plan for his survival. His ability to step around a corner worked only under extraordinary stress. More than likely, after an indeterminate time, it would bring him back to exactly where he was. It had been only by a fluke that his strange ability had taken him and Jay around a corner into Martin's traveler. He couldn't count on the same thing happening again.

He still had five cartridges in the rifle and with each of the cartridges he could bring down a more than adequate hunk of meat. Once it was down, however, he either would have to defend it or hide it against the scavengers, and it soon would deteriorate beyond any possible use. He could smoke it, of course, but he was not up on the procedure for the smoking of meat; he could salt it, but he had no salt. He was innocent of all the proper techniques to wrest a living from a land like this. He could, perhaps, find fruit or roots that could aid in his survival, but how could he know which of them would be safe to eat and which would poison him? So the problem, boiled down, came to how he could, day after day, hunt down and collect enough protein to keep his body functional.

That meant weapons that he could devise. And if that was to be the plan, he must get at it immediately, gaining some expertise in their manufacture and use before the last cartridge had been fired. The first step would be to find stone that could be worked. The sandstone ledges jutting out of the butte held nothing he could use. But there were other places where he might find the necessary stone.

Finally he halted his pacing and squatted down beside the fire. The wolves were feasting, burrowing into the ripped-open body cavity of the bull. From time to time they raised their blood-smeared muzzles to stare at him and then went back to feeding. In another couple of hours, it might be safe for him to walk out and claim his portion of the kill. The sun stood close to noon or a bit beyond. The vultures were gathering. A dozen or more of them circled high in the sky, dropping lower with each circle that they made.

The monster spoke again. Boone, be reasonable. Listen to me.

"I'm listening," said Boone.

I am robbed of all my senses. I cannot see and I cannot hear. All I can perceive is what you say to me and so far all that you have said has been most unkindly. I am nothing. I am a nothingness wrapped in nothingness. And yet I am aware of self. I could go on like this for uncounted millennia, knowing I am nothing, unable to reach out. You are my only hope. If you do not have mercy on me, I shall exist this way forever, buried by sand and dust with no other being aware that I am here. I shall be the living dead.

"You are eloquent," said Boone.

Is that all you have to say?

"I can think of nothing further."

Dig me out, the monster pleaded. Dig me out of the wreckage that I am and keep me with you. Take me when you go. Anything, just so I am not alone.

"You want me to rescue you?"

Yes, please rescue me.

"That might be only a temporary solution to your problem," Boone told the monster. "By your own act, I may be sentenced to stay here in this wilderness, as you term it. I may die here and you will be left alone again, facing the same fate that you face now."

Even so, for a time we would be together. We would not be alone.

"I think," said Boone, "I'd prefer being alone."

But there is always hope. Something could happen that would save us both.

Boone did not answer.

You do not answer, said the monster.

"There is nothing more to say. I'll have none of you. You understand that? I'll have none of you."

To have mercy on an ordinary enemy—yes, that would be nobly human. But this was no ordinary enemy. Trying to figure out, for his own peace of mind, what kind of enemy it was, he found he could put no name to it.

It could all be a trap, he told himself, and felt the better once he had thought of that. Out there, somewhere in that tangled mass of wreckage that had been the monster in its totality, lay one small component that could be the monster's brain or a fantastically complex computer that was the monster's essence. Should he paw among the wreckage to find and retrieve the essence, he well could become the victim of the monster, seized by a still-operative component that would make an end of him.

No, thank you very much, he said to himself; I am right, I'll have none of it.

The wolves had finished with their more voracious eating. Several of them had stretched out on the ground, looking uncommonly satisfied, while others still worried at the meat, but with no great urgency. The vultures were much lower in the sky. The sun had moved a considerable distance down the west.

Boone picked up his rifle and walked toward the kill. The wolves watched his advance with interest; when he moved up close, they moved away, then took a stand, doing a little growling at him. He waved the rifle gently at them, and they moved off a little further. Some of them sat down to watch.

Reaching the bull, he leaned the rifle against it and opened his jackknife. It seemed a feeble tool. The gut cavity of the bull had been ripped open, and some of the skin had been torn free of one of the hams. The flesh on the ham, Boone knew, would be tough meat. But there was little possibility that the knife blade would cut through the bull's tough hide to reach the better cuts. He'd have to take what he could.

He seized the torn hide with both hands and jerked with all his strength. The hide peeled back reluctantly. He set his feet and jerked again. It peeled off farther this time. The knife, to his amazement, did a better cutting job than he had thought it would. He sliced off a large cut of meat, laid it to one side, and then cut off another—far more than he could eat at one sitting, but this probably would be the only chance he had. Other wolves would drift in, drawn by the scent of blood, and vultures would drop down. By morning's light, there would be little left.

A huge wolf, bigger than any of the others, advanced toward the kill, snarling as it came. Others rose to their feet to follow. Boone picked up the rifle, shook it at them, roaring viciously. The big wolf halted and so did the others. Boone laid down the rifle and cut another slab of meat.

Never taking his eyes off the wolves, Boone collected the meat and began backing off. He moved slowly. Move too fast, he told himself, and the wolves might rush him.

The wolves watched, not moving, interested in what he would do next. He kept on backing off. When he was better than halfway to the fire, they rushed forward, closing in on the dead bison, snapping and snarling at one another. They paid him no further attention.

Back at the fire, he found a clean, grassy area and dropped the meat on it. Ten times more than he could eat at one time. He stood looking at it, considering what to do.

It wouldn't keep. In a couple of days it would be going bad. The thing to do, he thought, was cook it all. Cook it, eat what he needed, wrap the rest in his undershirt, bury the parcel in the ground, then sit on the hole where he had buried it. Unprotected, it would be dug up by the wolves, once they had finished off the bull. With him sitting on it, it would be safe. Or he hoped it would.

He set to work. Selecting stout limbs from the pile of juniper he had stacked for firewood, he trimmed them to proper lengths, sharpened their ends. He cut the meat into smaller pieces, thrust the sharpened ends of the limbs through them, impaling several gobbets of meat on each of the stakes. The fire had burned down to a bed of coals. He raked still-flaming chunks of wood to one side and used them to start another fire. He jammed the stakes into the ground, canting them to extend, with their freights of meat, above the coals.

He sat down and watched the cooking, adjusting the stakes from time to time. His mouth watered at the smell of the cooking meat. But mouth-watering as it might be, it wouldn't be tasty. He had no salt with which to season it.

The wolves were still quarreling over the carcass of the bull. A few of the vultures had dropped down, but had been chased off by the wolves. Now they sat, hunched, at a respectful distance, waiting for their chance at meat. The sun was just above the horizon. Night was coming on.

Out there on the plain lay the carcass of a bison that had been known in Boone's time only as a fossil. Further out would be other living fossils—mastodons, mammoths, primitive horses, and perhaps camels. Even the wolves feasting on the bison might be fossils.

Crouched beside the bed of coals, Boone kept close watch on the cooking meat. Pangs of hunger assailed him. Since the almost inedible oatmeal in the morning, he had eaten nothing. He had fallen on hard times.

When he had jumped into the traveler with Enid, he recalled, the thought had crossed his mind that they would go into the future, instead of to this world of extinct beasts and living fossils. Then the urgency of those last seconds at Hopkins Acre had driven the thought from his mind.

There would have been something to interest him in the future, but there was very little here. He thought about the future he had heard of at Hopkins Acre—a world almost empty of visible humanity, although humankind still was there as incorporeal beings, pure intelligence, with the survival factor that had made men the masters of the planet finally refined into small quantitive qualities that were no more than dust motes, if even that.

Change, he thought. Earth had undergone change during the nearly five billion years of its existence. What seemed at first small factors became in time significant in a process that no intelligence could pinpoint before it was too late to take measures to counteract.

Even given intelligence, the great reptiles could not have guessed what was happening to bring them to extinction sixty-five million years ago. Other forms of life had suffered extinction that could not be foreseen. He had read that the first great extinction had come two billion years ago when the first green plants converted carbon dioxide to oxygen, changing Earth's atmosphere from a reducing to an oxidizing medium, bringing death to most earlier, more primitive forms, to whom oxygen was poison.

There had been many times of dying; the species that had died in the past were a hundred times more numerous than those still living. Finally, up there in the future, it seemed the human race was dying. Perhaps it would still exist, but in a form that might cancel it as a factor in the further evolution of Earth.

Enid had told him that trees would supersede mankind, taking the place of man, once man was finally done. The idea was ridiculous, of course. By what process or capacity could trees take the place of mankind? Yet if anything were to replace humanity, it was perhaps fitting that it should be trees. All through history, trees had been friend of man—and man had been both friend and enemy to trees. Men had cut down the great forests wantonly; yet other men had cherished or, at times, even worshipped trees.

One of the stakes that held the gobs of meat above the coals tilted, its base shifting in the ground, and fell into the fire. Cursing, Boone snatched it off the coals. Holding the stake with one hand, he brushed the meat free of ash with the other. It must be done enough for eating. Gingerly, he slid one of the gobbets off the stake, bouncing it in his hand. When it was cool enough, he took a bite of it. For lack of salt it was tasteless, but its warmth and texture felt good in his mouth. He chewed it. It took a lot of chewing, but his stomach seemed very glad of it. Once he had eaten all he could, he laid the stake down on a patch of grass and took off his jacket, shirt, and undershirt. Stretching the undershirt out on the ground, he took up the other stakes and stripped the meat off them into a pile on the shirt. Threading the rest of the uncooked meat on the stakes, he set them above the coals, put on his shirt and jacket, and settled down to wait for the remainder of the meat to cook.

Darkness was creeping in. He could barely make out the wolves that still were clustered about the bison. In the east, the sky was flushed with the rising of the moon.

He watched the meat above the coals until it was done, pushed off the gobbets onto the undershirt, wrapped the meat well in it, used his knife to dig a hole, placed the meat into the hole, filled the hole even with the ground, tamped it down, and then sat upon the hole. Anything that wants that meat, he told himself, will have to go through me to get it.

He felt an expansiveness and a certain pride in himself. Whatever might happen in the days to come, he had done well so far. He had food for several days. Perhaps he should not have wasted the bullet, but he could not bring himself to regret doing it. He had given the bull a quick and decent death. If he had not, the wolves would have pulled the old bull down and started tearing him apart while he was still alive.

Maybe it made no difference, the wasting of the bullet. Any time now Enid would be back to pick him up. He thought about it for a time, trying to make himself believe it, but not successfully. There was a good possibility she would return, but an equally good possibility that she wouldn't.

He turned up the collar of his coat against the chill of night. Last night he'd had a blanket, but now he had none. He had only the clothes he stood in. He nodded, dozing, and woke with a start. There had been no reason to awake; nothing was amiss. He went back to sleep, the rifle cradled in his lap.

He stirred again, halfway between sleep and wakefulness, and he was not alone. Across the fire from him sat, or seemed to sit, a man wrapped in some all-enveloping covering that might have been a cloak, wearing on his head a conical hat that dropped down so far it hid his face. Beside him sat the wolf—*the* wolf, for Boone was certain that it was the same wolf with which he'd found himself sitting nose to nose when he had wakened the night before. The wolf was smiling at him, and he had never known that a wolf could smile.

He stared at the hat. Who are you? What is this about?

He spoke in his mind, talking to himself, not really to the hat. He had not spoken aloud for fear of startling the wolf.

The Hat replied. It is about the brotherhood of life. Who I am is of no consequence. I am only here to act as an interpreter.

An interpreter for whom?

For the wolf and you.

But the wolf does not talk.

No, he does not talk. But he thinks. He is greatly pleased and puzzled.

Puzzled I can understand. But pleased?

He feels a sameness with you. He senses something in you that reminds him of himself. He puzzles what you are.

In time to come, said Boone, he will be one with us. He will become a dog.

If he knew that, said The Hat, it would not impress him. He thinks now to be one with you. An equal. A dog is not your equal.

Sometimes dogs come very close to us.

But they are not one with you. There was another step to take, but it was never taken. Long ago man should have taken it. Now it is too late.

Look, said Boone, he is not one with me. The wolf is not the same as me.

The difference, Boone, is not as great as you may think.

I like him, said Boone. I have admiration for him and a certain understanding.

So has he for you. He sat nose to nose with you when he could have slashed your throat. That was before you killed the bull. He was hungry then. Your flesh could have filled his belly.

Can you tell him, please, that I thank him that he did not slash my throat.

I think he knows that. It was his way of saying he wants to be a friend of yours.

Then tell him I accept his friendship, wish to be a friend of his.

But Boone was talking to an emptiness. The Hat was no longer there. The place he'd sat was empty.

He was no longer there, Boone told himself, because he had never been there. It was all illusion. There was no one but the wolf.

When he looked, the wolf was gone as well.

Boone got to his feet. He was stiff with cold. He fed the fire more wood and stood close against it, soaking up its heat as new, vigorous tongues of flame flared up and ran along the wood.

He had slept for a long time. The moon had slanted far into the west. Moonlight reflected off the shattered skeleton of the monster. It had been a long time since the monster had bespoken him—if, in fact, it ever had bespoken him. Like The Hat, it could be fantasy.

A change had come over him, he thought. Short hours ago he had been a hard-bitten newsman who dealt only with facts. But now he fantasized. He talked with a hat, squabbled with a dead monster, and saw in a wolf a friend. Loneliness, he supposed, could drive a man to strangeness, but this soon? Here, however, the loneliness might be different than ordinary loneliness, compounded by the consideration that in all probability he was the only human within the span of two great continents. In his time many scientists believed that the first human had not set foot upon the western hemisphere for at least 10,000 years after this period. Somewhere in the vastness of Asia, barbaric tribes ranged the land, and farther to the west were other men who, in another 20,000 years or so, would begin to paint the first crude drawings of the fauna of their day in the caves of eastern Europe. Here he was a misplaced human, alone among wild beasts.

Warm now, he moved back and began to pace round and round the fire. He tried to think, but there was no beginning to his thoughts, nor was there any end. Like his walking around the fire, his thoughts went round and round.

The wolves were quarreling over the bison, although the quarreling was low-key; they were not putting their hearts into it. Far off, some animal was bawling, a steady, monotonous complaint. Up the slope in the juniper thicket, a bird chirped sadly. The moon hovered just over the western horizon, the east began to brighten, and another day was dawning.

When light came, he dug up the undershirt and took out some meat. Hunkered beside the fire, he chewed and chewed to break up the toughness of the fibers sufficiently to swallow safely. Finished, he went to the spring to get a saucepan of water, then up the hill to fetch wood for the fire.

The realization dawned on him that the days could be difficult to fill. He tried to think of chores that he could invent to keep himself busy. He could think of none that made sense enough to do them. Later he could set out to spy the land, but there was little point in that. Later he might have to do it, but now he had to be here when Enid returned or someone else showed up.

Going to the sandstone spur behind which the bull had been brought to bay, he lugged back to the camp slabs of stone fallen from the spur, as heavy as he could manage, and piled them on top the hole where the meat was buried. Quite possibly roving scavengers, sniffing out the meat, could move the stone to get it. But *his* wolves were too well fed to go to all that bother.

He set out to climb the butte, toiling up its face. Finally he reached the crest and looked out across the country. There was not much to see. Some miles off, a herd of herbivores were grazing, most likely bison. Skittering bands of other animals fled across the land like shadows. Tentatively, he identified them as pronghorns. What looked to be a large bear waddled along a dry stream channel. Otherwise, what he saw was a lot of empty land, cut here and there by dry watercourses and with the everlasting buttes rearing up from it. Here and there along the watercourses were groves of cottonwoods and some of the buttes showed dark splotches that could be thickets of shrubs or clumps of trees.

When he returned to camp, the wolves had left the bison carcass, now little more than bones and scraps of skin flapping in the breeze. A dozen or more vultures hopped about, pecking viciously at one another to guard the territory each had staked out, stripping off the last nourishment remaining on the skeleton.

Boone settled down to wait as best he could. Four days passed and there was no traveler. Boone did his chores. Several times he inspected the wrecked monster, circling it, keeping at a safe distance. He tried to reconstruct it in his mind, to connect the broken parts to one another. He could have done a better job of that if he had allowed himself to get closer to it, picking up some of the broken parts and inspecting them. But he shied away from that. The monster did not speak to him, and finally he became convinced it had never spoken to him, that his memory of its talk was a mental aberration.

By the end of the fourth day, several meals of the meat he had cooked still remained, but it was becoming tainted. He still remained too civilized for his system to tolerate tainted food.

On the morning of the fifth day, he tore a page out of the notebook he carried in his breast pocket and, using the pencil stub, wrote a note:

Gone hunting. Will be back directly.

He placed the note on top of the pile of rock that protected the buried meat and weighed it down with another stone.

Setting out with the rifle, he felt a lifting of his spirits. Finally there was something to be done, a chore that had to be done, that was not simply work made to fill the time.

After a mile or so, the wolf showed up, trotting out from the butte to join him. It fell in to his right, a hundred yards distant and slightly behind him; it seemed friendly and glad to be with him once again. He spoke to it, but the wolf disregarded the speaking and kept on with him, pacing him.

An hour or so out, he spotted a small band of pronghorns, grazing at some distance. To his left lay a dry stream bed. He slid into it, treading along as noiselessly as he could. The wash tended to the right, the direction that would bring him closer to his quarry. The wolf had descended into the dry wash with him and was trailing

along behind. Twice Boone halted and crept carefully up
the wall of the wash to check the pronghorns. They still
remained where he had first spotted them, feeding on
sagebrush and occasional patches of grass. They seemed
undisturbed, but the range was too great; he had to move
closer. He slid back into the wash and continued on his
way, cautiously, being careful where he set his feet. The
click of a pebble could trigger the pronghorns into flight.
As if sensing the stalk, the wolf slunk along behind him.
Ten minutes later Boone crawled up the incline of the
wash again. The pronghorns were much closer than he
had calculated they would be. He slid the rifle into position, selected the animal he wanted, lined up the sights,
and fired. The pronghorn leaped high into the air and fell
heavily. The rest of the band took off, bounding away,
only to stop a few hundred yards off, switching about and
looking back. When Boone climbed out of the wash, they
took off again.

With the wolf sitting to one side, Boone shouldered his
kill and set out for camp. The wolf trotted along to one
side of him, bearing the smug expression of a job well
done.

At camp Boone laboriously skinned the pronghorn,
stretching out the hide on which to place the cuts of meat.
Gutting the animal, he retained the liver, then dragged the
rest of the entrails and internal organs out to the bison
skeleton. The wolf got to work on the offering. Boone
sliced the liver, impaled it on a stake and slanted it over
a bed of coals. Then he set to work dismembering the kill.
He saved the loin and one ham; what was left he carried
beyond the camp and dumped. The wolf deserted the entrails and moved over to the more substantial feast.

At the campfire, Boone feasted on fresh meat and began
the cooking of what was left to store against the next few
days. This could not go on, he told himself. He was living
hand to mouth, and his ability to continue even this sort
of existence was limited to the four cartridges that remained in the rifle's magazine. Before they were gone,
he had to acquire another capability to feed himself. He
needed wood for a bow, tendons for strings, straight sticks

for arrows, stone to make the arrowheads and from which he could chip a knife, for the cheap jackknife would not stand up for long under the use to which he had to put it.

His knowledge about the making of a bow was almost nonexistent. Still he knew the basic theory and could manage. He could make a poor bow and it would do until, by trial and error, he could make a better one.

Tomorrow, he decided, he would set out in search of wood and stone. He considered briefly a search for wood for the bow in the juniper grove from which he had gotten firewood. Almost instantly, he gave up the idea. Juniper, at its best, was poor wood; and he doubted that in the entire grove he could find a piece that could be used to make a bow.

Two more wolves had showed up. Watching them, Boone tried to pick out *his* wolf and was unable to decide which of the three it was. By the time the sun had set, all the meat he had left out for the wolves had disappeared, and the wolves were gone.

But early in the evening, shortly after the fall of night, the wolf came back and sat across the fire from him.

Boone talked to it. "Tomorrow," he said, "I am going on a trip to find wood and stone. I'd be glad if you'd come along with me. It could be a hard trip. I have no way to carry water, but I'll carry meat and will share it with you."

It was ridiculous, he thought. The wolf could not understand a word he said, and yet talking to it made him more secure. It was good to have anything to talk to; a wolf was better than nothing. It was something that could share the fire with him.

He woke in the night and the wolf still was with him. It watched closely and companionably while he built up the fire. He went to sleep again with the wolf still watching him.

In the morning he wrote another note, a longer one this time:

I am leaving on a trip that may take several days, but I will be back. Please wait for me. A wolf may be traveling with me. If he is, do him no harm. He is a friend of mine.

He weighted it down on the rock pile and he and the wolf started out. They traveled west, heading for the butte on which Boone had detected dark splotches that he had thought might be small trees. It seemed no more than a good day's time away.

It was much farther. Late in the afternoon, Boone realized they'd not reach it by dark. He was tired and thirsty. They had come across no water. Perhaps, he told himself, they'd find water on the butte. He could get through the night without it. Dropping into a dry wash, he walked along it until he came to a place where it curved sharply, forming a pocket with high walls.

Collecting wood fallen from the cottonwoods, he built a fire. He selected three pieces of the meat and tossed them to the wolf. While the wolf gulped them down, he squatted by the fire and ate. The meat was tender and he had no trouble chewing it. The wolf finished and waited expectantly for more. He tossed over another chunk.

"That's all you get," he stated. "Share and share alike, and you've had more than I had."

Bone tired, he fell asleep soon after dark, the wolf stretched out across the fire from him. Dawn was near when he woke. The fire was out and he did not bother to start it again. He gave the wolf some meat and ate some himself. The sun was not yet up when they started out.

They reached the butte well before noon and began the climb. This butte was much larger than the one where he and Enid had camped; the climb was long and hard. The wolf found water halfway up. He came back with his muzzle wet and dripping.

"Water," said Boone. "Show me."

The wolf stood puzzled.

"Water!" said Boone. Sticking out his tongue, he tried to make lapping motions.

The wolf trotted off to the right, stopping now and then to look back. Was it possible, Boone asked himself, that it had understood? It was insane to think so, and yet he had shared the meat—would the wolf share water?

He had been thirsty for hours, it seemed; he had tried to wipe it from his mind, but now that he knew there must be water near, the thirst came raging back. His mouth and throat were dry and it was hard to swallow.

Ahead of him, a great outcropping of stone humped out of the slope. He tried to hurry, but the way was steep and the sun-dried grass was slippery. He went down on his hands and knees, scrabbling along, sobbing with his need of water.

The stone, he saw, was limestone, not sandstone. The limestone, he thought, must lie atop the sandstone strata that protruded from the other butte. Limestone would not serve as tool material, but in between its layers might lie veins of chert or quartz.

The wall of rock reared above him. Stunted cedar trees clung here and there upon its face. He crawled along the steep incline that came up to the base of the wall. Loose rock shifted under him. He had lost all track of the wolf, but he imagined that he heard the sound of running water.

He slipped, rolled, slid again, and suddenly stopped. Something gripped his right leg and an agonizing pain shot through it, a pain so terrible that it left him sick and gasping, gone in the gut, his dry throat retching, and nothing to come up.

He lay for a long moment while the pain slowly ebbed away, then tried to sit up. He couldn't; whatever pinned his leg held him tight against the ground, angled down along the slope. He tried to squirm around to see what was wrong with the leg and, as he moved, the leg screamed at him. Faint with the pain, he fell back upon the ground. When some of his strength came back, he tried once more, very cautiously. He was able to angle his head around so he could see back along his body. The leg was caught in a narrow crevice. The underlying limestone was close to the surface, barely covered by the rock fragments that had fallen from the face of the cliff. His right leg had plunged into a narrow crevice and he was trapped, held in the crevice almost to the knee.

What a silly thing to happen, he thought. He felt panic creeping up on him and pushed it back. All he had to do, he told himself, was to work his leg as gently as possible out of the rocky fissure that held it.

He tried to work the leg free. The muscles responded. He could move it, although it protested. Maybe a sprain; it didn't feel like a break. Probably gashed up quite a bit.

The wolf came inching down the steepness of the slope and stood with feet braced, looking at him and whining.

"It's all right," Boone croaked at him. "I'll get out of here in a while. Might take some figuring."

But he didn't get free in a while. No matter what he did, the leg stayed clamped in the fissure. The way he was sprawled out on the steep slope made the job hard. When he tried to maneuver his body into a more advantageous position, the agony of the leg left him weak and sweating. Finally he gave up, too weak, too pain-ridden, to go on. I'll rest a while, he told himself.

Rested, he tried again. But now it was nearly dark. The wolf had wandered off somewhere and he was alone. Once again he tried gingerly to work the leg free; when that didn't work, he lunged in a desperate effort to pull loose. The fire of pain slashed through him. He gritted his teeth and lunged again. The leg still held. He did not try a third time. He lay exhausted. He heard, distinctly now, the sound of running water. The pain of the leg screamed at him; the deep dryness of his thirst choked him.

He tried to reason with himself. He laid out a plan, but the plan did not progress far. He reached for the bundle of meat that he carried slung on his shoulder. The bundle was not there. Neither was the rifle.

Boone set his jaw grimly. He'd been in bad places before and he'd lived through them all. Among other things, he could step around a corner and be free. He tried to step around the corner. He squeezed his eyes shut, he tensed himself, and he drove his brain.

"The corner!" he screamed. "The corner! Where is that goddamned corner!"

There was no corner. He continued where he was. He let the tenseness ebb away and collapsed upon the ground.

He awoke much later. The stars were shining in the sky. A cold wind blew up the slope and he was half frozen. For a moment he did not know where he was, then it all seeped back. He was trapped upon this butte. He would never get away. He'd die here. He lay there, cold and hurt, his throat constricted by a raging thirst. Perhaps a little later he would do something about himself, but not now.

A gray shadow moved in the starlight. It was the wolf. It looked at him and whined.

"Promise me one thing," Boone said to it. "One thing is all I ask. Be sure I'm dead before you start to eat me."

Enid

7

It all had gone wrong, Enid thought. She never should have tried to operate a traveler. She should have known that she was not competent. And yet what could she have done? Back at Hopkins Acre, she had been left alone to wait for Boone, and there had been no chance to lay a course. She had simply told the traveler go—that was the one thing left to do. Then, later, the same sort of situation had arisen. Boone had yelled for her to save the traveler and she had fled. Now here she was, almost a million years into the future beyond the era where Boone was stranded—and she had not the least idea how to go back and pick him up.

It was Horace's fault, she told herself. Horace, who was so big on planning and who had planned so poorly. Each traveler should have had one person who was a skilled pilot—although, come to think of it, there had not been three of them who were skilled sufficiently. David was quite proficient. And Horace, although at his best he would be sloppy. Emma and Timothy would know nothing about it. When it came right down to it, there had been only two who could have run a traveler.

If the monster had not interfered and they had been given a chance to go about the planning decently, it all might have gone quite well. They would have decided where they would go when they left, and David, more than likely, would have programmed each of the travelers to go to the selfsame place and time. They would have known where and when they were going and they all would have gone together. If her traveler had been programmed, she would have had no trouble. It had been this repeated running in the dark that had been her undoing.

She looked again at the panel and the time designation was clear enough. But the spatial designation was all Greek to her. She knew when she was, but certainly not where. That first time, it had been Boone who had figured out where they were, although only the general area. The spatial designation had been on the panel, of course, but she could not read it. What she should have done, she realized now that it was too late, would have been to jot down the readings.

Locked somewhere within the recorder on the panel, the spatial designation of that place she and Boone had touched down still would be recorded. All she had to do was call it up, but she didn't have the least idea of how to call it up.

She slumped back in the seat, still staring at the panel. Why hadn't she, in all the time they'd spent at Hopkins Acre, asked David to teach her how to operate a traveler? He would have been glad to show her—she was sure of that—but she had never asked him because it never had occurred to her, not even once, that at some time she would have to use one.

She stared out of the vision plate, but the view was a restricted one and there was not much to see. She seemed to be located on some high point, for she looked out over a vista of rugged hills, with a river glint among them.

So she had gone and done it, she thought. At times, Horace and Emma had called her feckless and maybe they'd been right.

She had left a decent man stranded in the very distant past and there was no way she could return to rescue him. She was afraid even to try. She had made two blind jumps, one into the deep past, the other much deeper in the future. Henry had tracked them down in Dark Age Europe, but that, compared to this, had been a rather simple chore. She had left a trail, perhaps, that he could follow with any luck at all. One trail, but two—what could he do with two? She knew without question that she must stay where she was. If she made another jump, more than likely she would be lost forever. Even now, she thought, even with no more than two jumps, she still might be lost forever.

She rose from the pilot's chair and made her way to the port. When she opened it, she heard a strange sound, a little like the buzzing of a swarm of bees. When she stepped away from the traveler she saw what it was.

The traveler lay on a slope, some little distance below the top of a high ridge. On top the slope moved a band of people, and it was from them that the sound was coming—a thin babbling of many voices, all talking at once.

To her left and right, so far as she could see in either direction, the line of people moved along the ridge. The line was uneven. In some places the people were all massed together, then there would be a place where there were small groups of them or a few walking by themselves. All were in motion, right to left, in the same direction, but moving slowly.

Moving, not with them, but beside them, as if they were outriders of the procession, were strange and varied figures. Some of them had the appearance of being human; others did not appear human in the least; but all of them were alive and moving—crawling, humping along, rolling, scurrying frantically, striding, floating. A few were flying.

She drew her breath in sharply when she recognized what those outriders were. Some of those who had human appearances were robots, and undoubtedly others that did not appear to be human were robots as well. The rest of them were aliens. In the time that had been her home, there had been many aliens who had formed weird and not always understandable relationships with humans, but her own people, the outlanders, had as little as possible to do with them.

Enid moved out a short distance from the traveler and climbed a few steps up the slope that ran to the ridge where the procession walked its slow and awkward way. The land was high and dry. It had a sense of bigness and it seemed to stand on tiptoe to reach the very sky, which was deep and blue—the bluest sky she had ever seen, without a cloud to fleck its surface. There was a wind that blew strong and steady, rippling the cloak she wore. It had the breath of chill in it, as if it might have blown for a long distance over a cold and empty land, but the sun that stood at noon was warm. A smooth sward of grass grew beneath her feet, short and well-behaved grass that had no wildness in it. Here and there along the ridgetop grew occasional trees, each shaped and sculptured by the wind that must have blown there for centuries to bend them to its will.

No one noticed her. Not for a moment did her presence interfere with what was taking place.

A rite, she wondered, a religious pilgrimage, a celebration, perhaps, of some old mythology? But these, she thought, were no more than feeble guesses. Conceivably, there might be danger if she intruded, although, from where she stood, the procession seemed immune to intrusion. There was about it a solid sense of purpose.

A voice spoke at her elbow. "Have you come to join us, lady?"

Startled, she spun about. The robot stood close beside her. Any noise of his approach had been blotted out by the wind. He wore a human form and was extremely civilized. There was no crudity about him. He was a machine, of course; that could be seen by a single glance.

But in a strange way, he was nobly human. His face and body were human in the classic meaning of the term, and he was tastefully decorated, the metal of him incised in discreet little patterns that made her think of the exquisite etching on the barrels of the most expensive shotgun in Timothy's collection. Over his shoulder he carried a scraped, dressed-out hog, and underneath one arm he bore a large and bulging grain sack.

"I beg your pardon, lady," said the robot. "I had no wish to startle you. As I came up behind you I sought to make some sound to announce myself, but the wind, you know. You hear nothing in this wind."

"I thank you for your thoughtfulness," said Enid. "You did startle me, but not too violently and only momentarily. And, no, I did not come to join you. I have no idea of what is going on."

"It is all a matter of hallucination," said the robot, speaking bluntly. "What you see is a Pied Piper's march. Are you, perchance, acquainted with the ancient story of the Pied Piper?"

"Why, yes, I am," said Enid. "I read it in one of the books that my brother picked up. It is a story about a piper whose piping lured all the children from a village."

"This is the same," the robot said. "A Pied Piper's march, except there isn't any piper. It is the fault of all these aliens."

"If there isn't any piper, whom might they be following?"

"In their hallucinations, which I am convinced are supplied by the aliens, they follow dreams. Each follows a dream uniquely his own. I have told them and told them, and so have all the other robots, but they pay no attention to us. They disregard us and follow filthy aliens."

"Then why are you here? You are not alone; there are other robots here."

"Someone must take care of the humans. Someone must protect them against themselves. They left without provisions to feed themselves, without food or water, without sufficient clothing to protect them from the cold and damp. You see this shoat upon my back, this bag of meal beneath my arm? I scrounge the countryside, gathering what I can. It is not a job, I can assure you, that a robot of my integrity and sensibility could easily bring himself to do. And yet I must, for these foolish humans of mine are caught up in their silly dreams and pay no attention to their needs. There must be someone who will look out after them."

"What will be the end of it?" asked Enid. "What will happen to them? How will it all end?"

"I know not," the robot said. "I can hope only for the best. This may, at other times, have happened otherwhere, but this is the first time it has ever happened here. Much as I love my humans, begging your pardon, there are times when they can be the most thoughtless, most unreasonable forms of life existent. My age runs to many centuries, lady, and I have read the histories that cover untold centuries. The human race, according to the old historians, always has been thoughtless and unreasonable; but it seems to me that now they are gaily unreasonable, whereas before they were stupidly and perversely unreasonable. To be gaily unreasonable, to take joy from unreason, seems to me to be the worst form that perversity can assume."

"I'd have to think about that," said Enid. "I suppose you could be right."

Perversity, she thought. Could that have been what happened to the human race—a willing perversity that set at naught all human values which had been so hardly won and structured in the light of reason for a span of more than a million years? Could the human race, quite out of hand and with no sufficient reason, have turned its back upon everything that had built humanity? Or was it, perhaps, no more than second childhood, a shifting of the burden off one's shoulders and going back to the selfishness of the child who romped and frolicked without thought of consequence or liability?

"It would be quite safe, I am sure, if you are of the mind to go up the hill and have a look at them," the robot said. "I am sure there is no danger. They are not dangerous folk, only silly ones."

"I might like to do that."

"Or better yet, if you have the time, you might like to join with us—with my humans and perhaps a few assorted and disgusting aliens—when we break fast this night. There'll be roast pig and fresh baked bread and probably other edibles that my fellows will bring in. You need have no fear of intruding; you'll be with the family only. Come nighttime and all the different families will gather by themselves and eat the food their robots will bring in. You might like to meet my family. Other than for this silly exhibition, they are very beautiful. I have hopes this madness soon will run its course."

"I would like to do that," Enid said. "I am glad you asked me."

"Then come along with me and I will seek them out. They must be somewhere in the line, not too distant from us. Then I'll hunt out a place for camping and make ready for the feast—perhaps at a spot some distance ahead so that they will be not too far off when this insanity is suspended in the face of dark."

"They don't march all night?"

"No, of course not. They have not taken leave entirely of their senses."

"I'll go with you," said Enid. "But I don't want to join the march. I'd be out of place there. Going with you, I might be able to help you set up camp."

"No need of that," the robot said. "There are others of us and all of us are good workers. But I'll be glad to have you come with me. Since we are going to be together for a while, you might call me Jones."

"I am glad to know your name," she said. "You might call me Enid."

"I'll call you Miss Enid. Young females are entitled to the 'Miss.'"

"I thank you, Jones," she said.

All this time they had been walking up the hill together and now were close to the line of march. The procession, Enid saw, was following a faint track that ran along the ridgetop, the sort of path that ordinarily would have seen but little use, followed only now and then by lonely wayfarers hurrying along in the hope of reaching shelter by the fall of night.

The procession stretched in both directions as far as she could see. There were occasional empty gaps in it, but in no case were the gaps so large as to wipe out the sense that this, indeed, was one vast procession.

Each and every person walked as if walking alone, paying no more than courteous attention to those who were moving with them. They walked with their heads held high and confident, looking ahead rather than upward, as if there were something that they would see at any moment and they were entirely confident that they would not be disappointed. Their expression was serenely expectant and there was about them a subdued rapture—although, she told herself, in no way a holy or religious rapture. This was not, as she first had thought it might be, a religious procession.

There were no children. There were teen-agers and the middle-aged, the old and the very old who hobbled on canes or levered themselves along on crutches.

With them ran, scurried, humped, and hobbled a great array of aliens—not as many as there were humans, but enough to make a continuous impression on the watcher. There was a wraithlike creature that floated, bobbing along, now on the same level as the human marchers, now above them, changing its shape constantly. There was a three-legged creature that stalked along as if mounted on stilts, with a body that had no features on it, but looked like just an ordinary box. There was another that was at once a wriggler and a ball—a wriggler that twisted along like a slithering snake, twisting its way among the humans' marching feet and legs, then at intervals rolling itself into a ball that moved gently and serenely. There was a head, a head alone that was mostly one eye and a mouth, scampering all about, as if it might be in a hurry without knowing where to go. There were many others.

The humans paid no attention to the aliens—it was as if the aliens, to them, were simply other humans. The aliens, in turn, paid no attention to the humans, as if they were well acquainted with these humans, who were nothing to be wondered at.

Enid had the impression that all of them, humans and aliens alike, were watching for something, but that there was no single sign they watched for, as if each sought a personal revelation.

She looked about for Jones, the robot, and could not locate him. There were other robots, but few of them mingled with the humans and the aliens in the line of march. Mostly they stayed off to the side of the procession. She kept on looking for Jones, but there was no sign of him. Perhaps, she told herself, she should hurry forward along the line of marchers, in the hope that she could catch up with him. She was hungry, and hot pork and new-baked bread sounded awfully good. It had been silly of her to have lost contact with him. She started trotting along the side of the line, but after a few steps she stopped. She had not observed the direction Jones had taken; she might be moving away from him rather than closer. A voice spoke, almost in her ear, a twangy, nonhuman voice that used human words.

It said, "Kind human, would you perform a small task for me?"

She jerked herself around, involuntarily jumping to one side as she turned.

It was an alien, as she had known it would be, but slightly more humanoid than most aliens were. Its head, bent forward on a long and scrawny neck, was a cross between that of a winter-gaunted horse and a woebegone hound dog. It stood upon two badly bowed legs and its torso was a warty bloat. Its two arms were long and limber, twisting like a pair of performing serpents. The ears flared out like trumpet bells. Two groups of eyes were mounted on its forehead; each with several irises. The mouth was wide and the lips were slobbery. A pair of gills, one on each side of the scrawny throat, bellowed in and out as it breathed.

"I am to you," it said, "a disgusting sight, no doubt. As humans once were to me before I became accustomed to them. But my heart is kind, and my honor of the best."

"I have no doubt of that," she said.

"I approach you," said the thing, "because, of all the humans here, you seem not preoccupied with what is going on, impelling me to believe that you'd be willing to waste a small amount of time on me."

"I cannot imagine anything that I could do for you," she said.

"But of a surety you can," it insisted. "A very simple task which, because of the perplexity of the chore, I cannot do myself. I have not enough . . ." The woebegone horseface hesitated, as if searching for a word. "Let us say that someone was tying up a package with a piece of string and was having difficulty because of lack of hands when it came to the tying of the knot. And that person says to you, will you hold your finger so upon the crossing of the string so I can tie the knot. In a somewhat different manner, that is what I would ask of you."

"Because of the lack of hands?"

"Not because of the lack of hands, but the lack of another facility for which I have no word that you could understand. This is my fault and not yours."

Enid looked at it, puzzled.

"You still fail of understanding?"

"I'm afraid I do. You must tell me more."

"You see all those humans out there, processioning in all seriousness, all of them striving, all of them seeking, but seeking different things. A marvelous painting, perhaps, that one can put upon a canvas. Or a piece of music that will be listened to by many other music lovers. Or an architectural model that someone out there has been striving to draft for years."

"So that is it," said Enid. "That is what they are looking for."

"Yes, assuredly. I had thought you knew."

"I knew they were looking for something. I did not know for what."

"It is not the humans only who are looking."

"You mean that there is something you seek? And you need some help? Sir, I cannot comprehend in what manner I can help you."

"I have sought an idea, trying time after time to run it to the ground, and each time a little short. So when I learned of this processional and its seeking out, I said to myself, if it works for humans, surely there must be a modicum of hope it also would work for me."

"And has it worked?"

"I think it has. I think I have it all in mind, but I cannot tell unless I find someone to hold a finger where the two strings cross."

"Except it's not a finger. And it's not a string."

"That is correct, fair lady. You catch on rapidly and you listen closely. Will you listen further?"

Enid looked around quickly. There still was no sign of Jones, the robot.

"I will listen further, closely."

"First of all," said Horseface, "I must be honest with you. I must tell you sorrowfully of my fraudulence. All the other aliens here attending this procession make up a group of special selection. They have been brought along because they have the power to elevate human sensitivity to high hallucinatory levels. Given such soaring hallucinations, the participatory humans then can grasp the pattern of the great art toward which they strain. Furthermore, there are among these sundry aliens some who have the power to guide the humans in a materialization of their visions—to create a painting from the mind without any painting being done—a short cut, one might say, between conception and execution. Or the power to create music, the realistic sound itself, without the aid of score or instrument."

"But that's impossible," cried Enid, suddenly envisioning a shower of painted canvases falling from the sky to the sound of music coming out of nowhere.

"Not impossible in every case," said Horseface.

"This is all very honest of you," said Enid. "But you told me that you are fraudulent. Why?"

"Because I joined this procession, not to work for the humans, but rather for myself. I had thought perhaps that the fervor of this assemblage would spur and supplement my ability."

"What you are trying to say is that you were in this procession for yourself, in the hope that it would give you the edge you needed to develop the idea that you have. And that while it apparently has given you that edge, you still are unable to accomplish it for the lack of someone to hold a finger on the string."

"Admirably you outline the situation in most exact detail. Having understood, are you of a mind to help me?"

"Tell me first what this object is you have the need to develop."

"That, alas, I cannot do since it involves concepts not understandable to a human without much instruction being given."

"It would not be detrimental? It would be of harm to no one?"

"Look at me," said Horseface. "Do I appear as one who would be willing to do harm?"

"Looking at you, I cannot tell."

"Then please take my word. The object would be of harm to no one."

"And if I am able to help you, what would I get out of it?"

"We'd be partners in it. You'd own half of it, have equal rights in it."

"That is generous of you."

"Not at all," said Horseface. "Without your help, it will never come to be. So now will you permit me to explain what you must do to help me?"

"Yes, I think I will."

"Then close your eyes and think at me."

"Think at you?"

"Yes, think at me. I'll think back at you."

"I've never, in my life, thought at anyone."

"It is not difficult," said Horseface. "You close your eyes and, concentrating all your mind, think of me."

"It sounds terribly silly," said Enid, "but I suppose it's worth a try."

She closed her eyes and concentrated about thinking at him, but had a feeling far back in her mind that she was making a bad job of it since she did not know how to think at someone.

But she felt him thinking at her. It was a little terrifying, though somewhat like hearing Henry in her mind; she hung in there and did not try to pull away. There was nothing she could lose, although she doubted very much she had anything to gain. It was all an exercise in absolute futility.

But a picture formed inside her mind that she could not have possibly thought up by herself. It was a picture of a complicated structure made up of and hung together by many colorful lines. The colorful lines all were thin and had a rather dainty look about them, but the structure, which she could not see too well because there was too much of it, had the feel of being most substantial. She seemed to be standing in the very center of it, with it stretching so far to every side of her that she could not see the end of it.

"Now, right here," said the invisible Horseface, speaking in her mind, "is where you lay your finger."

"Where?" she asked.

"Right here," he said, and when he said it she saw exactly where she should lay her finger and she laid it there, pressing down hard as one would press hard upon the crossing of two strings that tied up a package.

Nothing happened, nothing that she noticed right away. Somehow, however, the structure all around her seemed to become more solid, and the wind had quit its blowing. All this time she had been keeping her eyes on her finger to make sure she was holding tight against the string that wasn't there.

Horseface spoke to her, not speaking in her mind, but aloud. "All right," he said, "the job is done. There is no longer any need of holding the finger."

She looked up and there he was, some little distance from her, climbing up the bare bones of the structure as if it were a ladder. She heard a shout beneath her and looked down. The procession was all spread out below her, and all the people were looking up at her, shouting, waving their arms, crying in amazement.

Frightened, she reached out and grasped one of the colorful bars that went into the making of the structure. The bar she grasped was lavender and it tied into two other bars, one of them lemon yellow and the other a deeply glowing plum. It was solid in her grasp. Wondering where her feet were, she glanced down and saw that they were planted firmly on another bar, a red one as substantial as the lavender one she gripped. All around her, everywhere she looked, were other bars; the structure quite surrounded her. She looked out through it at the hills and valleys and saw that the ridgetop, with its snaking procession, was only a small part of the landscape that lay beneath her.

The structure tipped smoothly over on one side and she found herself spread-eagled over the landscape, facing down toward it. She gasped and felt panic reaching out for her, but the panic went away when she realized she was as comfortable in that position as she had been in the other. Her orientation, she realized, was keyed into the structure, not the land that she had left. She looked around quickly to try to locate the traveler, but she couldn't find it.

The structure tipped back to where it had been before. It had started to grow little dangles and spangles all over it with no specific pattern. Horseface was clambering down toward her, like an awkward spider swarming down a web. He reached her level and stood peering at her.

"What do you think of it?" he asked "Is it not beautiful?"

She gulped. "This was what you were trying to make?"

"Of course," he said. "I thought that you would know."

"What is it?" she asked. "Please tell me what it is."

"It is a net," said Horseface, "useful for the fishing of the universe."

Enid crinkled up her face, staring at what he called a net. It was a flimsy thing and it had no shape.

"Certainly," she said, "you would not go fishing the universe in so slight a thing as this."

"Time means nothing to it," said Horseface, "nor does

space. It is independent of both time and space except as it makes use of them."

"How come you know so much about it?" demanded Enid. He did not look to be the sort of creature that would know too much of anything. "Did you study somewhere? Not on this Earth, of course, but . . ."

"I studied at the tribal knee," said Horseface. "There are old stories and very ancient legends."

"You can't depend on legends with a thing like this. You must have the knowledge, know the theory and the basic facts."

"I made it, did I not? I told you where to hold your finger on the string?"

Enid said, weakly, "Yes, you did."

It was changing as she watched it, losing some of its flimsiness, gaining strength and form, although not as yet an impressive strength and form. The ornaments with which it had been sprinkled changed from spangles, growing into objects, no longer merely glinting ornaments, but objects that had some relationship with this slab-sided structure Horseface called a net, although she could not figure out, for the life of her, what the relationships might be. What bothered her the most was that he called it a net and it certainly had no resemblance to a net. She tried to think of something that it might resemble and came up with nothing.

"We will travel in it," Horseface told her, "from one planet to another, without a tick of time, without a touch of space."

"We can't cross space in it," said Enid. "There is nothing to protect us. We'd die in the cold and emptiness. Even if we could, we'd arrive at some unknown planet and plunge into an atmosphere that would choke us or fry us or . . ."

"We would know where we were going. There'd be no unknowns to us. There are charts to follow."

"Where do such charts come from?"

"From long ago and far away."

"Have you ever seen them? Do you have them now?"

"There is no need to possess them physically or to see

them. They are a part of my mind, a genetic part of me, passed on to me by my forebears."

"You're talking about ancestral memory."

"Yes, of course. I thought that you would guess. Ancestral memory, ancestral intelligence and knowledge, the knowing of what went into the net, or should go into the net."

"And you claim this net of yours can do many wondrous things?"

"How wondrous not even I can know. Time means nothing to it nor does . . ."

"Time," said Enid. "That is what I am getting at. I lost a friend in time. I know the time factor, but not the space."

"Nothing to it," said Horseface. "It is a very simple matter."

"But I told you I don't know . . ."

"You think you do not know. But the chances are you do. All you need to do is bespeak the net. Let it pry into yourself. It can find the forgetfulness."

"But how can I talk with it?"

"You cannot talk with it. It can talk with you."

"How do I let it know that I want it to talk to me? How can I be sure we can communicate, the net and I?"

"You thought at me when you said you couldn't and you thought upon the knot . . ."

"Now that it's all done, now that you have your precious net, can you tell me what I really did? There wasn't any knot and there wasn't any finger."

"My dear," he said, "there is no way I can tell you. Not that I would not if I could, but there is no way. You may have called into play some ability you are not aware you have and which I was not sure you would have. Even when I talked about the laying of the finger, I was not entirely sure that it would work. I only hoped it would."

"Well, then, let's forget the jabber. There is no way of getting sense from you. I want very much to get back to my friend again and to do that you say I talk with this silly net. Please tell me how to start."

"Most assuredly I will," he said. "All in proper time.

But first there is an errand must be run and once the errand's done . . ."

He reached out and took hold of one of the ornaments scattered all about the net.

"Duck your head and hang on tight," he said.

Nothing happened and she raised her head and opened her eyes. The planet was pink-and-purple and the sky was golden-green.

"You see!" Horseface said triumphantly. "We are here and nothing happened to us."

Enid drew in a cautious breath, shallow at first and then more deeply. The air seemed to be all right. She did not choke on it; it did not strangle her and it had no bad smell.

"What's the matter with you?" he asked. "Are you indisposed?"

"Not at all," said Enid, "but the sky can't be that color. There is no such thing as a deep green sky. The land is bad enough, although it can be pink and purple, I suppose, but the sky cannot be green."

Although, she told herself, the sky *was* green. She was alive, and everything was all right, perhaps, because she didn't know anything at all about what was going on.

Horseface started clambering down the net, the lower corner of which hung just above the ground.

"I won't be long," he told her. "I'll be back directly. You wait here for me. Don't go wandering off. Stay close."

The land was pink-and-purple. There were purple grasses and pink trees and, despite its coloring, the land was as flat and as drab and uninteresting as any she had ever seen. It stretched out on all sides to a hazed horizon that was a sickly blend of pink and green and gold and purple. Except for occasional trees and a number of scattered mounds, the land was empty. Nothing moved upon it, not even a flittering bird or butterfly. It was empty with a vengeance.

"What is this place?" she asked of Horseface.

"Its only designation," he said, "is a symbol on a chart. I would have no idea how to pronounce the symbol.

Maybe it is a designation that is not meant for anyone to speak."

"And how did we get here in so short a time and without any . . ."

"We were translated here," he said and, having reached the ground, turned his back on her and said no more, going across the land in a loping fashion, with his grotesque shadow bouncing and bobbing, much blurred at the edges. The bloated red sun in the green haze of the sky shed too little light to make a sharp and proper shadow. The entire planet, Enid thought, was a mite too garish and not in the best of taste.

She climbed down a short way, then stopped to look the place over a little more closely. Horseface had disappeared into the distant haze, and she was alone. Below here, there was no sign of life she could detect except for the grass and trees. There was only the level sweep of the land and the scattered mounds.

She slid to the ground, surprised to find it solid under her feet. From the look of it, she had expected to find it spongy. She moved away from the net and began walking toward the nearest mound. It was a smallish one, looking like a pile of rocks. She had seen such piles on Earth where the husbandmen dug the stones from the ground and piled them to clear more land for planting. But those piles had been made up of dull-colored stones of all sizes, from pebbles to weighty boulders. Here the rocks seemed to be all small and many glinted in the sun.

When she reached the mound, she knelt down beside it and picked up a handful of the pebbles. She raised her hand and opened it, spreading out her fingers to make a flat palm, with the pebbles lying before her eyes. The stones, catching the light of the red sun, blazed back at her.

She held her breath, and her body tensed, then slowly relaxed. She knew nothing about gems, she told herself; she couldn't have distinguished a shattered piece of quartz from a diamond. And yet it was unbelievable that all the brilliance and fire of the stones could come from no more than common pebbles. A reddish one, a little smaller than a hen's egg, flashed brilliant red from a corner where a sliver had been broken off. Beside it, a pebble split in half seemed to quiver with a throbbing blue. Others gleamed with the glow of green, rose, amethyst, and yellow.

She tipped her hand and let them go, scintillating as they fell. If they were truly gems, they would bring a fortune back in certain periods of mankind's development. But not in the time from which the family had fled. In that time, alll precious things, all rarities, and all antiquities had lost their value. There had been no money and no jewels.

She wondered if Horseface had known of these piles of gems, heaped so carelessly and in such quantities by an unknown people. But no, she told herself—Horseface was seeking something here, but it was not these stones.

She started walking toward a second pile of pebbles, but did not stop when she reached it. There were other such piles, all alike except for some variation in size. She knew now what they were and what she'd find in them. Perhaps it was time to travel just a little farther to see what might lie beyond.

Although not aware of it at first, she must have been climbing a slight slope, for quite suddenly she came to where the land broke and fell away into a tangle of grotesque formations, cliff faces of raw earth, deeply eroded stream beds, and a group of pyramids, all straight lines that tapered to points.

She stood at the edge of the land where the slope broke and stared fixedly at the pyramids, remembering something she had once read—that there was no such thing in nature as a straight line; such straightness must suggest artificiality. The pyramids did have the look of architecture. The edges that marked the corners were definite, and the sides that led up to the apex were smooth.

As she looked, she saw the sparkle in them. But that would be impossible; to build such pyramids so exactly as they should be with pebbles or gems would be ridiculous, if it could be done.

She moved up the slope. As she came closer, there could be no doubt at all—the pyramids were built of gems, or what she guessed were gems. From close up, the whole structure before her quavered with a myriad of multicolored sparkles.

She advanced to the pyramid, blinking as it flashed red and green and purple in the light of the sun. She did not care for the purple—she had seen enough of purple, pink, and sickly green on this planet. But there was a yellow— a primrose yellow, clean and bright—that seemed to stop her heart and made her suck in her breath. It came from a stone larger than an egg and smooth, perhaps polished by some ancient river flowing over it.

Before she could think to stop herself, her hand went out and her fingers tightened around the stone. As she lifted it, the entire slope of the pyramid came down as if it were liquid. She skipped aside to escape the rush of rolling pebbles.

Something squeaked nearby. When she looked to see what it was that had made the noise, she saw them at the sagging corner of the pyramid, peering at her out of their popeyes. Their round, soft, fuzzy mouse ears quivered and they stood on tiptoe, horrified at what had happened to the pyramid.

They had popeyes, mouse ears, and a softness about the triangular faces, but their bodies were angular and harsh, with a vague hint of spiders carved out of wood. Carved, Enid thought, out of the seasoned driftwood that could be found beached along the shores of old rivers, gray, knobbed, and twisted wood with all the twists worn smooth and shiny as if someone had spent long hours giving it a polish.

She spoke to them in a kindly fashion, frightened and repulsed by the driftwood bodies, but drawn to them by their fuzziness of face, by the large and liquid eyes, and by the quiver of the ears.

They spooked away, their spraddling driftwood legs prancing, then switched around again to stare at her. There were a round dozen of them. They were the size of sheep.

She spoke again, as softly as before, and held out her hand to them. The movement of her hand did it—they swirled about and ran, in dead earnest this time, making no motion as if to halt and look at her again. They fled down the tortured slope and disappeared into one of the deep erosion gashes and she lost sight of them.

She stood there, beside the pyramid that was no longer neat. The green sky lowered over her and she clutched in one hand the large pebble with its glow of cowslip yellow.

I've made a mess of it, she thought, as I've made a mess of everything the last few days. She walked around the corner of the shattered pyramid and stopped in astonishment.

Spread out on the purple grass were rectangles of white fabric, and grouped among the spread-out rectangles were colorful hampers made, perhaps, of metal. And the thought came to her—the poor things were having a picnic when she had so rudely interrupted them.

She walked forward and nudged one of the pieces of fabric with her toe. It lifted off the ground, falling back in folds. As she had thought, it was fabric. Tablecloths, to be spread down upon the grass, forming a clean surface on which the food would have been spread out.

It was strange, she thought, that the concept of a picnic should have come into being on this planet as well as on the Earth. Although here, of course, all this might mean something else entirely—it might not even be concerned with eating out of doors.

She dropped the yellow stone into a pocket and bent to examine the contents of the hampers. There was no doubt that this picnic, if that was what it might be called, had to do with eating. There was no question in her mind that what she saw was food. There were fruits, apparently freshly picked from tree or bush. There were evidences of cooking—blocks and bricks and loaves—and in one of the hampers was placed a huge bowl of what probably was a salad, a tangled mass of leaves and gobs of quivering slimy matter. A fetid effluvium rose from the bowl.

Almost gagging from the smell, she stood up and stepped back, taking several deep breaths to clear her nose. Then, as she glanced around, she saw the box.

It was a small black box, perhaps a foot square and six inches in depth, lying on the ground just beyond what she had decided was the tablecloth. Most of it seemed to be of metal, but the side facing her was of what appeared to be a gray, opaque glass or crystal. She could see no way to open it. And she had no time to experiment with it. Horseface would soon be returning, and she didn't want him to find her gone.

She was still staring at the box when the face of it suddenly lighted, to show an image of Horseface toiling across the grass, bent almost double by the weight of a huge chest that he carried on his back.

Basic television, she thought, and another parallel with Earth. A picnic and a television receiver. On the plate, Horseface had slipped the chest from his back and set one end of it on the ground while he wiped his steaming face. The chest was apparently a heavy load to carry.

Had the driftwood spider-things been watching him all the time and could they have known of her as well? They had seemed genuinely surprised when they peeked around the pyramid to see her.

As she thought of them, she saw them in the plate. The image of Horseface flipped off, and there they were, toiling down the narrow bottom of a dry canyon. There seemed to be something grimly purposeful in their traveling.

We'd better get out of here, she told herself. Somehow she had the feeling that the sooner gone the better. She'd go back to the net and wait for Horseface. As soon as she thought of him, he was on the plate, again trudging along under the weight of the chest.

Strange—as soon as she thought of someone, he was on the screen. Mental tuning? She could not know. But this box was more than simple television. It was, perhaps, a spying apparatus that could penetrate into unguessed places and unknown situations.

She lifted the box, which was not heavy, and started rapidly down the slope, suddenly realizing that she might have betrayed a trust in leaving the net unguarded. When she finally saw it still there, a flood of relief flowed through her and she began to run.

She glanced to her right to see Horseface still plodding toward the net with the chest upon his shoulder. She felt an unexplained urgency to leave this planet quickly and assumed that Horseface must share her feeling, perhaps with good reason. The chest could not be his. He was stealing it.

She reached the edge of the net and tossed the television box onto it. The box was large enough to fit firmly there. Now Horseface was running heavily toward her, gasping and panting, with the chest bouncing on his shoulder.

She leaped on the net, balancing on it, reaching out to seize the chest and steady it as he hoisted it from his shoulder, thrusting it toward the net. She caught hold of a leather handle on one end of it and braced herself, hauling on the handle to make sure the chest stayed on the net and did not slide off it.

It struck the net and bounced, beginning to slide toward the edge. She dug in her heels and hauled at the chest, pulling it sidewise to stop the slide.

Out of the corner of an eye she saw the writhing of something deep purple rear out of the purple grass, and tentacles reached out. Horseface bleated in terror and ducked away, leaping for the net. His hands caught the edge, and he pulled himself part way up it, his legs dangling in the air. Enid grasped one of his arms and hauled. The purpleness fell toward them. Enid stared, stricken, at the gape of mouth, the sharp and gleaming teeth, the writhing of tentacles, and the malicious glint of what could have been an eye. Under them, the net jerked violently as a tentacle grasped its trailing edge.

Feet set, Enid heaved on Horseface and he came into the net, sliding along it. The net was rising, the purpleness dangling from it, clear of the ground now, but almost indistinguishable against the purple of the grass. The tentacle still grasped the net. Enid's hand fumbled blindly in her pocket for the yellow gemstone. She raised it and slammed it down against the tentacle. The purpleness shrilled in pain and the tentacle fell away. She watched but did not see the purpleness hit the ground. It was a purpleness blending into purpleness, and there was nothing to be seen.

Horseface was crawling swiftly up the net. He had grasped one of the leather handles of the chest and was hauling it behind him.

The net was rising in the air, and Enid began crawling on it, getting away from the edge. The televisor was sliding toward her and she reached out to grasp it. It flickered at her; when she looked down at it, Boone was there. He was in a place of grayness and seemed to be gray himself and there was a gray wolf with him.

"Boone!" she cried at him. "Boone, stay there! I will come to you!"

Corcoran

8

Jay Corcoran stepped out of the traveler into a marvelous late-April springtime. The traveler lay in a small mountain meadow. Below it was a narrow valley with a silver streak of water. Above it towered the knife-edge hills. New leaves with the soft greenness of early growth clothed all the trees, and the meadow wore a carpet of pastel-blooming wildflowers.

David came up to stand beside him. "We traveled a bit further than I had intended," he said. "I had no time to set a course. I just got out of there."

"How far?" asked Corcoran. "Not that it matters very much."

"Actually, I don't suppose it does," said David. "Closer, however, than I'd really like to the era from which we came. We're now, in round figures—take or give a few hundred either way—975,000 years beyond the beginning of your reckoning. As to where, probably somewhere in what you would call the colony of Pennsylvania. Perhaps you've heard of it."

"In my day," said Corcoran, "it was no longer a colony."

"Give me a little time to figure it and I can pinpoint where we are within a mile or two and the time within a year or less, if you are interested."

Corcoran shook his head. He pointed at the ridgetop up the slope from the meadow where they stood.

"Something strange up there. A certain irregularity. Could it be a ruin?"

"Could be," said David. "Up this far in time, the entire Earth is littered with old, forgotten places. Worn-out cities, roads that outlived their usefulness, and shrines and other places of worship, deserted when religions changed. You want to climb up and see?"

"We might as well," said Corcoran. "From up there, we could spy out the land."

That the hilltop, indeed, was crowned by a ruin became apparent when they were no more than halfway up the slope.

"Not much left of it," said David. "A few more centuries and it will be a tell—a mound. A lot more like it, scattered all about. What it was, no one will ever discover. Up here there are no archaeologists. The race has lost all interest in what it was. The bulk of history weighs too heavily. Somewhere, I would suppose, there is tucked away a written account that would tell us what this ruin was and give a full history of it. But no one will read it. There are now no historians."

Almost at the summit, they came up against a wall, or what was left of it. It was tumble-down, no part of it rising more than ten feet or so. To come up to it, they picked their way carefully through fallen blocks of stone, many of them half-buried in the ground.

"There has to be a gate somewhere," said Corcoran.

"It's bigger," said David, "than it seemed looking at it down in the meadow."

Following the wall, they came upon the gate. An old man sat flat upon the ground to one side of it, leaning back against the wall. His tattered clothes fluttered feebly in the little breeze that blew across the ridge. He wore no shoes. His white beard came down across his chest, and his hair, as white as the beard, bunched about his shoulders. All that showed of his face was forehead, nose, and eyes.

They stopped stock-still at the sight of him. He stared back at them with no great surprise. He made no motion; all he did was wiggle his naked toes at them.

Then he spoke. "I heard you coming from a long way off. You are clumsy creatures."

"I'm sorry we disturbed you," said Corcoran. "We had no idea you were here."

"You were not disturbing me. I allow nothing to disturb me. For years there has been nothing that disturbed me. I was a prospector at one time. I roamed these hills with sack and spade, seeking out whatever treasure I might find. I found some, but not much, and finally it occurred to me that treasure is worthless. Now I converse with trees and stones, the best friends that a man can have. There are too many people in the world, worthless kinds of people. All they do now is talk among themselves, with little purpose other than their love of the sound their voices make. Everything is done for them by robots. I have no robot; I live without the benefit of robot. And the little talk I have is with trees and stones. I don't talk much myself. I am not in love with the sound of my voice as so many others are. Rather than talk, I listen to the trees and rocks."

All the time he had been talking, his body had been sliding down the wall against which he leaned. Now he hunched himself upward into a more erect position and shifted his conversational gears.

"At one time," he said, "I roamed the stars and talked with aliens, and the talk of aliens, I can tell you, is all gibberish. My team and I evaluated new planets and wrote weighty reports, all filled with hard-won data, to be delivered when we returned to the planet of our origin. But when we returned to Earth, only a few remained who had any interest in what we had found. The people had turned their backs on us. So I turned my back on them. Out in space, I met aliens. I met too many of them. There are those who will tell you that aliens are brothers under the skin to us. But I'll tell you truthfully that most aliens are a very nasty mess . . ."

"In all the time that you were in space," asked David, interrupting, "or here on Earth, for that matter, did you ever run into any talk about aliens who were called the Infinites?"

"No, I can't say that I ever did, although I haven't more than passed the time of day with anyone for years. I'm not what you would call a social person . . ."

"Is there anyone else, not too far away, who might have heard of the Infinites?"

"As to that," the old man told him, "I cannot say, but if you mean is there anyone who might be more willing than I am to talk with you, you'll find a group of ancient busybodies a mile or so down the valley below this mountain. Ask them a question and they'll answer. They talk unceasingly. Once they hear a question or get their teeth into any proposition, they will never let it go."

"You don't do so badly yourself," Corcoran said. He turned to David. "Since we're here, maybe we should take a walk through the ruins before we hunt up the people in the valley."

"There is nothing to see," the old man told him. "Just a heap of stones and old paving blocks. Go if you wish, but there is nothing worth the looking. I'll stay here in the sun. The trees and stones are friends of mine, and so is the sun. Although there can be no talking with the sun. But it gives warmth and cheer and it asks nothing in return, and that is a friendly thing to do."

"We thank you, then," said David, "for the time you have given us."

Saying that, he turned about and started through the

gate. There was no trail or road, but there were open places in the clutter of fallen stones. The old man had been right; there was not much to see. Here and there old walls still stood, and skeletons of ancient structures still clung to some of their former shapes, but nowhere was there a hint of what the ruin might have been.

"We're wasting our time," said David. "There is nothing here for us."

"If we didn't waste our time," asked Corcoran, speaking tartly, "what would we do with it?"

"There's that, of course," said David.

"There is one thing that bothers me," said Corcoran. "Here we are, almost a million years beyond my time. There is a million years between you and me. To you I should seem a shambling, uncouth primitive; to me you should seem a sleek sophisticate. But neither of us finds the other strange. What goes on? Didn't the human race develop in all those million years?"

"You must take into account that my kind were backcountry people," David said. "The hillbillies of our time. We clung desperately to the old values and the old way of life. Perhaps we overdid it, for we did it as a protest and might have gone overboard. But there were sophisticates up here. We built a great technical civilization and explored space. We came to terms with politics. No feuding nationalists were left. We arrived at a full social consciousness. No one in the world we stand in now lacks a place to sleep, food to eat, or medical aid, although now there is seldom need of it. The diseases that killed you by the millions have been wiped out. The human lifetime has been more than doubled since your time. Given a good look at this society, you might be tempted to call it utopia."

Corcoran snorted. "A hell of a lot of good utopia did you. Your time achieved utopia and now you are going to pot. I wonder if utopia might be what is wrong with you."

"Perhaps it is," said David, speaking mildly. "Rather than the fact of utopia, however, the acceptance of it."

"You mean the feeling that you have it made and there is nowhere else to go."

"Maybe. I'm not sure."

They walked along for a while, then Corcoran asked, "What about the others? Can you get in touch with them?"

"There's not much that you and I can do, but Horace has Martin's ship, and it has a communications system. He could do some checking around. He'd have to be careful about it. There undoubtedly are a number of groups like ours, scattered throughout time. Maybe none of them are any better off than we are. Whoever sent the killer monster against us would have sent monsters out against them as well. If there are some of them left, they probably would be wary about answering any calls."

"You think the Infinites sent the killers out?"

"I would suspect so. I can't think of anyone else who would have."

"But why? The Infinites drove you, helter-skelter, back into time. You can't pose much of a threat to them."

"It is possible," said David, "or the Infinites might think of it as possible, that we could all regroup and at a later date come back and set up a new society. We might not do this until after the Infinites were gone, and in that possibility they might see an even greater threat. If they left any of us behind there always would be the possibility, in their minds at least, that, once they were gone, we'd be likely to undo their work."

"But their work's already done."

"Not until the last human is either dead or has assumed incorporeal status."

All this time they had been climbing up the slope toward the ridge top. There still was little worth the seeing. The shattered stones lay all about them, and growing among them were bushes and small trees. In occasional patches of soil not covered by the stones, flowers grew and bloomed, many of them wild, but some of them survivors from the gardens of the fallen city—a scattering of pansies, tulips in an angle formed by two still-standing walls, and a gnarled lilac laden with sweet-smelling sprays.

Corcoran halted by the lilac bush. Reaching up, he pulled down a branch, and sniffed the heady scent of the tiny clustered flowers.

It all was the same, he thought. There was little change in this world of a million years ahead. The land was the same. There still were flowers and trees, all of them familiar. The people were little changed, if changed at all. Long as it might seem, a million years was too short a time for noticeable physical evolution. But there should be intellectual change. Maybe there was. He had seen few people of this far future—only the old man at the gate and David and his family.

He stepped away from the lilac tree and continued along a short span of wall only partially fallen. Coming to the end of it, he saw that the ridge top was a short distance off. There was a strangeness about the ridge top—a faint haziness that hung above the serrated line of ruins standing in stark outline against the sky. He slowed his walking, came to a halt, and stood staring up at the haziness that was beginning to assume the form of a gigantic, circular, free-standing staircase winding up the sky.

Then he saw that he was wrong. The staircase was not free-standing; it wound around a massive tree trunk. And the tree—good God, the tree! The haziness was going away and he could see it more clearly now. The tree thrust upward from the ridge top, soaring far into the sky, not topping out, but continuing upward as far as he could see, the staircase winding round it, going up and up until the tree trunk and the staircase became one thin pencil line, then vanished in the blue.

David spoke to him, "Is there something up there?"

Corcoran came back to reality, jerked back by the words. He had forgotten David.

"What was that?" he asked. "I am sorry; I did not hear you well."

"I asked if there was something up above the ridge. You were staring at the sky."

"Nothing important," said Corcoran. "I thought I saw a hawk. I lost him in the sun."

He looked back at the ridge. The tree still was there, the staircase winding round it.

"We might as well go back," said David. "There is nothing here to see."

"I think you're right," said Corcoran. "It was a waste of time to come."

Even looking at the hilltop, David had not seen the staircase tree. And I, thought Corcoran, did not tell him of it. Why the hell should I not tell him of it? Because of the fear that he would not believe me? Or because he had no need to know? The old, old game—never give anything away, but keep your knowledge to yourself against that day you have a chance to use it.

This was another example of that cockeyed ability that had made it possible for him to see Martin's traveler when no one else could. The traveler had been there, and he knew the tree was there as well; but this was private, privileged knowledge and he'd keep it to himself.

David was starting down the hill and, after a final look to make certain the tree was there, Corcoran followed in his wake. The old man was gone when they reached the gate, and they went down the hill to the meadow where the traveler awaited them.

"How about it?" asked David. "Shall we hunt up that village the old man told us of?"

"I'm willing," said Corcoran. "We should be doing something to find out what the local situation is. As it stands, we're operating in a vacuum."

"What I'm particularly interested in learning," said David, "is whether the Infinites have made their appearance yet. It was about this time that they first showed up, but I'm hazy on specific dates."

"You think the people in a small village might know? This area has the look of being out of touch."

"There'd be rumors. All we need to know is if the Infinites have showed up. The most flimsy rumors will tell us that."

At the edge of the meadow they found a trail that led down into the valley where a chuckling river flowed. David, in the lead, turned downstream. The going was easy. The valley was open and a fairly well-traveled path ran along the river.

"Can you give me some idea of what we'll be getting into?" asked Corcoran. "What, for instance, is the economic setup?"

David chuckled. "This will shock you down to your toenails. Basically, there is no economy. Robots do all the work and there is no money. I suppose that you could say what little economy there is is in the hands of robots. They have taken over everything, take care of everything. No human has to worry about how to get along."

"Under such a system," asked Corcoran, "what do the humans do?"

"They think," said David. "They think long and well and when it comes to talking, they talk most eloquently."

"Back in my own time," said Corcoran, "the farmers would go to town and drop in at a cafe for a cup of coffee. There'd be some small businessmen as well, and all of them would sit there and settle the fate of the world, each of them convinced he knew what he was talking about. Of course he didn't, but that made no difference. In his own niche, anyone can be his own philosopher."

"But not your people, not everyone . . ."

"We were the minority," said David. "The stupid fools who couldn't understand and wouldn't go along. We were the troublemakers, the thorn in the side of decent people, the loudmouths . . ."

"But, as I understand it, you weren't really troublemakers."

"No," said David. "We just set a bad example."

They were walking up a low hill. When he reached the crest, David stopped. Corcoran came up to him, and he nodded down the hill.

"There's the village," he said.

It was a small, neat village. A few of the houses were of respectable size, but the others were rather small. There were not many of them, perhaps more than a dozen, but not more than twenty. A narrow road formed the village street. A bridge spanned the stream, and the road beyond the stream snaked its way across flat bottomland checkered by fields and gardens. Beyond the bottomland, hills rose up again.

"A self-contained community," said Corcoran. "Isolated. The robots, I imagine, grow the food and tend the herds."

"Exactly. And yet the humans here, with their scaled-down needs, have everything they want."

They went down the hill and came to the road that formed the village street. There an old man walked, making his slow and careful way. No one else was in sight.

A robot came out of a small building that stood at the edge of the village. He headed directly for them, striding purposefully. When he came close, he stopped and stood facing them. He was a plain robot, businesslike, and with no fanciness to him.

"Welcome to our village," he said, without any preamble to cover social niceties. "We are glad you came. Will you step in with me and enjoy a bowl of soup? That is all we have today, that and honest bread, but there is plenty of it. We have been out of coffee for some time, but can offer you a stoup of our finest ale."

"We accept your hospitality with deep gratitude," David said, stiffly. "We hunger for companionship. We are on an extended walking tour and have fallen in with few. When we heard of your village, we came out of our way to visit you."

"There are gentlemen here," the robot told them, "who will be glad of discourse with you. We are a contented place and isolated, which affords us time for weighty cogitation. We have thinkers here we would array against any in the land."

He turned about and led them to the small building from which he had emerged. He held the door to let them in.

A counter ran along one wall, with stools arranged before it. In the center of the room stood a large, round table on which sat several flaring candles. A half-dozen men sat about the table. Large soup bowls had been pushed to one side and replaced with steins. Despite the candles, the room was dark and stifling. In all the building, there were only two small windows to let in the light.

"Gentlemen," said the robot, in a voice of somber pronouncement, "we have visitors. If you will, please to make elbow room for them."

The men at the table shoved their chairs closer together to make room for their visitors.

For some time after the two sat down, there was silence, with the others at the table looking them over closely and perhaps a bit suspiciously. In turn, Corcoran studied the faces before him. Most of them were older men and most wore beards. But they were cleanly, respectable men. He thought that he could catch the scent of bath soap; their clothing was plain and clean, although patched here and there.

An old man with a shock of snow white hair and a beard of alarming frostiness finally said to them, "We have been discussing the escape of mankind from the treadmill on which we had been placed by our former economic and social circumstances. All of us are convinced the escape came barely in time. This seems to be the one thing on which we are agreed, for each of us has developed divergent viewpoints on how and why it all came about. The world, we are agreed to start with, had become so artificial, so air-conditioned, so sterilized and comfortable, that a human no longer was a human, but a pet, computer-kept. Have either of you, perchance, had any thoughts on this?"

Bingo, thought Corcoran. Just like that. No introductions, no questions about who you are and what you might be doing, nothing about how glad we are that you happened to drop in, no small talk at all, no preliminaries. These men are fanatics, he told himself, and yet there was no sign of fanaticism—no wild gleam in their eyes, no tenseness in their bodies. As a matter of fact, they seemed to be calm and easy men.

"We have thought on it, of course, from time to time," said David, speaking as quietly as the old man with the frosty beard. "But our thoughts have been more directed toward why mankind, to start with, had gotten itself so trapped. We have sought for cause but there are so many factors and all of them so jumbled that true assessments are very hard to come by. In the last few months we have been hearing some snatches of rumors about a new school of thought which urges incorporeality as the final answer to all of mankind's problems. This is new to us. Being out of touch for too long, we may only now have stumbled on a thought that has been spoken for some time. We are hard pressed to arrive at the sense of it."

All the others at the table leaned forward with interest.

"Tell us what you know of it," said the frosty beard. "What have you heard of it?"

"Almost nothing," said David. "Only whispers here and there. No explanations. No details of what is going on. It has left us puzzled. We have heard a strange designation mentioned—Infinites. But we do not know what is meant by that."

A man with a head entirely lacking hair, but with a huge black walrus mustache, said, "We have heard of it as well, probably not a great deal more than you have heard. Wanderers passing through have brought the word. There was one who held that incorporeality would finally bestow upon mankind the immortality that has been always sought."

The robot brought two large bowls of soup and set them down in front of Corcoran and David. Corcoran picked up a spoon and tried the soup. It was warm and tasty. Some sort of meat, beef from the taste of it, noodles, carrots, potatoes, and onions. He swallowed a second spoonful with fine appreciation.

A third man, this time one with a wispy beard, was saying, "It is not hard to appreciate why such a notion should have wide appeal. Death has always seemed a shameful thing. Attempts to arrive at longevity have been a partial protest against the shameful ending of a life."

"As I understand it, incorporeality would, or at least could, mean the loss of individuality," a somewhat younger man said disapprovingly.

"What have you got against togetherness?" asked the wispy beard.

"What we are talking about," said Frosty Beard, "is the human mind. If it were possible to achieve incorporeality, the human mind would survive and the body be discarded. If one were to think about the proposal deeply, he might come to see that the human mind, the human intelligence, is all that really matters."

The younger man asked, "But what would the mind be without a body? The mind may need a vehicle."

"I'm not certain the mind needs a vehicle," said Frosty Beard. "The mind may be something entirely outside the parameters of the physical universe. We have, it seems to me, been able to explain all but mind and time. Facing these, mankind falters."

The robot brought steins of ale to David and Corcoran. He put down a cutting board and knife and slapped a loaf of brown bread onto the board. "Eat," he said. "It is good and healthful food. There is more soup, if you wish it. More ale, too."

Corcoran cut a thick slice of bread for David, another for himself. He dipped the bread into the soup and took a bite. It was excellent. So was the ale. He settled down to enjoyment.

David was speaking again. "There was this matter of the Infinites. We've heard the term, but nothing whatever of what the Infinites may be."

The old man with the frosty beard answered. "Like you, we have heard only rumors. It sounds like a cult, but there are suggestions it is not entirely human. There is a whisper of alien missionaries."

"There is little evidence to support a full discussion of this matter," said Wispy Beard. "Notions arise at times, flourish for a while, and then flicker out. Incorporeality, you say—but how is it to be accomplished?"

"I would think that, if mankind wishes to become incorporeal, a way can be found," said Walrus Mustache. "There have been many times when man has accomplished matters which it would have been better for him not to have tried."

"It all goes back," said Frosty Beard, speaking in a judiciary tone, "to a human characteristic we have pondered on many a long evening—the insatiable push of mankind toward a state of happiness . . ."

Corcoran let the talk go drifting on. He mopped up the last of his soup with a swab of bread, then emptied the stein. He straightened in his chair with his gut as full as possible, short of stuffing it.

He glanced around the room and saw for the first time that it was a hovel. It was small and bleak, without ornament, with little thought of comfort, a robot's idea of a dwelling place, simply an area of space enclosed against the weather. The workmanship was good; it would be good if put together by robotic labor. The table and the chairs were made of solid, honest wood. They would last for centuries. But aside from honest labor and honest wood, there was nothing else. The soup bowls and steins were the simplest pottery; the candles were homemade. Even the soup spoons were fashioned from carved and polished wood.

Yet these men of the village sat at this rude table in this rude hovel and discoursed on matters that were far beyond their ability or power to influence in any way at all, happily mumbling over considerations when they well might have no information on which to fabricate the basis of their talks—although, he told himself, he could be no proper judge of that. But it was, he thought, nothing to be greatly wondered at. It was all done in an ancient and honorable tradition that ranged back as far as history ran. In ancient Athens, idle men had met in the agora to engage in pompous talk; centuries later, idle men had sat on the porches of American country stores and talked as pompously as any old Athenian on matters they did not understand. In English clubs other men had sat over their drinks, mumbling to one another.

Idleness ran to talk, he thought, and men were entranced by the brilliance of their own thoughts. These men here were idle, made so by a computer-robotic society.

David was rising from his chair, saying, "I fear that it is time for us to go. We would tarry longer if we could, but we must be on our way. Thank you for the food and drink and for all the talk."

The men at the table did not rise. They did not offer

hands to say good-bye. They looked up briefly and nodded, then went back to their interminable discussion.

Corcoran rose with David and started for the door. The
robot, there before them, held it open.

"Thanks for the soup and ale," said David.

"Any time," the robot said. "You are welcome any
time."

Then they were out in the street, the door closing behind them. The street was empty.

"We found what we came for," said David. "We know
now that the Infinites are here, that they are in place and
beginning their mission."

"I feel sorry for those men back there," said Corcoran.
"Such pitiful bastards. Nothing to do but sit around and
talk."

"You have no need to pity them," said David. "They
may not realize it, but they have found their happiness.
They are truly happy men."

"Maybe so, but it's a horrible way for the human race
to end."

"It may be what the race was driving for all the time.
Through all of history man was always looking for some
method that would do his work for him. First the dog, the
ox, the horse. Then machines and after that computers
and robots."

Dusk was just beginning to creep into the valley when
they reached the meadow where the traveler lay.

As they approached the traveler, a misty scatter of shining motes moved out to meet them. Corcoran, the first to
notice it, stopped short. He felt the hair at the nape of
the neck begin to bristle in atavastic fear, then suddenly
realized what was taking place.

"David," he said, speaking softly, "we have a visitor."

David drew his breath in sharply, then he said, "Henry,
we are glad you turned up. I had hoped you would."

Henry floated across the grass and came up close to
them.

You laid me a long trail, he said. I had far to go.

"How about the others? What traveler were you in?"

I was in no traveler, said Henry. I remained at Hopkins

Acre. I knew you'd all go separately and I'd have to track you all.

"So you planned to start from scratch."

That I did. It is well I did. There have been complications.

"Well, you found us. That's a start. But why did you track us? You must have known we'd be able to take care of ourselves. You should have taken Enid's trail. She had the least experience, would be at the greatest risk."

That is what I did, said Henry. She has disappeared.

"How could that be? She would have waited for you. She would have known you would track her down."

She did not wait. She reached her first destination, then left. I fear she fled the monster. At her first destination lies the monster, dead.

"Dead? Who would have killed the monster?"

"Perhaps Boone," said Corcoran. "Boone was with her. He was running for her traveler with the monster close behind him. I tried to go to help him, but you seized hold of me and tossed me in the traveler."

You will not let me tell it all, wailed Henry. You must break in with all your jabbering. There is more to say.

"Well, say it then," said David, somewhat impatiently.

She left alone. I am sure of that. Boone was left behind.

"That doesn't sound right. She'd not have deserted him."

I can be sure of little, Henry said. I have only my deductions. I came upon the destination far in the past from Hopkins Acre. Fifty thousand years into the past, in the southwest of North America. The traveler was gone, but there was scent of it. The traveler had left a week or more before.

"Scent?" asked Corcoran. "Does he trail the travelers by scent?"

"I do not know," said David. "Neither does he, I would suppose, so there is no point in asking him. He has something you and I don't have and I wouldn't make a guess."

I can do it, said Henry. I know not how; I do not ask. Will you let me now continue?

"If you please," said David.

I looked about. There was a campfire that was fairly recent. Two days, three, not more than four. There was a rock cairn beside it. A piece of paper was held down on the cairn by another stone placed on top of it. I could not lift the stone nor could I insert enough of me to learn what, if anything, was inscribed upon the paper. I suspect it was a note left for others who might come. A short distance off lay the wreckage of the killer monster and a few strides beyond that the skeleton of some great beast, an oxen of some sort from the looks of it. It had enormous horns.

"There was no sign of Boone?" asked Corcoran.

None. I looked, but in all honesty, I must confess, for no great length of time. I was much too concerned for Enid. The trail was long and hard, but I found the second destination where her traveler had landed.

"And Enid wasn't there," said David.

Neither she nor the traveler was there. The traveler had not taken off; it had been taken off. I found skid marks on the ground; I found wheel tracks. It had been dragged off and placed on a vehicle. I tried to work out the trail, but I was never able to track it to the end.

"You looked for Enid, too?"

I checked, making many wide circles. I pried into every corner. I peeked in every cranny. Not once did I get an impression of her. If she had been in the area, I would have known it.

"So she's really lost. And someone has a traveler who shouldn't have it."

"There's a good chance," said Corcoran, "that they don't know what they have. Someone found it, was intrigued by it, and hauled it off fast, before the owner could come back—figuring, I suppose, that later on they'd have a chance to try to work out what it is."

David shook his head.

"Look," said Corcoran, "how many time travelers are there in the world? How many people before your time knew time travel was possible?"

Corcoran could be right, said Henry. You should listen

to him, David. He has a good head on his shoulders. He looks facts in the eye.

"At the moment," said David, "there is no good reason to debate the matter. For the moment, Enid is out of our reach. Her traveler's gone and so is she. We'd have no idea where to look."

My suggestion is to go back to the prehistoric site, said Henry. There we can look for Boone. He may have some clue that will help us find Enid. She may have said something to him that could be significant.

"Can you get us there? Have you the coordinates?"

Very closely there. I have the location coordinates. I worked them out carefully before I left. And the time coordinates are off by very little.

"I think you're right," said David. "We may find something there to work on. Otherwise we'll be thrashing around with no idea what to do."

Corcoran nodded. "It's the one thing we can do," he said.

David stepped through the door of the traveler, reaching out a hand to grasp Corcoran by the arm and haul him through.

"Get that door closed," he said, "and get set. Once Henry gives me the coordinates, we're off."

Corcoran closed the door and went forward, watching while David wrote down the coordinates in his log book as Henry gave them to him. David reached his fingers out to the instrument panel. "Hold on," he warned, then came the shock and darkness, the deep, unforgiving darkness. And almost instantly, it seemed, David was singing out again: "We're there."

Corcoran found the door and fumbled with it, finally got it open and tumbled out. The sun battered down out of a molten sky. The buttes stood up against the melting blue. The sagebrush shimmered in the sundance of the sand. Out on the plain lay the whitened skeleton of some great beast.

"Are you sure this is the place?" David asked of Henry.

It is the place. Walk straight ahead and you will find the ashes of the campfire.

"There's not any cairn," said Corcoran. "You said there was a cairn close by the fire and a note weighed down."

You're right. The cairn's not there. But the stones of which the cairn was built lie scattered on the ground. Something knocked them over.

Corcoran walked forward. The stones were scattered on the ground and there was a hole dug in the center of the scattered stones. The ashes of the campfire showed white against the sand.

"Wolves or foxes," said Corcoran. "They scattered the stones to get at the ground beneath them. There must have been something buried underneath the cairn."

"Meat," said David. "Boone must have cached some meat there and built the cairn to keep off the wolves."

Corcoran nodded. It sounded reasonable.

"The note should be here somewhere," said David. "It all checks out. The ashes of the fire. The skeleton of the large animal. That pile of junk over there must be what is left of the killer monster."

They looked for the note and did not find it.

"It's hopeless," David said. "The wind blew it away. There's no chance of finding it."

Corcoran stood and looked out across the plain. Far off, a dust devil swayed like a dancing snake. Just within the limit of vision dark dots danced in the shimmer of heat. Bison, Corcoran told himself, although it was no more than a guess; there was no way the unaided human eye could have made out what they were. The skeleton, he knew, was a prehistoric bison. The skull lay canted, resting on one horn, the other angled in the air. No other creature than a bison, he thought, could have horns like those.

Had Boone killed the bison? If that was the case, he must have had a large caliber rifle, for no other kind could have dropped that large a beast. And if he had a rifle, had it been he, as well, who had downed the killer monster? Corcoran shook his head; there was no way he could know.

"What do we do now?" asked David.

"We have a look around," Corcoran told him. "We may meet Boone returning from wherever he may have been. We may find him dead. Although it's hard to think anything could kill him. After all the risks he has taken, all the scrapes that he's been in, the damn fool should have died years ago. But his life is charmed."

"I'll climb the butte," said David. "From the top I might be able to see something that will give a clue."

"It would help if you had binoculars."

"I doubt we have. I'll go and see."

David walked back toward the traveler; Corcoran headed for the heap of scrap that had been the killer monster. He stayed well clear, walking a wide circle around it, though there was no threat or menace left in the scattered metal. Yet an awareness that seemed no proper part of him warned him to keep his distance.

David came back from the traveler. "No binoculars," he said. "Horace dumped the stuff in hurriedly; no thought went into it."

"I'll climb the butte, if you'd rather," said Corcoran.

"No, I'll do it. I'm very good at climbing."

"I'll walk along the base of the butte," said Corcoran. "I don't expect to find anything. This whole business has a peculiar ring to it. I'm beginning to wonder if Boone might not have left with Enid."

"Henry doesn't think he did."

Corcoran choked back an observation not entirely complimentary to the glittery Henry. Instead, he asked, "Where is Henry? He hasn't said a word for a long time now, and I have caught no glimpse of him."

"Come to think of it, neither have I. But that means nothing. He'll be back. He's probably doing some poking around."

David was carrying a shotgun. He must have picked it up when he went looking for the binoculars. He extended it to Corcoran, holding it upright by the stock. "Here, you might have more use of it than I have."

Corcoran shook his head. "I don't expect to run into any kind of trouble. I'll be careful that I don't. And you be damned sure that you don't pick the wrong target.

There probably are critters here a shotgun would mean nothing to."

David tucked the gun comfortably under his arm, seemingly glad that Corcoran had not taken it. "I have never fired this gun or any other gun," he said, "but on my walks at Hopkins Acre, I got accustomed to carrying one. This particular gun has become a part of me. I feel better, more myself, with it underneath my arm. The gun has never been loaded when I carried it."

"Take my advice," said Corcoran, in some disgust, "and load it. I suppose you carry shells?"

David slapped a pocket of his jacket. "Right in here. A double handful of them. Even back at Hopkins Acre, I always carried two shells. I took them out of the gun, Timothy insisting that it always should be loaded when it was in the rack."

"It is senseless to carry a gun if you don't intend to use it," said Corcoran. "What's the use of packing a gun unless it's loaded? My old man told me long ago, when he gave me my first gun—don't ever point your gun at anything, he said, unless you mean to kill it. I took that as good advice and never in my life have I pointed a gun at anything unless I was prepared to kill it."

"I often pointed this gun," said David, "but I never killed. I pointed it at hundreds of birds that the dogs put up, but I never pressed the trigger."

"What are you trying to prove—that you are finally civilized?"

"I've often wondered myself," said David.

Wandering along the base of the butte, Corcoran found a seepage flow that had been scooped out, forming a basin into which the water flowed. He came unexpectedly upon a badger that hissed at him before it waddled rapidly away. He became aware that a wolf was following him and paid it no attention. It kept on following, never getting closer than it had been, never falling back.

Nothing else happened. He found nothing of any interest. After a time, he turned about and followed the curve of the butte back to where the traveler lay. Before he turned back, the wolf had disappeared.

The sun was not far above the western horizon. Using some of the wood from the pile that remained beside the old campfire, he started a blaze. He went to the seepage basin and brought back a pail of water. When David came down off the butte, he was frying sizzling bacon in one pan and cooking flapjacks in a second.

David flopped down on the ground, the gun across his lap. "There is nothing," he said. "A few grazing herds far out on the plain, and that is all. This is the loneliest place I have ever seen."

"Pour yourself some coffee," Corcoran told him. "I have enough flapjacks for you to start. Help yourself to the bacon. The plates and cups are over there on the blanket."

Halfway through his first helping of cakes, David asked, "Any sign of Henry?"

"Not a peep from him."

"It's strange for him to go away without saying anything about it. Or to stay so long."

"He got an idea, maybe, and went to try it out."

"I hope so," said David. "There are times I'm not sure I understand Henry. He's my brother and all that, but try as I may to see him as blood and bone, he's no longer blood and bone—my brother still, but a highly unusual human being. He allowed himself to get snared by the Infinites, by their sleek, fine talk. But the process didn't take. Maybe Henry was too knotty, too warped a personality for it to take hold of him."

Corcoran tried to be comforting. "Don't worry about him. Nothing can happen to him. Nothing can lay a mitt on him."

David made no response. A few moments later he asked, "What do you think we should do now? Is there any point in staying here?"

"It's too early to say," Corcoran said. "We've been here only a few hours. Let's wait at least through tomorrow. We may have new thoughts by then."

A soundless voice spoke to them.

You seek a man called Boone? it asked.

After a startled moment, Corcoran said to David, "Did you hear that?"

"Yes, I did. It wasn't Henry. It was someone else."

I am the mind, the voice said, of what you term a killer monster. I can help you with this Boone.

"You can tell us where he is?" asked Corcoran.

I can tell you where he went. But first we strike a bargain.

"What kind of bargain, monster?"

Cease calling me a monster. It is bad enough to think of me as such, but to say it to my face is rank discourtesy.

"If you are not a monster, then what are you?"

I am a faithful servitor who does no more than carry out my master's will. It is not mine to question the rightness or the wisdom of his will.

"Don't bother to apologize," said David. "We know who you are. You lie in the tangle of wreckage that was once a killer monster."

There you go again, calling me a monster. And I made no attempt to apologize.

"It sounded to me as if you did," said Corcoran. "Let's get on with your bargain."

It is a simple bargain. Straightforward and no frills. I tell you where to look for Boone, but before I do that you must lift me from this wreckage of my former self and engage in all sincerity to take me elsewhere, away from this dreadful nothingness.

"Why," said David, "that is an easy bargain to be struck."

"Easy on," Corcoran cautioned. "Ask yourself how much faith you're willing to accord this junkyard voice."

"It seems a fairly simple thing," said David. "He knows where Boone is and is willing . . ."

"That's the point. He doesn't claim he knows where Boone is. He tells us he'll tell us where to look for him. Those are two different things."

"As a matter of fact, they are. How about it, sir? How precise would be your information?"

I would help you in any way I could. The aid I offer will not be limited to the finding of Boone.

"What other kinds of help? In what regards could you be of aid to us?"

"Forget it," Corcoran growled. "Pay him no attention. He is in a tight spot and he'll promise anything to get out of it."

But in all human charity, wailed the monster, you must take pity on me. You must not condemn me to endless eons of no contact with external stimuli. I can not see; with the exception of this telepathic talk, I cannot hear. I feel no heat or cold. Even the passage of time is blurred. I cannot differentiate between a second and a year.

"You're in terrible shape," said Corcoran.

Indeed I am. Kind sir, please empathize with me.

"I'll not lift a hand to help you. I'll not lift a finger."

"You're being hard on him," said David.

"Not as hard as he was on Athens. No harder than he would have been on us if he'd had the chance—if he'd not bungled it."

Bungle it I did not. I am efficient mechanism. My luck ran out on me.

"It certainly did," said Corcoran. "It is still running out. Now shut up. We want no more of you."

It shut up. They heard no more of it.

After a time, David said, "Henry has not come back. You and I are left alone. The monster-mind says it has information. I think it reasonable to believe it does. It was here when Boone was here. It may have talked with him."

Corcoran grunted. "You are trying to convince yourself that you should show a measure of magnanimity to a fallen enemy, that you should act nobly and be a gentleman about it. It's your neck if you want to risk it. I wash my hands of it. Do whatever you damn please."

The sun had set and deep dusk was flowing in. Somewhere out in the emptiness, a wolf howled and another answered. Corcoran finished eating. "Give me your plate and the silverware," he said to David. "I'll go down to the seepage basin and rinse them off."

"Want me to come along as guard for you?"

"No, I'll be quite safe. It's just a step or two away."

Squatting beside the dug-out basin, Corcoran rinsed off

the dishes. In the east, the moon was riding low. Off in the distance, a half-dozen wolves had joined in lamenting their hard and sorry lives.

When he got back to the fire, David had the blankets out. "It's been a long day," he said, "and we should get some sleep. I'll stand first watch. I imagine we should keep a watch."

"I think we should," said Corcoran.

"I'm worried about Henry," David told him. "He knows that in a situation such as this we should not divide our forces."

"He's probably only delayed," said Corcoran. "By morning, he'll be back, and everything will be all right again."

He wadded up his jacket to use as a pillow and pulled the blanket up. Moments later, he was asleep.

When he awoke, he was lying on his back. Above him, the sky was growing lighter with the first touch of dawn, and David had not called him to take his turn at watch.

Damn him, Corcoran thought. He knew better than that. He doesn't have to prove that he can take it or that he's a better man than I am.

"David!" he shouted. "Damn it, what do you think you're doing?"

On the butte, the birds were singing, saluting the first brightening of the east. Except for the singing, there was no sound at all, and the flicker of the dying fire was the only motion anywhere. Out on the plain, the white bones of the bison gleamed in the soft dawn light; and a little way to the right of them, he could make out the junk heap that marked the death of the killer monster.

Corcoran stood up, shaking off the blanket that had covered him. He moved toward the fire, reaching out for a stick of wood to use in rearranging and consolidating the scattered coals. He crouched down before the fire and it was then he heard the slobbering sound that sent a wave of terror through him. It was not a sound he had ever heard before and he had no idea what it was, but there was about it a freezing quality that held him rigid. It came again and this time he was able to turn his head to see where it might come from.

For a moment all that he could see was a pale blob crouched over a dark blob on the ground. He strained his eyes to see the better but it was not until the pale blob lifted its head and stared straight at him that he recognized it for what it was—flat cat face, tasseled ears, the gleam of six-inch fangs—a sabertooth crouched above its prey, feeding with that horrible slobbering to indicate the toothsomeness of what it was ingesting.

Corcoran knew the prey. Out there, under the claws and fangs of the sabertooth, lay David!

Grasping the stick he had picked up from the pile of wood, Corcoran rose. He shifted the stick in his hand, getting a better grip. It was a puny weapon, but was the only thing he had. The cat also rose to its feet. It was much larger than he had thought. It was fearsome in its size. It stepped over the dark blob that was David and took a few steps forward. It stopped and snarled, the down-curving fangs gleaming in the growing light. The cat's forelegs were longer than its hind legs; its back sloped and the beast seemed to slouch. There was light enough now for Corcoran to make out the speckled coat, brown splotches on light tan.

He did not stir. After its few steps, neither did the cat. Then slowly, deliberately, as if not yet decided, it pivoted about. It slew-footed its way back to its prey, lowered its head, nuzzling the dark blob and arranging the catch so it could get a firm grip. Then the cat's teeth sank into the blob and lifted; and the cat began to move away, taking its time, turning its back on the man beside the fire.

Corcoran watched, unable to move a muscle. The cat broke into an effortless trot. It held its head high so that its dangling prey would clear the ground. But even so, one leg fell down and dragged, and the cat stumbled once or twice when one of its front paws tripped over the dragging leg. It went along the base of the bluff, around an extending spur that ran off the butte into the plain, and disappeared.

Not until it was gone did Corcoran move. He crouched

down before the fire and fed wood into it. The wood caught quickly and flames leaped high. Still crouching, he swung around to see that the traveler still lay where it had landed. Thirty feet or more beyond the fire lay the shotgun. He had not noticed the gun before. It had been too dark, and, in any case, he had been so occupied with watching the cat he had seen nothing else. He did not move to pick it up. The paralysis of fear still held him.

Slowly the enormity of what had happened struck him full force. Killed by a sabertooth! Killed and eaten by a sabertooth. Killed, not in anger or defense, nor yet in thoughtless killing fury, but killed for the sake of the meat upon the bone.

David was dead. David who? Shocked, Corcoran realized he'd never known the family name. The folk at Hopkins Acre had never mentioned it, and he had never asked. He called the roll: David, Enid, Timothy, Emma, and Horace. Although that wasn't right; Horace's family name would have been different.

David had not called him, had let him sleep. If he had called me, Corcoran thought, it might have been me instead of him.

He tried, in his imagination, to lay out how the death might have happened. David might have heard something out beyond the fire in the predawn darkness and have stepped out to investigate. He might have been taken by surprise or he might have seen the cat. Whatever the situation, he had not fired the gun.

If it had been me, Corcoran thought, I would have fired. If I had walked out from the fire and run into a sabertooth, I would have used the gun. A shotgun would not be the weapon of choice to use against a sabertooth, but at close range, while it might fail to kill, a shotgun certainly would dampen the killing urge of even so large an animal. David had not used the gun, perhaps because he had never fired it, perhaps because he was too civilized to use it, even if he'd had the chance. To him the gun was not a weapon—it had been a walking stick.

The poor damn fool, Corcoran told himself.

He left the fire and walked out to the gun. It had two

shells in the breech; it had not been fired. He cradled it in the crook of his arm and walked out farther. A boot lay on the ground and inside the boot, a foot. The bones were shattered, broken by the crunching teeth of a feeding animal. A little further on he picked up a torn jacket. Around it were scattered other shotgun shells, lying where they had fallen. Corcoran gathered them up, put them in his pocket. There seemed nothing else left of David. He walked back to the boot with the foot enclosed and stood there, staring at it. He did not stoop to touch it. It would be, he told himself, messy to pick up and he shied away from it.

He turned back to the fire and hunkered down. He should eat something, he knew, but he had no urge for food. His mouth tasted sour and foul.

Now what should he do?

He was certain that he could operate the traveler. He knew where David kept the logbook; he had watched David program the control panel for the jump to this place.

But where to go? Back to his own twentieth century, washing his hands of this whole affair? He thought about that. The idea had some attraction, but he felt an uneasiness about it. Thinking of it, he felt like a deserter. Boone was somewhere in this crazy quilt of time, and he should not leave until he was certain he could be of no help to his friend.

He thought about the sabertooth and being alone in this forsaken place, and it was a thought that did not please him. But he weighed it all against the need to be here if Boone should return from wherever he had gone. And Henry, too, perhaps, although Henry had no need of a traveler to move through all of time and space. Henry, he decided, had no need at all of him.

He considered the sabertooth and saw that the cat was an incidental problem, not to be taken account of in any decision he might make. The cat might not return. Even if it did, there now was a weapon in the hands of someone who knew the use of it. With the gun in hand, he told himself, he would not be as vulnerable as David. At night he could sleep in the traveler, with the door closed tight against marauding carnivores. There was food to last for a time and water in the seep-hole. He could stay, he knew, as long as he might wish.

Full dawn had come and he bestirred himself. He went to the seep-hole for a pail of water; he went to the traveler for food. He squatted by the fire to bake a pan of cornbread, boil coffee, and fry bacon. Hell, he told himself, it's just a camping trip.

He tried to feel sorry for David, but could dredge up little sorrow. The horror of the death—or, rather, the horror of the circumstances of the death—sent a shiver through him, but he forced himself not to dwell on it. The quicker he could wipe it from his mind, the better it would be.

There was a titter in his mind. It came from somewhere outside of him. Heh-heh-heh, it laughed.

Anger flared within him.

"Bug off," he told the monster.

Heh-heh-heh, the monster tittered. Your friend is dead and I am still alive.

"You'll wish a million times that you were dead before this is all over."

You'll be dead yourself, the monster chortled, long before I am. You'll be bone and dust.

Corcoran did not answer. A whisper of suspicion came to him. Was it possible the monster could have lured the killer cat to David?

It was silly on the face of it. He was paranoid, he thought, for even thinking of it. He ate breakfast, then washed and dried the pots and plates, using his jerked-out shirttail to do the drying. On second thought, he went to the traveler and found a shovel. Digging a hole, he buried the boot with the foot inside it. For sanitary reasons, he explained to himself; the action was not intended to be ceremonial.

Wrapping a chunk of cornbread in a handkerchief, he put it in his pocket. In the traveler he rooted through the flung-in supplies, looking for a canteen and finding none. In lieu of a canteen, he filled the pail half full of water.

It was an awkward thing to carry, but the best that he could do.

Packing the shotgun and the water pail, he walked out onto the plain. A few miles out he turned to his left and began to walk a circle route, with the butte as the center of the circle. He kept a sharp lookout for any sign that Boone had passed that way.

Twice Corcoran found what he thought might be a human trail. He followed each and could not be sure. Both trails finally petered out. It was useless, he told himself. He had known all along that it would be useless—but even convinced of the uselessness, still he had to try. He and Boone had gone through a lot together. They had, at times, stuck out their necks for one another. Boone was the closest thing to a friend he'd ever had. He'd not had many friends.

At times he came on wolves that grudgingly moved out of his way, sitting down to watch him once he'd passed. A deerlike animal sprang out of a clump of bushes and dashed away. He passed within a mile of a small herd of bison. In the distance he glimpsed what looked like mastodons, although they were too distant for him to be certain. There could be mastodons here, he told himself; it was the proper time for them.

When the sun stood directly overhead, he halted and squatted in the shade of a tree. He munched cornbread and drank lukewarm water from the pail.

Probably he should go back to the butte. He had set out with the intention of describing a circle around it. He already had completed the western sweep of the circle. To the east lay nothing, just the plain stretching vast, flat, and empty, finally to merge with the sky. If Boone had gone anywhere, he would have gone west, where other buttes loomed up; he would not have gone into the nothingness of the east. Corcoran pondered the matter. Perhaps what he should do was backtrack himself, covering virtually the same ground, keeping a sharper lookout for a clue he might have missed before.

He finished the cornbread and had another lukewarm drink. He was readying himself to rise to his feet when he felt the presence. He froze and listened. There was nothing to be heard, but the presence was still there.

He spoke hesitantly, unsure.

"Henry?"

Yes, it is I, said Henry.

"You know of David?"

Yes, I know of him. As soon as I returned, I knew. And you were missing. I set out to find you.

"I'm sorry about David."

I sorrow also. He was a brother who cannot be replaced. He was a noble man.

"Yes. A very noble man."

A cat got him, said Henry. I tracked it and I found it, worrying his remains. There was little left. Tell me how it came about.

"He was standing guard. When I awoke I found what had happened. I had heard nothing. The cat carried him away."

There was a grave. A very small grave.

"A boot," said Corcoran. "With a foot inside of it. I buried it."

I thank you for your act. You did what the family would have done.

"You know where the body is. I could take a shovel and scare off the cat . . ."

It would be meaningless. An empty gesture. I see you have the gun. He did not use it?

"He must have been taken by surprise."

In any case, Henry said, he would not have used it. He was too gentle for this world. This venture has gone badly. For all of us. First Enid lost, then Boone.

"You know of Boone? You have news of him?"

I found where he had gone, but he was not there. A rifle was there and a pack he had carried, but he was gone. A wolf, I think, had been with him. I am sorry, Corcoran.

"I think I know what happened to him," said Corcoran. "He stepped around another corner. I only hope he stays where he went and does not come popping back."

What do you intend to do now? There is no point in staying here.

Corcoran shook his head. Yesterday he'd thought briefly of what he could or should do. He had thought of going back to New York. He had rejected this idea out of hand; Boone had been lost and must be found. Now Boone was still lost, he realized, with very little chance of finding.

He thought of the twentieth century and again rejected it. Never in his life had he turned his back on any adventure until it was all played out. This adventure, he reminded himself, was far from being all played out.

He could return to Hopkins Acre. The coordinates, he was sure, could be found in David's logbook. Living in the Acre would be comfortable. The servants and the tenants still would be there. It would be a place where he could be secure and rethink the situation and, perhaps, arrive at a logical plan for further action. It was possible, as well, that some of the others would be returning there.

But there was that other place where the ruins of a city topped a peak and a massive, sky-piercing tree lanced up to tower above the ruins, with a spiral stairway running around the tree. There must be some mystery there, perhaps not as he had seen it or remembered that he'd seen it, but surely something that needed looking into.

Henry was waiting for an answer. Corcoran could faintly detect the shimmer of him, a cloud of sparkles gleaming in the sun.

Instead of answering Henry's question, he asked a question of his own. "As I understand it, you stopped short of incorporeality. Can you tell me how it happened?"

It was a piece of bad judgment on my part, said Henry. I let the Infinites talk me into it. I took to hanging around with them. Curious, I would guess, wondering what kind of things they really were. Very strange, you must understand. They are marginally humanlike, or the glimpses that I caught of them seemed humanlike. You don't see them. You scan them now and then. They float in and out, like ghosts. But see them or not, you hear them all the time. They preach at you, they reason, they implore, and they plead. They show you the path to immortality and recite the endless comforts and triumphs of immortality—an intellectual immortality, they say, is the only way to go. All else is gross, all else is sloppy and shameful. No one wants to be shameful.

"They sell you a bill of goods?"

They sold me, said Henry. But they sold me in a moment of weakness. When the weakness went away, I fought them. They were shocked to their very core that I should have the temerity to resist them, and that was when they really got to work on me. But the harder they pounded on me, the stubborner I got. I broke away from them. Or maybe they gave up in disgust. Maybe I was taking more of their time than I was worth, and they heaved me out. But when I got away, the process had gone too far; I already was halfway to incorporeality; I was stuck somewhere between. I was the way you see me now.

"It doesn't seem to bother you."

There are disadvantages and advantages, and I take the view that I am somewhat ahead, that the advantages may outweigh the disadvantages. At least, that's what I tell myself. There are many common, human things that I cannot do, but there are abilities no other human can command, and I make the most of those abilities, ignoring what I've lost.

"And what do you intend to be doing now?"

There still is one part of the family that I must track down. Horace and Emma—and Timothy, who was hustled aboard the traveler by that big bully of a Horace.

"Have you any idea where to look?"

None at all. I'll have to track them down.

"Can you use the traveler in your tracking? I could operate it for you."

No, I must do it on my own. I must go back to Hopkins Acre and pick up the trail from there. It will be faint and thin, but it will still be there. You say you can operate the traveler?

"Yes. I know where the logbook is and I watched David punch in the coordinates when he set the course for here."

It might be best for you to go back to Hopkins Acre.

I think the place is safe. Some of us could come back for you. We could do that, knowing where you were. The coordinates would be written in the logbook. You are sure you can run the traveler?

"I am certain," Corcoran said. "I don't think I'll go to Hopkins Acre. Later on, perhaps, but not immediately. I want to go to the place where you found David and me. There is something there that needs looking into."

Henry did not ask the question that Corcoran was sure he would. Rather, there was the impression of a shrug.

Well, all right, said Henry. You know where you're going and I know where I'm going. We'd best be on our way.

Suddenly, Henry was gone.

Corcoran rose to his feet. Boone no longer was in this time and place, and there was no reason to stay on. He knew where he was going and, as Henry had said, he should be on his way as soon as possible.

When he reached the camp, the place was deserted. There was no sign of the cat and not even any wolves. Corcoran picked up the pots and pans beside the ashes of the campfire and flung them on the blanket; then, lifting the blanket, he flung it all over his shoulder.

A voice talked at him. Heh-heh-heh, it said.

At the sound, Corcoran spun on his heel to face the pile of junk.

The tittering kept on.

Corcoran headed for the junk heap.

"Cut out that goddamned tittering," he shouted.

The tittering cut off and a pleading began.

Dear sir, you are about to leave. You gather up your things to leave. Please take me with you. You will not regret it. Many things I can do for you. I can pay back your kindness. I will be your eternal friend. The taking of me will in no way impede your going. I am of little weight and will not take up much space. You need not search for me. I lie in back of the wreckage of my body. I am a brain case, a highly polished sphere. I would look well displayed upon a mantle. I would be a conversation piece. For me you would find many uses. In times when you are alone and desirous of companionship, the two of us could hold instructive and entertaining conversations. I have a good mind and am well versed in logic. There would be times I could serve as your advisor. And always I would be your friend, filled with loyalty and gratitude . . .

"No, thank you," Corcoran said, turning on his heel and walking toward the traveler.

Behind him the killer monster went on wailing, pleading, begging, and promising. Then the wailing fell off and a storm of hatred came.

You scaly son of a bitch, I'll not forget you for this. I'll get you in the end. I'll dance upon your bones.

Corcoran, unscathed, continued to the traveler.

Boone

9

A cold nose woke Boone, and he tried to jerk himself erect. His leg screamed at him, and he choked back the answering scream deep inside his throat. The wolf, whining, sidled away. All around the southern horizon, the stars glittered coldly at him. His clothes were damp with the chill of frosty dew.

From where he lay he looked over the moon-silvered plain that he had crossed, more desert than plain, although there was some grass and other pasturage for small game herds. Somewhere, perhaps to the east, there would be grassy plains where enormous herds would range. But here the herds were small and the predators few.

"You're out of place," he told the wolf. "You could find better eating elsewhere."

The wolf glared at him and snarled.

"That's no way to carry on a conversation," Boone told it. "I do not snarl. I've never snarled at you. We have traveled together and fed together and the two of us are friends."

He had been holding himself propped up on his arms, but now he relaxed and eased himself to the ground, turning his head so that he could watch the wolf—not that he feared the wolf, he told himself; it was simply the inclination to maintain touch with the only companion that he had.

He had been asleep and how could he have slept under such conditions—his leg trapped in a rocky crevice and a watching wolf that waited for him to die so that it might feed? Yet, he thought, he might be maligning the wolf, for they were friends.

His leg hurt, no longer a scream, but a dull, tooth-gritting ache. He felt like hell—his leg hurt, his gut was empty, his throat burned, and his mouth was dry. He needed water badly. Somewhere, not too distant, he was certain that he heard the sound of running water.

The wolf had sat down, its bushy tail wrapped neatly about its feet, its head canted to one side, and its ears tipped forward.

Boone closed his eyes. He let his head settle more firmly against the ground. He tried to close out the pain. Except for the sound of running water, all was silent. He tried to close his ears against the sound of the water.

What a hell of a way to end, he thought. Briefly, he dozed.

And snapped back to awareness.

He was on his knees, no weapon in his hand and none to reach for. Tearing down upon him was the mounted horseman that came deep out of his memory, a giant of a man astride a small but wiry horse. The horse, its teeth bared, was as purposeful and grim as the man who rode it.

The horseman's mouth was open in a scream of

triumph, his teeth flashing in the firelight that seemed to appear from nowhere. His great mustaches streamed back in the wind of his rush, and the gleaming, heavy sword high above his head was beginning to come down.

Then the wolf was there, rising in a leap, foam-flecked jaws agape, aimed for the horseman's throat. But it was too late, far too late. The sword was coming down and nothing in the world could stop it.

Boone landed with a thump and sprawled. His eyes were filled with grayness. The surface beneath him was smooth; when he crawled upon it, he knew his leg was free—his leg was free and he was no longer where he had been, trapped on the steep slope of a butte, with an upthrust of stone behind him and the sound of nearby running water.

The sound of running water still was with him and he crawled toward it. Reaching it, he flopped upon his belly and lowered his head to drink, retaining sense enough to force himself to limit the drink to several swallows, then rolling away from the edge of the water.

He lay upon his back and gazed up into the grayness of the sky. Fog, he thought. But it was not fog, he knew; it was a gray sky. Everything was gray. He took stock of himself. The leg that had been trapped was sore, but there was nothing broken. The edge had been taken off his raging thirst. His gut was empty. Otherwise he seemed to be all right.

It had happened again; he had stepped around a corner.

But what had been all that business of the mounted horseman with the streaming mustaches and the down-sweeping sword? There had been no such horseman, could not have been such a horseman on that world of the distant past. His subconscious, he thought—the complexity, the mystery, and the sneakiness of the human brain. There had been no present, instantaneous danger that would have been necessary to trigger the stepping around a corner. His subconscious, to save his life, to make it possible for him to step around a corner, had summoned up the mounted warrior, the outrageous barbarian, so that his brain could react automatically. Thinking of it, it didn't seem quite the correct and logical answer. Yet, he told himself, logic or not, it didn't actually matter. He was here, wherever here might be, and that was all that counted. The question now was whether he could stay here and not, after a time, be plunged back into the prehistoric world. Always before he had gone back to the point of origin, except for that last time when he, accompanied by Corcoran, had stepped into Martin's traveler and had stayed there, not going back to the Everest room that had already crumbled. Perhaps, he thought, the pattern had been broken. He'd been here for quite some time.

He crawled back to the water and drank again. The water was good, cool, clean, and flowing. Slowly he hoisted himself to his feet. The leg that had been trapped in the crevice supported him. It ached and smarted, but basically it was as normal as it had ever been. He had been lucky, he thought.

He looked around. There was a good deal of substantiality in the place. In other instances, except for the Everest, which had been a special case, around the corner had been a filmy, foggy place, with all structure blocked out and smothered by the fog. Here there was no fog. The fog, if there ever had been any, had cleared away. The place still was gray, but a grayness with form and structure.

He stood on a plain. The plain undoubtedly ran to a horizon, but there was no way of knowing, for the grayness of the sky came down to the grayness of the plain and the two could not be separated. The stream from which he had drunk meandered down the plain, coming from nowhere and flowing into nowhere. Down the plain, as well, went a road, not meandering, but straight as a road could run. It was gray as well, but was marked by two darker streaks that appeared to be wheel marks. The wheel tracks were neat, regular and straighter than any actual track could be.

"What the hell kind of place is this?" Boone asked, speaking aloud, not expecting an answer and not getting one.

The road ran two ways and he probably should follow it, but in which direction?

The entire situation was wrong, he told himself. He had no idea where he was or where to go. There was no way to know how long he'd been here. There was water, but no food.

He moved away from the stream and walked out into the middle of the road. He knelt down and felt what he had taken to be wheel marks. While his eyes could not define the elevation of the darker streaks, his fingers told him they were raised an inch or so above the level of the surface. In texture, they seemed to be made of the same material as the surface, but raised above it. Could they, he wondered, be rails? Maybe if he waited long enough a conveyance of some sort would come along, running on the rails, and he could catch a ride on it. That, he knew, was nothing he could count on.

Standing in the middle of the road, he made his decision. He would follow the road in the same direction that the stream ran. He would go with the flowing water. Water, he recalled someone saying long ago, ran toward civilization. Follow a stream and you would eventually find people. That could be right, but logic might not apply to this place. Walking in either direction, he might arrive at nowhere. Perhaps there was nowhere to arrive at.

He trudged along for a while, but nothing changed. The water course still ran along the road, now close to it, now farther off, as it meandered about the plain. There was just the road and brook.

He heard a clicking behind him and swiftly turned about. The clicking had sounded like and was the click of toenails. A wolf was close upon his heels. *The* wolf? Looking at it, he could not tell. This wolf was gray and the other wolf had been gray, but that was not significant, for here everything was gray. He held out his arms and the sleeves of his jacket were gray. His jacket, before he had come here, had been tan.

The wolf had halted and sat down, not more than six feet from him. It wrapped its tail around its feet and cocked its head at him. It grinned.

"I'm glad you like it," said Boone. "Maybe you can tell me where we are."

The wolf said nothing. It kept on sitting there and it kept on grinning.

"I think you're the wolf I know," said Boone. "If you are, snarl a bit at me."

The wolf lifted its lip in an instant snarl, then went back to grinning. When it had snarled, it had flashed a lot of teeth.

"The same old wolf," said Boone. "So let the two of us get moving."

He started striding down the road, and the wolf moved up beside him, walking along with him. It was good to have the wolf here, Boone told himself. After all, it was better to be walking with a friend than with a stranger.

Nothing happened. Nothing changed. Boone kept striding along, and the wolf kept padding with him, and they might just as well have been standing still; no matter how far they walked, it all stayed the same.

He wondered where Enid was and why she had not returned. What could have happened to her?

"Do you remember Enid?" he asked the wolf. The wolf did not answer him.

Far down the road a dot appeared. The dot grew larger.

"There is something coming," Boone told the wolf.

He stepped off the road and waited. It was, he saw, a vehicle of some sort, running on the tracks.

"It's going the wrong way," he told the wolf.

The wolf yawned. It might as well have said, "What difference does it make? How do we know which way is the right way?"

"I don't suppose we do," said Boone.

The dot became a trolley car, a very funny trolley car, open to the weather, although a striped canopy hung over the two seats, one of them facing forward, the other facing back. There was no operator; the car ran by itself.

The trolley slowed, but it did not stop.

"Up you go," Boone told the wolf.

The wolf leaped up and sat down on one of the seats.

Boone jumped in and sat down beside the wolf, both of them facing forward. The car picked up speed.

The car was gray, of course. The canopy was striped only in the sense that the alternating stripes were light gray and dark gray. The gray car went rocketing through the land, with the gray wolf and the gray man sitting on the trolley's seat beneath the flapping canopy.

Finally, on the left hand side of the track and very far ahead, a cube loomed up and became larger as they sped along. The car began to slow, and now it could be seen that the cube was a building, with three tables set outside and chairs around the tables. Someone sat at one of the tables; when the car came to a halt, Boone saw that the person at the table was The Hat, who had sat across the campfire from him and had talked with him about the brotherhood of wolf and man. The Hat's great conical hat was still the same, so huge that it rested on his shoulders and concealed his head.

The wolf jumped out of the car and trotted over to The Hat's table, sitting down and staring at The Hat. Boone got off more slowly and walked to the table, taking the chair opposite The Hat.

I have been waiting for you. I was told you would be coming, The Hat said.

"Who told you?"

That doesn't matter. What does matter is that you've arrived and have brought along your friend.

"I did not bring him," said Boone. "He came all by himself. He was the one who sought me out."

You are meant for one another, said The Hat. I told you the two of you were friends.

"It appears this might be an eating place," said Boone. "How do we go about getting something to eat?"

Your needs are known. It is already on the way.

"For the both of us?"

Of course. For the both of you.

A squat service robot rolled out of the door of the building. A tray rested on top of its squared-off head. It stopped by the table and, lifting its arms, transferred the tray to the table.

"This plate is for the carnivore," said the robot. "How do I serve it?"

"You place it on the ground," said Boone. "He eats most naturally that way."

"I did not cook the meat."

"That is right. He likes it raw and bloody."

"And I cut it into mouth-size pieces for easy handling."

"That was thoughtful of you," said Boone. "You have the thanks of both of us."

The robot set the large plate of raw meat on the ground and the wolf began gulping it down. He was hungry; he gulped it fast and without the nicety of chewing.

"He is hungry," said the robot.

"So am I," said Boone.

Quickly the robot unloaded the tray on the table in front of Boone—a huge and sizzling steak, a baked potato with a pot of sour cream, a salad with cheese dressing, a dish of green beans, a piece of apple pie, and a pot of coffee.

Boone said to The Hat: "This is the first civilized food I have seen for a week or more. But I'm surprised to find good twentieth-century American cooking in a place like this."

We know our customers, said The Hat. We fit our cuisine to them. We knew you and the wolf would be our guests.

Boone, ignoring the salad, started on the steak. He spooned cream into the baked potato. He asked, speaking with his mouth full, "Can you tell me where we are? Or are you bound to silence by some foolish secrecy?"

Not at all, said The Hat. For all the good it does you, you're on the Highway of Eternity.

"I have never heard of it."

Of course you haven't. You were not supposed to. You or any other human.

"But we are here. The wolf and I."

The Hat said, sadly: There was reason to believe it would never happen. The lesser breeds, we thought, were barred. There was but one chance in many millions that the evolutionary process could stumble on the kind of freakishness that you have. Once the universe was stable.

One could cipher what might happen. One could plan. But that is true no longer. Not with you, it isn't. Random biological processes have made a jest of reason.

Boone kept on eating. He was too hungry even to try to be polite. Wolf had finished gulping down his plate of meat and now lay comfortably beside it, only a couple of feet away so that he would be close by if anyone should bring another bait of food. His hunger had been dulled, but little more than dulled, for Wolf was a hard animal to stuff to the point where he could no longer eat.

Boone gulped and swallowed. He spoke to The Hat. "You said the Highway to Eternity?"

That is not what I said. I said the Highway of Eternity.

"Small difference," Boone told him.

Not so small as you might think.

"Well, it doesn't matter," said Boone. "If I followed this road, would I reach Eternity? And what is Eternity? What would I find at Eternity? Who, I ask you, would want to reach Eternity?"

You're already in Eternity, said The Hat. Where did you think you were?

"I had no idea," Boone said. "But Eternity!"

It's a good place to be, said The Hat. It is the end of everything. When you are in Eternity, you have arrived. There is no use of going further.

"I'm supposed to just settle down and stay?"

You might as well. There is no place else to go.

There was something terribly wrong, Boone told himself. The Hat was lying to him, making sport of him. Eternity was not a place; perhaps it was no more than something that some ancient philosopher had thought up, but not a point in space and time. And the road did not end at this little eating place; it kept unrolling into the gray distance. There were obviously other places to go.

The steak and potato were finished. He pushed the platter to one side and pulled the plate of salad in front of him, reversing the usual course of eating. He did not care for salad, although when hungry, as he had been and still seemed to be, he would eat it.

The Hat had not spoken for some time. When Boone

glanced across the table, he saw that The Hat had fallen with his hidden face upon the table. His arms, which had been resting on the table top, had slipped off and now dangled from his shoulders.

Startled, Boone rose to his feet and stood staring down at the collapsed figure.

"Are you all right?" he asked. "What has happened to you?"

The Hat did not answer, nor did he stir.

Stepping swiftly around the table, Boone seized him by a shoulder and lifted him. The Hat dangled limply in his grasp.

Dead, Boone thought. The Hat was dead—if he had ever been alive.

He let loose his hold and The Hat collapsed, falling back upon the table. Boone went to the cube and walked through the door. The service robot stood with his back to him, puttering at what appeared to be a stove.

"Quick!" said Boone. "Something's happened to The Hat."

"He collapsed," the robot said. "Someone let the air out of him."

"That's exactly it. I think that he is dead. How did you know?"

"It happens," said the robot. "It happens all the time."

"When it does, what do you do? What can be done to help him?"

"I do nothing," said the robot. "It's no concern of mine. I'm just a service robot. All I do is wait for customers to come rolling down the road. They almost never do. I keep waiting for someone and no one ever comes. It's all one to me. When, and if, they come, I am here to serve them. That is all I do. I can do nothing else."

"The Hat? What about The Hat?"

"He shows up now and then, but he needs no service. He does not eat. He sits at the table, always that same one. He never talks to me. He sits at the table and keeps staring down the road. Sometimes he collapses."

"You do nothing for him?"

"What is there to do? I leave him sprawling there and then, after minutes, hours, or days, he's gone."

"Where does he go?"

The robot shrugged, an elaborate shrug, greatly overdone.

Boone turned about and went out the door. Wolf had pulled The Hat off the chair and was hauling the limpness all about the area, as a pup might drag a rag at play. Tossing The Hat high in the air, Wolf caught him by the middle before he reached the ground and shook him viciously.

A doll, thought Boone, that was what The Hat was, a crudely fashioned rag doll that ranged extensively in time and space and might serve as a voice for someone or something else, acting the part of a dummy for an unknown ventriloquist.

Standing by the table, watching Wolf at play with the rag doll that had been The Hat, he shivered in a chill that came from deep inside himself, a psychic chill that he knew in all honesty came from being scared to death.

When he first had reached this land, he had wondered into what strange place he had been hurled. Now the wonder came on him again, this time a distilled and ghastly wonder. The land or place or condition was stark and alien and he wondered why he had not noticed it before. He felt naked and alone against a menace that he could not even guess at, although there was no apparent menace and he was not alone—Wolf was with him.

Wolf stopped his play with The Hat and looked across the fallen doll, grinning at Boone, happy to have a toy, happy not to be alone. Boone patted his thigh and Wolf came padding at the invitation to sit close beside him. Boone reached out and stroked the head of his partner and Wolf did not draw away.

The coldness, Boone was surprised to find, had melted, and the gray landscape was no more than a gray land once again.

Wolf whined. He was pressed hard against Boone's leg and Boone could feel the nervous trembling of the animal's body.

"What's the matter, boy? What is going on?"

Wolf whimpered.

Looking down at him, Boone saw that Wolf's head was tilted upward, staring at the sky, which was no sky at all, but a lowering grayness pressing against the grayness of the land.

"There is nothing up there," Boone told Wolf. "Not a thing at all."

Even as he spoke, however, he saw that he was wrong. There was something up there in the grayness, slowly taking form. It was simply a wavering shape that looked for all the world like a badly woven carpet undulating in the grayness.

He watched as the flapping carpet sank closer to the ground, seeing finally that it was not a carpet, but a very open net with two figures crouched upon it.

Then it was on the ground, billowing as it settled down, and a woman leaped off it, running toward him with her arms outstretched.

"Enid!" he yelled, leaping forward to catch her.

They were in one another's arms and she was pressing close against him. Her face was muffled on his chest and she was saying something, but her words were so mumbled that at first he was unable to make them out. Then he did. ". . . so glad I found you. I did not want to go and leave you, but you yelled at me to go and save the traveler. I was coming back to join you. I intended to come back, but something happened and I couldn't."

"It's all right," he told her. "Now you are here and that is all that matters."

"I saw you," she said, lifting her face and looking up at him. "I saw you in a place of grayness and you were gray and there was a gray wolf with you."

"The wolf's still here," said Boone. "He is a friend of mine."

She stepped a pace away and looked closely at him. "You are all right?" she asked.

"Never better."

"What is this place?"

"We're on the Highway of Eternity."

"What in the world is that?"

"I don't know. I never got it straight in mind."

"It's a different place. It isn't Earth."

"I think not," said Boone, "but I don't know where or what it is."

"You stepped around another corner?"

"I suppose I did. Lord knows, I tried hard enough."

The second figure that had been aboard the net had clambered off it and was coming toward them. It had two legs and two arms and seemed, in other ways, to be humanoid, but it was no human. Its face was that of a scrawny horse and the expression that it wore overflowed with misery. Its ears flared out from either side of its elongated head. It had two groups of eyes scattered in blobs upon its forehead. Its neck was thin and gaunt. Its legs were bowed so badly that it spraddled in its walking. Its arms had no elbows, but looked somewhat like rubber hoses. A pair of gills pumped on either side of its throat. Its body was a warty barrel.

"Meet Horseface," Enid said to Boone. "I don't know what his name is, but that is what I call him and he doesn't seem to mind. Horseface, this is Boone. The one I told you of. The one we came to find."

"I am pleased that we have found you," said Horseface.

"And I'm pleased that you're both here," Boone told him.

The robot was emerging from the cube with a tray balanced on his head.

"Are you hungry?" Boone asked. "I see food is here."

"I am starved," said Enid quickly.

As they sat at the table, Boone turned to Horseface. "This is human food. It may not be to your taste."

"In my wandering," Horseface assured him, "I have learned to gulp down anything that has nutrients."

"I brought you nothing," the robot said to Boone. "You just bolted down a tremendous meal. I brought the wolf another plate of meat. He looks all squeezed with hunger." The robot set down the plate of cut-up meat for Wolf. Wolf dived into it.

"He's a glutton," Boone said. "Wolf can eat half a bison without pause for breath."

"Is he one of those that hung about the camp? One of those who were pestering the poor old bison?" Enid asked.

"None other. After you left—no, before—he cozied up to me. I sat up the first night, and there he was, nose to nose with me. I said nothing of it because I thought I was hallucinating."

"Tell me about it. What happened to the killer monster and the brave old bull?"

"You have a story of your own that I want to hear."

"No, you first. I'm too hungry now to talk."

Wolf had finished eating. Now he walked away and began worrying The Hat.

"What is that thing Wolf has?" asked Enid. "It looks like a silly doll."

"That's The Hat. I'll tell you of him. He's a big part of my story."

"So get on with it," said Enid.

"In just a moment," said Boone. "You told me that you saw me. In a place of grayness, you said, and the wolf was with me. Would you mind telling me exactly how you saw me, how you knew where I was?"

"Not at all," she said. "I found a televisor. I'll explain that later on. The televisor shows you what you want to see. You think at it. So I thought about you, and there you were."

"It may have showed me in the grayness. But it couldn't have told you where to find me."

"The net did that," Horseface told him. "Flimsy as it may appear, it is a wondrous mechanism. No, not a mechanism. Nothing nearly so clumsy as a mechanism."

"Horseface made it," said Enid. "He made it in his mind and . . ."

"You helped," Horseface insisted. "Had it not been for you, there would have been no net. You held the finger so I could tie that final, all-important knot."

"This sounds interesting and mysterious," said Boone. "Tell me all of it."

"Not now," said Enid. "First we finish eating. Now tell us whatever happened to you since you yelled at me to leave, with the killer monster charging down upon us."

Boone settled down to the telling, marshaling the facts as concisely as he was able. As he finished, Horseface pushed his plate away and wiped his lips with the back of his hand.

Wolf had finally finished his play with The Hat and was using it, all bunched up, as a pillow. He blinked yellow eyes at them.

"The Hat, the way you told it, was alive," said Enid.

"He's disconnected now," said Boone. "I don't know how to say it better. He's nothing but a puppet. A ventriloquist's dummy."

"You have no idea who the ventriloquist might be?"

"Not a hint," said Boone. "You're wasting time. Tell me what happened to you."

When she had finished with her telling, he shook his head. "A lot of it makes no sense. There should be some sort of pattern, but there isn't. None that I can see."

"A pattern there is," said Horseface. "Likewise a pinch of reason. The three of us have been brought together with the chest I found on the pink-and-purple planet."

"You stole it," Enid told him. "You did not find it. You stole it. I know very well you did."

"Well, I stole it, then," said Horseface. "Perhaps I only borrowed it. That is a softer term and more acceptable."

He sprang from his chair and went shambling toward the net.

As they watched him struggling with the chest, Boone asked, "Have you any idea who he might be?"

"He is a thing of many wonders," Enid said. "I have no idea who he might be or what might be his origin. But he has great ideas and perhaps some knowledge, although not of the human sort."

"Can he be trusted?"

"As to that, I cannot tell. We'll have to go along with him and watch him."

"Wolf seems not to dislike him. I'm not sure he likes him, but he shows no dislike of him."

"You have confidence in Wolf?"

"He could have eaten me, up there on the butte. There was not a thing to stop him. We'd been on short rations and he was hungry. But I don't believe he even thought of eating me."

Horseface came back to the table, bent over with the weight of the chest upon his back. He thumped it to the ground.

"Now we'll see," he said.

Enid asked, "By that, you mean you don't know what it is?"

"Oh, I know what it is. But not the shape or form of it, or what the manner of its use."

He bent and unlatched the locks. The lid of the chest popped open and a mushy dough surged out. The dough ballooned and then collapsed, falling down all around the chest, and still the mushiness kept pouring out of it, as if it had been compressed within the chest and now had been freed and was in a hurry to escape.

The dough kept coming. It overflowed the area where the tables and chairs had been placed and began to envelop the cube. The robot came charging out, fleeing the invasion of the doughlike mass. Boone grabbed Enid by the arm and hustled her down the road. Wolf came scampering to range himself beside them. There was no sign of Horseface. Off to one side, the net had lifted and was moving away, flying low, a few feet off the ground. After flying several hundred yards, it settled down again. The forefront of the dough was closing in upon the trolley, and the car began backing away, gaining speed as it went rumbling down the tracks.

Now, however, the dough was changing character. Instead of continuing as a solid mass, it was becoming porous and somewhat honeycombed. All the time, however, it continued to spread out. It crawled along the ground and billowed in the air. Its size increased enormously. Sparkling points of light showed up in it, as well as large areas of smudged blackness and some misty swirls that were shot with brightness. Some of the points of light grew brighter and others moved away, becoming dimmer as they moved. All through the entire mass there was a sense of movement, of shifting and changing.

"Do you know what it is?" Enid asked.

Boone shook his head.

"Have you seen Horseface? Is he still in there?"

"I suspect he is," said Boone. "The damn fool let it catch him."

The chest no longer could be seen. It had been buried by the mass that was changing to a misty filminess and was growing larger, although at a slower pace than it had shown before. It was now a sparkling, shimmering soap bubble.

"Here he comes," said Enid, her voice tense and low. Looking in the direction of her pointing finger, Boone saw Horseface, faint and tenuous in the bubble, but sturdily stumping his way toward them.

Finally he broke free, as a man might break free of a mass of cobwebs, and spraddled toward them.

"It is the galaxy," he called to them. "A chart of the galaxy. I had heard of such charts, but never such as this."

He halted and stared at them, his blobs of many eyes goggling, then turned half-around and started stabbing one rubbery finger toward the bubble.

"See the stars," he said. "Some shining with a fierce brightness, others so dim they barely can be seen. Note the clouds of dust, the haze of nebulae. And there, the straight white line spearing straight for the heart of the galaxy, is your Highway of Eternity."

"It's impossible," said Enid.

"You see it and yet you cry impossible. Can you not see the glory and the immensity of our galaxy?"

"It's a galaxy, all right," said Boone. "And the white line is there, although I'd never have guessed it to be this highway we are on."

"It is, I tell you," Horseface insisted. "In my people's legend there was mention of a highway that ran among the stars. Although the legends, every one of them, fell short of telling why the highway might be there or whence it might lead. But now we follow it. Now we go and see."

Boone had another long look at the blob and there seemed no doubt that it did represent a spiral galaxy. In shape it was approximately oval, thicker in the center than at the edges, although not so neat and disciplined as the photos he had seen of spiral galaxies. It was, however, clearly a sprawling spiral with misty arms flaring out, thinner and more wispy than the central area. One of the spiral arms came twisting out around the place where the tables had been standing. Rather vaguely, the tables were still visible there.

Horseface moved away from them, sidling closer to the chart, stooping and peering at it, examining it.

Wolf stood close beside Boone and, when Boone looked down, he saw the shivers that ran through the animal's body. No wonder, he told himself. It was spooky enough for anyone. He reached down to pat Wolf on the head. "Easy, boy," he said. "It will be all right. Everything's all right." Wolf moved closer to him, and he wondered if what he said had been correct. He could not be sure that it was all right.

He said to Enid, "He talked with you, didn't he, about charts and maps?"

"He talked of a lot of things," she said. "Some of it nonsensical. At least, it sounded so to me. I can't remember all of it. He talked mostly of genetic maps, of maps implanted in his mind or his consciousness."

Horseface came lumbering back to them. "Shall we have a look?" he asked.

"You mean into that thing?" Enid asked. "You mean walk right into it?"

"Of a certainty," said Horseface. "How else will we know? The white line leads someplace. We go to find that place it leads to. It was put there for a purpose."

"We could get lost in there," protested Enid. "We could flounder around for days."

"Not if we follow that white line. We follow in, then we follow back."

"If we are going in there, " said Enid, "there is something that I want."

Having said that, she ran swiftly toward the net.

To go and have a look into that maelstrom of mistiness was the last thing Boone wished. On the surface it was simple enough, no more than a representation put together by a technology and an art that had yet been unthought of in his time. There was about the chart a scary alienness that he could not cotton to. What if a man got tangled up inside of it with no way to get out? Follow the white line, Horseface had said, and that would be all right should the white line stay in place. However, what if the white line were no more than bait to lure prey into a trap?

Enid came back, clutching a small black box. She held it up to show to Boone. "This is the televisor that I found at the picnic. I thought it might be good to have if we went into the chart."

"It's a piece of foolishness," said Horseface.

"No, it's not. It showed me where Boone was and told us how to get here. It's another pair of eyes and, in there, we'll need all the eyes we have. It shows you what you want to see."

Her allusion to another pair of eyes, Boone thought, was somewhat off the mark, for while she and he each might have a pair of eyes, Horseface had a double handful of them—two clusters of eyes which probably were far more than the equivalent of a pair of human eyes.

Wolf whined softly and Boone looked down at him. Wolf was scared, he thought, and if he had any sense, he'd be as scared as Wolf.

"Well, are you coming?" Enid asked.

"What is there to see? Horseface says the Highway of Eternity leads to where we want to go and that's all we need to know. Just jump onto the trolley and follow along the Highway."

"That's ridiculous," Enid told him. "On the trolley, it would take half of forever to get anywhere at all. When we go, we'll travel on the net, and neither time nor distance means anything when you travel on the net."

"That's well and good," he said, seeking a delay from

stepping into that crazy chart, "but when we start, what are we looking for?"

"Why, the Infinites," she said. "The home planet of the Infinites. That is what this is all about."

Until she said the word, he had quite forgotten about the Infinites. A great deal of time and scenery had passed between mention of the Infinites and here. But she, of course, would be the one to remember, for she had lived for centuries hunkered against their threat.

"This is the first I've heard about seeking out the Infinites," he said. "You have been hiding out from them for years, and you and I fled for our lives to escape their killer monster."

"I've had some thought about it," she told him, "and it seems to me that we can't stay hiding from them. We'll go and seek them out. We have the net and Horseface and we may find others who'll help us out against them."

"I never would have guessed," said Boone, "that you were so warlike."

"Are you coming or not?" asked Horseface, speaking gruffly. "If we are going on the net eventually, we should have some idea of what we're getting into. The chart should give us at least a hint."

"You have full confidence in that chart of yours?" asked Boone. "How can you be sure that it is accurate?"

There had been a time on ancient Earth when mapmakers, with an airy blitheness, had placed upon their maps as actualities many features that were no more than myths or products of their own free-ranging imaginations.

"My honor upon it," said Horseface. "This construct was made by a knowledgeable race who knew whereof they spoke."

"You knew them?"

"I knew of them. They were spoken of to me upon my grandfather's knee and there was other word of them from the sages of my people."

Boone looked down again at Wolf and Wolf was no longer there. Glancing back over his shoulder, he saw Wolf sitting some distance up the road. He had found The Hat and it was hanging limply from his jaws. Wolf didn't want to go into the chart, and there was no reason to drag him into that misty mess.

"Okay, Wolf," he said, "you wait right there for me."

The other two were moving into the chart, Horseface ahead and Enid trailing after. Boone hurried to catch up.

It looked like a space filled with spider webs, but there were no webs. There was not a thing at all. When Boone stepped into it, he could no longer feel ground beneath his feet. It was as if he were walking on nothing or, more likely, that his feet had suddenly gone dead and he could feel nothing when he put them down.

To one side of him burned a large red globe, and he ducked away from it; in doing so, he came face to face with another bright-burning jewel of incandescent blue. Before he could duck the other way, he walked straight into it. There was no sensation, no feel of heat, no indication that the stars were even there. He chuckled nervously. He had ducked a red giant and run smack-dab into a much hotter blue star. Did this chart contain a representation of every star, every wisp of gas, and every drift of dust in the galaxy? On the face of it, this seemed impossible. He seemed to remember having read somewhere at some forgotten time that there were more than a hundred billion stars in the Milky Way. There could not possibly be that many represented in the chart. Given that many, even with the smaller stars no more than the size of motes of dust, the entire area would be packed so solid there would be no walking through it. So much, he thought, for Horseface's claim of accuracy.

"Watch the white line that we trace," said Horseface. "It lies at the height of your hips, close to your right side." Boone glanced down and there it was, a thread of white, a lifeline back to the world of gray where Wolf waited for him with the limp and frazzled Hat hanging from his jaws. There stood the cube and somewhere nearby the robot who might cook another meal for them if they should get back.

I don't believe it, he told himself. I don't believe a word of it. I'll admit to none of this. It simply isn't happening.

But it was happening. He was walking in a place where

he could not feel the ground when he put down a foot, proceeding through an area that was not only illusory, but imaginary, where there were glowing stars and drifts of dust and gas, all of which one could see, but could not touch nor feel. Now there was something else—a sound, a singing. The stars were singing to him—the music of the spheres, the hiss of hydrogen, the ditty of radiation, the carol of time, the canticle of space, the hum of dust, and the chanty of vast emptiness. The horrible part of it was that there was nothing there. This was no reality; it was at best the wizardry of representation, of a construct that was entirely abstract.

He saw that he had fallen behind the other two. Through the haze he could barely make out Enid; Horseface he could not see at all. We've been walking for hours, he thought, and that was ridiculous, for this chart in which they walked could not have had a diameter of much more than several hundred feet.

He struggled to catch up, plunging ahead. No longer did he try to duck the stars or the spidery webs of gas, for now he could accept that they weren't there. But in spite of nothing being there, there seemed to be some sort of substance that tried to hold him back. It was as if he were desperately trying to wade through a rushing torrent.

Ahead of him loomed a drift of thicker-than-ordinary dust. Despite knowing that there was no rift of dust, he tried to lower his head and duck beneath it, but it was deeper than it seemed and it blinded him. The stars had all pinched out, and he plowed into the blackness as if he were butting head-first into a wall, his legs driving him forward, still with the pressure of the unknown torrent pushing back against him.

He burst from the dust cloud and there was light, far more light than there had been before. Its source, he saw, was a brilliant, glowing star to the right of him, all misty around the edges.

Beside him Enid said, "A nova. Maybe even a supernova. So obscured by the dust cloud that it can't be seen from Earth."

In the moment that she spoke, he saw the other star

that was so close it seemed he could have put out his hand to touch it. It was unspectacular—a faint, tiny yellow star. The thing that made him notice it was that someone— someone?—had painted or drawn a precise X over it, as if that someone had picked up a fine-point pen and marked it, distinguishing it from all the other stars in the galaxy, marking it so that if it be seen again, it would be recognized as a very special star.

"Boone, did you hear me?" asked Enid. "What is the matter with you?"

He did not answer, but stepped forward, circling, so he could see the star from another angle. As he moved, the X moved with him. He changed his position, and the X changed its position, too. Viewed from any angle, the X still showed, centered on the star. That, he thought, was impossible. It must be an illusion . . .

Enid grasped him by the arm. "Horseface has gotten ahead of us. And, Boone, where is the line? We've lost the white line. It's nowhere to be seen."

He turned in response to the pressure on his arm and the hint of fear in her voice. She was looking all about, searching everywhere for the vanished whiteness of the line.

"It's not here," she said. "In our rush and all the wonder of this place . . . What do we do now?"

Boone shrugged. "We'll retrace our steps and look for it. We'll find it."

But he had little confidence they would. It was so thin a line, so insignificant, that they might not pick it up.

A short distance away hung a great white star, spinning madly on its axis, while around it swung a much smaller star, white and bright, but its brightness paled by the brittle glory of its larger companion. The small star was spinning so fast that its motion was a blur, rotating in a mad dance about its huge fellow, while between the two of them extended a brilliant ribbon of flaming energy, flowing from the larger body to the smaller one. A B-type star, Boone thought, circled by a white dwarf.

"We can't go back," said Enid. "Right now we can't

go back. We have to go on and find Horseface. He'll help us find the line.''

She hurried ahead and he followed her. They seemed now to be going up a a hill and that was insane, Boone told himself. In this galaxy there weren't any hills. Swirls of dust curled about their ankles, and the stars, it seemed, were much thicker now and a lot of them were bloated red.

There was no question now that they were climbing a long, steep hill. They labored up the slope and reached the crest. Just beyond the crest they found Horseface. He was standing, gaunt and hunched, staring straight ahead.

They stopped and stood staring with him at the swirling darkness ringed by flashing, sparkling flares of light.

"A whirlpool!" gasped Enid. "It's spinning. It's a whirlpool."

"This is the core of the galaxy," Horseface said. "This is the very center of everything there is. A huge black hole eating up the galaxy. The end of everything."

A bitter wind was blowing, although there should not have been a wind. It had the icy chill of emptiness, the black glacial kiss of death. It could be, Boone thought, the black frost of defeated Time fleeing from the anni- hilation eating at the center.

"You said the end of everything," Enid objected. "It can't be the end of everything. Of this galaxy perhaps. But there are other galaxies. There are endless galaxies."

"There may be those who know," said Horseface. "I am not among them. Nor were any of my people."

"How about those who fashioned this thing we're in? Those who made this chart?"

"Maybe," Horseface told her. "Maybe not. Perhaps the truth might shrivel up the soul. Or there may be no answer."

"Then to hell with all of it," said Boone. "I am going back."

"We can't go back," Enid reminded him. "We lost the line. The thin white line, remember? We lost it."

Horseface mumbled, startled. "The line? You say we lost it? I had all forgotten it."

"So had we," said Enid.

"It can't be that much of a problem," Boone said. "This chart we're in, spread out even as it is, can't possibly be more than a few miles in diameter, not more than two or three, perhaps. My impression, back on the Highway, was that it covered only a few hundred feet. If we walk in a straight line in any direction, we should soon be out of it."

Horseface rumbled at him, "There are no straight lines here. There is only twisting convolution, a trickery of the senses."

"You went straight to the center," said Boone. "You ran ahead of us, aiming for the center. You got where you wished to go. There were no twisting convolutions . . ."

"True," said Horseface. "I went to the center. I had heard legends. The center held great interest, and my intuition took me there. Long ago I had heard of the black nothingness and . . ."

"That is nothing new," Boone told him. "The people of my time knew about the center. They knew of the great turbulences in the centers of most galaxies and there were those who said black holes and . . ."

"This is getting us nowhere," said Enid. "Our problem is to find the white line."

"We don't need to find the line," said Boone. "We can get out without it. All we need to do is walk a straight line. Doing that, we will find the edge."

"You did not listen to me," Horseface said. "I told you that this straight line you speak of cannot exist here. All is twisted, braided about, a meander of great complexity."

"You're trying to tell us we can't get out?"

"Not that. Blunder about enough and we shall get out. But it will be no easy task."

It was all nonsense, Boone told himself. The problem, despite all this talk of great complexity, was a simple one. Yet when he looked about he could see, in part, what Horseface meant. There were too many landmarks—no one star, no single misty glow, no twisted blackness that he could remember—too many to remember. And there was a twistiness to everything.

As if she sensed what he might be seeing, Enid said, "Certainly there is something that you can remember."

"There is," said Boone. "There was a star with an X upon it."

"An X?"

"Yes, an X. As if someone had painted an X upon it. It was an ordinary star, a very ordinary star. A main sequence star. Yellow. Probably a G star, like our sun."

"You never mentioned it to me."

"I forgot it when you said we had lost the white line."

"You saw no star with an X upon it?" Horseface asked Enid.

"No," she said. "I didn't. Who would go around painting an X upon a star?"

Horseface asked Boone, "Anything else that you remember?"

"No, not really," said Boone.

"Simple, then," said Horseface. "I have been standing in this place, never moving, staring at the black hole, since I first arrived. So we have a point of reference. When you came upon me, was I standing with my back to you?"

"That is right," Enid answered. "With your back to us."

"Elementary, then," said Horseface. "I will turn one hundred and eighty degrees, and we will go downhill from where we are."

Boone shrugged. It seemed much too elementary. It took no note of other factors. But he could think of no other way that they could go.

"We might as well try it," he said.

All three of them turned about and started down the hill. The going was easier. There was no surging current to buck. Boone still could not feel a solid surface when he put his feet down, and the stars still sang, but he paid no attention to any of it. They came down off the hill, and he kept on going. He was hurrying, eager to get out of this maze of illusion.

Behind him, Enid cried out suddenly. "The line," she called. "Here is the line again!"

Boone turned around and saw the two of them standing still, as if stricken, and staring at the line. He looked to his left and there, also, was the line. He was on one side of it and they were on the other and it seemed to him quite apparent that he had walked through it without any notice of it.

He walked back to where they were standing and all three of them stood there, staring at the line.

"Now," said Enid, "we can follow it back and come out where we started. How lucky that we found it."

"It stands to reason that we would find it," said Boone. "We were walking a straight line."

Horseface snorted. "A straight line, you say. I told you and I told you . . ."

Boone did not listen to his tirade. Glancing up the hill, he saw again the flare of the nova, or perhaps the supernova, that Enid and he had seen going up the hill. Off to one side of it was a little yellow star.

He started up the hill again, heading for the yellow star.

"Where are you going?" Enid called to him.

"Come on up," he said, without glancing back, his eyes steady on the little yellow star. "Come on up, and I'll show you the star with the X upon it."

He was feeling foolish even as he said it, for it might not be the star with the X upon it. There were a lot of yellow stars. You saw them everywhere.

But there had been no need to worry. It was the star with the X inscribed upon it.

"Of some importance," said Horseface, coming up to stand beside him. "Otherwise, why is it marked?"

"It's just like a million other stars of its class," said Boone. "That's why it seems so strange. That's why I was sure my eyes were playing tricks on me. One of these stars is just like all the others."

"Perhaps it is not the star that is important," suggested Horseface. "Perhaps it may have a planet and the planet is important. But we can't see a planet."

"Just a minute," Enid said. "There may be a way . . ."

She lifted the black box that she carried and aimed it at the star. Immediately as she lifted it, she drew her breath in sharply.

"That was it," she said. "There is a planet."

Boone stepped up behind her and stared into the vision plate. As he did so, the planet that was being showed expanded to fill the plate. It went on expanding until they could see only part of the surface—and what was on that surface.

"A city," Horseface said. "The planet has a city."

Huge structures speared up at them.

"This is it," said Horseface, his voice hushed but gleeful. "This is where we go. This is were the line led."

"And when we get there?" asked Enid.

Horseface answered with another question, "How is one to know?"

And that was right, thought Boone—how was one to know short of going there?

Enid lowered the televisor and the plate went blank.

"Back we gallop," said Horseface, "tracing close upon the line. Then we get upon the net . . ."

"Wait a second," Boone cautioned. "This is something we want to talk about. We should give it thought."

Horseface, however, did not stay to listen. He was galloping off, following close upon the line.

Boone looked at Enid. "You are right," she said. "We'll have to talk it over."

"Then let's get out of here," said Boone.

They went more slowly than Horseface, but, even so, they hurried. Both of them were anxious to win free of the chart.

Ahead of them they made out faintly the grayness of the land they had left behind them. Then they caught the loom of the cube and the tables surrounded by the chairs. And just beyond the tables and the chairs, the outline of Wolf, with the flat-headed robot standing side by side with him.

When Boone finally felt the impact of the surface beneath his feet, he knew that he had left the chart behind him. He walked a few paces forward and said to Wolf,

"How are you, boy? What is going on?" Wolf was sitting on his haunches. The Hat, still limp and mauled, lay in front of him.

There was no sign of Horseface, but the trolley, Boone saw, was coming down the tracks; and someone was sitting on the forward seat.

Timothy

10

The door unfolded outward and became a ramp. Horace walked through the door, but stopped with his feet only one step out.

Behind him, Emma shrilled, "Where are we?"

"I wouldn't know," said Horace. "There is no one here to ask."

Although, he realized, *when* might have been the better question.

He should have known better, he scolded himself. Sure, they had been in a crisis situation, but there still would have been time to set the course. There had been no time, of course, to think it through, to give his action the consideration that he would like to have given it. But too hasty a rush to escape the ravening monster that was snapping at their heels was inexcusable.

It was not that he had been frightened, he assured himself. It had been no more than solid good sense to get out of there as quickly as he could. There were many things, Horace told himself, that could be said of him: pompous, probably, for at times he might seem a pompous man; stubborn, but in most cases stubbornness was a virtue, not a fault; and fuddy-duddy, maybe, for he was in all things a very careful man. The one thing that could not be said of him was that he was a coward.

After all, he thought, everything had been fine until the two from the twentieth century had burst upon the scene. More than likely, though, the fault had been Martin's. Martin should have known what was going on. But it was apparent that he had not known, had no inkling of it until Corcoran had tipped him off by telling him that someone was snooping around in London, asking about a place called Hopkins Acre. And what had he done then? He had bolted, he and Stella. Thinking this, Horace felt better. He had found someone on whom he could fasten all the blame. He, himself, now was entirely innocent of any blame at all.

He took a few more steps down the ramp, but still stayed on it just in case a quick retreat was called for.

The traveler lay on the slope of a hill, just below the crest. Below was a small valley in which stood a sprawling black building, only one storey high, but with many angles and extensions, as if after its construction a number of haphazard additions had been tacked onto the original structure.

Looking at it, with something of a shock, Horace realized it was one of the many monasteries that had been built by the Infinites. They might not, in fact, have been monasteries in the strictest sense, but people had called them that because the Infinites had looked considerably like little, hobbling monks.

Nothing stirred in the valley. It was an empty place. Patches of grass grew here and there, and some thickets of small growth; but there were no trees, although there were some rotting stumps where there had been trees at one time.

The sun had been behind a heavy bank of clouds. Now, as he watched, the clouds parted for a moment and the sun shone through. All along the crest of the circling hills, reaching far into the sky, was a sparkle and a twinkling, as if someone had hung the sky with glittery tinsel.

Behind him, Timothy spoke quietly, almost matter-of-factly. "There you see," he said, "what is left of millions of our race. Each of those little sparkles is an incorporeal human, put in place and waiting through all eternity."

"You can't be sure of that," said Horace, fighting against the horror and the beauty of it. "You have never seen an incorporeal being."

"I have seen our brother Henry," said Timothy. "He is a cluster of those sparkles, a human who didn't make it to the final phase of his incorporeality. Had he done so, he would have been one sparkle only and not the many that he is."

Timothy was right, Horace told himself. Timothy was always, and irritatingly, right.

"If I read the dial correctly," said Timothy, "we are far into the future, some fifty thousand years beyond that time when we fled into the past."

"So the Infinites won," said Horace. "So this is the end of it. We humans didn't stop them."

Emma spoke to them from the doorway. "You two down there get out of the way. Spike is coming out. There isn't room for all of you."

Horace looked quickly over his shoulder. Spike, looking more than ever like a revolving porcupine, already was rolling down the ramp. Horace stepped quickly to the ground and over to one side of the ramp, Timothy moving with him. Spike started rolling down the hill.

"He'll get down there and stir up trouble," said Horace. "He always was a troublemaker. The Infinites in the monastery haven't seen us yet."

"We don't know if they have or not," said Timothy. "There may be no Infinites. From the evidence up there on the hill they have done their job and left. This probably is only one array of the incorporeals. Throughout the world there may be many others."

Emma came down the ramp to join them. "We waited too long," she said. "We should have left before. Then we could have picked our time and place and not gone off so frantically, not knowing where we'd end."

"I am going back," said Timothy, "as soon as I am able. I made a mistake in coming along with you. There are all my books and notes and . . ."

"I notice," Horace told him, coldly, "that you didn't linger in your going. You damn near ran over me. You were scared out of your britches."

"Not really. Perhaps only slightly apprehensive. An automatic defensive mechanism, that is all it was."

"We never did get around to burying Gahan," said Emma. "That's a shameful thing. We just left him lying there, all wrapped up in canvas on his bier and the grave still open."

Spike had reached the foot of the hill and was rolling steadily across the plain toward the monastery.

A few fleecy clouds had moved over the sun. The brilliant glitter of the crystal latticework that crowned the hills and soared into the sky glimmered less brightly.

Timothy looked up at them speculatively. "Just motes of thought," he said. "Dust-size philosophers. Tiny theoreticians generating dreams of greatness. No physical functions to consider, only the fine-tuned workings of the human mind . . ."

"Oh, shut up!" yelled Horace.

Something crunched on the hill above them and a loosened pebble went bouncing down the slope. All three turned toward the direction of the disturbance. A robot was coming down the hill toward them. His metal body shone dully in the weak sunlight, and he had an axe slung across one shoulder.

He raised a hand in salute to them. "Welcome, human ones," he said in a deep voice. "It has been long since we have seen one of you."

"We?" asked Horace. "Then you are not alone."

The robot came down the slope to a position where he was slightly downhill from them and swung around to face them.

"There are many of us," the robot told them. "Word is spread of you and there are others coming, thankful for the sight of you."

"Then there are no humans here?"

"A few, but only a few," the robot said. "Scattered very widely, hiding out. A small band here, another there, not too many of them. There are too many of us now. Very few of us have humans we can serve."

"So how do you pass your time?" asked Horace.

"We chop down trees," the robot told him. "We chop down all we can. But there are too many trees; we cannot chop them all."

"I do not understand," said Timothy. "Once you chop them down, what do you do with them?"

"We roll them all together and set fire to them once they are dry enough to burn. We destroy them."

Another robot came clumping down the hill and ranged himself alongside the first. He took his axe off his shoulder and, placing its head upon the ground, leaned upon the handle.

He started off as if it had been he, and not the first robot, who had finished talking. "The labor is arduous," he said, "because we have none of the marvelous labor-saving mechanisms you humans once devised. At one time, there were robots with technical knowledge, but now they all are gone. Once the humans retreated to the simple life to cultivate their minds, there was no need of them. All the humans needed then were very simple robots—gardeners, cooks, and others of that ilk. Those were the ones who were left, as the humans began to disappear."

Other robots were streaming down the slope, each one carrying a tool. They came singly and in twos and threes, and all of them grouped themselves behind the two who stood facing the humans.

"But tell me," said Timothy, "why this selfless devotion to the destruction of trees? You make no use of them once you cut them down. Surely you have no reasonable quarrel with trees."

"They are the enemy," said the first robot. "We fight against them for our rights."

"You mouth madness," Horace shouted. "How can simple, unassuming trees be enemies of yours?"

"You must surely know," said the second robot, "that once all men are gone—and now they're almost gone—trees will supersede them as the dominant race of Earth."

"I have heard some talk of it," Timothy told the assembled robots. "Loose and speculative talk. I never paid it much attention, although our sister, Enid, thought it a splendid idea. She feels that, as a dominant race, trees would not be aggressive and would do little meddling with other forms of life."

"It's all blathering," yelled Horace. "Enid is noted for her fuzzy thinking. Why, a tree has no sense—no sense at all. It can't do anything. It stands there and grows and that is all it does. After a time, it falls down and rots, and that is the end of it."

"There are certain fairy stories," Emma said, speaking in her most timid voice, which was very timid.

"Fairy stories are nonsense," yelled Horace. "All of this is nonsense. No one but a stupid robot would believe it."

"We are not stupid, sir," said the second robot.

"I suppose," said Timothy, "that your animosity toward the trees is occasioned by the belief that you should be the ones to supersede the humans."

"Why, yes, of course," said the first robot. "That is exactly what we think. It stands to reason we are the ones who should take the humans' place. We are an extension of the race. We were made in the image of the race. We think the thoughts of humans and our behavior is patterned after humans. We are the heirs of humans and are being cheated of our heritage."

Emma said, "Spike is coming back. And there is something with him."

"I don't see him," Horace said.

"They're coming around the far corner of the monastery. The thing with Spike is bigger than he is. He's bobbing along behind it. They are heading this way."

Horace squinted his eyes and finally he made out the two of them. He recognized Spike immediately from his erratic, bounding progress, but for a time he could not make out what the other was. Then something flashed in the weak rays of the sun and there was no doubt at all. Even from as far away as he stood, he could see the spider web and the single gleaming eye.

Emma said, "It is a killer monster. Spike is playing with a killer monster. He plays with everything."

"He is not playing with it," said Horace, choking with a sudden wrath. "He's herding it. He's driving it to us."

Down the slope from him, there now were fewer robots, he noted, than there had been before. Even as he watched them, they continued to dribble away, leaving by ones and twos and threes, not seemingly in any hurry, but simply walking off, going up the hill.

He asked Timothy, "What kinds of guns did you put in the traveler?"

"I put in no guns," Timothy told him. "You attended to that detail. You raided my gun collection without a word to me. You simply grabbed up guns, as if they belonged to you."

Emma shrilled, "All the robots are leaving. They are running away. They'll be no help to us."

Horace snorted. "I never thought they would. They are a weak-bellied tribe. I never counted on them."

He started purposefully up the ramp. "I think there was a thirty-naught-six," he said. "Not as big a caliber as I might have liked, but if the cartridges are high-power, that should handle almost anything."

"The best thing we can do," wailed Emma, "is get into the traveler and leave."

Timothy spoke sharply. "We can't go without Spike. He is one of us."

"He's the one," said Emma, tartly, "who is causing all the trouble. He is always causing trouble."

The robots all were gone. The slope below the traveler was empty; not a one of them was left. It didn't matter,

Horace told himself after a quick look around. Even if they'd stayed, they would be no help. A flighty bunch of people.

The monster, herded along by Spike, was closer now. The two of them had covered half the distance between the monastery and the foot of the hill.

Horace swung about and went up the ramp into the traveler. The guns were there, as he had thought they would be, their barrels protruding from beneath the pile of blankets—a shotgun and a 30.06 rifle.

He grabbed the 30.06 and eased back the bolt. A cartridge was seated in the breech and the magazine was loaded.

For some little time, there had been a faint commotion somewhere outside, the soft sound of running feet and the rattle of disturbed pebbles bouncing on the hillside. Horace had been conscious of it while he had inspected the rifle, but now, suddenly, the commotion swelled and boomed. A rock that must have been larger than a pebble banged with a loud metallic clamor against the traveler. Outside the doorway Emma was yelling, although he could not make out the words.

He spun heavily about and lunged for the doorway. From outside came not only Emma's bellowing, but the heavy pound of many feet and the thudding sound of heavy objects being hurled against the ground.

It could not be the killer monster being driven up the slope by that unspeakably perverse Spike, for when Horace had ducked into the traveler, the two of them still had been far out on the plain.

As he set his feet upon the ramp, he saw a scene of milling nonsense, with what seemed to be hundreds of robots, many of them loaded down with tools or logs. Those with logs were busily engaged in carrying them to several spots, where they hurled their loads down upon the ground and, turning swiftly, fled up the hill again.

Other robots with shovels, picks, mauls, or axes were making the dirt fly in all directions as they went to work.

Long logs were rammed into deep holes, canted at sharp angles to the steepness of the hillside. Other logs were being shaped by flashing broadaxes into squared timbers. Augers bit into wood, driving holes for heavy wooden pegs, while other gangs of robots toiled to heave the timbers into place, forming what seemed at first glance to be senseless structures.

Timothy said, quietly, "Do you realize that we are witnessing what amounts to the mounting of a Roman defense line? Short, flanking fortifications, with ditches dug in front of each fort, so situated as to support one another. Those other structures are catapults, designed to break up enemy attacks in force. The total defense could well be based on a classic Roman model. However, they seem to be rather overdoing it."

All around the line of hills that enclosed the circular valley where the monastery stood, other gangs of robots labored at their chores. Here and there, tendrils of smoke rose from campfires the robots had kindled. If the signs meant anything, this robot legion was settling in to stay.

"I cannot believe these robots are students of Roman history," said Timothy. "The story of the Roman Empire would be no more than a pinch of history scattered in a pile of blowing dust. But the same thinking and the same principles of engineering are as basic today as they were in very ancient times."

"But why?" screeched Emma. "Why are they doing this to us?"

"Not to us, you ninny," Horace shouted. "They are doing it for us. They are protecting us. Unnecessarily." He shook the rifle in a clenched fist thrust above his head. "We could have protected ourselves short of their interference."

Out on the plain beyond the slope a small whirlwind was zigzagging, darting here and there.

"It's Spike and the monster," Timothy explained. "The monster, seeing what is happening, is trying to get away, probably back to the safety of the monastery. Spike is just as determined he will drive it up the hill."

"It is all utter nonsense," Horace roared. "Why should Spike want to drive the monster up to us? He knows what kind of thing it is."

"Spike was always insane," Emma said. "David used to stick up for him every now and then, and Henry always had a good word for him. But to me he is just a big nothing."

One of the robots was climbing up the hill toward them.

The robot came to an abrupt halt at the foot of the ramp, upon which Horace stood. He clicked his metal heels together and raised his right arm in a brisk salute. Looking straight up the ramp at Horace, he said, "The situation is secured, sir. We have it well in hand."

"To what situation do you refer?" asked Horace.

"Why," said the robot, "the Infinites. The dirty Infinites!"

"We're not even sure," said Timothy, "that there are any Infinites. All we saw was the killer monster."

"There is the monastery, sir," said the robot, stiffly, as if somewhat miffed by any questioning of his word. "Where there is a monastery, there are always Infinites. We've been watching this place for years. We have been keeping tab on it."

"How many Infinites have you sighted?" asked Horace.

"Not a single one, sir. Not so far, we haven't."

"How long have you been watching?"

"Not all the time, you understand. But off and on, for two hundred years or so."

"In two centuries you have seen no Infinites?"

"Yes, that is true, sir. But if we'd been watching all the time . . ."

"Oh, come off it," Emma said. "Cut out the silly games."

The robot stiffened violently. "My name is Conrad," he said, "and I am the commander of this exercise. We are doing nothing more than our primary function, the protection and the care of the human race, carrying out our duty, I might say, with precise competence and dispatch."

"Very fine, Conrad," Horace said. "Please do carry on."

The monster and Spike had ceased their dusty waltz

and stood together, neither of them stirring. The robots, so many now that the circling hill seemed to be covered with them, still were energetically building a solid defense, ringing in the central valley where the monastery stood.

"Well, I guess there is nothing we can do about it," said Emma. "I might as well go in and see to some food. Are either of you hungry?"

"I am," said Horace. He was always hungry.

She went swiftly up the ramp and Horace came slowly down it to stand beside Timothy. "What do you make of it?" he asked.

"I am sorry for them," said Timothy. "They've been here for centuries without a human to take care of."

"And, suddenly, here we are," said Horace, "dumped slap-dab in their laps."

"That's about it. No humans at all, and then, all at once, three humans who seem utterly defenseless to them, and coming under threat. Part of it an imaginary threat, for it appears quite definite that there are no Infinites. But the killer monster is real enough and extremely dangerous."

"So they went hog wild."

"It's natural that they should. Here they've been, out of work for years and years."

"They've not been standing idle. They cut every tree they find, they grub out stumps and tend bonfires where they burn the logs."

"Made work," said Timothy. "To do it, to put any muscle into it, they must sell themselves on the belief that trees would follow humans as the planet's dominant life force."

"You don't believe that tree business, do you?"

"Well, to tell you the truth, I am of two minds about it. That trees should assume a position of dominance has a certain appeal to me. They probably would work out better than the humans, the dinosaurs, or the trilobites, all three of which turned out rather badly."

"The whole idea is crazy," protested Horace. "They'd just be standing there, they'd not be getting anywhere."

"You forget," said Timothy, "that they would have billions of years. They could afford to sit and let evolution have a chance. That was the trouble with the human race. We couldn't wait, so we short-circuited evolution. But it is a mistake to put evolution down as being too slow. See what it did in less than a billion years, from the first bare flicker of life to a highly intelligent animal. One that proved too smart for its own good . . ."

"There you go again," howled Horace, "putting down your own kind."

Timothy shrugged. Perhaps, he told himself, Horace might be right. He was putting down the human race. But the fact was that it had put itself down. Men had been a bungling band of primates. In the course of human history, there had been glory and accomplishment, but there had also been too many fatal errors. Man had made every error that was possible.

The sun was going down behind the western hill. Timothy ambled slowly down the slope, leaving Horace where he stood. As he approached the first fortification, the laboring robots dropped their tools and sprang swiftly to attention.

"It's all right," said Timothy. "Pay no attention to me. Continue with your work. You are to be commended. You are doing very well."

The robots went back to their work. Conrad, sighting Timothy, hurried up the hill to meet him.

"Sir, we have them now," he said, "surrounded on all sides. We're looking down their throats. Let them so much as wiggle and we'll be down upon them."

"Good work, Captain," said Timothy.

"Sir," said Conrad, "I am not a captain. I'm a colonel. A full colonel, sir."

"My mistake," said Timothy. "I apologize. I intended no offense."

"And none was taken," said the colonel.

From the door of the traveler, Emma yelled that dinner was ready.

Timothy turned about and went swiftly up the hill. He was hungry; it had been a long time since he'd eaten.

On the table Emma had placed a plate of cheese, another plate of ham, a large jar of jam, and a loaf of bread.

"Do the best you can," she told the other two. "It all is cold. Either the stove is not working or I don't know how to use it. It resisted all my efforts."

"We'll make out," said Horace.

"You'll have to drink water," Emma wailed. "There is tea and coffee, but without a stove . . ."

"It's all right," Timothy comforted her. "Think no further of it."

"I looked for beer. But there wasn't any."

"Water will be fine," said Horace.

They sat down and began to eat. It was not too bad. The cheese was aged and crumbly, melting on the tongue, the ham robust and tasty. The jam was brambleberry and, despite its heavy freight of seeds, was excellent; the bread was crusty and substantial.

Emma nibbled on a slice of cheese and munched a slice of bread slathered with jam. Between two bites, she asked, "What do we do now?"

"For the moment," Horace told her, "we stay right here. This traveler is luxurious by any standard. It will serve as a shelter and a base of operations."

"How long?" Emma quavered. "I don't like this place."

"Until we learn what's going on. That situation out there seems chaotic to me, but in a few more days, it may resolve itself, and then we'll know what we should be doing."

"For my part," said Timothy, "I am going back as soon as possible."

"Going back to where?" asked Emma.

"Back to Hopkins Acre. I never meant to leave. If I'd had time to consider it, I never would have left."

"But the monster!" Emma cried in horror.

"By the time I get back, the monster will be gone."

"Why would you want to go back?" asked Emma. "I can't understand. It could be dangerous back there."

"My books are there," said Timothy. "And notes that I worked years upon. I still have work to do."

"Your work is finished," Horace told him harshly.

"No, it's not. There is still much to do."

"You were working for a hoped-for future. You thought you could find a way for humans to reverse their course, to profit from the old mistakes and to make a new beginning. Don't you understand you failed? *This* is your future, and in it humanity, or the greater part of it, has been converted to those sparkling points of light you see up in the sky. The Infinites have done their work and left."

"But some people are still here. We could start over."

"Not enough of them," said Horace. "A few one place, a few somewhere else, all of them hiding out. Some in the past, some in the present time. The gene pool is too small for starting over."

"It's no use talking to him," Emma said. "He is the stubborn one. Once he gets an idea in his head, he never will let loose. No amount of talking and no kind of argument will convince him otherwise."

"We'll talk again tomorrow," Horace said. "After a good night's sleep."

Timothy got to his feet. "Can I have some blankets? I'll spend the night outdoors. The weather's clement, and it's not too cold. I'll sleep beneath the stars."

Emma got him blankets. "Don't wander off too far," she warned him.

"I never wander," he told her.

Night had fallen. The blackness of the monastery was swallowed by the darkness around it. The robot campfires gleamed all around the hills, and over all was the twinkling of the sky. Staring up, Timothy was able to make out some stars, but only a few of the brighter ones, for the glitter of the points of light served to blot out the dimmer ones.

He found a small, benchlike terrace on the hillside. It was fairly level and would serve well as a bed. He folded one of the blankets as a protection against the ground and pulled the other blanket over him.

He lay flat upon his back, looking at the glittering points in the sky. He was content to watch. Up there, he saw the final phase of the human race. As segments of pure thought, humanity could survive the extinction of both time and space at the end of the universe. The intelligence of man would remain untouched in the emptiness and would persist forever. But persist for what? He tried to conjure up what might come, if anything could, after time and space were gone. He could think of nothing.

He had said to Horace that men had been impatient with evolution, that they had not been content to wait. Had he been wrong in saying that? Had the works that men had created and the dreams they had held been as truly evolutionary as the slow process by which the small pulse of life had come to man himself? Had the intervention of the Infinites done no more than help man along the evolutionary track he had been meant to follow? Had that first faint stir of life in some shallow sea been irrevocably aimed at the glinting sparkles set out overhead? Could the universe all along, in its glory and its wonder, have been only a hothouse in which to grow intelligence?

If that were true, then the human race had been the Chosen People. Yet there would not have been one Chosen People, but many Chosen Peoples. Rather than relying upon a single race, there would have been an attempt to bring about many different intelligences, for one could not be certain of survival. Through foolish, perhaps inevitable mistakes, many would have died upon the way. Others could have taken such unfavorable turns that deliberate elimination of them would have been the only answer. Like many creatures of Earth, which spawned thousands of eggs to insure that a few of their progeny would survive to adulthood, so must evolution have spawned vast numbers of intelligent races to make certain that a few, in the end, would win to full development.

It could not be, Timothy told himself. This was foolishness, a mad thought even to entertain for a moment.

But why had humanity taken such a step at a time when the stars were firmly in its grasp and when mankind seemed about to reap the benefits of the journey along the highway of technology? Why had man faltered? Had there been a racial tiredness, a shying away from an implied responsibility which, in the light of past achievements, he should have been fully capable and anxious to assume? Standing face to face with the unlimited space and opportunity which stretched before him, had man stepped back in fear of failure? Or in fear of something else?

Timothy tried to put a stop to thinking and make his mind a blank, for he realized that all he was doing was building up a troublesome confusion inside himself, and that there were no conclusions to be reached. He shut his eyes and fought to purge the tenseness from his body. Finally the thoughts that had been surging in his skull did slow. He went to sleep, but it was a fitful slumber. Time and time again he came half awake, puzzled by where he was, listening to the shuffle and murmur of the legion still at work upon the forts, disturbed by the pulsing ripples in the sky—and then, recalling where he was, went back to sleep again.

Then someone was shaking him by the shoulder and speaking to him in a querulous voice. "Timothy, wake up! Wake up, Timothy! Spike has disappeared."

He sat up, throwing the covering blanket to one side, wondering at the urgency of the voice, knowing it was Emma who was shaking him to tell him that Spike had disappeared. He was considerably puzzled. Spike was always disappearing. Back at Hopkins Acre, Spike had been gone a good part of the time. They'd not see him for days on end and had never worried about him. In good time, in his own time, he would show up again, as frisky as ever, never harmed by absence.

The land was silvered by the first light of dawn. The valley floor still lay in half darkness. Smoke dribbled up from the fires built among the forts. Why, Timothy wondered, should robots be so intent on building fires? Certainly not for cooking, for they never ate. Probably this fire building was only another evidence of a robot's ever-present urge to ape man, its creator.

Horace was standing a hundred feet or so away, talking with Conrad and a gaggle of other robots. Horace was shouting gruffly, but that meant nothing. Horace always shouted and his voice was almost always gruff, a studied affectation to show how tough he was.

Emma whined at Timothy, "Spike is causing trouble again. He always causes trouble. I don't know why we put up with him all these years."

Timothy staggered to his feet. He put up his fists to scrub his eyes of sleep, then walked slowly toward Horace and the robots.

Hearing his approach, Horace turned to face him. "It's Spike again," he shouted. "He's playing games. He is hiding out somewhere. He thinks we'll come and look for him. Playing hide and seek."

Conrad spoke more softly than Horace, but his words were clear. "The only place he can be is the monastery. Both he and the monster are gone. They're in the monastery."

"Well, then," yelled Horace, "why are you bothering us? Why didn't you go and look in the monastery?"

"Not me," said the robot commander. "The monastery is not our business. It is human business. If you go in, we'll go with you, but we won't go alone."

Timothy came up and joined the group. "You are sure," he asked Conrad, "that they didn't sneak through your lines?"

"It would have been impossible. We were on watch all night. We had the two of them in sight all the time; then suddenly they were gone."

"What were they doing all the time you were watching them?"

"They were playing games, it seemed. They were chasing one another, first one and then the other. They were taking turns at it."

"Spike is hell on tag," said Horace. "He likes nothing better. I'm not going to waste any time on him. After a while he'll get tired of it and come dragging back."

"He's played us fools for years," said Emma, joining them. "We'd be fools again if we went looking for him."

Timothy said, "This situation is slightly different. I think we should have a go at it. This time he may be in trouble."

"No!" howled Horace. "Not a foot! I'll not take a blessed step."

"Maybe Timothy is right," said Emma faintly, not sure she should be saying it. "After all, he's family. We let him stay with us."

"If you don't want to go," Timothy told Horace, "then I'll go alone. The two of you stay here. Give me the rifle."

Horace took a long step backward. "I won't give it to you. You don't know how to handle it. You'll end up shooting off your foot."

"It's my rifle, Horace."

"Yes, you own it. Which doesn't mean you know how to use it."

"Then I'll go without it."

"No, you won't," yelled Horace. "I won't let you go alone. There's no telling what sort of scrape you'll get into and no one there to get you out of it."

"If you're going with him," Emma told Horace, "then I'm going with you. I won't be left alone in this howling wilderness."

"I'm obliged to you," said Timothy, speaking to Horace. "I'll be glad to have you with me."

"I'll organize a company," said Conrad, "to furnish you support."

"There's no need," said Horace, stiffly.

"I insist," Conrad told him. "We provide protection here. We'll continue to provide it."

Conrad turned about and began snapping orders. Robots wheeled into line, standing stiffly at attention, each shouldering the tool it had been carrying—a shovel here, a crowbar there, pickaxes, a heavy iron maul, a posthole digger . . .

"Since you are determined to make fools out of all of us," Horace growled at Timothy, "let's get it over with."

Timothy started down the slope, with Horace, rifle carried slantwise across his body, to one side and Emma stumbling along behind. In the rear came the clanking legion with sergeants or their equivalents calling out the marching cadence.

Timothy went down the slope, fighting the steepness of it, driving in his heels to maintain his balance. Small stones and pebbles dislodged by the marching legion-

naires went skittering past him, bouncing and rolling and
raising little spatters of dust.

Where was Henry? he wondered. If Henry were only
here, he could infiltrate the monastery and spy out the
place. Then, if it were necessary that the others of them
should enter it, they wouldn't be going in blind.

They reached the bottom of the hill, and the company
of robots split into two files, to march on either side of
them toward the monastery.

Conrad, who had been striding on ahead, snapped out
a command, and the two files of robots halted. Conrad
came striding back to the humans. "You stay here," he
said. "I'll send out scouts."

He bellowed another order and four robots went running ahead. "There must be a door, maybe more than one
door," Conrad said. "There has to be a way to get into
it."

"This is foolishness," protested Horace. "There isn't
any danger."

"Not that one can see," Conrad told him, "but there
always is a chance of danger in any new situation. There
could even be a planned and studied attempt to make it
appear there is no danger. In any case, it never hurts to
be just a trifle cautious."

Timothy turned around to look over his shoulder. There
were other robots on their way to join them. They came
tumbling out of the defense lines they had built upon the
hill, running madly. Others were streaming across the
plain, hurrying to catch up with Conrad's squad.

"The rest of them are coming to join us," he said to
Horace. "The entire gang of them."

Horace turned around to look. He grunted his disgust
with robots.

They waited. A waiting silence settled over them. There
was no sound of wind, no chirring of insects. Finally one
of the scouts came running around an irregular corner of
the building. He pulled up in front of Conrad and said,
"Sir, we have found an entrance. An open door. There
were other doors and they were locked; we did not try to

force them. We thought it would be wiser nót to. Then we found the open door.''

"Did you enter?"

"Again, we thought it better not to. The others are waiting for the full company to arrive."

"Well, thank you, Toby," Conrad said. "You acted wisely." He said to Horace, "Are you ready to proceed?"

"We've been ready all the time," said Horace. "It was not our decision to stand here and dawdle."

The column lurched into motion and the three humans marched inside their lines, with the reporting scout hurrying on ahead. They came to the monastery and skirted its outer rim. Close up, it was a dowdy building. The outer walls appeared to be constructed of some metal that was beginning to rust. The walls had no windows, but at intervals there were doors and all of them were closed.

Finally they came to the door the scouts had found. It opened into the main building.

"We'll wait here," said Conrad. "I'll send in a squad to have a look, and then we can go in."

They waited again and finally one of the squad members appeared at the door and beckoned.

"We go in, but, please, without unseemly haste," said Conrad.

They went in without unseemly haste. The company of robots spread out, scouting ahead.

The interior was lit by a greenish glow. When Timothy looked for the source of it, he was unable to locate one. The light, he decided, emanated from the walls and the domed ceiling.

At first glance, there was nothing much to see. The one vast room into which they had entered seemed empty. Open doors here and there led into the various additions that had been tacked onto the original main structure. Robots kept ducking into the doors and almost immediately returning, as if to indicate they had found absolutely nothing.

As his eyes became accustomed to the faint green light, Timothy made out a pockmarked section of the floor. The pocks were lopsided circles or scooped-out holes. But there was no furniture of any kind—no desks or chairs, no storage bins, no filing cabinets, no machines.

No machines, of course! He was thinking in terms of humans and this was an alien building, constructed for alien purposes. One would not expect to find desks, chairs, or filing cabinets. But there should be other items—alien items—and there were none of these.

Emma nudged him in the ribs. "Look up there," she said. He looked where she was pointing and saw the strange objects hanging from the ceiling. There were hundreds of them, all suspended by strings or cords. They fluttered in the slight circulation of air that flowed in the building.

"They look like Infinites," said Emma.

"If they are," said Conrad, who was standing just a little distance off, "there is no life in them. I can detect no life. If there were life, even a little, my senses would tell me so. If they are Infinites, they are dead and hung up to dry."

Since entering the building and walking a short distance into it, they had scarcely moved. Now, from deep inside of it came a humming of excitement.

"The boys have found something," said Conrad. "Let us go and see."

The four of them hurried forward, coming upon the robots, who had formed into a circle and were watching something with exclamations of wonder.

"Let us through," said Conrad, speaking sharply. "What is going on? Make room for us."

The robots parted, and there, in the center of the circle, Spike and the killer monster were dancing a rigadoon. But whether it was a dance or a combative circling, with each opponent waiting for an opening to attack the other, there was no way to determine. They jigged and skittered, moving very fast, making tentative lunges at one another and then turning quickly aside.

"Stand back, the rest of you," screamed Horace. "I'll put an end to this!"

He had the rifle halfway to his shoulder when the building rocked so violently that the humans and many of the robots were thrown off their feet. As he fell and skidded on the tilting floor, Timothy heard the slamming of a door.

He fell into something. When he attempted to scramble out, the texture of whatever he had fallen into was so slick that he could find no purchase point to hoist himself out of it.

As suddenly as it had started, the bucking of the building ceased and Timothy realized that what he had fallen into was one of the holes scooped out of the floor. His body fitted the hole neatly and he thought that if a man could curl up in it, the hole would be a restful place to sleep. Perhaps that was what it was; conceivably all these holes were beds for Infinites. Being somewhat smaller than humans', their bodies must have fitted into the holes most trimly.

"Are you stuck in there?" Conrad asked, bending over him.

"No, not stuck. It's just difficult to get out. Lend me a hand, if you will."

Conrad extended a hand, pulled him free, and set him on his feet.

"I think," the robot said, "that we may be in trouble. I suspect we have been moved."

"Moved?"

"The building moved."

"It threw me off my feet."

"I think it did more than that."

Someone had opened the door by which they'd entered, and robots were pouring out of it, fleeing from the building. Horace, who apparently had stepped outside, came back through the door, fighting his way against the rush of fleeing robots. Coming toward Timothy, he waved the rifle in the air and bellowed, "The building was a trap. It sucked us in and then it took us somewhere else." He asked Conrad, "Have you any idea where we are?"

Conrad shook his head. "Not the least," he said.

Timothy stood confounded, not sure what was going on, what Horace might be saying. "Somewhere else?" he asked. "There should be no problem. A matter of some miles, perhaps."

"You fool," said Horace, harshly, "that is not what I meant. Not miles. Light years, more than likely. This is not our planet. We're not on the Earth. Take a look outside."

Horace grabbed him by the arm and jerked him roughly, propelling him toward the door.

"Go out and look!"

Timothy staggered toward the door, thrust forward by Horace's broad hand between his shoulder blades.

It was dusk or dawn. The air was crisp and fresh, and the sky looked strange. The land lay in folds; rolling hills led to other, ever-higher rolling hills, fading to a far horizon line. Above the horizon hung a bloated yellow moon.

Perhaps there was something about it that Horace had seen to make him think it was a different planet. To Timothy it appeared a quiet place, with no peculiarities. The air was breathable and the gravity like that of Earth.

One of the robots asked, "Is everyone out? Clear of the monastery?"

"Everyone is out," replied another robot voice.

"Controls?" Horace was yelling. "Did anyone spot controls?"

"Controls?"

"Yes, controls, something to operate the monastery. To control and guide it."

"No one did, I'm sure," Conrad answered. "It's not a vehicle. There would be no controls."

"It moved from there to here," cried Horace. "It moved. Otherwise, how are we here?"

"It is beginning to break up," said another robot. "It is cracking at the seams. Listen to it."

They listened, and the groaning and the screeching of the structure could be heard—the rending of too-ancient metal.

"It barely held together to get us here," said Conrad. "This is the end of it. A few years more and it would not have moved at all."

"Damn it!" Horace bellowed. "Damn it! Damn it! Damn it!"

"I agree with you," said Conrad, speaking quietly. "There are times when nothing works out right."

Timothy turned about and walked free of the crowd packed in front of the collapsing monastery. It was just as well, he thought. If the monastery had proved, in fact, to be an operative traveler, there would be no telling what sort of harebrained scheme Horace would cook up. At least here they were momentarily safe and in an environment that up to now had been congenial. They could breathe and move about, the temperature was not oppressive, and probably there would be food of some sort they could eat.

He was standing on a hillside and there was turf beneath his feet—but what kind of turf? It still was too dark to see, although to his right the sky was becoming lighter. Horace had said they were on another planet, but there was nothing as yet to support his assertion. The hills looked like Earth hills. It still was too dark to see much of anything.

Someone moved up the hill toward him and he saw that it was Emma. He walked down to meet her. "Are you all right?" he asked.

"I'm all right," said Emma, "but I'm frightened. Horace says we are no longer on the Earth. He says there are two moons and Earth does not have two moons, and I don't understand at all how it could have happened."

"Two moons? There's only one moon. It's hanging in the west. Or what I take to be the west . . ."

"There's another directly overhead," said Emma. "It is a smaller moon."

He craned his neck to look and there the moon was, directly overhead. As Emma had said, it was a small moon, less than half the size of Earth's moon. So that is how Horace knew.

The monastery still was groaning. The eastern sky was brighter than it had been before. In another little while the sun would come popping up.

"Have you seen Spike?" Emma asked.

"Not a sign of him."

"He's off playing his silly games with that stupid monster."

"I'm not sure they're games," said Timothy.

"What could it be but games? Spike always was playing some foolish sort of game."

"Yes, you're likely right," he told her.

The gang of robots that had been massed downslope from the monastery were withdrawing, trooping down the hill to a point where the incline leveled out to a valley floor. A sharp command rang out and the robots began swiftly shifting into military conformations.

The dawn light had strengthened and it was possible to see a little better. The surge of rolling hills lost the starkness of the night, their profiles softening. Looking first at them in the dark, he had envisioned them as green hills, but now he saw there was no greenness in them. They were tawny, the color of a lion or a cougar, beneath a violet sky. Why should a sky be violet—not a small part of it, but allover violet?

Horace came clumping up toward them. He stopped just downslope, the rifle slung in the crook of his arm.

"We've been had," he said, angrily. "We were kidnapped and flung into this place, wherever it may be."

"But we are not alone," said Emma. "We have the robots with us."

"A tribe of fools," said Horace. "A pack of stumblebums."

"They'll be some help," said Timothy. "Conrad strikes me as competent—he can get things done."

"We have lost everything we had," cried Emma. "All the stuff that was in the traveler. The blankets! And all the rest of it! The skillets and the pots!"

Horace put an arm around her shoulder. "They brought the blankets and some other stuff," he said. "We'll manage somehow."

Sobbing, she clung to him; clumsily he held her, patting her back. Timothy watched uncomfortably. It was the first time in all his life he'd seen Horace display even the slightest affection for his sister.

The east was brightening rapidly, and now it could be

seen that a river ran through the valley that lay between the hills and that small groves of trees grew along the river and on the lower slope of some of the hills. They were funny trees, however; they had the appearance of giant ferns or overgrown rushes. On the hills above the valley, the tawny growth that could be grass billowed in the wind. Good pasture, Timothy thought, but there were, so far as he could see, no herds of herbivores nor, in fact, any single grazer.

A metal plate slid from the collapsing monastery and skated for a few feet down the hill. The structure, by this time, had completely fallen in upon itself to become only a heap of flattened metal.

Down in the valley the robots' military formation had broken up. All that remained of it was a phalanx, the hollow square, Timothy thought, that had been classic, from Alexander's Macedonians through the centuries to Napoleon's last stand at Waterloo. The rest of the robots were scattering like scurrying bugs fleeing from the center. Apparently they were setting out as scouts to look the country over.

Three of them were heading purposefully up the hill toward the humans. The three reached them, placing themselves in such a way as to partially surround them. One of them spoke, "Sirs and madam, Conrad has sent us to escort you to the safety of the camp."

"You call that hollow square a camp?" growled Horace.

"'We are out searching for fuel to make a fire. Others will bring in water and what else may be needed."

"Well, all right," Horace agreed, grudgingly. "I don't know about you two, but I'm hungry."

He started down the hill with Emma trotting at his side and Timothy following.

The sun had cleared the horizon by now. Glancing over his shoulder, Timothy noted its similarity to the sun of Earth—perhaps a little larger and a little brighter, although that was hard to judge. In a lot of ways, this planet was much like Earth. Underneath his feet grew fine-textured grass intermixed with a vinelike ground cover.

From the hollow square below them rose a wisp of smoke.

"They found fuel," said Horace. "Something that will burn. We'll have a hot breakfast after all."

Inside the protective square, Conrad told them about the fuel. "Wood," he said, "from the fern trees. Not as good a wood as one might like, but it burns, giving heat and light. A hollow center surrounded by a pith, but a fairly dense pith. Also we found coal."

He thrust his hands out to show the coal, shattered slabs of shiny black.

"We dug it out of a rock formation in the river bank. Not topnotch coal, more like lignite, but coal. We'll keep looking as we travel and we may find better coal. Between poor wood and poor coal, however, we have fire. Back on Earth most of the coal had long since been mined and burned."

"Travel?" Emma quavered. "Where will we travel?"

"We have to travel somewhere," Conrad told her. "We can't stay here. We have to find a place where we can get shelter and food."

"Food?"

"Yes, of course, madam, food. The little that you have will not last."

"But it might be poison!"

"We'll test it," Horace said.

"We have no way to test it."

"I agree," said Horace. "No laboratory. No chemicals, no knowledge of chemistry even if we had the chemicals. But there is a way. We'll use ourselves as guinea pigs."

"This is one you'll have to do yourselves," said Conrad. "Robots cannot help you."

"We'll take a tiny bite," said Horace. "We'll test the taste. If it tastes bad, burns the tongue, or puckers up the mouth, we'll spit it out. If it tastes good, we'll swallow a tiny piece of it, then we'll wait and see."

One of the robots cried out a warning, gesturing up the hill. A vehicle—a flier—of gleaming metal was streaking down the hill toward them. It flew only a few feet above the ground. It swooped upon them and passed over them, then turned sharply to bank against the hills beyond the river. It swung around and followed the slope of the opposite hills to cross the river at a point somewhat upstream from them, then came about to come skimming down the stream, no more than ten feet above the ground, passing almost directly above the hollow square of robots. It continued down the river for some distance, then lazily climbed up the range of hills, flying far above them until it finally disappeared.

"We're being watched," said Conrad. "They came to look us over."

"What can we do about it?" Horace asked. "What should we do to protect ourselves?"

"We'll keep close watch," said Conrad. "We'll look out for them."

Late in the afternoon, the scouts who had gone down the river returned to report that the stream finally flowed into an extensive swamp. During the night, the upriver scouts came back. The hills, they said, gave way some miles ahead to a high plateau, with mountains thrusting up in the distance.

"That's what we needed to know," said Conrad. "We go upriver."

In the morning they started out. As the hills closed in on the stream, the going got harder. Thick veins of coal lay in the sheer rock faces along the stream. The trees began to change. Those that looked like giant ferns and rushes grew fewer. Honest, earth-type trees took over. The hills persisted. They lay in ranges, separated by narrow valleys, each range rising higher. Conrad did not push the march. He and Horace bickered from time to time, but never went beyond the bickering.

They came on food that was fit for human consumption—a couple of kinds of tubers, a yellow fruit that was fairly common, beans that grew in stubby pods on a crawling ground vine. The testing of each food was done in a gingerly fashion. Some possibilities were rejected out of hand—they smelled or tasted bad. Horace picked up a touch of gastritis from berries that he sampled; that was the only nasty episode. The robots brought in small mammals; all but one proved good eating. The fish they took from the streams they came upon smelled so foul that they did not try them.

The robots made hunting weapons, but the bows were awkward and the arrows often failed to fly true. They essayed flint-napping, but from the lack of proper stone and technique, most of the projectile points turned out lopsided. Yet the ranging robots did manage to bring in some game.

The good weather held. No clouds showed in the violet sky. The days were hot, the nights only slightly cooler.

Finally the hills ended, and they came out on a great, flat, dry plateau sprinkled with buttes, with the white-blue of distant mountains poking above the horizon. Carrying water in casks laboriously fashioned out of native wood, the band started across the level plain. Tempers were beginning to run short.

There had been no further sighting of the ship that had buzzed them when they first arrived, although Timothy had the eerie feeling that they were being watched.

Several times they caught a momentary sight of Spike and the killer monster outlined against the sky. Although he could not be certain, Timothy had the impression that Spike had gained some sort of ascendancy, harrying the monster, driving him.

The plain seemed endless. Day after day they plodded along, and little changed. The mountains kept their distance, never seeming nearer. There was nothing but endless distances. At the foot of one of the buttes they found a small, reluctant spring and from it collected sufficient water to fill the empty casks. The small stream that flowed from it ran less than a quarter mile before it disappeared into the thirsty ground. Horace groused continually; Emma wrung her hands. Conrad paid small attention to them; he kept the march moving, boring ever deeper into the barren wasteland.

Late one searing afternoon, the flatness of the plain broke, dipping down into a canyon. From the lip of the break, they sighted, at the bottom of the canyon, a ribbon of a river, flanked by narrow strips of vegetation on either side. To their left a massive butte reared up, its western slope cut sheer in ages past by the ancient river that had carved the canyon. Between the edge of the slope and the steepness of the canyon wall lay a level bench with the crumbling ruins of what at one time would have been a small town.

They wasted little time upon the ruins. Scurrying robots found a narrow path that led down to the bottom of the canyon, and the party made its way cautiously along the trail which wound its way along the face of a towering cliff of rose-red rock. At the bottom of the trail, the cliff turned in upon itself, forming an extensive rock shelter. From the opening of the shelter came a drift of cooler air, providing some relief from the blasting of the sun.

Conrad, followed by the three humans, stepped off the trail to enter the shelter.

"Here," said Conrad, "we will tarry for a time. It's not all I'd hoped we'd find, but at least we'll have some protection while we plan our further move. The water from the river is only a little distance off. Along its banks, we may find food that humans can consume."

Emma sat down on the stone floor. "This is good," she said. "We're away from the sun until it sets late in the day. And we won't have to measure out the water. Maybe I can even have a bath."

"It's better than nothing," Horace said in a grudging tone. "It is better than the open plain."

The next day an exploring robot found the junkyard. It lay against the base of the cliff that hemmed in the canyon. It was broad of base and extended halfway up the cliff. He ran back to the party, shouting the news. Everyone hurried to explore the discovery.

Most of the junk was metal. Originally, undoubtedly, there had been a lot of other trash, but over the ages since it had been dumped, the less durable items had wasted away and disappeared. Only the metal, some strangely shaped stones, and a few large pieces of wood remained. The strange thing about it was that most of the metal had not deteriorated. It remained bright and shiny; there was no sign of rust.

"An alloy," said Conrad, "that was unknown on Earth. Most of it, all of it, perhaps, as good as the day that it was junked."

The metal came in all shapes and sizes—simple pieces of scrap, isolated machined parts, broken instruments and tools, metal formed into convoluted shapes, and massive blocks of metal. Some of it was recognizable in a general sort of way; most of it made no sense at all. The robots spread the more easily accessible parts on the ground and wandered about through the outspread display, vastly puzzled as to what they were seeing.

"An alien technology," said Conrad. "It might take us forever to figure out what some of this could be."

It was apparent that the junk must have been thrown from the bench above the canyon, possibly by the inhabitants of the forsaken town that now lay in crumbling ruins.

"It seems to be a lot of stuff to be discarded by so small a town," said Horace.

"It may have been a public dump serving a large area," said Timothy. "At one time all that plain we crossed might have had many other towns. Perhaps it was an agricultural area and well populated. Then the rains failed and the economic base was gone . . ."

"We can use the metal," Conrad told him. "We can make machines we need."

"You mean we'll huddle here while you concoct machines. What kind of machines?"

"Tools, for one thing."

"You have tools. You have spades and shovels, axes and saws, crowbars and posthole diggers . . ."

"Weapons," Conrad said. "Better weapons than we have. Better bows. Arrows that fly true. This metal is strong but flexible. Maybe crossbows. Spears and lances. Catapults."

"A hobby!" Horace growled. "You have found a hobby trove and . . ."

"Likewise," said Conrad, continuing, "we could contrive a wagon to transport water for you, and what food we can gather. We have robots who can haul the coach and wagons. We might, as well, be able to contrive an engine run by steam . . ."

"You're out of your skull!" Horace shouted.

"We'll think on it," Conrad told him. "We'll put our brains to work . . ."

In the following days they put their brains to work. They squatted in huddles. They drew designs in the sand. They mined coal from a site a mile or so away, set up a forge, and got to work. Horace fumed and fretted. Emma, remembering the days spent crossing the plateau, was satisfied to stay where there was water and protection from the sun. Timothy went exploring.

He climbed the trail and spent long hours snooping through the ruins of the town. Pawing through the sand and dust, he came up with occasional artifacts: primitive weapons; rods up to three feet long, made of metal that was flecked with rust; and strangely shaped ceramics that might have been idols. He crouched and looked at what he'd found and the artifacts added up to nothing. Still, the ruins had an abnormal fascination for him, and he went back again and yet again.

Here, God only knew how many centuries ago, had lived an intelligence that had developed a social and an economic sense. What kind of intelligence, the ruins gave no clue. The doors giving access to the buildings were circular and so small that it was a chore for him to wriggle through them. The rooms were so low that he had to go on hands and knees to explore them. There were no stairs to the upper storeys, but metal poles too slippery for him to climb.

Finally he climbed the massive, chopped-off butte. Its slopes were littered with precariously perched boulders waiting for no more than the slightest push to send them hurtling down. In between the boulders was treacherous, shifting scree that he had to scrabble over, being careful of the boulders.

It made sense, he told himself, that the people of the town might have maintained a watch post on top to spy out the approach of strangers, or to watch for game herds, or perhaps for other purposes that he could not bring to mind. But when he reached the top, he found no watch post. The top was a flat plane of stone, sand, and clay. No plants grew in the sand or clay, no lichens on the rock. The wind keened over it, and it was as desolate a piece of real estate as he had ever seen.

Below him the country spread out in a wonderful array—the brown and yellow of the flat plain over which he had traveled in the robot march, with other buttes, darker in appearance than the plain, dotted here and there. To the west was the gash of the rose-red canyon, and beyond the gash, far off, the blue loom of jagged mountains.

He walked to the edge of the western extension of the butte's top and looked down into the canyon, thinking he might see some sign of the activity of the robot legion; but he could glimpse no sign of activity. The blueness of the river writhed through the canyon floor, bordered on each bank by a strip of green. Beyond the river, the redness of the canyon wall tipped upward toward the yellow flatness of the continuing plateau.

And now he'd have to climb down off this butte—and must proceed most carefully, for the descent could be more dangerous than the climb.

He heard the click of a stone behind him and spun around. His heart tried to leap into his throat, choking him. Charging toward him was a killer monster, and behind the monster was Spike, rolling swiftly in an erratic pattern.

Timothy leaped quickly to one side to get out of the way of the oncoming monster. The monster, apparently seeing for the first time the yawning gulf before him, dodged as well, bearing down upon the human. Quickly Spike moved to head it off and the monster turned again in the opposite direction. Timothy stubbed his toe and fell upon his side. Out of the corner of his eye he saw the monster, fighting desperately to stop its headlong progress, go over the edge of the chopped-off butte. For a moment it seemed to hover in mid-air, then plunged out of sight.

Scrabbling erect, Timothy rushed to the lip of the precipice in time to see the monster strike a clump of boulders that clung to the face of the butte. It struck and bounced, dangling momentarily in the air, and began to come apart. Shattered fragments exploded in all directions and began raining across the face of the slope. The scattered segments went tumbling down the incline above the canyon floor, with the various parts battered into even smaller pieces.

Timothy turned to look for Spike, who was just a few feet away, dancing a jig of final victory, spinning and revolving, leaping high into the air, and skittering along the ground.

"You and your goddamned games!" yelled Timothy, although he knew, even as he spoke, that if it had ever been a game, it had been a deadly one.

"So you finally ran him down," said Timothy. "You never stopped the chase. You tried, that first day, to run him up the hill to us, knowing Horace would use a rifle on him; and when that failed, you kept on running him."

Spike had ceased his jigging and was standing now, rocking slowly back and forth.

"Spike," said Timothy, "we underestimated you. All these years, we took you only for a clown. Come on. We'll go down and join the others. They will be glad to see you."

But when he moved, Spike rolled to intercept him. He moved again, and Spike headed him off.

"Goddamn it, Spike," he shouted. "Now you're herding me. I will not stand for it."

He heard a faint humming and turned around to find what it might be. A shining aircraft was skimming toward them, like the one that had buzzed them their first day on the planet. It lowered gently to the ground and rested there. The top of it slowly levered up. In the forward section sat a monstrosity. A proportionately small head sprouted out of broad shoulders. What started out as an upturned nose split into twisted twin antennae. The skull swept back to a point that was tufted by angry red feathers, resembling misplaced wattles. A single compound eye protruded between the nose and the spearlike termination of the skull. The head turned toward Timothy and a chittering came out of it.

He took a careful, tentative step toward the flier and its monstrosity of a pilot. Curiosity consumed him. Here was intelligence again, but of a higher order, more than likely, than that represented by the ruined town. Spike moved around him to one side, then quickly reversed his course and spun to the other side.

"You can quit driving me," said Timothy. Spike did not quit; he kept up his double spinning. Timothy took another forward step and yet another. He was not being driven, he told himself; he was moving on his own. He wanted a close look at the alien craft. Spike kept pressing him forward.

"Oh, all right," said Timothy. He walked up to the rear part of the flier and laid his hands upon it. The metal was warm and smooth. He rubbed his hands along it. Inside was what appeared to be a passenger compartment. There were no seats, but the floor and sides were padded, and along the inside of the compartment ran a set of rails that might be hand holds for passengers.

But this was far enough; he was not about to get into this contraption. He turned about to face the spinning Spike and as he did, Spike rushed swiftly at him. The backs of his knees struck the edge of the flier and he went over backward, tumbling into the passenger compartment. Like a flash, Spike leaped in, the compartment cover came down with a bang, and the flier was taking off.

Suckered, Timothy told himself. Abducted by Spike and the hideous pilot and headed for a place not of his own choosing. He felt a little fear, but not much. What he felt was outrage.

He scrambled to his knees and, holding the rail, looked out through the canopy. Below him was the receding eastern rim of the canyon wall, the rose-red rock shining in the sun.

The family had been scattered and now it was further scattered. He wondered vaguely whether it would ever come back together. The chances were, he told himself, that it would not. They were being moved about like pieces on a game board. Someone or something was using them as pawns.

He recalled Hopkins Acre and how he had loved the place—the ancient baronial home, his study with the walls of books and the desk overflowing with his work, the broad sweeping lawn, the groves of trees, and the brook. It had been a good life, and there he had done his work; but thinking back on it, he wondered what his work had amounted to. At the time it had seemed important, but had it really been? Added all together, what had it amounted to?

The canyon had disappeared well beyond the eastern horizon and now they were flying at a low altitude over the endless desert of the high plateau. As Timothy watched, however, some of the dry brownness went away, and again he saw the billowing yellow of the prairie grass, interspersed at intervals by streams and groves of trees. The aridity of the desert land was being left behind.

Ahead the mountains loomed, much higher than they had seemed before, peaks stabbing at the sky, bare rock faces staring out across the land. For a moment it appeared the flier would crash straight into the mountain wall, then there was space ahead, with looming walls of rock to either side hemming them in. For breathless moments the flier hung between the walls of rock; suddenly there was openness ahead and the machine nosed down over a wide green valley that lay in the bosom of the mountains. For a short distance, a high ridge ran along the valley floor, and halfway up its slope was a wall of soft and pearly white that humped continuously along the ridge. On top of the ridge was a cluster of white buildings rising many storeys high, and among the trees all around the clumped skyline were what he took to be residences. Some of them seemed to be low-slung barracks, others were compounds enclosing huts, still others looked no better than slums, and there were some that he could not figure out.

The flier skimmed along the ridge, following its slope until it reached the top. Then it began to drop toward a wide green lawn, at one side of which stood a house. It settled on the lawn and the canopy came up. The pilot chittered at them and Spike rolled out on the lawn. Somewhat confused, Timothy followed him and stood beside the flier. Looking up the slope of lawn, he stared at the house, drawing in his breath in astonishment. With a few differences, it was the house on Hopkins Acre.

A gangling creature that had a slender body, bowed legs, and dangling arms was coming down the slope toward them. It headed straight for Timothy and stopped in front of him. It said in English, "I am your interpreter and companion and, I trust, your friend. You may call me Hugo, which is not my name, of course, but I understand it is a name that comes easily to your tongue."

Timothy gulped. When he could speak, he asked, "Can you tell me what is going on?"

"Everything," said Hugo, "in its own good time. But first, accompany me to your domicile. There a meal awaits."

He started up the lawn, with Timothy trailing after and Spike gamboling to one side of them. Behind them the flier was rising from the ground.

There were certain variations, but for all intents and purposes, the place appeared to be another Hopkins Acre. The lawn was well groomed, the trees well placed, the contour of the land very similar. There was one incongruity—everywhere one looked mountains rose against the skyline, while at Hopkins Acre the nearest mountain had been hundreds of miles away.

They reached the house and climbed the wide stone stairs to the massive door. Spike had deserted them and was skittering happily down the lawn.

Hugo pulled open one of the doors and they stepped in. Inside there might be differences, but it took some time to see them. Ahead of them lay the dark drawing room, with shadowy furniture crouched within, and beyond was the dining room with the table set and ready.

"There is a saddle of mutton," Hugo said. "We understand it is a favorite dish of yours. A small one, but there are only the two of us to eat it."

"But mutton—here!"

"When we do things here," said Hugo, "we do them properly, or as closely as we can. We have immense respect for the varying cultures that reside within this community."

Timothy stumbled across the drawing room to come to the dining room. The table was set for two and there was a clatter in the kitchen.

"Of course," said Hugo, "you will not find the guns of Horace in the gun room, although there is a gun room. There is your study, also, but quite empty, I'm afraid. We could not duplicate your books and notes, for which we are regretful, but there are certain limitations that could not be surmounted. I am certain there is material we can furnish that will replace the books."

"But wait a minute," protested Timothy. "How did you know about Horace and his guns, about my study and my books, and about the mutton? How did you know all this?"

"Think a moment, if you will," Hugo told him, "then make an educated guess."

"Spike! We harbored, all these years, a viper in our midst?"

"Not a viper. A very diligent observer. If it had not been for him, you would not be here."

"And the others? Horace and Emma? You pounced on me. How about the others? Can you go back and get them?"

"We could, I suppose. But we won't. You are the one we want."

"Why me? Why should you want me?"

"You'll learn of that in time. I promise you it will be nothing bad."

"The other two are human, too. If you want humans . . ."

"Not just humans. A certain kind of human. Think on it and tell me true. Do you like Horace? Do you admire the way he thinks?"

"Well, no. But Emma . . ."

"She'd be unhappy without Horace. She has grown to be very much like Horace."

It was true, Timothy admitted to himself. Emma did love Horace, and had come to think as he did. Even so, it wasn't right that the two of them be left in that arid desert while, he supposed, he'd be living here.

"Please take your place at the table," Hugo told him. "Your place is at the table's head, for you are the lord of the manor and so should conduct yourself. I shall sit at your right hand, for I am your right hand person. You have perceived, perhaps, that I am a humanoid. My bodily system works much the same as yours does and I ingest my food as you do, although I must admit that I had some trouble in adjusting my palate to the sort of food you eat. But now I have come to enjoy the greater part of your fare. Mutton is my favorite dish."

Timothy said, stiffly, "We ate many other things."

"Oh, I know very well you did. Spike, I must tell you, missed very few details. But now let us sit and I shall ring the kitchen that we are here and hungry."

Timothy pulled out the chair at the head of the table and sat down in it. He noted that the tablecloth was clean and white as snow, the napkins correctly folded. Somehow that made him feel more comfortable. Hugo rang the kitchen bell and sat down at Timothy's right hand. "Here," he said, reaching for a bottle, "we have an excellent port. Would you care for it?"

Timothy nodded. Three other humanoids, almost exact copies of Hugo, came out of the kitchen. One of them carried a platter bearing the mutton. He saw that some of the meat had been sliced and that was one thing, he thought with indelicate glee, that Spike had bollixed up. No one sliced a roast or a bird in the kitchen; the carving of good meat was reserved as an important table rite. Another brought in a tureen of soup and served it, ladling it into the soup bowls set at the two places. The third put down a large dish of vegetables beside the roast.

The soup was excellent, a rich broth with vegetables, strips of ham, and noodles. With the first spoonful of the soup, hunger came upon him and, forgetting good manners, he ladled it into his mouth with unseemly speed.

"Good, isn't it?" asked Hugo. "That Becky is turning into a cook of no mean skill, but it took a lot of training."

He chattered on. "Your ménage does not have the command of the language that I have. They can understand the simpler words and can speak after a fashion, but are beyond any real conversation. It is a pity that you are not telepathic, but then I would not have the pleasure of being in your service."

"Are most people in this community telepathic?" Timothy asked.

"No, but a good percentage of them are, and we have the Basic. But you don't know the Basic, and it would take some time to learn."

"The Basic?"

"A common language. A contrived language combining easily spoken words from many languages. Lacking in grammar, of course, and not elegant, but one speaking Basic can be understood. There are many species here who do not communicate by sound, nor, in fact, by telepathy. However, ways have been worked out by which all can be understood."

They finished their meal and pushed back from the table. "Now," said Timothy, "would you mind telling me exactly where we are? What sort of place is this?"

"That might take some extensive explanation," said Hugo. "For now, let me say that we are a galactic center composed of many cultures from widely scattered planets. We are thinkers and investigators. We try to make some sense of the universe. Here in this center, we meet and converse, in whatever way, as equals. We pool our thinking and our theories and discoveries. Questions are posed and defined, and ways are sought to answer."

"Then you missed with me; you came up a blank. I'm no great thinker and I am slow. I chew on thoughts before I write them down or spit them out. Mathematics is a complete mystery to me and I know no science. What little I have figured out, I did on my own. I had no training. I hold no academic degrees. My fascination is with history

and philosophy. I tried, during many years, to come
to an understanding of how my race took the course it
did, and I came up with very little. I can't imagine how
Spike . . ."

"He saw more in you than you see in yourself."

"I find that hard to believe. Spike always seemed a silly
thing. He played silly games. He had one game where he
jumped from square to square, except that there weren't
any squares. They were imaginary."

"Much of what we see in the universe," said Hugo,
"starts out as imaginary. Often you must imagine something before you can come to terms with it."

"We are mumbling in circles," said Timothy. "We are
getting nowhere. I accept this place as what you say it is
and I realize that I'm a misfit in it. So tell me why I'm
here."

"You are to provide us evidence."

"What kind of evidence? What is expected of me?"

"I can tell no more," said Hugo. "I have been in-
structed to tell you no more of it. Tomorrow I shall take
you where you are supposed to go. But it grows late, and
I believe we should retire."

For hours Timothy lay in bed before he went to sleep,
his thoughts spinning in his skull as he went over, time
after time, what little he had been told by Hugo.

It was rational, of course, that there should be a galactic
center where the intelligences of the galaxy could pool
their knowledge and work together toward their mutual
good. But what would the problems be, what the questions asked? Thinking on what they might be, he could
marshal many in his mind, but on examination of them,
some seemed lacking in necessary depth and others
sounded plain ridiculous. His human view was too narrow; human culture had been shaped by tunnel vision.
Although, he thought, that must necessarily have been
true, originally, of all the cultures that were represented
here.

Finally he went to sleep. Then someone was shaking
him awake. "I am sorry, sir," said Hugo, leaning over
him. "You were so sound asleep it seemed a shame to

wake you. Yet breakfast is ready and we must be on our way. I have a surface vehicle and it is a very pleasant drive."

Grunting with displeasure, Timothy roused himself and sat on the edge of the bed, reaching for the clothes that he had hung on the chair.

"I'll be right down," he said.

Breakfast was bacon and eggs, both done as he liked them. The coffee was acceptable.

"Do you grow coffee here?" he asked.

"No, we don't," said Hugo. "We had to scurry around to find it on one of the planets colonized by your people millennia ago."

"Those colonies were successful and still exist?"

"They are thriving. After a hard initial period, of course."

"You got all this food from those colonies?"

"Enough for a while," said Hugo. "We also got cattle, hogs, chickens, and the seed to grow corn, wheat, and a long list of vegetable crops. We have resources and a vast file of information. We were told to spare no effort. We spared none."

"Just to feed one man? Or are there other humans here?"

"You're the only one," said Hugo.

The ground car was waiting outside, and they got into it, with Hugo at the controls. Other residences showed up along the road, mostly screened by heavy growth. On the lawn of one that seemed to be mostly underground, half a dozen woolly creatures rolled and tumbled happily in childish play.

"You'll meet all sorts of people here," Hugo told him. "You'll be surprised how quickly you become accustomed to them."

"You sound as if I'm to be a permanent resident. I had the feeling that you would throw me out, once you used me."

"Never that. Once the interview is over, we'll supply you with informational material so you can get to work again. Your work will probably involve thinking about problems and solving them or suggesting approaches by which to tackle them."

Timothy grunted.

"You don't like it?" Hugo asked.

"You shanghaied me—you and that unspeakable Spike who must have spied on us for years."

"You were not singled out. We seek information and talent on many planets. Information can be garnered from most worlds, but talent is rare."

"You think I'm talent?"

"You could be."

"But the talent you find often could turn out not to be at all what you expected of it. What do you do then?"

"We keep them on. We owe them something. We always pay our debts."

They passed a miniature pink castle standing on a hill, all gussied up with battlements and towers, with brave pennons flying.

"A fairy castle," said Hugo. "I think I have the right word. Up in that castle are an accomplished people who see the universe as a complex mathematical structure and are working on it. There is some hope that in time they may supply the necessary key."

The road now joined a hard-surface highway and there were other cars—not many of them; there was nothing like a traffic jam. In the distance loomed a clutter of tall buildings, rising clean and crisp, with no fanciness about them.

"That is where we're going?"

Hugo nodded. "In your language, you'd call it an administration center. That's where much of the work is done, although many of our people work in their homes or in retreats tucked among the hills. But here is where it all comes together. There are laboratories, observatories, libraries, instrument and machine shops, and conference rooms. And certain other facilities that in your language I cannot put in words."

They came into the center and wheeled along the wide boulevards. Cars were parked upon the streets. Vast parks opened up, separating the buildings. A few monstrosities moved along the sidewalks, some of them arrayed in colorful and outrageous clothing, others innocent of clothing. There were humpers, crawlers, skitterers, and striders. Some carried bags and cases, and one of the humpers dragged a cart laden with stacked paraphernalia.

"This place," said Timothy, "seems almost like Earth—the streets, the parks, the buildings . . ."

"The problem of partitioning working areas is quite a simple one," said Hugo. "You take so many cubic feet of space and enclose it. Here the buildings were erected with one thing in mind: to make them as simple and functional as might be possible. To have been anything but simple might have offended some of the cultures that are represented here. There was no pleasing everyone, so we've done our best to please no one, using humdrum architecture with straight and simple lines."

He pulled over and stopped in front of the entrance to one building. "Here is where you go. I'll walk you to your place of appointment, but I can't go in with you. You enter alone. You'll be in a small room with one chair. Sit down and wait. Don't be uneasy. After a few moments, it will seem all right."

The room was close to the entrance. The building seemed nearly empty. They halted in front of a door, and Hugo turned back toward the entrance. Timothy pushed gently at the door, and it swung open easily.

A small room, Hugo had said; and it was a small room, but an attractive one. Carpeting covered the floor and there were decorations on the walls. The chair faced a wall entirely covered by one such decoration. Timothy walked across the room and sat in the chair, studying the decoration. It was a gaggle of soft colors. It was loaded with designs, but all of them were small and tangled up with one another. He could not tell where one ended and another began.

A voice spoke to him, seeming to come out of the wall. "Welcome to the Center. Your name is Timothy. Do you have another?"

"I have a family name, but my family never used it in

recent years. First names were enough. The family name is Evans."

"Very well, Mr. Evans," the voice said, "this is an inquiry into a situation concerning which you have some knowledge. We have heard many witnesses, but none whose testimony should bear more weight than yours. Please answer frankly and forthrightly."

"To the best of my knowledge and ability, yes."

"Fine, then we'll proceed. For the record, you are Timothy Evans, human from a planet you call Earth. Until recently, you have lived there all your life."

"That's correct. Why don't you show yourself? I dislike talking with a wall."

"My not facing you directly is a courtesy, Mr. Evans. You have been here only a short time and have met only Hugo. Given a few more days to meet others, you may understand. While I am, I assure you, a friendly and compassionate creature, I would appear to you a monster. There are others. A panel of us is listening to you, although I am the only one who talks with you. Most of the panel would also be monsters in your eyes. A row of monsters staring at you. Now can you appreciate our attitude?"

"I can," said Timothy. "It is considerate of you."

"So let us get on with the questions. You are acquainted with certain missionaries your people called the Infinites. What did those missionaries preach or advocate?"

"They sought to convince people that it would be advantageous to trade their corporeal bodies for an incorporeal state."

"In instances where they convinced people of their thinking, did they have the ability to affect this transformation?"

"Yes."

"You say that as if you are positive."

"I am. I came upon a place recently where many incorporeal beings were affixed—or seemed to be affixed—to some kind of lattice in the sky. Also, a brother of mine entered the transformation process, but it didn't take . . ."

"You mean the Infinites failed in your brother's case?"

"Either that or he pulled out of the process. I never quite got the straight of it. He would say one thing one time, then something else the next."

"What effect did that have upon your brother?"

"He became a shadowy person, composed of many shiny sparkles. My understanding is that if he had continued in his transformation, he would have been condensed to a single sparkle."

"The incorporeal beings you saw upon the lattice that you mentioned were single sparkles?"

"There were many single sparkles. They were located above a former Infinite dwelling place which we called a monastery."

"Please explain that to me."

"Monasteries are houses occupied by clerical orders that we call monks. Monks wear distinctive habits, and the Infinites looked like little monks, so we called their places of residence monasteries."

"We may come back," said the voice, "to certain specifics once again. But I would like to get to the crux of the matter now. It appears from what we have learned that the greater part of Earth's human population indeed became incorporeal. Your family didn't. How did that come about?"

"We fled the Infinites. We fled into the past. My family were not the only fugitives. There were many others. I have no idea how many."

"You fled in time. That means you had time machines."

"We stole the process for constructing the machines from the Infinites. We had no part in developing time travel. We simply blindly followed a pattern. We knew almost nothing of the technology."

"Why should you have fled? The vast majority of the Earth's population did not flee."

"We were a different kind of people, different in our outlook. We were the outlanders—the hillbillies, if you know that term?"

"I think I do. The disadvantaged people who, because

of environmental factors and cultural outlook, lagged behind. Perhaps with reason."

"Entirely with reason," said Timothy. "We kept sight of the old values which the rest of the population had abandoned."

"Therefore you could not accept the philosophy of the Infinites?"

"We gagged on their philosophy. It went against our grain."

"Yet, once again, most of Earth's people accepted it."

"The rest of the people completely abandoned the old values. They rejected technology, which in many ways, had served them in good stead and could have served them better if they had bothered to develop a stronger ethical code. They walked away from progress. In all fairness, I must say that progress, in certain instances, was detrimental. Yet it lifted us from beasts to a fairly reasonable and decent society. We scrapped nationalism, we conquered almost every disease, and we arrived at an equitable economic policy."

"Still these other people walked away from what you describe as the old values at the very point when they could have brought about a nearly perfect society. What happened? Did the race grow old and tired?"

"I've wondered about that off and on. There were, I would suspect, no data upon which a conclusion could be based. The strangest thing about it is that there seemed to be no one who was preaching it; there were no advocates of the change in attitudes, no one pushing for a new life style. The idea seems to have dribbled along until, after some years, everyone seemed to be doing nothing except sitting around and talking. They had the idea that they were engaged in great philosophical discussions, but actually all they were doing was talking. Through the history of mankind there have always been cults. They'd spring up here and there and would flourish briefly, but in the end they all faded out. But the abandonment of progress was not a cult. Each man seemed to decide suddenly for himself that progress was meaningless and technology not worth the cost. It was almost as if a contagious disease had struck.''

"Could it have been a disease?''

"No one ever hinted that it was. In fact, there was almost no discussion about it. The attitude was accepted and that was the end of it.''

"So the society was ripe for the Infinites.''

"Apparently. Not too much attention was paid to them at first. Then their philosophy began catching on quietly. There was never any great uproar about it. It went slowly, but grew in strength as the years went on. It was, you might say, a quiet catastrophe. The human race, in its history, had faced a number of possible catastrophes. There was a time when we nearly poisoned our world environment by the use of chemicals, but came to our senses just in time to escape that fate. We could have been wiped out by war, but found the way to peace at the last possible moment. But in the Infinite catastrophe, we lined up and went willingly to our doom.''

"There were people, however, who did not go willingly.''

"Not too many. A few. A few thousands went out into space to find other planets. Some of us fled into time. By the time we fled, the Infinites had started to push hard. They saw the chance, I suppose, of converting an entire race of people. By the time I was born it was beginning to get rough for dissidents like us. All I have told you of events before that is the history I was told.''

"The history could have been colored by prejudice.''

"To some extent, I suppose. We were becoming defensive in my day.''

"What arguments were used by the Infinites to persuade members of your race to accept the transformation?''

"They offered a certain kind of immortality. An incorporeal being could not die. It could survive the death of the universe. It would be immune from all physical ills. Free of the body, the mind would soar. That, the Infinites said, was the true goal of any intellectual being. Intelligence was the only quality that counted. Why contend, they asked, with the physical world—all its dangers and disappointments? Slough it off, they said, and be really free."

"That must have been compelling logic for many."

"For most of them," said Timothy.

"But not for you and your fellows? You still thought of it as wrong?"

"I find it hard to characterize exactly what our feelings might have been. I can only sum it up by saying we felt a great revulsion at what the Infinites were doing."

"You feared and hated them? You thought of them as enemies?"

"Yes."

"How do you feel about it now that it apparently is over, that the Infinites have accomplished what they set out to do?"

"It's not all over," said Timothy. "The human race still lives. There are human colonies on other planets that I am told are doing well, and there are a few dissidents hiding in the past."

"What do you feel for the humans who went the route the Infinites pointed out?"

Timothy hesitated for a long moment. Finally, he said, "Perhaps they had it coming to them. I would guess they asked for it. They turned their back on what the race had done."

The voice said nothing. Timothy waited, then asked, "This is what you wanted to talk with me about? May I ask your interest?"

The voice said, "This is an inquiry into the purpose and the motive of the Infinites. We have questioned many others."

"Other races that were victims of the Infinites?"

"Some of them were."

"But are the Infinites still pursuing their missionary efforts?"

"Not for some time. We have segregated them on their planet. They are being held in quarantine while we proceed in this inquiry. You must recognize that while we here at the Center respect the free will of any people, we still must take some note of where a too-aggressive free will may lead."

"The creatures that we termed killer monsters. What of them?"

"They were hired hands. Enforcers," said the voice, "that the Infinites, in their arrogance, hired to carry out their wishes. The killers have not been segregated, but are being destroyed. Such an element cannot be tolerated. A few are still free, but we hunt them down. Your friend, Spike, destroyed one of the last of them."

"I saw him do it," Timothy said.

"It was the arrogance of the Infinites that brought our attention to them. There is, in this galaxy, no room for arrogance. Almost anything can be tolerated, but not arrogance."

Again the silence.

"Is that all?" asked Timothy.

"For the moment," said the room. "Later, we'll talk further. You now are one of us. It is high time that we had a human here. Go back to your house and there you'll find informational material that will tell you in some detail who we are and how we function. From time to time, we'll call on you to consider certain matters with us."

After a time Timothy rose from his chair and walked slowly to the door. Down on the street Hugo lounged against the car, waiting for him.

Timothy Evans, human, newest member of Galactic Center, walked down the steps to the waiting car.

Henry

11

The trail had been long and hard to puzzle out, but here was the end of it, and everyone was gone. On the rim of a cuplike valley, the traveler stood empty. Over the dished impression gouged into the earth hung a covering dome of sparkle. Henry knew instinctively that each of the sparkles in the dome was one incorporeal human.

The situation was puzzling. The ones he had been tracking had been here, rather recently, but they had left without a trace. As Enid had also left no trace.

The traveler was empty of the supplies that Horace had put in it. So, Henry told himself, their leaving had not been precipitant. The leaving had been planned; there had been time to collect their supplies and take them wherever they had gone.

The entire slope of the bowllike depression was strangely pitted, with a number of crude devices planted on the slope. A hurriedly constructed defense line, more than likely, but what had been here to defend against?

He found and identified the spoor of Emma, Horace and Timothy, and Spike's scent as well. Also he found the abundant traces of many other beings. Humanlike footprints were pressed into the dust; examining them closely, he was convinced they were not human footprints.

Down on the floor of the bowl he came upon a rectangular impression where a building might have rested not too long before. Associated with it was a faint odor he had known long ago—the smell of Infinites.

The family was gone. Enid had disappeared, David was dead, and now the other three were missing. He was left alone in this far future place.

If only he could cut back along the time line to the moment when the three of them had first come upon this place—if he could do that, then it would be simple. But he knew it was impossible. Time could be traveled in quite freely but it could not be used in areas where interference with a sequence of events was possible. He could, in all reasonableness, recognize the need for such restriction; but when he sought to grasp the machinery of its operation, he could think of not a single principle that might apply. Was it possible, he asked himself, that the principles of the universe were, after all, based on simple ethics?

He floated, running all of it through his mind. He was without family or friends, engulfed in a world he did not know or like. He could go back to Hopkins Acre, but now it would be a lonely place, haunted by visions of the past, an acreage in which he would be lost. He could track down Corcoran, the single person who was left, but Corcoran was not family. He was no more than a stranger who had stumbled into Hopkins Acre.

He should be up there, he thought, with all those other glittering points of light; for better or for worse, he should be one of them. Long ago, through his obstinacy and pride, he had bungled that; he did not belong with them. Perhaps he was better off than they. He once had thought that and he might have been right.

Again he took up the chore of quartering in all directions, like a hunting dog, in the faint hope he might pick up the trail again. It was a hopeless task. The trail ended in the scooped-out valley.

Corcoran

12

Corcoran followed the path up from the meadow where the traveler had landed, coming to the crumbling wall that had once surrounded a long-forgotten city. He might be engaged in a wild goose chase, he warned himself. When he had stepped from the traveler, he'd stood and had a long look at the hilltop ruins, and there had been no tree. Yet he was sure now that he had not imagined it.

Probably he had to position himself correctly to see it. He had been able to see the traveler outside the wall of the Everest only when he looked for it at a certain angle. It might be the same way with the tree. He must stand in a certain place and look for it at a narrow angle before he could see it.

He shifted the shotgun from one hand to the other, resuming his climb. He reached the gate, half expecting to find the old man there, but he saw no one. Perhaps the old spaceman was off somewhere in the hills, talking to his trees and his rocks.

Corcoran picked his way through the rubble and came into the city, finding the path that he and David had followed. Still there was no tree.

He continued making his way through the tangled ruins, working up the slope.

On the hilltop, he glimpsed a wavering in the sky and when he took another step he saw the tree—that incredible, massive tree that soared high into the sky. When he took another step, the tree came clearer and he saw the staircase that wound its way around it.

Sobbing in his effort, he plunged up the hill toward it. Stay there, he pleaded with it, stay there, do not go away.

It stayed there, assuming more reality as he clambered up the hill to reach it. Finally he collapsed at the foot of it, gasping from the physical effort of running up the hill. He put out his hand and laid the palm against the bark, which was rough and solid, as real as any tree, no different from any other tree except for its height and girth.

The stairs, he saw, were constructed of solid metal and had, as well, an outside railing.

He rose from the ground and moved toward the stairs, then halted and sat down again. Not, he told himself, until I have my breath back, not until I'm ready. He laid the gun on the ground and slipped the rucksack off his shoulder. Opening it, he checked its contents—food, a canteen of water, a heavy jacket, a blanket for extra warmth, and a length of rope he could use to tie himself to the stairs if he should have to spend the night on them.

He repacked the sack and leaned back against the tree. Not until I'm ready, he insisted to himself. Down the slope lay the ruins and below them the valley where he and David had walked a path to reach a tiny town.

Fifteen minutes later he rose, slipped into the rucksack,

picked up the gun, and started up the staircase. The climbing was not difficult. The treads were at proper intervals, and the rail was stout and sturdy, helping him along and giving him a feeling of security.

He did not look down or back until he was forced to rest. Then he peered through the railing, and was surprised at the distance he had climbed. He had to crane his head out between the railing supports to see the ruins that lay at the base of the tree. From his height, they appeared to be no more than a huddle of gray stone. The broken wall that ran around them showed as a thin and jagged line. Beyond the ruins lay a green tangle of rugged hills and ridges with no break showing in them except the occasional glint of rivers that ran in valleys between the hills. Looking upward along the tree trunk, he could see no end to it. It speared upward until it disappeared in the blueness of the sky.

He climbed again. When he stopped the second time to rest, he found with some surprise that he could not make out the ruins that lay at the base of the tree. The rugged hills that stretched away in all directions no longer showed distinct lines of elevation. The bole of the tree had shrunken to some extent, although it was still of much greater girth than even the largest ordinary trees.

He must, he estimated, be at least three miles above the surface. That was impossible; no man could climb to such a height with only two stops for rest. And he had detected no drop in temperature or noticeable change in the density of the air. More than the size of the tree seemed to be beyond all rules he knew.

He had been debating whether to continue the climb, wondering what he was trying to prove and what he expected to find. But these mysterious effects surrounding the tree decided him. He must continue. Somewhere up there, he told himself, there must be an answer to the puzzle of the tree. He had come this far and he could not stop now. He would always wonder what he had missed by not going to the top.

The sun was only an hour above the horizon when he took up the climb again, and below him the land lay in darkness except for one high ridge. Some time later, he realized he had forgotten the gun he had rested butt down on one of the steps. But he did not need the gun and felt no need to return for it. He went on climbing, finding that the going was easier now, unhampered by its weight. As he climbed, the sun went down and dusk came on—not a blue dusk such as he was accustomed to, but a gray one. Soon, he knew, he would have to stop, tie himself securely to the stairs with the length of rope he'd brought, have something to eat, and try to sleep. He was fairly sure, however, that he would get but little sleep.

As he climbed, he was still trying to consider the puzzle of the tree, the stairs, and the mysterious forces that somehow seemed to prevent normal fatigue on his part and to hold the atmospheric pressure constant around him. Calm reason should tell him that there could be no such tree as this and no staircase that rose around it for miles into the air, circling around and around to nowhere.

But there was such a tree, though he seemed to be the only one who could see it, using the strange vision he had developed after the accident that should have killed him. David had seen no tree, and the old man, who seemed much concerned with trees, had not mentioned it. Surely if anyone else had seen it, the fact of its existence would be common knowledge, a wonder to be advertised worldwide and much talked about.

Thinking of all this, he lost some of his concentration and did not pay enough attention to his climbing. His toe caught the edge of a step, and he stumbled. Falling, he reached out a desperate hand to catch the rail . . .

Something seemed to stitch across his consciousness, like a flash of lightning striking. Everything went black. Then it was gone . . .

There was no rail. He scrabbled wildly to catch hold of the stairs so he would not go tumbling down. There wasn't any stair; he lay upon a flatness.

Puzzled and frightened, he levered up the forepart of his body from the flatness. All he saw was the flatness and a grayness. The tree and its encircling stairs were nowhere to be seen.

He rose to his knees and looked around him and still all he saw was gray flatness—gray fog swirling over a gray, flat ground. Except there was no swirling; there seemed to be no fog. He could see where he was; there was nothing to stop his seeing, but there was nothing to be seen.

Carefully, he rose to his feet. In front of him, a short distance away, was what seemed to be a line running across the gray land. He walked toward it. When he reached it, he saw that it was a road that was only a slightly different shade of gray from the land on which it lay. It ran in either direction from where he stood and was arrow-straight. In the center of it were two parallel darker streaks that had the look of trolley tracks, something that he recalled from his earliest childhood. To confirm the nature of the tracks, a trolley of very primitive design came out of the distant grayness and bore down upon him. It carried on its top a striped awning and, despite its rickety appearance, it made no sound at all. As it approached him, he stepped out of its way and it went running past him; but after going only a short distance, it came to a sliding halt and then reversed itself. When it reached him, it stopped. Without even considering that he should do otherwise, he clambered aboard and took a seat.

There was no question that the trolley was taking him to an unknown destination, but it was better, he thought, to be proceeding toward an unknown place than to stay where there was nothing to be seen but an unending grayness. Even riding on the trolley, the grayness still persisted. There was nothing to be seen, but in a little while he saw, some distance off, a cubicle of some kind and people moving about. Tables and chairs stood in the space between the cubicle and the trolley track, although some of the tables and chairs were partially obscured by a filmy cloud that was spangled by many points of light.

The trolley moved at a stately and sedate pace down the rails and when it came closer he saw that two of the people had seen its approach and were staring at it. One of the people seemed familiar to him and a moment later, recognition of the man burst suddenly upon him. Not waiting for the trolley to come to a halt, Corcoran leaped out of it and went running down the road.

"Tom!" he shouted. "Thank God, man, it's you. What are you doing here?"

He came up to Boone and grasped him by the shoulders. "I went hunting you," he said. "Finally I had word about you and . . ."

"Simmer down," said Boone. "Everything's all right. You remember Enid, don't you?"

Corcoran looked at the woman standing by Boone's side. "Why, of course, I do."

Enid held out her hand to him. "It's good to see you, Mr. Corcoran. This is a far cry, isn't it, from Hopkins Acre?"

"It surely is," Corcoran agreed.

"And here is Wolf," said Boone. "I guess you don't know Wolf."

Corcoran looked where Boone was pointing and saw the gray wolf grinning at him.

"Not Wolf, perhaps," he said. "But I saw some of his kinsmen back in that place where you killed the monster."

"I did not kill the monster," Boone told him. "It was the bull that killed the monster; then I shot the bull."

Corcoran shook his head. "It seems I don't know what is going on."

"Neither do we," Enid told him. "We're still trying to get it ciphered out."

"Let's sit down at this table here," said Boone. "From all the banging and the clatter that is coming from the cube, it would seem that the robot who runs this wayside rest is busy with a meal."

As the three headed for the table, Horseface came bumbling out of the fogginess of the galactic chart and made his way toward them.

"The chart," he told Boone, "is making its way back into the chest with no help from me. Which is a thing of luck, for I am sure, had I essayed the chore, I would have bungled it. And who, may I inquire, is this personage who has joined our party?"

Boone said to Corcoran, "Meet our friend Horseface."

Horseface rumbled at him, "I am pleased to meet you, sir."

"My name is Jay Corcoran," Corcoran told him. "I'm a longtime friend of Boone."

"Well," said Horseface, "we are all together and safely back at base. I don't mind saying I am glad our force is augmented by this friend of Boone. And here is Wolf. And The Hat."

The Hat was sitting at the table, erect in his chair, no longer slumped over. His hat was still pulled across his face, if he had a face.

Looking more closely at him, Boone observed that he was somewhat rumpled, apparently from Wolf's play. Here and there, toothmarks showed.

The robot came up to the table with a tray balanced on its head. "I have naught to offer you," he said, "but pig hocks and sauerkraut. I trust you can get along with that. For the carnivore, I have a plate of hocks without the kraut. I mistrust that he would relish the kraut."

"He'll eat anything that is of animal origin," said Boone. "But I am sure you are correct about the kraut."

Enid, sitting next to Boone, put her hand on his arm.

"Do you like kraut?" she asked.

"I like it well enough," he answered. "I have learned to eat almost anything."

"Horace was the one who really liked his hocks and kraut," said Enid. "He always made a pig of himself when we had them. He got grease up to his elbows."

Corcoran changed the subject. "Can anyone tell me where we are? What is this place?"

"The Hat said it's the Highway of Eternity," said Boone.

"He must have been kidding you."

"I don't think so. He seems to know. If he says it's the Highway of Eternity, I'll go along with him."

"You stepped around one of your corners to get here?"

"That I did—when my subconscious worked up a

dream to scare me enough. Wolf came along with me.
And what about you? You didn't step around a corner."

"No. I climbed a tree—a big tree with a staircase winding around it. What happened then, I'm not quite sure."

"That's ridiculous," said Boone.

"No more ridiculous than your corner stepping."

They ate in silence for a time and finally pushed aside
their plates. Wolf had finished more quickly and was
curled comfortably at Boone's feet.

Enid asked Corcoran, "Will David be coming soon? He
was with you in the traveler, wasn't he?"

Corcoran squirmed uncomfortably. "I have sad news,
Miss Enid. David is dead. I'm sorry. I . . . I'm very
sorry."

For a moment, she sat stricken, saying nothing. She
sobbed, then fought to regain control. "Tell me what
happened."

"Henry came to us. He'd found where you and Boone
landed, but you were both gone. He tracked your traveler
into the future and found that you had been there, but
had left. So the three of us went back to the prehistoric
period, hoping that we . . ."

"But how . . . ?"

"A sabertooth," said Corcoran. "David had his shotgun and he killed it when it attacked us. But it reached
him before it died."

"David killed by a sabertooth?"

Corcoran nodded dumbly.

"He never would fire a gun," she said. "He went hunting, but always with an empty gun. He took the shells
out."

"Back there," said Corcoran, "I insisted he keep it
loaded. When the cat came at us, he acted to protect both
of us. If he hadn't, the cat would have killed us both."

"You were with him when he died?"

"Just for a moment. He was almost dead when I
reached him."

"Did he say anything?"

Corcoran shook his head. "He didn't have the time. I
buried him as best I could. A rock-lined grave with stones

on top. I said some words over him. I'm not sure the right ones. I'm not good at that."

"And Henry?"

"Henry left before it happened. He went to track down the third traveler."

Enid rose from the chair. She said to Boone, "Will you walk with me?"

"Certainly," said Boone. "Whatever you may wish."

They moved out from the area, Enid clinging to Boone's arm. Wolf trailed along behind them.

At the table, when they were out of hearing, Horseface said to Corcoran, "I have a feeling that what you told was not the entire truth. You embroidered it."

"Of course I embroidered it. What would you have done? I was asleep when the cat killed him. It carried him off to eat. Would you tell that to his sister?"

"I would not. You have a kind soul."

"I'm a stupid coward," said Corcoran.

Down the road, Enid said to Boone, "I don't want to cry. David would not have wanted me to dissolve in tears."

"Go ahead and cry," said Boone. "Crying sometimes helps. I feel like crying myself. I liked David. During the short time I was with him, I liked him very much."

"In the family," she said, "he was my favorite person. We could talk together and we had our private jokes. David seemed happy-go-lucky, but he was never silly. He was an expert with the traveler and ran errands for us to other times. He brought books and the guns for Timothy, liquor for Horace, other stuff for Emma. I never asked him to get anything for me, but he always brought me gifts—jewelry, a book of poetry, perfume.

"And now he's dead. Buried in the prehistoric past. And he fired a gun. I never thought he could. He was too civilized, too much the gentleman. But when it came to life or death, he did.

"Now I'm going to cry. I don't want to, I shouldn't— but I am. Please hold me, Tom, while I cry."

The crying lasted for a time, but finally lessened and

came to an end. When it was all done, she lifted a tear-streaked face, and Boone kissed her gently.

"Let's go back," she said.

When they reached the table again, Horseface and Corcoran were sitting where they had been before, talking to each other.

"We've been discussing further moves," Corcoran said. "What should we do next? Neither of us has any sound ideas."

"Going is no problem," Horseface told them. "The net will take us wherever we may list."

"We could return to Hopkins Acre," Boone suggested. He looked At Enid. "Would you like that?"

She shook her head emphatically. "There's nothing there."

"There was that star we found," said Boone. "The one with the X painted on it. It has an inhabited planet. Enid's television showed that."

Horseface rumbled doubtfully. "You think that it's important because it has the X. So did I at first, but I'm not so sure now. The X could be meant to warn us to stay away."

"I hadn't thought of that," Boone admitted. "It could well be. Like the signs of a cross marked on the doors of plague-stricken houses in the Middle Ages."

"I would much like to visit the center of the galaxy," Horseface suggested. "We could go in the net . . ."

Boone had leaped to his feet. Behind Horseface and Corcoran, a faint flicker glimmered in the air, and there was a thump. A traveler came to rest just beyond the table.

The rest of them, except for The Hat, jumped up. The Hat continued sitting, saying nothing.

"That's my traveler!" Enid shouted. "It is the one I lost, the one I left behind."

"The one that was stolen from you," said Corcoran. "Henry told me that he found the traveler had been hauled away."

"But if it was stolen," Enid asked, "why should it be here?"

The port came open and a man stepped out, staring about and then looking at them. Corcoran moved toward him. "Martin," he said. "Fancy meeting you here. Is Stella with you?"

"No, she has other interests now," Martin answered. He seemed uncertain, as if confused at what he saw.

Enid asked quietly, "Is this the Martin who held the outpost for us in New York?"

"None other," Corcoran answered. "He ran away when I told him someone was inquiring about a place called Hopkins Acre."

"And now he has stolen my machine."

"You are Enid, aren't you?" Martin asked. "Yes, you must be. I did not steal your traveler. I purchased it from the man who stole it. An ignorant man. Scared as well. The key was still in it, but he was afraid to turn it on. He had no idea what might happen and was glad to sell the traveler for a pittance. Since I then had two machines, I took this one, and Stella kept the other."

"You found Enid's machine and now you come to us," said Boone. "Tell us how you did it."

Martin glanced around again, then shrugged. "There are ways," he said vaguely.

"I'll bet there are," said Corcoran. "And you'd be the one to know them. For whom are you working now?"

"For no one. For myself. I'm working on my own," Martin answered.

"And doing well, I suppose?"

"Not too badly. Corcoran, I can't understand your hostility. I always paid you well, gave you a lot of business."

"You conned me," said Corcoran. "You conned everyone."

A face peeped out of the traveler.

"An Infinite!" cried Enid. "You have an Infinite in there!"

Martin turned and yelled at the peeping Infinite. "All right! I told you not to show yourselves until I called you. But you couldn't wait, you had to look. Now you might as well come out."

Three Infinites tumbled out of the traveler and stood

in an awkward line. They were crazy-looking creatures, not more than four feet tall and rigged out in what appeared to be black robes and cowls. From under the cowls, pinched features peered out.

"So you're working for them now," said Boone.

"At the moment. They are all refugees. The Infinites are held in some kind of quarantine by a group called the Galactic Center, which has taken it upon itself, with no authority, to imprison them on their planet. These three managed to get loose. I heard of their plight and agreed to help them."

One of the Infinites stepped forward and spoke in a liquid voice. "We plead your understanding. You are members of a race to whom we gave our services. We made most of your race immortal, free of any threat. We are a highly moral people, doing good for others and asking nothing in return. Now we are victims of injustice, seeking friends who will stand with us and speak on our behalf against the cruel and unjust quarantine . . ."

"You feel you are ill-treated?" Enid asked, too gently.

"Yes, we do, milady."

"And you want us to help you?"

"That is our earnest wish."

"You drove us into exile," said Enid, "and when we fled, you sent killer monsters to hunt us down . . ."

"We three, the most of us, had nothing to do with killer monsters. There was a certain faction among us, bloated by arrogance . . ."

"Those of bloated arrogance are still with you?"

"We suppose they are. But we had nothing to do with them. They are a separate problem. We three are refugee ambassadors who seek understanding and help."

Boone asked Martin, "How much do you have to do with this?"

"Almost nothing," Martin said. "I only hire conveyance."

Enough of this, a voice said in their minds.

"Who was that?" asked Martin, startled.

"It's The Hat," Boone said. "That's the way he talks, directly to you without bothering with spoken words."

"Just a moment," said Enid. "Before we go further, I want this Martin to hand me back the keys to the traveler."

"I think that's a reasonable request," said Corcoran. He looked at Martin, who fidgeted, uncertain, then fumbled the keys out of his pocket and handed them to Corcoran. Corcoran took them to Enid and gave them to her.

"I would not have tried to get away," said Martin, trying to restore his ruffled dignity.

"Of course you wouldn't," said Boone. He turned to The Hat. "I'm sorry for the interruption. You were about to say?"

I was about to say, said The Hat, that there is only one logical destination for us. Not the core of the galaxy, nor any star with an X upon it, whatever that is. Who ever heard of a star with X painted on it?

"It was on the chart," said Horseface. "One star had an X marked on it."

"So what place would you suggest?" asked Boone.

"If you are going anywhere," announced the robot, coming out of his cubicle, "I am going, too. For too long I have stayed here with no one showing up except this Hat, who never so much as passes the time of day with me. I'll take my stove and the mechanism that supplies the food I cook. You'll need me along, or you might starve. There's no telling where this crazy Hat will take you. He never eats and knows nothing of comforts or necessities. He is . . ."

"That is quite enough," said Boone. "You've convinced us." He turned to Horseface and asked, "Will the net hold all of us?"

"Indeed," said Horseface. "The net will take us."

"What will we do with the traveler?" Enid asked.

"It will be safe here," Horseface told her. "The net is far better."

"But where are we going?" asked Corcoran. "That Galactic Center sounded attractive, if anyone knows how to reach it."

We go to the planet of the Rainbow People, said The

Hat. The Infinites ask for justice and justice they will find there.

"I don't give a damn what the Infinites want," Boone said. "We need some place where we can get some answers. There have been too many daft places and mad happenings. This road, Jay's tree . . ."

You are confused? asked The Hat.

"Considerably."

Then we go to the Rainbow People, said The Hat. They can supply answers.

"Very well," Horseface growled. "We'll go to the Rainbow People. So let us load the net with what we take and climb aboard."

Something bumped against Boone's leg. He looked down at Wolf.

"You, too," he said. "We'll take you along, but stick close to me. This one could be creepy."

Horace

13

The robot swung the axe, severing the rope that held the ballista cup in place. The great arm, responding to unleashed tension, swung up swiftly, hurling the boulder that lay in the cup against the wall. Against the wall, but not flying over it. At the impact of the boulder, the wall rang like the clanging of a mighty bell. The boulder came tumbling down the slope from which the wall rose. Robots scattered, getting out of the way of the rolling stone, which barely missed the ballista before coming to a halt.

Two primitive steam engines, earlier used to haul the

ballista into place, stood a little distance off, panting under their head of steam.

Conrad plodded slowly to where Horace stood.

"It's no use," the robot said. "We aren't going to be able to heave a stone over that wall. It's the configuration of the wall that defeats us. It flares up and out at the top and we are forced to position the machine too far back to give us the arc we need. And besides, to tell you the honest truth, which I have told you many times before, I fail to grasp the point of it."

"The point," said Horace, "is that somehow we're going to attract the attention of whoever is living in the city. They can't just sit there and ignore us, as they have been doing all this time. They have to be made to recognize that we are here and come out to talk with us."

"I'm not quite sure why you are so set on that," Conrad told him. "If I were you, I'd be inclined to be better satisfied if they continued to pay no attention to us. We don't know who or what they are. Once we attract their attention, if we do, we may be sorry that we did."

Horace glowered up at the wall. It was a monstrous structure, looming high into the sky, a milky white barrier that ran for miles all around the ridge top, closing in the city.

Emma said, a little piteously, "Why don't we let it be, Horace? You have become obsessed with it. You spend all your time scheming at how you are going to get at those people."

"They know we're here," Horace fumed. "They send out flyers every now and then to look us over, then go back. We are knocking at their door and we get no answer. That's not right, I tell you. That simply isn't right. This is the first time in my life I have been ignored and I won't stand for it."

"I don't know what else we can do," said Conrad. "We have modified the boulder-thrower and we still can't pitch anything over the wall."

"If we did," said Horace, "they'd pay us some attention. Toss a few boulders over that wall and they'd pay attention to us."

"Why don't you come over to the tent," suggested Emma. "Sit down for a while. Eat something, maybe. You haven't eaten for hours. You must be hungry."

Horace paid her no attention. He kept staring at the white, defiant wall.

"We've tried everything," he said. "We circled the entire wall, looking for doors or gates. We built fires and sent up smoke signals. Someone would have seen them. They ignored the signals. We tried to climb the wall and it can't be climbed. It's smooth. There is no place a man can get hold of it. It isn't stone and it isn't metal. It looks more like a ceramic. But who can make a ceramic that can withstand a thrown boulder?"

"Whoever is in there can," said Conrad. "Don't ask me how they do it."

"We talked about a tower that would reach the top of the wall," said Horace, with a question in his voice.

"It wouldn't work," said Conrad. "It would have to be high. We have trees from which we can make timber, but not the kind of timber to build the tower you have in mind. Also, there is the question of anchoring its base securely."

"We also talked about a ramp. I suppose that's out of the question, also."

"There is no way we could move enough dirt to build that sort of ramp."

"I suppose so," said Horace. "If we only had a flier."

"Look," said Conrad, "my robots and I have done the best we can. We built steam engines, and they are working well. We can build almost anything that runs on the ground, but air travel is beyond our skills. We don't know the theory; we couldn't machine the parts. And the energy? You couldn't power a flier with wood and coal." He hesitated for a moment. "I don't know how long we can keep the ballista working. We're running out of rope. Every time we use it, we waste ten feet of rope."

"You can splice rope."

"That we have done," said Conrad. "But each time you splice it, you lose a few feet of it."

"We could make more rope."

"We can try. The material we've tried has not worked out well."

"You see," said Emma. "It isn't any use. The wall has got you stopped."

"No, it hasn't!" Horace raged. "I'll find a way to beat it. I'll force the people in that city to pay me some attention."

A robot standing nearby said, "There is something coming."

When they turned around to look, they saw that a flier from the city was approaching for a landing.

Horace leaped into the air, waving his arms in triumph.

"Finally," he yelled. "Finally someone is coming out to talk. That is all we ever wanted. Just someone to come out and talk."

The flier landed and the passenger was getting out of it—a human, not some kind of crummy alien. There was an alien in it, but it stayed in the flier. More than likely, Horace told himself, the alien was the aviator.

Emma started forward uncertainly, then stopped and stared, as if not believing what she saw. Then she moved again, running toward the man who had climbed out of the flier.

"It's Timothy," muttered Horace, talking to himself. "Wouldn't you know it would be Timothy?"

Then he was hurrying forward, with Conrad trailing along behind him.

"So it's you," said Horace, sourly, coming up to Timothy. "What are you doing here? We thought we'd seen the last of you."

"Isn't it wonderful!" gushed Emma. "He's back with us again."

Timothy thrust out his hand, briefly meeting Horace's unwilling clasp.

"I see you're still at it, Horace," he said. "As uncouth as ever."

"I don't suppose," said Horace, "that you are here to extend an invitation."

"I'm here to tell you to cut out your inane doings. We'd appreciate it if you'd halt your banging on the wall."

"We?"

"The others in the city. And myself, of course. All your life you've embarrassed me and you still are doing it."

"There are people in the city?" Emma asked breathlessly. "People just like us?"

"Not people just like us. In appearance, some of them are fairly dreadful. But they are people and your throwing rocks at them has them somewhat perturbed."

"So they don't like it, huh?" said Horace.

"Some of them are outraged."

"Who are those monsters in there? Just what is this place?"

"This," Timothy told him, "is the Galactic Center."

"Then what are you doing in there?"

"I am one of them. I'm the only human member of the Center."

"You mean you pretend to represent the human race."

"I represent no one. All I can do is present the human viewpoint. That is all they ask."

"Well, then since you are one of them, why don't you just invite us in? That's all we want, to have some attention paid to us. All you've done is ignore us. We've been knocking at the door—that's all we've been doing."

"Hammering, you mean. You never knock, Horace. All you ever do is hammer."

"You mean you won't do anything for us?"

"I'd take it upon myself to invite Emma with me. She'd be more comfortable inside the city than out here."

Emma shook her head. "I'll stay with Horace. I thank you, Timothy, but I am staying with him."

"Then I guess I can do no more."

"You mean that's it?" asked Horace. "You just come out here and threaten us and that is all there's to it."

"I don't intend to threaten you. I only ask you hold it down."

"And if we don't hold it down?"

"Next time, it won't be me who comes. It'll be someone else. They may not be as courteous as I have tried to be."

"You certainly have not been the soul of courtesy."

"Perhaps not," said Timothy. "At times, it is something of a strain to be courteous to you."

"Stop it!" screamed Emma. "Stop it, the two of you! You're acting as you've always acted. At one another's throats."

She turned to Horace. "You! You say you've been only knocking at the door. It's more than that. It's throwing stones at windows. That's what you've been doing. Throwing stones at windows."

"One of these days," said Horace, "I'll break a window. Once I do that, the city will pay attention to me."

"I'll tell you what I'm willing to do," said Timothy. "I'm willing to go back to the council once again. I'll try to put your case to them. It's barely possible I can get you and Emma in, but not the robots."

"That would be all right with us," said Conrad. "We're not the ones who want in. We are doing it for Horace. We'd be just as satisfied to be left out here. We've got an entire planet to fool around with. A chance to build a robot society. A chance to make something of ourselves. There is a lot of good farmland here. We could grow food for the city. There are a lot of other things to do."

"How does that sound to you?" Timothy asked Horace.

"Well," said Horace reluctantly, "if that is what they want."

"Back on Earth," said Conrad, "we had our war with the trees. If we were still back there, we'd go on fighting trees. But here it makes no sense to fight against anything at all. Left on our own, we will make out. We'll begin to build a life. There is no end to the possibilities of what we might be able to accomplish."

Timothy looked at Horace, who shuffled his feet, saying nothing. He looked like a man who'd had the wind knocked out of him.

"So I'll go back and do what I can," said Timothy. "But if they let you in, you'll have to behave yourself, you'll have to keep your mouth shut. No more troublemaking. I have a house much like the one at Hopkins Acre. You'll be welcome there. It's a pleasant place to live. If you get obnoxious, you'll be restricted to it. Is all this satisfactory to you?"

Emma answered for him. "It's satisfactory to him. I'll see it is. I'm tired of this wilderness. So you go back, Timothy. Do the best you can for us."

The Rainbow People

14

Where the net had landed, huge up-thrust blocks of ice-white crystal humped up to make a serrated skyline above the plain, which was also made of white crystal blocks, laid like paving stones. The sky was so deep a blue that it was nearly black. The horizon seemed too near and was marked by a line of purple. Naked space came down close to the surface of the planet, with only a puny shield of atmosphere sandwiched between the surface and emptiness. Yet breathing was not difficult. It looked cold, but it was really shirt-sleeve comfortable.

No one had yet said a word. Boone turned slowly, looking around. There was nothing to see but the crystal blocks encircling the tiny plain on which they'd landed. There seemed to be no sun, although there was light and warmth.

Color flickered briefly above the skyline, then was gone.

"What was that?" asked Enid.

No one answered her.

"There it is again!" cried Enid.

This time the flicker persisted and climbed in a curving arc above the notched horizon, bending over and reaching down. It glowed and steadied, forming an arch of pastel color that loomed high above the surface.

"A rainbow!" Corcoran said. "This is the place."

"It is not," rumbled Horseface, "a simple rainbow. Mayhaps it could be the Rainbow People."

As they watched, more rainbows formed. They flickered out of nothing, then reached into the sky, bent and formed their arches. They clustered, rainbow bisecting rainbow until the plain picked up the colors, glowing with the soft light that glimmered in the sky.

Although the rainbows seemed stable enough, there still was about them the sense of not being fixed. There was a feeling of a certain delicacy, a misty ethereality, as if they were a phenomenon that was not meant to stay.

The robot had hauled his equipment off the net and was working on his stove, paying no attention to the rainbows. Enid and Corcoran stood not far away, staring up into the sky. The Hat was hunkered down close against the surface. Horseface loomed over him.

"One of us isn't here," said Boone, startled at the fact of the missing one. "Martin isn't here. What happened to him?"

"He fell through the net," said Horseface. "The net let him go."

"And you said nothing about it? You never even mentioned it?"

"He was not meant to be with us. The net knew."

"The Infinites are still here," said Corcoran.

The three of them, huddled together, were standing quite apart from the others.

"I think it's horrible," said Enid. "You say Martin fell. You are sure you didn't shove him?"

"I was far from him. I could not reach him to shove."

"I, for one," said Corcoran, "shall shed no tears for him."

"Have you any idea where he could be?" asked Boone.

Horseface shrugged elaborately.

The Hat spoke to them. I speak not for myself, he said. I am the tongue of the Rainbow People. Through me, they speak to you.

"But where are the Rainbow People?" asked Boone.

They are the ones you call the rainbows, said The Hat. They welcome you. Later they will talk to you.

Enid asked, "You mean the rainbows, the things we call the rainbows, are the people that you told us of?"

"They don't look like people to me," said Corcoran.

Wolf moved close against Boone's leg and Boone spoke softly to him. "It's all right," he said. "Stick close. It's you and I together."

"That is all the Rainbow People have to say to us?" asked Enid. "That we are welcome, and later they will talk?"

That is all, The Hat informed her. What further do you wish?

The robot said, "Hamburgers are all that I can manage on quick notice. Will you be satisfied with them?"

"If they are food," Horseface told him, "I'll be satisfied."

Above the horizon the clumped rainbows lost their intensity, the color fading out. Then they were gone. The fading of the rainbows, Boone thought, had taken some of the warmth away. He shivered as he thought it, even while he knew there was no reason for the shiver. The place was as warm as ever.

It was The Hat, he told himself, that got us into this. The Hat had not allowed consideration of the suggestions that had been made by others. The Hat might even be a

Rainbow agent—he knew who they were, where they might be found, and he was the one who spoke for them.

"I vote," he said, "that we get on the net and leave. Just what the hell are we doing here?"

"So you feel it, too," said Corcoran.

We came here, said The Hat, for the judging of the Infinites. To the only court that could hear them fairly, the one judiciary with the knowledge to render them their justice.

"Then let's get it over with," said Corcoran. "Let us get them judged and leave. Better yet, let's just leave the Infinites here to receive their justice. I, for one, don't care one way or the other how the verdict will turn out."

"But I do," said Enid, sharply. "These were the ones who wrecked the human race. And I want to know what is to happen to them."

The judging is not all of it, The Hat told them. There may be here something of interest to all the others of you.

"I can't imagine what," said Corcoran.

The Rainbows are an ancient race, The Hat said. One of the first, if not the first, people of the universe. They have had the time to evolve beyond anything you can even guess at. Their knowledge and their wisdom encompass more than you can conceive. Now that you are here, it would be well to hear them out. It will demand of you no more than a little of your time.

"The most ancient people of the universe," said Boone, then said no more. For if they were the most ancient people, then they had been given the time to work out their evolution to what probably was its ultimate condition.

His mind spun as he thought of it. It seemed fantastic—and yet, perhaps no more fantastic than what the humans had accomplished in a few million years, lifting themselves from cunning, but endangered, beasts to a position from which their shrewd and sharpened minds, linked with dextrous hands, had enabled them to take charge of their planet, devising means by which they could survive the animosities of an environment that could turn hostile without notice.

But the Infinites, he thought—good lord, if what the Infinites claimed was true, then the incorporeality they offered was proof against any physical condition, while the Rainbow People, if they had not advanced beyond the energy form they were taking here, still could die of entropy. On the day the universe flattened out to a state where there were no differences, when space and time and energy stood still, the force by which the Rainbow People survived would be gone and they would die with the universe.

And The Hat had claimed that these Rainbow People were the ones who could and should stand in judgment of the Infinites!

Yet, Boone wondered, could it be possible that the Infinites, while able to offer a perfect survivor system to others, were unable, for some reason, to use it for themselves? The Infinites, standing back there on the Highway of Eternity, had cringed, begging help and mercy.

Here they were cringing still, the three of them. They had formed a circle, facing one another, so that their robes seemed to be a part of a single organism.

They had begun a dolorous chant that held within it the sound of loneness and lostness. It was not a death chant, for a death chant, even at its worst, strikes a defiant note. The chanting of the Infinites had no defiance and no hope—it was a dirge to the end of everything.

Out of the stillness that hung over and enclosed the chant, a voice with no sound, and no inflection said: Your sin is that you have erred. You Infinites have sinned because of pride of self. There is no question that your technique is of the highest quality, but you used it too soon. You have condemned members of a race to a lower state of intellectuality than was their destiny. The people of the planet called the Earth were not in the final stages of their development, as it seems you thought; they were simply resting. Given time, which you did not give them, they would have developed a new intellectuality. In acting too soon, you have made them junior citizens of the universe. Of this, you stand condemned and cursed. You shall be returned to your people so that you may inform them of this judgment. Their punishment, and yours, is that you shall know and accuse yourselves throughout the remainder of your racial life of the injustice you have done.

The voice ceased. The Infinites did not stand huddled like a small black tent; they were not there at all.

Corcoran let out his breath, as if he had been holding it for a long time. "I'll be damned," he said.

"Anyhow," said Horseface, "we are done with them. Now that judgment has been passed, let us leave this place." Having said this, he began to climb aboard the net.

There were seven of them, Boone told himself, ticking off each of them—Enid, Corcoran, Wolf, Horseface, the robot, The Hat and, last of all, himself. There had been eleven of them, but Martin had fallen through the net, and the three condemned Infinites were gone.

"We become fewer and fewer," he said, speaking to himself. "Who will be the next to go?"

You cannot go, said The Hat. There is further still to come.

"Hat, we've had enough of it," said Corcoran. "Enough of you and your Rainbow People, enough of judgments and delay. We have played your little game longer than was wise."

Wolf came sidling over. Boone squatted down and threw an arm around the animal. Enid moved to the two of them and leaned over them. She started to say something. Then she disappeared.

Boone no longer was on the angular whiteness of the crystal world. Instead he crouched, Wolf still within the circle of his arm, at the head of a deep and wild ravine flanked by towering hills that sloped sharply upward into a pale blue sky. The hills were covered by ancient, twisted trees and embedded boulders that thrust like gray, shaven skulls out of the sloping terrain. A boisterous wind was blowing up the ravine. Far in the distance, down the savage gully, Boone could see the glint of sun on water.

He rose to his feet, gazing all about him. The crystal world was gone; no single feature of it remained. He and

Wolf were quite alone in this different place. The others were not there.

He had, he thought, stepped around another corner, although there had been no reason he should have done so. There had been no danger and no threat; he had been aware of none. He had done nothing, he was sure, to bring him and Wolf to this other place.

He spoke to Wolf. "What do you think of it? What have you to say?"

Wolf made no answer.

"Boone!" a voice called. "Boone, are you here? Where are you?"

"Enid!" Boone shouted.

There she was, up the hillside from them, running down the slope that was too steep for safe running.

Boone plunged up the hill toward her. She started to fall and he leaped to catch her. But even as he leaped he himself was falling, the loose soil giving way beneath the driving effort of his lunge.

They tumbled down together to where Wolf waited. Sitting up, only a few feet apart, they burst out in laughter, half-apologetic laughter at the silliness of what had happened. Boone tried to sweep back a lock of hair that had fallen across her face. His dirt-smudged hand, dirtied in the fall, left a streak of soil across her nose.

"What happened?" she asked. "What brought us here? Did you duck around another corner?"

He shook his head. "I didn't duck around a corner. There was no threat, nothing that could have triggered me."

"Then what?"

"I don't know," he said. He moved closer to her and reached out a hand. "Your nose is dirty. Let me wipe it off."

"And the others?"

"I suppose they're where we left them."

"Boone, I'm scared. Can you tell me where we are?"

"I don't know," he said. "And I'm as scared as you."

They sat side by side, staring down the wild, wind-whipped ravine. Wolf sat solidly, determinedly in front of them.

The soundless voice of the Rainbow People spoke to them, from no direction, out of nowhere, the words ringing in their minds. There was no threat in the voice and no assurance. It was a dead, flat voice.

Listen closely to us, it said. Let us talk of the universe.

"It would be presumptuous of me to talk of the universe," said Boone. "I have no knowledge of it."

One of you, the voice said, has given thought to it.

"I have given it no thought," said Enid. "But there have been times I have pondered on it. I have wondered what it is and the purpose of it."

Then pay attention, said the voice. Listen very closely.

And then came a rush of thought that beat savagely against them. It was an overpowering force, a gush of half-heard words and wordless thoughts filled with information.

Boone felt his legs buckling under him, as if he stood against a strong and deadly wind that battered at his body and his mind.

"Oh, my God!" he whispered and collapsed upon the hillside. As if through a veil, he saw Enid sitting just a few feet distant and tried to crawl to her, trying to reach some warmth and oneness that he lacked in this storm of information that pounded steadily against him.

Then the storm lifted and was no more, and he lay sprawled on the dirt. Wolf was crouched close against the slope, whining to himself.

Crawling, Boone reached Enid and hoisted himself to a sitting position. She sat frozen, as if not knowing he was there, not knowing she was anywhere. He reached for her and pulled her within his arms. She came close against him and he held her hard.

"Do you know what happened?" he asked. "Do you remember any of what they said?"

She whispered at him, "No, I don't. I feel it all tamped hard inside me, but I know none of it. My mind is full to bursting . . ."

Another voice shouted at them—a rough, loud voice—a voice that could be heard and was made of honest words.

Boone leaped to his feet. Something was flapping in the air above them and he saw that it was the net. Horseface stood upon it, riding on its flapping like a drunken sailor erect upon a storm-tossed boat.

"Move swiftly," Horseface roared at them. "Climb upon the net. We will leave this place as soon as you are on the net."

The net was fluttering lower and Boone, lifting Enid off her feet, threw her bodily upon it. Wolf already was in the air, leaping for it. Horseface came to its edge and reached down a hand. "Up you come," he said, grasping Boone's outstretched arm and jerking him through the air to a place beside him.

Corcoran was on the far side of the net, hunkered down and fiercely hanging on to it. The robot was wailing. "All my equipment gone!" he howled. "All of it left behind. Without it, how am I to feed you?"

"We had to leave in a hurry," growled Horseface. "That shoddy sham of crystal was dissolving beneath our feet."

"How did you know where to reach us?" Enid asked.

"That visor you stole on the pink-and-purple world," Horseface said. "It was lying face up on the net. I looked at it, wondering at the same time where you could have gone, and I saw you here in the glass. When I saw you, the net knew where it was and came here to pick you up."

Corcoran shouted at him, "Where are we going now?"

"Where we should have gone in the first place," said Horseface, "had we not listened to The Hat. To that star the chart showed, the one with the X marked on it."

"And The Hat?" asked Boone. "He's not with us."

"Most unfortunate," said Horseface, unctuously. "He was unable to reach the net in the time remaining."

Henry

15

The bloated redness of the sun hung above the world—a nearly empty world, a world without grass or other vegetation except for the lone, ancient tree that stood down the ridge from Henry. He floated, his sparkles pulled together as if he cringed against this forbidding world, although he was not cringing. In his years of wandering, he had seen too much to cringe.

The sky was dark, the kind of darkness that would come with an approaching storm, although here there was no storm nor any hint of one.

The end of the world, he wondered, the beginning of

the end, with a dying, now unstable sun undergoing the
first stages of a red giant sequence?

The tree down the ridge cast no shadow. And for the
first time in his life, Henry experienced utter silence. No
bird was crying in the sky, no insect chirping from the
ground, and there was no soughing of a wind. Everything
stood still.

Then a voice spoke within him: You are a stranger here?

If he had still possessed a body, his surprise would have
made him gulp. But there was no way that he could now.
He answered, calm and clear: Yes, I am a stranger. I have
only now arrived. Who is it that speaks to me?

The inner voice said, I am the tree. Why don't you come
to me and rest within my shade?

But you have no shade, said Henry. This bloated sun
casts no shadow.

I speak from olden habit, said the tree, harking back to
that time when I did have shade to offer. It has been so
long since I have bespoken another that I now forget. I
am inclined at times to stand here in my loneliness and
make loud and senseless declamations. I am simply talking to myself, since there is no one else to speak to.

I do not need your shade, said Henry, which is well,
since you have no shade. But your company I need and
your information, if you will favor me with it.

Saying which, he floated to a position close to the lonely
tree.

What information do you wish? the tree asked of him.
My store of it may not be ample for you, but I'll give you
what little I may have.

You are a sentient tree, said Henry, and you bolster a
belief some ancient humans had. My long-lost sister, I
recall, believed quite firmly—and the others of us thought
unrealistically—that trees would follow man. Now, meeting you, it occurs to me that she could have been correct.
She was a most perceptive person.

Does it happen you are human? asked the tree.

A partial human, Henry told him. A fragmented one.
A beaten-up human at the best. Which leads me to another
question. What has happened to the clustered sparkles

that at one time were stationed in the sky? Once there were many of them.

I recall them faintly, said the tree. Searching far back in memory I bring them to my consciousness. There were many lights in the sky. Some of them were stars and some of them were what you term the sparkles. There still are stars, and in a little time we'll see them. When the sun sinks to just above the horizon in the west, they'll begin appearing in the east. The sparkles you will not see; they have been gone for long. They drifted off. They became less and less. I'm sure they did not die; they only drifted off, as if they were going elsewhere. Can you tell me what humans were? Were they all like you?

Not at all like me, said Henry. I am, you must understand, a freak. I started out to be a sparkle, but it didn't take. It's a long story. If we have the time, I'll tell you.

We have all the time there is.

But the sun?

I'll be withered up and dead, all trace of me vanished, before the sun is any actual danger. In time to come, it will kill the planet, which is close to dead already. Not for some little time.

That's good to hear, said Henry. You asked me what a human was. I take it there are no humans now.

Once, very long ago, there were creatures that were formed of metal. Some said they were not humans, but copies of humans.

Robots, Henry said.

They were not known by that name. I can't be certain they existed. There are many stories told. One was that the metal creatures tried to eliminate the trees by cutting them down. There was no explanation of why they should have tried, or evidence that they did.

The robots now are gone?

Even metal, said the tree, does not live forever. But you and I are here, and we are talking. Perhaps we could be friends.

If you wish it, Henry said. I have not had a friend for far too long.

Then let it be so, said the tree. Let us settle down and

talk. You said that some thought trees would follow man. Does that mean take the place of man?

That is what it meant. Even then, an untold time ago, there was a well-founded perception that the human race would end and that something else must take its place.

Why must something else take its place?

I cannot tell you that. There is no solid rationale for it, but the belief seemed to be that there must be a dominant race upon this planet. Before men were the dinosaurs and before the dinosaurs were the trilobites.

I have never heard of either dinosaurs or trilobites.

They didn't amount to much, said Henry. The dinosaurs were big and perhaps there were not too many of them. The trilobites were small and there were a lot of them. The point is that all the trilobites and the dinosaurs died out.

And man took the place of dinosaurs?

Not immediately. Not all at once. It took a little time.

And now myself, a tree? I am dominant?

I think perhaps you are.

The strange thing, said the tree, is that I never thought of myself as dominant. Perhaps at this late date, dominance is of slight importance. Was it different with the trilobites, the dinosaurs and men?

I don't know about the trilobites, said Henry. They were a stupid lot. The dinosaurs were a stupid tribe as well, but they had a hunger in them. They ate everything in sight. The humans had a hunger, too; they controlled everything.

We had no hunger, said the tree. We got our living from the soil and air. We interfered with no one, had no enemies, and were enemies to no one. You must be mistaken; if it takes great hunger to be dominant, we were never dominant.

Yet you can think and talk.

Oh, yes, we did a lot of that. Time was, when there were many of us, we raised a storm of chatter all across the world. We were the wisest things in all the world, but we did not use our wisdom. We had no way to use our wisdom.

Can you tell me, perhaps, asked Henry, some of that wisdom?

You come too late, the tree told him sadly. I grow old and senile. I am swamped with forgetfulness. Perhaps it required a community of effort and of thought and chatter to hold the wisdom intact. Now there is no community. You come too late, my newfound friend; there is nothing I can give you.

I am sorry, said Henry.

Another failure, he told himself. The trilobites, the dinosaurs, and men, at least upon this world, had failed. And the trees as well. Even if the trees had persisted and gone on, they'd still have been a failure. Wisdom of itself was useless. If there were no way to act upon it, it had no value.

You are troubled, said the tree.

Yes, troubled, Henry told him, although I don't know why I should be; I should have known the end.

The Family

16

Timothy leaned back in his chair and thrust his long legs out in front of him.

"Finally, after months," he said, "I'm beginning to catch on to what is going on here. I'm learning the basic galactic language. Hugo has been a help to me from the very start, of course. He has guided me, counseled me, and seen that I met other beings who have been of help to me."

"Don't be taken in by all of this," Emma told Enid. "He still follows his old habits. He stays in his study for days at a time, not even coming down for meals. Some of Hugo's people had to carry them up to him, and now that silly robot that came with you carries them up to him and . . ."

"The robot has been a great help ever since he arrived," said Hugo. "My people worked very hard to run the kitchen and do other chores around the place, but the robot moved immediately to take over. He is a wizard at cooking and he seems to have the knack."

Horace grumbled from the far side of the room. "He still doesn't know how to turn out a good saddle of mutton."

"Do you have to complain all the time?" Emma asked tartly. "If it isn't the cooking, then it is something else. You remember, don't you, what Timothy told you when he agreed to bring us here. Don't make any trouble, he asked. That's all he asked of you."

"He also told me," yelled Horace, "to keep my mouth shut. All I ask of you, he said, is to keep your big mouth shut."

"I must say," said Timothy, "that you've not done too well at it."

"Except for complaining all the time," said Emma, "he's not done too badly. He's not set a foot off the property and he's not quarreled with any of your ridiculous neighbors. I don't see how you put up with them."

"So far as I am concerned," said Enid, "I cannot see any need to step off the property. This place is simply perfect. Except for the mountains, I don't see much difference between it and Hopkins Acre."

"You are right," said Corcoran. "It is as pleasant a place as I have ever seen. It reminds me much of Hopkins Acre. Boone and I, of course, were only there for a short time, but . . ."

Boone said to Horseface, "I can't imagine how you knew that the star with an X marked on it would lead you here."

"I told you," Horseface rumbled. "The X made me to think it must be a special place, so I headed for it."

"But you were the one who suggested that the X could have been meant as a warning," said Corcoran.

"It could have been," Horseface agreed. "But sometimes I like to take big chances."

"For my part," said Timothy, "I am glad you took the chance. It was lonely here, among all the aliens, considerate as they may have been. Now the family, what is left of it, is together again."

"Have you had any word at all of Henry?" Enid asked.

Horace answered, "No word at all. Henry you could never tell about. Despite what the rest of you may say, he was a spook. Always slipping in and out."

"There goes that big mouth again," said Emma. "You never did like Henry. You were always saying terrible things of him. I would think you would be different now. Henry may be dead."

"Henry dead!" Horace roared. "He'll never die. There never was a thing that could get to him."

"The last I saw of him," said Corcoran, "he told me he was leaving to find you people who were in Martin's traveler."

"Well," said Horace, sourly, "he never found us. He probably found something else that interested him."

They sat in the drawing room, taking their ease at talk following a splendid lunch. From the dining room came the subdued clatter of the staff clearing away the china and the silver.

Timothy waved at the bar. "Anyone who wants a refill, help yourselves."

Horace heaved himself up and stalked to the bar for more brandy. He was the only one.

Corcoran said to Timothy, "You seem contented here."

"I am well content," Timothy told him. "There is an old familiarity to the house and grounds. And I have work again. Why don't you stay here with us? I am sure Center would, without difficulty, find a place for you."

Corcoran shook his head. "My home is back in the twentieth century. I have a business there and I find myself anxious to get back to it."

"You have decided, then," said Boone.

"Horseface has agreed to take me. You won't be going with us?"

"No. I think I shall stay here."

"And you, Horseface?" asked Enid. "Will you be coming back to us?"

"Perhaps on visits, if you are willing to have me. But there are many things to see, light years to travel, and far places to poke into."

"Before you go, there's one thing you must tell me."

"Please ask."

"What really happened to Martin? You said he fell through the net. I think you shoved him off."

"I never laid a hand on him," protested Horseface. "I only told the net."

"You told the net to throw him off?"

"You make it sound so heartless."

"Well, it was heartless, wasn't it? You dumped him into space."

"That I did not do," said Horseface. "I told the net to dump him into another place and time. On Earth, in the twenty-third century."

"Why there?"

"I wish the man no harm. I just wanted to get rid of him, to put him where he cannot leave and start trouble. He will have no traveler, so once there, he has to stay."

"One thing still puzzles me," said Corcoran. "Who the hell was Martin? I had been under the impression that he somehow was connected with Hopkins Acre and the others in your group—the Pleistocene and Athens. Some sort of outpost man. But when he learned that someone was asking about a then nonexistent place—Hopkins Acres— he took it on the lam. The next we saw him, he was working for the Infinites, carting them around in a stolen traveler."

"Not stolen," objected Horseface. "He claims he paid for it."

"Still it was stolen," said Boone. "It had been stolen from Enid. Probably not by Martin, but by someone else."

"As I recall it," said Horace, nastily, "it was you, Corcoran, who told him someone was inquiring about Hopkins Acre."

"He had hired me," said Corcoran. "I did a job for him, that's all. He paid me handsomely for what I did. I have been wondering since how he got that money. Not from you folks, certainly. My impression is that you had nowhere near that kind of money."

"Are you sure it was real money?" Horace asked.

"It could have been," Enid said. "He had two travelers—the big one and the one Stella took. When you can travel through time, it isn't hard to locate treasure, to win lotteries, or use some such means to get money. That's how David got the small amounts he needed to pay for the supplies he brought back to us from his trips."

Timothy nodded. "I doubt we'll ever know who Martin was. Undoubtedly, a very devious man. I must tell you that we had full confidence in him, although we never liked him. David met him in New York and took him in dislike. Not a nice man. Very far from being nice."

"He was a traitor," Horace stated. "When he heard there might be trouble for us, he deserted us."

"As I say," said Timothy, "we'll probably never know. Are you fairly sure," he asked Horseface, "that you got rid of him? He'll not rise again to plague us?"

"He is trapped," said Horseface. "Without a traveler, there is nowhere he can go."

"We all feel better now that you've told us what you did with him," said Enid. "Thanks for telling us. There is one more thing you can do for us."

"Name it, Miss Enid," Horseface said. "My debt to you never will be paid in full."

"Could you pick up the traveler we left on the Highway of Eternity and bring it back to us? A traveler is a handy thing to have."

"Also," said Timothy, "Center would like a look at it."

Wolf emerged from a corner where he had been sleeping off a plate of beef, bumbling across the room to collapse beside Boone's chair.

"He wants out," said Enid.

"He isn't asking yet," said Boone. "Just thinking about it. Making up his mind. When he's made it up, he'll ask."

Horace heaved himself up and crossed the room for another refill of brandy.

"One thing I forgot to tell you," Timothy said. "Something that I ran across while going through some tapes and papers. A copy of a document dating from the twenty-fourth or -fifth century. It's the first reference to Earth that I have run across since coming here. Earth isn't mentioned by name, of course, but certain internal evidence indicates that it was the Earth. The document tells of the rise of a religion that centered around a mysterious artifact. The account is not clear on its actual nature, but it seems to have served as a sort of messiah that railed against technology and preached a philosophic attitude of reaching within to find one's true self and rejecting materialistic progress. Does that sound familiar?"

"Of course it does," said Enid. "It was that attitude that undermined the human race and set us up for the Infinites."

"The time span's too long," Boone objected. "Ideas don't survive a million years. They lose validity and become obsolete."

"I'm not so sure," Timothy told him. "If the cult spread widely at first, it would survive among some—particularly if the artifact endured for a long time. And when certain social stresses occurred—as they tend to do repeatedly—the hard core of the cult that survived could spread it further. Look at the belief in magic, which kept being put down by rationalism and popping up in various guises almost to our time."

"I suppose it could happen," Corcoran admitted. "Certainly, cults related to belief in magic were multiplying in my period."

"Our people never knew of it," said Emma. "If it was there, we should have heard of it."

"But the attitudes it taught were there," Timothy told her. "Maybe in time it did die out—because its purpose was accomplished. The people had already accepted its teaching. It could have gradually become a part of the public consciousness. People could have forgotten the origin of it and believed that the philosophy developed from it was the result of their own inescapable logic, their own finely tuned intelligence."

"I don't believe a word of it," said Emma. "It's just an ancient myth."

"It may well be," Timothy conceded. "But it's more than commonly interesting."

"You seem to have fallen into a niche that was made especially for you," Corcoran told Timothy.

"I was afraid at first," said Timothy, "that all the work of the Center would be so strange that I could find no place where I could fit in. But even my sketchy knowledge of Earth's history seems valuable to the study being made of how cultures grow or fail. Center is deeply concerned with what enabled the Infinites to succeed in their efforts. Time travel is another matter in which Center is concerned. There were rumors that the Infinites had it, of course, but they never revealed its nature. And now that the Rainbow People have taken them over, all contact with them has been cut. But if we could secure the traveler that was left on the Highway of Eternity . . ."

"I pledge you," Horseface promised, "that it will be placed within your hands."

"Better yet," suggested Timothy, "if we could have your net for just a little time. Just to look at it."

Horseface shook his head. "I'm sorry, but I will not let it go, even for a moment. It is a heritage of my people. Sages from my deepest past rose up in my mind to help me gain it, and I could not ask them to give that help to others."

"I understand," said Timothy. "In your place I would do the same."

"Was it difficult," asked Enid, "to work with the aliens at the Center?"

"At the beginning," said Timothy, "but not now. I have become accustomed to them and they to me. At my first direct contact with them, I was not allowed to see them because they feared I would think them monsters." He shrugged his shoulders. "Many of them still are monsters; but face to face, I no longer shrink from them, nor do they shrink from me. I work with them in comfort.''

Wolf rose to his feet, wriggling closer to Boone, laying his muzzle in Boone's lap.

"Now he's asking," said Enid.

"I do believe he is. I'll open the door for him."

"No," said Enid. "I'll take him out. It is getting stuffy in here. I need a breath of air."

She rose and spoke to Wolf. He followed her appreciatively.

"I'll be right back," she said. "A breath is all I need."

Boone spoke to Wolf. "Be a decent animal," he said. "Don't chase anything. Behave yourself. Don't you raise a ruckus."

Then the two of them were gone.

Horace rose, heading again for the brandy bottle.

"Don't you think you've had enough?" suggested Timothy. "It's still early in the day."

Emma blazed at him. "Why do you have to keep on humiliating him?" she asked. "You humiliated him when you brought us here. You've kept on ever since. You talk to him exactly as Boone talked just now to Wolf. Behave yourself, he said."

"That's what I did tell him," said Timothy. "It was part of the bargain that we made. I couldn't leave you out there in that howling wilderness and you wouldn't leave without him. So I talked with the council at Center . . ."

"He worried about Conrad and the robots," Emma said. "He had grown very close to them."

"I couldn't have convinced Center," Timothy told her, "to allow that gang of robots in. In any case, they would not have come. They'd be miserable here. Out there they are doing all right by themselves. They're breaking a large acreage on a virgin prairie that they found and they'll be raising food for Center."

Horace, paying no attention to the argument, was re-filling his glass. Emma went over to him and took him by the elbow. "Come on," she said. "We don't need to stay here and be insulted. We'll go upstairs. Maybe you can catch a nap."

Without protest, Horace went up the stairs with her. He took along the bottle.

When they had disappeared, Timothy stirred uncomfortably. "I must apologize," he told the others, "for this unseemly family squabble. It or other versions of it happen all the time. What I said to Emma is true. I couldn't leave her outside the walls. It took a lot of persuading for the council to agree to letting Horace in. He'd been making a nuisance of himself for months."

"Think nothing of it so far as we are concerned," said Corcoran. "Boone and I, back at Hopkins Acre, saw Horace at his finest. We can understand."

"Center is happy with the robots," said Timothy. "They'll solve some awkward food problems. They have a pair of steam engines and have built some gang plows. They're plowing the prairie and harrowing it—several thousand acres, if I remember correctly. By this time next year, they'll be raising tons of produce."

Corcoran changed the subject. "You've told us of what happened to you after you left Hopkins Acre, landing on the rim of the crater, with the monastery down on the floor. What I don't understand is who moved the monastery here while you were in it."

"It must have been the Infinites," said Timothy. "They left it booby-trapped, set for anyone who walked into the monastery. We were the ones who sprang it."

"It seems strange that they would set it to come here," Corcoran objected. "Has it occurred to you that the trap could have been set by those here at the Galactic Center?"

"I asked, and they claim no knowledge of it. I guess we'll never know who did it," Timothy said. He shrugged and changed the subject. "When Horseface brings us Enid's traveler, it should be possible to pick up the other two machines we know about. But, while Horace read the dials when he landed at the crater, he can't remember. What about the machine you left near the ruined city?"

Corcoran shook his head. "I can't help you. I had the logbook David kept, but I left it in the traveler."

"Well, we'll keep working on it," Timothy said. "We may find some way to locate at least one of them."

Corcoran asked, "What about the Rainbow People? You said the Center had never heard of them until we brought word."

"We were totally unaware," Timothy admitted. "I think some effort may now be made to contact them, but it may prove to be too difficult."

"I would think it might," said Corcoran. "The Hat said they were the oldest intelligence in the universe."

Boone pushed himself out of his chair. "If you'll excuse me," he said, "I think l should go out and see if Wolf is causing any trouble. He requires some looking after."

He waited for a moment, but none of the others seemed to have an urge to join him. They were content to remain exactly where they were.

Once out the door, he saw that Enid was sitting in one of the several lawn chairs that stood halfway down the parklike slope that lay before the house.

When he reached the chair, he bent over to kiss her. She put up her arms and held him there. He kissed her again—a much longer kiss.

"I was waiting for you," she whispered. "Why did you take so long?"

"We got to talking."

"When you're with Timothy, you always get to talking."

"I like the man," said Boone. "He's an easy man to like."

"Pull over a chair and sit down here beside me," she said. "We have a lot to talk about."

Far down the slope, just above the road that ran at the bottom of the property, Wolf was nosing around, investigating shrubbery.

"Tom," asked Enid, "how much do you remember of what the Rainbow People forced into our heads?"

"A little," said Boone. "It's coming back to me in bits and pieces. They packed it into us in an indigestible mass, but now it's beginning to float up."

"They gave us a body of knowledge," she told him,

"that should have taken days to absorb. We haven't talked about it, but maybe it's time we did."

Boone nodded. "Maybe. I still can't understand why they chose us."

"They must have discerned that I had been pondering on the significance of the universe for years. You, I think, were recognized as a trained information gatherer. What do you remember?"

"Not too much yet. What I seem to remember most clearly," said Boone, "is that certain very special conditions are needed in a universe to produce life. Most of the physics and chemistry still escape me, but there was something about the ways unstable stars were possible. In addition to stable ones, such stars were needed to go supernova to spray out the heavier elements that made life possible."

Enid crinkled her forehead. "I remember some of that. But it makes my head ache just to think of it. They seemed to be telling us that the universe was formed as a sort of factory to create life, out of which—at least out of some life—intelligence would sprout. They seemed to regard the universe as a machine to produce life and consciousness. Without consciousness and intelligence, the universe would lack meaning."

"They also talked about the origin of the universe—not as theory, but as if they knew. But it's beyond me, although, even in my time, the astrophysicists were tracing things back to a fraction of a microsecond after the beginning of the universe. In your time, Enid, had that final fraction been traced?"

"I don't know. Remember, Tom, we were the hillbillies of our culture," she said. "The Rainbow People spoke about a higher order of intelligence, an instinctive intelligence that did not rely on reason. They spoke as if they had reached that higher level. Maybe we can't ever understand all of what they said."

"Perhaps. But more will become apparent and understandable as time goes by, I think," he told her. "We have to wait."

And maybe, he thought, they could never understand

fully. Maybe even the Rainbow People could not reach a full understanding of life and the universe. But he knew they were still searching. Here, at the Galactic Center, others were seeking answers in different ways. The end was still hidden. Yet the drive to know existed. So long as the drive to learn existed, there was hope that the puzzle of universal purpose would eventually be solved.

They sat quietly side by side, holding hands. The warmth of the sun beat down on them, and they could smell the perfume of the flowers blooming in scattered beds. There was contentment in the sweep of the lawn.

"Corcoran and Horseface will soon be leaving," Enid said. "I hate to see them go. Timothy told me that Center could use them, and he will also miss them. I thought you might be leaving, too, even when you said you would stay. But today, you promised Center you would remain to study here."

"That was my excuse to stay. I had to tell them something," said Boone. "I couldn't bring myself to tell them the real reason—that I'm staying because there is a woman I found in time and have learned to love."

"You never told me that before," she said. "I've known I loved you since you held me while I wept for David. I needed strength and you gave me strength and understanding."

"I couldn't tell you before," Boone told her. "I'm good with hard words, words of facts. But other words do not come easily to me."

Down at the foot of the lawn, a commotion erupted.

Boone leaped to his feet. "Wolf!" he yelled.

"He's got something," said Enid. "He's chasing something."

Wolf emerged from a thicket. He tossed something in the air and caught it in his mouth, then came trotting up toward them. It was The Hat, hanging limply from his mouth.

Wolf dropped The Hat before them. He pranced with happiness.

"He's got his old plaything back," cried Enid. "He has found his doll."

The Hat came alive and sat up.

You do not understand, The Hat said. Then he collapsed again.

Wolf scooped up the limp doll and went serenely up the lawn.

Martin

17

Martin pulled the clanking, battered vehicle off the road and steered it down a gentle slope to the bottom of an arroyo. The battery was low again and would take some hours of recharging from the solar panels before it could be built up to even a marginal efficiency. When he braked the car to a stop on the flat floor of the gulch, he noted with some satisfaction that the machine would be fairly well hidden from the road. There was very little travel in this miserable country. But even so, it would be best to conceal the vehicle; beaten-up as this one was, it still had components that could be stripped, if its owner were unable to defend his property.

A utterly miserable world, he told himself, with no money, no credit, few, if any, opportunities, and only the slightest sense of law; each man was his own law, if he had the muscle to enforce it.

There was a worldwide economic depression, if Martin's judgement was correct. He could not be sure, since he had no data, and no one seemed to know what was going on. There still was radio, he had been told, although in the sun-scorched, shabby hamlet near which he had been deposited, no one had a radio set, let alone a television, if there still was such a thing as television. When he had asked about newspapers, the residents of the village had looked blankly at him. They had never heard of newspapers.

When, weeks before, he had come plodding down the path that led into the village, the people had shied away from him, gathering in clumps to stare at him as if he were some wild animal come from his lair among the distant buttes. After a time, one aged, tottering man, who seemed to hold some measure of leadership, had come up to him and talked in a tongue that he could understand, although filled with unfamiliar intonations and words. Hearing what Martin had to say and not believing him, the old man had thrust a finger close to his brow, moving it in circles to indicate one afflicted with a feeble mind.

They had, out of the goodness of their hearts, given him food to eat and a place to sleep. In the days that followed, he learned from talk with some of them that he was on Earth and in the twenty-third century, although they did not know the actual year. Hearing this, he inwardly damned the Horseface monstrosity, since he was sure that it had been Horseface who had hurled him off the net.

He managed for some weeks, although he was not sure how many. In that village, it was ridiculously easy to lose count of almost everything. He helped in hoeing corn, a chore little to his liking, and in carrying water to the corn from a small, reluctant stream that gurgled its slow, difficult way across the land about a half mile from the village. He learned to set snares for rabbits and tried to achieve some proficiency in archery, but with small success.

In his talk with the villagers he learned of a road, scarcely better than the track he had followed to the village, that lay some distance to the north, a track which eventually reached a wider road that ran straight east and west; by following that, one would finally come to cities. Martin suspected those would be no more than slightly larger villages, but with more people in them and somewhat easier living. From mention of less and less employment, of the slackening of trade activity, and of the disappearance of all money, he deduced that he was in a land and century deep in a worldwide economic collapse.

It had been by accident that he found the beaten-up solar-powered vehicle, sheltered in a lean-to built against one of the ramshackle huts that made up the village. Examining it, he became convinced that it still had in it some degree of operating life. When he tracked down its owner, it was apparent that the man had no further use for it; there was nowhere he wished to go and he had no idea of how to operate it. After much dickering, it cost Martin his wrist watch, for which the man had no more need than for the vehicle; the time of day was of no interest to the people of the village.

Now here he finally was, sitting in an arroyo, waiting for the beaten-up machine to recharge its batteries. Yesterday he had reached the wider road of which he had been told, recognizing it as what was left of one of the great transcontinental highways which had plunged across the nation, coast to coast. He had headed west, for he believed he had landed somewhere in the American southwest. It should thus not be too far to the Pacific area, where he might find some of the larger cities, pitiful at the best, but better than the village he had left.

During the one day he had been on the main highway, he had been passed by only three cars. One of them had been solar-powered, but a later model and much better designed than his. The other two cars had been propelled by internal combustion engines. The sweetish smell of their exhausts led him to believe that they burned alcohol as fuel.

Now off the road, parked on the flat floor of the arroyo, he climbed wearily from the single bucket seat of his car. Even on the smoother surface of the ancient freeway, his vehicle provided a rough and punishing ride. Every one of his muscles, it seemed, ached from the pounding he had taken.

He walked a few feet from the car and stretched. The arroyo was silent. There was no wind and not even any insect sounds. The high sky above him was pale blue. In it was a single high-soaring bird, maybe an eagle, more likely a buzzard. On either side of the gulch, the walls came down, sluiced and streaked by erosion, crumbling at the edges in the fierce blast of sunlight. Here and there small boulders and thin stone strata thrust partway from the soil. At the foot of the walls, where they joined the now dry streambed floor, lay scattered mounds of fallen stone.

Just beyond where he stood the arroyo bent, swinging around abruptly to take a different direction. He followed it and stopped, staring at the wall to his left. Protruding from the wall were the dead whiteness of old bone and the burnished gleam of ancient horn. A skull buried beneath the surface had been revealed by the erosion of the wall.

It was a bovine skull, but the skull was too massive and the one projecting horn too heavy and too long to ever have belonged to even the largest of the longhorns.

It had to be a bison, but not a bison of the Old West. What he was looking at, he told himself, was a prehistoric bison, one of the monstrous brutes that had been hunted by the first men in America. Looking at the floor of the arroyo beneath the skull, Martin saw the fractured whiteness of other bits of bone. How long ago, he wondered, had this buried beast cropped the prairie grass? A prairie then, but a desert now. Twenty thousand years, he told himself, probably more than that. There might have been a time when such a discovery would have the promise of some profit. But if the world of the present was actually in the shape he had deduced, there'd be no profit now.

A small buttress of the wall, a section that for the moment had resisted the power of rushing water, thrust out a few feet into the gully. As he stepped around it, the flare of reflected sunlight caught him in the eyes. He halted, puzzled. The flare had come from something embedded in the wall. The flare was gone, but whatever was embedded there still glittered.

He advanced slowly and stood in front of the shining object. It was a sphere, highly polished, looking for all the world like one of the crystal spheres used by phoney fortune tellers. It was the size of a basketball and its surface was so smooth and reflective that he saw the image of himself reflected in it with the sort of reflection that a curved mirror would project.

He raised his hands to lift it from the wall and it spoke to him.

Kind sir, it said, take me in your hands and hold me. Give me the warmth of other life and your loving kindness. I have been alone so long!

Martin froze, his hands still extended, but not moving to pick the sphere from out the wall of earth. His teeth chattered with sudden fright. Something had spoken to him, deep inside his mind, for he was sure there had been no sound of words—the same sort of speech as was used by that doll-like simpleton, The Hat.

Free me, the voice pleaded. Lift me down and keep me. I shall be a friend to you, a faithful servant to you. I ask no more than that you keep me with you. I could not bear the agony should you reject me, should you walk away from me.

Martin tried to speak. The words rattled in his throat.

Fear me not, the voice said. As I am, I have no power to harm you and, if I had, I would have no wish to do so. I have waited for so long, for a long eternity. Please, kind sir, have mercy on me. You're the last and only hope I have. There will be no other chance for me. I cannot face foreverness alone.

Words finally came to Martin, gulping, hurried words,

as if he feared he could not get them out. "What are you?" he asked. "Are you really speaking to me?"

I am really speaking to you, said the sphere. I hear you in my mind and speak to you from my mind. Your spoken words mean nothing to me. I can hear no sound. Once I had an auditory sense, but that long since is gone.

"But what are you?"

My history is a long one. Suffice it now to say that I am an ancient artifact from a mysterious race of which there is now no record.

The damn thing is lying, Martin told himself.

The sphere protested: I do not lie to you. Why should I lie to you, my rescuer?

"I did not say that you were lying. I spoke not a word to you."

The thought lay within your mind. I thought that you spoke to me.

"My God," said Martin, "you read my mind. Can you read the minds of everyone?"

That is my manner of conversing, said the sphere. And, yes, I can read the mind of any thinking creature that is close enough.

"All right," said Martin. "All right."

He advanced a step and lifted the sphere from the wall. It left behind it the imprint of itself. It had a good heft to it, a feeling of solidity, but it was not heavy. He held it for a moment, then placed it gently on the smooth floor of the arroyo, squatting down beside it.

Kind sir, asked the sphere, does this mean you'll keep me?

"Yes, I think I'll keep you."

You never shall regret it, said the sphere. I shall be the best friend you've ever had. I will be your . . .

"Let us not talk of it now," said Martin. "We'll talk about it later."

He picked up the sphere and walked along the gully, heading for the car.

Where are we going, sir?

"I'm taking you to my car," said Martin. "I'll place

you in it. Then I have a few things to do. I'll leave you
there, then later I'll join you."

You will return? Kind friend, you will return?

"You have my promise," Martin said.

He placed the sphere in the car and walked away, back
down the arroyo, well beyond the point where he'd found
the sphere. This will be far enough, he told himself. It
can't read my mind over such a distance. Or, at least, he
hoped it couldn't. He had an idea by the tail and he needed
time alone to think it out.

This was something new, he told himself. There must
be profit in it. It could be the key, wisely used, to a better
life in this godforsaken world. His mind skittered rapidly
as he thought about it. He took the idea and turned it
round and round. The sphere had possibilities, a lot of
possibilities, and he had to think of them long and hard.

In this benighted world, there must be something one
could offer that would have some appeal. The world was
filled with hopelessness, and maybe that was it. The people could not be promised riches, for there were no riches
to be given. The hope of riches would be an empty hope
and everyone would know that. But hope itself—pure and
naked hope—that might be something else. If there were
some way to give them hope, they'd buy it. They'd flock
in thousands for a whiff of hope. But it would have to be
more than a namby-pamby hope. It must be such as to
touch off a howling fanaticism.

He thought about fanaticism and that it was hard to
come by. He paced back and forth, thinking of hope and
fanaticism and what he might gain by arousing a hopeful
fanaticism. Somewhat easier living, perhaps, but not a lot
of money. What could be gained, perhaps, would be position and power. Given position and power, a canny man
could do a lot.

He wrestled with the idea he had snared and the mystery of an ancient artifact, although he still did not entirely
buy that the sphere was really an ancient artifact.

A dash of religion might turn the trick. That, by God,
was it—religion! A new messiah and an ancient artifact
performing in a sacred mystery atmosphere.

He squatted down and thought about it. He'd have to take it easy to start with, he told himself. No big splash, no circus background. Start small and humble and let the crusade grow by word of mouth.

To make it go, he would have to tell the people what they wished to hear. By slow degrees he must find out what they wanted, then feed them what they wanted.

There was one question still: What was the sphere? Not an ancient artifact from a long-lost race, as it had told him. Although, true or not, it was a good approach to what he had in mind. He tried to think of all the things it might be and rejected them one by one. He was wasting time, he told himself. He did not need, right now, to know what the sphere actually might be. He could use it without knowing.

He went back over the plan and thought it through, point by point, searching for glitches that could trip him up. He found none that he could not circumvent. After all, a hopeless people, offered hope, would not question it too closely. They'd be eager for it, they would lap up a promised salvation and would scream for more. Worked out right, he told himself, the scheme was foolproof. It would take a great deal more thinking and more planning, and he would give it those. He'd think it out in every detail before he went ahead with it. It was a solid and workable plan, and he was the one who could work it out.

He rose from his crouch and headed for the car. He had been in the arroyo longer than he'd thought. The sun was about to set.

You came back, the sphere shrieked joyously at him. I had thought you might not. I agonized you might not.

"No need for you to have agonized," said Martin. "I am here."

He checked the battery and it was up, as up as it would ever get. He moved the sphere to the well beside the seat and climbed in to start the car.

"One question," he asked the sphere. "How about your ethics? Have you any ethics?"

What are ethics? asked the sphere. Please explain to me.

"Never mind," Martin told it. "You'll do. We'll make a team together."

He turned the car around and headed for the road.

Horseface

18

orseface sat at ease at a table that stood in front of the cafe hut, now empty of the robot and equipment. Near him floated the net with the chest in which the galactic chart had been locked away. The visor that Enid had thought she stole was on the table, close to hand. The trolley car still stood on its track, waiting for the next passenger, who might never come. And around all this was wrapped the foggy grayness of the Highway of Eternity.

As he had done many times before, Horseface pondered on the Highway. So far, all his pondering had come to nothing, and he supposed it always would. He wondered who or what had engineered this never-ending thread of road, yanked askew and canted out of normal time and space. He had first heard of it very long ago and very far away, from an incredible creature that seemed to mock all the needs and qualities of life. It was this incredibility who had called it the Highway of Eternity, but who did not answer when he asked the reason for the name.

"Don't go looking for it," the incredibility had warned him. "It cannot be found by looking. It must be stumbled upon."

Horseface had stumbled upon it millennia ago and, curiously, had then found its representation worked into the ancient galactic chart. But he was sure his race had never built it, though they had been aware of it.

Having stumbled upon the Highway, he had decided it might make a place to sit and ponder his various choices of action. He had installed the hut with the tables and chairs, and had put the robot in charge. Since the tracks were there, he had placed the trolley on them and had rigged alarms so that he would be notified should someone or something appear along this section of the Highway.

For many centuries, nothing happened. Then, only a few years before, the alarms had been tripped by Boone in his first stepping around a corner. That strange happening had seemed to provide a possible key for which Horseface had been looking to solve the problem presented by the humans at Hopkins Acre.

He had been hopeful, but not completely convinced, until Boone's second appearance. Then he had recognized that he was witnessing an entirely new talent in a race from which he had not suspected such talents. The talent itself was less important than the fact that within the race there existed a capacity to develop masked new capabilities in an evolutionary mode. With his realization of that, Boone had become central to his project.

Now that project, Horseface told himself, was finally underway, working out far better than he had hoped. What now remained were years of monitoring and close watching to make certain no hitches developed, but he would have help with that. Spike and The Hat would be accepted by the family, as Spike had been for years.

Horseface chuckled as he thought of that. Galactic Center had considered Spike their undercover agent, and he had been inserted into the family at the moment they were about to flee into the past to escape the Infinites. Spike's reports to Horseface had reinforced his hunch that this band of humans was worth his close attention.

Of course, there was no guarantee that he would not fail in this project as he had failed in others in the past. Intelligence, it appeared, had a miserable chance of developing to its full capacity. There had been other races he had tried to help over long centuries of effort, and each had been a failure. There had been races he had not helped who had failed as well. The Rainbow People had failed finally because they had lost all true values by repressing their emotions until such emotions had shriveled away. The Infinites had become lost in their drive toward their fanatical crusade. Even Horseface's own people had failed when their too-successful search for immortality had caused a sacrifice of racial fertility that left him, finally, as the last surviving member of his race.

A soft plopping sound jerked his attention from his reminiscenses. The Hat stood opposite him, shaking himself as a dog would shake off water. With the shaking, his disarranged garments fell into their accustomed places. The Hat sat down carefully.

I am not deserting my post, The Hat told Horseface. I shall return and carry on my duties. I come to escape the wolf. He tosses me about and shakes me. He walks away, making me hope he has deserted me; then he turns and pounces on me. His teeth have battered and chewed upon me, and . . .

"You must put up with it," Horseface said. "It is a rôle you must play. While you seem only a ragged doll, they will not suspect you spy upon them. Consider the rôle I must play. I must act a clown, talk as they would expect from an uncouth alien, tell them untruths, and play seedy tricks upon them."

Like the trick he had played upon the little Enid, making

her believe she must hold her finger upon a point while he tied a knot. He had gained her confidence by making her feel she helped to create the net, which, of course, had been there all along, needing only his thought to make it visible.

And to convince her of her importance on the net, he had let her believe that she was stealing the visor he had placed on the pink-and-purple world where he had left the chart chest. The compulsion to go to it had been put into her mind while she believed they were both thinking at each other. Then he had let her think she was saving him from the purple monster that was only trying to ride the net with them.

You need not have done any of it, The Hat said, if you had minded your own business. But you *must* interfere in the lives of others. No one seeks your advice or help. You are simply an objectionable busybody.

"Perhaps I am," Horseface admitted. "But I cannot do otherwise, when a small push might place some race on the path toward a full development of the intellectual powers possible."

And I have helped you, said The Hat. I have even acted on my own many times. That is how I got in trouble with the wolf. There your precious Boone was, stupidly dozing by his campfire, with the wolf edging up on him. The wolf would have torn out his throat in another minute had I not taken over its small mind and engulfed it with a sense of brotherhood for Boone and doglike devotion to him.

"Yes," said Horseface. "You did well, as I have said before. You did well in programming the travelers whenever the family fled in them. Even when you programmed Martin's to bring him and the Infinites here, you did well—although I did not think so when he first appeared."

And I saved Corcoran while you were in the chart, The Hat added. I watched him and when I saw he was about to fall, I zapped him unconscious and brought him to the ·Highway. And now I become a plaything for the wolf so that I can spy on your chosen Enid and Boone. It is not a proper reward for . . .

Horseface interrupted. "Tell me, do you see any signs that the two of them will mate?"

They have done so already, The Hat answered. I think Enid is feeling guilty that it took place before the rite they term a wedding. I do not understand this wedding business.

"Don't try," Horseface told him. "The sexual ethics of all races make little sense. And the syndrome that humans call love is beyond all understanding."

But The Hat was no longer listening. The Hat had collapsed into his rag doll phase and lay limply across the table.

Poor little tyke, Horseface thought in sudden sympathy. Perhaps he had been used hardly and deserved a rest.

Horseface recalled the day he had found the creature, tucked away in a display niche of an ancient museum of his own people, perhaps left against a time when the race would be gone. He had glanced at The Hat and passed on, unwilling to load himself down with relics of the past. Later, however, he had gone back to retrieve the doll. He never ceased to bless the urge that led him to do so, for The Hat had strange abilities beyond any he could understand, such as the power to move and carry across space and time without such aids as the net.

So Enid and Boone had mated and the die was cast. It was, Horseface knew, a genetic gamble, but better than many other gambles he had made. Horseface knew much about genetics.

From their union, there was a chance that a new race would spring—an offshoot of humanity that combined the evolutionary trend shown by Boone and the toughness of that small group of humans who had stubbornly dared to resist the menace of the Infinites.

He had admired that stubbornness and he had helped the rebels, recognizing the promise in them. He had supplied them with one of the most simple of the time machines developed by his race as an ancient forerunner of the net. The Infinites had time travel, of course, but theirs were such complicated devices that the rebels could not have understood them. Lying again, Horseface had let the rebels believe they were stealing it from the Infinites.

That was before he discovered Boone in a stroke of pure luck. But having discovered him, there had been the problem of getting him in contact with the Hopkins Acre family. More shifty-footed maneuvers had been called for—a whisper of rumor to Martin to send him to Corcoran and another rumor for Corcoran to take to Martin to scare him into leaving without his larger traveler.

Horseface had learned of Corcoran's weird vision before and of his friendship with Boone. A little prodding of Corcoran had sent the man to the Everest to gaze at Martin's suite and see the traveler.

Corcoran, Horseface admittted to himself, could have been a mistake. He had expected Boone to step around a corner into the traveler alone, leaving Corcoran behind. He had underestimated Boone's talent. But fortunately, Corcoran had caused no trouble. The discovery of the strange tree had been a danger point, but all had worked out well in the end.

Someday, Horseface told himself, he must take the time to find out what Corcoran's tree really was, though he could probably never learn what race or people was responsible for it, nor why it had been placed in that period on Earth.

In the end, he decided, all comes out better even than he could have hoped. There was still work to do, of course. He would have to find mates for the yet unborn children of Boone and Enid. Perhaps suitable ones could be found on one of the planets colonized by the humans. But the big job was done.

Idly, he pulled the visor closer to check on Martin. He seemed to have an odd compulsion to keep track of Martin, though the man was stashed away where he could not escape. Still, Martin was a slippery character.

In the visor plate, he saw the interior of a temple filled with starry-eyed worshippers. Martin, decked out in gold and purple vestments, stood before an ornate altar. The killer monster's brain case rested on a pedestal against the altar, glowing in the flickering light of many candles.

It was apparent that Martin was in the middle of a spirited harangue. Suddenly he flung up his arms and the crowd leaped to its feet, mouths open in what must have been wildly happy response.

Martin had it made. He had the power that he had wanted and no one to challenge him. He was safely trapped in his own self-glorification. And yet, Horseface knew with some disgust, he'd keep on checking on Martin.

There was still one more chore to do now. It was not necessary, perhaps, but in all decency it should be done. The visor showed the far future now, where a glitter of sparkles rested in the faint shadow of an ancient tree while the world swirled slowly in its orbit around a swollen, blood-red, dying sun.

As Horseface began to clamber onto the net, The Hat came awake again and sat up groggily.

What are you doing now? he asked.

"I'm bringing Henry back to the family," Horseface told him. "I don't know what Henry may think about it, but the rest of the family will be glad to see him. Do you want to come along?"

The Hat shook his head. There you go again, he told Horseface. Interfering. Still a busybody.

The net vanished, and The Hat collapsed upon the table, a limp, lumpy, and much-abused plaything.

About the Author

Clifford D. Simak was born and raised in south-western Wisconsin, a land of wooded hills and deep ravines which he often uses as the background locale for his stories. Over the years he has written more than 25 books, and he has some 200 short stories to his credit. A retired newspaperman, Simak lives in Minnesota. His most recent novel, also published by Del Rey Books, is *Special Deliverance*.